NO-SIGNAL AREA

NO-SIGNAL AREA

ROBERT PERIŠIĆ

Translated by ELLEN ELIAS-BURSAĆ

Seven Stories Press
New York · Oakland

Seven Stories Press
140 Watts Street
New York, NY 10013
www.sevenstories.com

LIBRARY OF CONGRESS CATALOGING-IN-PUBLICATION DATA

Names: Perišić, Robert, 1969- author. | Elias-Bursać, Ellen, translator.

Title: No signal area / Robert Perišić ; [translated by Ellen Elias-Bursac].
Other titles: Područje bez signala. English
Description: [New York] : [Seven Stories Press], [2019] | Originally published as Područje bez signala in 2015. | Translated from the Croatian.
Identifiers: LCCN 2019025284 | ISBN 9781609809706 (paperback) | ISBN 9781609809713 (ebook)
Classification: LCC PG1619.26.E683 P6413 2019 | DDC 891.8/3354--dc23
LC record available at https://lccn.loc.gov/2019025284

9 8 7 6 5 4 3 2 1

TRANSLATOR'S NOTE

The first translation of *No-Signal Area* was the result of a class assignment for a group of twenty-five students in the English department of the Faculty of Humanities and Social Sciences in Zagreb. Their professor, Alex Hoyt, submitted their translated excerpts to the Zagreb publisher, who passed them on to Seven Stories Press. I was grateful for the students' substantial efforts when I later translated the novel.

—E.E.B.

NO-SIGNAL AREA

I

HER VOICE WAS breaking up. *How... our relationsh... on't kn... was thinking... whose...* The words were surfacing, crackling, like a person drowning in the waves. "Must be a no-signal area," he said.... *eep appearing and disapp...*

He glanced at the phone. The only remaining signal bar blinked, then vanished.

The Japanese SUV had good shocks, so he was able to browse the newspaper he'd bought early that morning at a newsstand near the border. Sometimes he liked reading the newspapers in countries that had been socialist. There was a magical-thinking feel about them, part real and part unreal. Feeble recall, an addled mind, vestiges of defunct policies. A little like places out in the sticks marked by roadside plastic flowers or crosses.

They drove by the occasional roofless house mired in the dense weeds that had been flourishing since the recent war. On the charred walls one could still make out the signatures of those who'd ransacked it, the symbols and names of the army units, flaunting their misdeeds.

The poor blew up the poor. The poor took their revenge against the poor, and the poor became even poorer.

Spiral poverty, he thought. Perhaps I, too, had a hand in this.

Was *spiral poverty* even a phrase? Had he made it up? He couldn't remember. Not that it mattered. He toted his language along with him wherever he traveled and used it as he pleased.

In front of them again stretched a dip of a valley surrounded by sharp peaks and a cramped small town—a place they would have traversed speedily had they not been stuck behind a school bus that spewed greasy smoke, filled with kids.

On the back seats of the bus a crowd of teenagers played an old game. A kid with big ears was staring through the smudged window at the Japanese SUV. Somebody slapped him on the ear and then everyone threw their hands up, like, who? me? He was supposed to guess who. And he couldn't.

Big-Ears stared, distracted, at the SUV's tinted windows and foreign license plate, bracing for the next slap.

From the SUV, Oleg looked at the boy's dazed eyes. The eyes of the people, he thought.

"That bus has been creaking since the eighties."

"Like everything else here," said Nikola.

But, surprise, Big-Ears guessed who. So now it was his turn. They switched seats. A zit-faced kid was next. Big-Ears slapped Zit-Face, but—not like that, man, patience, patience—he was busted right away.

"You're definitely weak in the strategy department," said Oleg; Nikola shot him a glance.

"Not you," Oleg told him.

Again Big-Ears was slapped. The mounting frustration was written all over his face. Oleg suddenly wanted to let him know whose hand slapped him, but no, the kid wouldn't understand the gesture anyway if he tried. While he was getting slapped the kid stuck out his tongue at them, a little risky: he easily could have bitten it off.

"Pass the bus."

"It's a solid line. And there's a speed limit."

Big-Ears was now showing his friends the car and the foreign plates, so all the kids started showing them something along the lines of a national symbol. Oleg knew more or less what they were shouting at them while making faces.

"Big-Ears spotted a foreign threat," Oleg said to Nikola.

"What?"

"Pass them already, fuck the speed limit!"

On they drove, and put off stopping till they reached a roadside café on the first floor of a deserted two-story building; the sign said STRADA.

They sat down inside.

But I shot a man in Reno just to watch him die . . .

"Hey, someone in here's listening to Johnny Cash."

"Well, looks like nobody's around."

From behind the bar stepped a slim, long-legged young woman in knee-high black boots, a cigarette dangling from her mouth.

"Greetings, God b'with you, praised be Jesus, As-Salaam Alaikum, what'll you be having?" she bent over between them, cheerfully oblivious of her cleavage, and wiped the table. Just then the long plug of ash on the cigarette between her lips dropped onto the table. She quickly took the cigarette from her mouth, scooched down, and puffed at the ashes. "*Theeere* you go!"

When she brought the drinks she asked, "Where are you off to?"

Oleg said they were going to the town of N.

"Oh? Why there?"

"Business."

"Heh, heh, good one!"

"You don't believe me?"

"I'm from there."

"Want to hitch a ride with us?"

"Can't you see I'm busy here?" she said, walking toward the bar.

He looked around the bar.

"What's your name? I'm Oleg, this is Nikola."

"Lipša."

"Funny name."

"What's so funny about it?" she said.

"How about the cell phone number of one of your girlfriends? We'll need a guide."

She waved away the smoke and measured him up. "You mean an escort?"

"No, we're good boys," said Oleg. "We're bringing in foreign capital."

"Take my number, then. And give me a buzz me when you lose your way out there in the big city."

They wanted to get to N. before dark, so they finished their drinks.

"Three-fifty," said Lipša.

Oleg gave her a twenty and turned to go. "Keep the change."

She ran after him with his change, calling, "Come on, man, that's, like, money."

As Nikola was starting the car she watched them from the doorway, a cigarette in her teeth, her arms folded, under the broken STRADA sign.

A few feet away a long car was covered in snow, possibly a Volvo, with a flat front tire.

Through the leafless trees, there were clouds the color of ash floating in from the west, and distant, soundless lightning.

"That's one fabulous woman," said Oleg when they got going.

Nikola sighed, as if he were thinking about something he wasn't in the mood to share. But then he said, "That's no woman."

"What, then?"

"Woman is a serious concept."

Oleg burst out laughing. From the heart. "Now, that's more like it!"

"Like what?"

"You've been so glum since this morning. But you can be fun."

"I meant that."

"I know."

This conversation is such a crock, thought Nikola.

"You're the most romantic guy I know."

Nikola considered denying he was romantic. What about his life was so romantic? What does romantic even mean?

What was Oleg getting at—that Nikola was a fool, a wimp, what? Maybe he was a romantic, but there was no point in talking with Oleg about this.

Still, he said, "So what's so romantic about my life?"

"Dunno," said Oleg. "I wasn't claiming a romantic can actually pull off romance."

"Aha."

✦ ✧ ✧

"There was this thing in Siberia, near Tobolsk."

"Near what?"

"Tobolsk. Well, I mean, nothing's near there, but Tobolsk was the nearest…"

"Wow, so helpful."

"You haven't heard of Tobolsk? That's where Križanić published his treatise on grammar. In 1665!"

"Who knew."

"I know, I've been there."

"How did we get onto this?"

"I don't know, we're driving in the middle of nowhere so that reminded me."

"Of what?"

"Right! You interrupted me. I was saying. In the place near Tobolsk, a town there, even more backwoods than this, a man, listen to this, he told me that for a million bucks he could get me a bomb."

"What kind of a bomb?"

"Atom."

They drove over a sizeable pothole and were shaken up. Now they were driving along a deep gorge by a river. There was a light drizzle of sleet.

"Only a million?" said Nikola, with a firm grip on the wheel.

"That's what I asked the guy. Only a million?" He blew out some smoke while looking down at the riverbank below, where there were countless plastic bags, snared, mistletoe-like, on the brambles. He'd expected pristine nature here, so he scowled at the plastic bags.

"Know what he said to me?" Oleg asked.

"Mmm?"

Oleg looked at Nikola, letting the swirl of smoke in the car serve as a dramatic flourish.

"So I tell him: *Only a million*? And you know what he says?"

"Come on, what?"

"He says, '*Yes. It's only a small bomb.*'"

Oleg stubbed out his cigarette and lit another.

After some time, Nikola asked, "Do you think he was actually serious?"

"Listen, I didn't pursue it . . . Russia was a mess . . ." Oleg thought for a moment and then added with a chuckle, "Either he was serious, or he was screwing with me."

"Fuck, man, that's not so funny."

"What can I say? I didn't pursue it. My grand contribution to humanity."

"Such a hero."

"Hey, what do you think? What if I had brought a *small bomb* to the geniuses here, how far would it have gone?" Oleg chuckled again.

Damn his sense of humor, thought Nikola. In the gorge only the white plastic bags still flashed from the brambles by the dark river. Then the roads branched and the SUV began a long climb.

Oleg sank deep into thoughts: the weird night in that hotel near Tobolsk, where he ended up with a stunning black-haired belle, a Russian-speaking indigenous woman. She'd turned up next to him by the bar at a sleazy nightclub during the evening, and he hadn't known whether or not she was a hooker—he hadn't solicited her, which didn't mean someone else hadn't, because the people he was working with had their own, sometimes unconventional, forms of hospitality. He talked up all sorts of drivel, said he was a sea captain—though the sea was very far away, and frozen to boot—he told her he was from Krems in Austria, though that, too, was very far from the sea, but none of this bothered her. He was wondering: was she a hooker he was being set up with, or did she find him amusing, did she trust him? She had a look in her eyes as if she were really attracted to him, it was maybe even a naively in love kind of look, which could possibly have been genuine since she desperately wanted to ditch where she was and go somewhere else, to the world he stood for and she gazed at, enthralled. He wondered about this, downing vodka after vodka, telling her about the seas he'd sailed, the rigging on his boat, and something he'd been through on a trop-ical isle, lacing into his ramblings the plot of *Mutiny on the Bounty*, which was based on a true event, but he relied only on the movie, telling her of the island's native women, beautiful like her. This was where he lost track of the plot and launched into babble about the upsides of the culture there, which, he said, didn't frown on free love, it was, he said, an altogether different world, a world he'd come to know and become a part of, and the whole time he kept wondering if she truly believed him or was just putting on an act. But as time passed, many vodkas later, he wondered less and less, so they ended up at a hotel and had magnificent sex—though he had no condoms on him, but he couldn't resist. Besides, he'd assumed (still thinking she might be a hooker) that she'd have condoms, but she didn't. They kept drinking from the minibar, and she, as he remembered it, said she was of Mansi lineage or some such thing, an ethnic group from there, so he revealed his true identity, at which she flinched, saying she'd had a child with a compatriot of his, and used the word Mantyer, and at first he thought this was a name, or maybe her ex's surname. Mantyer, Mantyer, she kept repeating as if he were supposed to know what this was, and eventually he figured it must be Monter, a company from back home that was also doing business there. Damn it, all she knew was the name of the firm. She was probably messing with him. She was probably a hooker who made up silly stories to match the silly stories he told her. Or maybe she was a particularly romantic hooker, who kept forgetting she was a hooker so she had unprotected sex with a fellow national of his who had a name she couldn't pronounce, and only remembered the name of his company? Or she was so dense that her mind-set went beyond stupidity to a whole other way of life, like the movie he was telling her about, so he was beginning to feel he was one of the sailors from the movie, which was very different from the role he played in real life, but he liked it so much that he could fall in love with her, and—what with one thing and another—he made love to her again, like a man head over heels in love. But dammit, what was he supposed to do with these feelings for a hooker, or romantic hooker, or otherworldly soul who had a child with a Mantyer in a town where he'd been offered an atomic bomb? So maybe that was why he got so drunk that he no longer knew who she was or who'd sent her to sleep with him, or whether someone had sent her at all, or whether she was crazy, because at one point, when they were already extremely drunk—they'd emptied the minibar—she wrapped her arms around him and sobbed, telling him he was the love of her life and she knew he was going to go and leave her behind, and that wasn't fair, and he should think again, and he'd see wrong from right. But he was already so sozzled that he couldn't think, he just kept smiling and nodding, he was probably sobbing, too, yes, yes, he probably was, and furthermore he kept thinking all night about the little bomb, the little bomb he eventually decided not to mention to anyone, though he was told always to tell everything, to report on every offer, and he was told this in a serious tone, backed by serious consequences. Nikola didn't know any of this when he said "Such a hero," but there was no point in explaining it all to Nikola, just as there was no point to how, the next morning while she was sleeping, he'd packed his things and taken off, leaving her some cash, a lot of cash if she really was a hooker after all, or not much cash at all if she wasn't, or even if she was a crazy hooker who kept forgetting she was a hooker, but he didn't know any of this and he was afraid of finding out about it, sober, just as he was afraid of finding out about the little bomb. So he paid up for the room, and after seeing the receptionist reach for the phone, he stormed out of the hotel and into a cab, and told the driver to step on it and raced all the way to Tobolsk in a panic that was probably overblown, especially since he wasn't altogether sure just what it was he was running from, but running he was.

2

WASHED-OUT REDDISH rooftops and a battalion of square-shaped buildings stood on the plateau at the foot of a mountain rising into the fog like a big hand reaching for help. A creaky iron bridge, slush on a narrow sidewalk, a man stooped by the weight of a shopping bag. An empty seesaw in a playground stripped bare, next to it a man with a dog. The man was staring at them as if they were something new. He probably knows every car in town, thought Oleg.

Then a small square intersected by a road, and a snarl of flags on the three-story town hall, and three kids out in front of a bar, standing with their backs hunched in the cold, in short jackets, with their hands stuffed in their pockets, scheming. Oleg felt as if he knew them, as if he were watching the rerun of an old TV show with fresh eyes.

He couldn't hold back the memories: he'd grown up in a place exactly like this.

He knew the limits of this life. Old feelings of familiarity welled up inside him.

The feeling of being far away from everything, yet penned in.

Nature all around you, yet you don't see it.

Isolated—that's the word. Nowhere, yet trapped.

I'd have lost my mind if I'd stayed, thought Oleg. Then he thought, no—in reality, I probably would have been careful and made sure not to lose my mind. Lowered the bar. Taken the shit. Fallen in love with a bimbo.

Well, maybe not a bimbo—a nice girl, one who would've had a therapeutic effect on me.

The skeleton of a factory loomed in the distance. Amid landscape sloping slowly toward the mountain, the industrial plant looked like an abandoned fortress from another era.

He mused about how socialism had evolved in the sticks where he grew up. Then abruptly he could envision his parents' home in the late seventies when they panicked over the "situation" and kept track of all the symptoms, the little signs cropping up on TV. What's going on in the center of the country?

How's the president's health? It had been—he remembered the feeling well—nearly impossible to imagine the president dying.

Funny, but such a thing had felt like the end of the world.

And then, later, the world did end.

They drove up to the house they'd rented by phone ten days earlier; a man who worked in Germany had built a vast manor, his dream house.

Some people dream of their houses and all the architect does is tspoil their vision.

In addition to a few domes, the house had pointy gables, archways, and round balconies, a balustrade of white pillars with miniature lions at the corners, and a remote-controlled gate out in front of a patched-up driveway.

Oleg stared, and thought the house looked as if a very modern witch lived inside. Then he said, "This is our fairy-tale castle."

The man who welcomed them, Isa, the dreamer's brother, said, "Nice way of describing it."

The house looked out over a turquoise gas station keeping guard by the main road.

"Open till midnight," said their host. "This is the last place to fill up within a sixty-mile radius."

"Terrific," said Oleg. "Are kids buzzing around here till late?"

Isa looked at him as if wondering how he knew, then said, "Well sort of. The ones on scooters. But the noise isn't too bad."

They were expecting to pay the rent right away, but Isa insisted they only take care of business after a little drink. This was the custom. He invited them to try some homemade quince rakija in his somewhat more modest abode across the road, where they entered a dark, wood-paneled dining room and sat down at a massive, newly built round table. A boy spreading margarine on a slice of bread didn't respond to the guests' greetings, but glanced at them sideways, as if he'd already heard bad things about them. Then he slipped out to kick a ball around with a bareheaded friend in a roadside patch of grass: little goals with rocks as goalposts. The offsides—frozen snow.

Nikola watched them out the window; he saw puffs of their breath in the winter light, feeling at an arm's length from it all, distant, at which point anxiety started inching from his gut upward toward his head, grabbing him by the throat.

He went to the bathroom, rummaged through his pockets, and took a Xanax.

The mirror had a gold-plated frame.

The door didn't creak on his way out.

Oleg asked their host if he knew any of the engineers from the old factory, and the host mentioned a Sobotka. Isa wasn't sure where the man lived, but he did say Sobotka could be found around town.

As he was sitting back down, Nikola realized he'd neglected to wipe the sweat from his forehead. He dabbed at it with a tissue.

Two empty shot glasses and one, Nikola's, full of rakija, were on the table, with all the light shining only on them, and Isa shot him a diagnostic look, like a doctor or a mechanic ("What? something wrong?").

Nikola downed his shot. Oleg said, "Thanks for the rakija, superb! But we must be going!"

He walked through the old town center with small steps.

A small town can be ruined if you pace through it with too long a stride; you sense this without thinking and your pace shrinks till you're nearly standing in place. He walked along the cobblestone street where the two old empires had rubbed elbows, reluctantly, both as if they were losing momentum: they'd come this far, many miles from home, and were beginning to wonder what the point had been to all the adventure. There they stayed, forced by the other empire to dig in, and they'd been facing off ever since, centuries later, giving an inch now and then, a step here, a step there, bumping up against each other like two heavyweights staggering in a stranglehold, aching for the bell, almost cronies in their desperate exhaustion.

"Come on, Niks, you're staring at it like it's Paris."
"Right."
"Tired from the drive?"
"Sure am."

A small town has its eye-contact logic; he was reminded of this by every passerby. In a big city people's gazes float, hover, spark, while around here, scrutiny ruled the space, blazing like high beams. Every guy they met seemed to need to look them over while slogging through the slush; each made sure to look them right in the eye, check them out.

The stares seemed routine. Nobody took any pains to be circumspect.

Nikola found this irritating; he wished he could shake free of their stares the way a dog shakes off water after a swim.

Oleg thought there was disrespect in the way they were being inspected. Apparently we don't come across as threatening enough, he thought.

Something to attend to. He had walked down back alleys and passed by people when he'd been careful to avert his eyes.

He felt a momentary urge to turn around, walk away and never come back, but he knew he mustn't breathe a word of this to Nikola. He glanced over: Nikola's brow had begun to relax.

"Food, drink, women."

"Excuse me?"

"Keep these things firmly in mind," said Oleg brightly. He saw the sign: RESTAURANT HAIDUCI, and rubbed his hands together in glee.

"Finally!"

They walked into the perfectly preserved 1980s interior, and took seats in a booth.

The waiter kept urging Oleg to order the fish, because he assumed Oleg was an import from abroad; Oleg found this mildly offensive.

"So what's with all the plastic bags down by the river? Were they thrown there on purpose?"

"What can I say?" said the waiter with a helpless shrug. "The pea brains upstream allowed there to be dumps in all the wrong places, then the floods hit last fall."

"And nobody's out there cleaning it up?"

"Hmmm," the waiter was startled. "Well, who?"

He stopped mentioning the fish.

The meat, however, was delicious.

They inquired in passing about Sobotka, with no success.

Later they asked about him at two little shops, huddled side by side, selling local handicrafts. They'd survived industrialization and stood there now like joyless champions. One was a coppersmith, selling copperware and hammering out ornamental bowls. The other sold only slippers, soft and warm, in lively colors and designs. There were so many slippers in the shop that just looking at them left you feeling all cozy. "People must have a thing about slippers here," said Oleg.

"Right," nodded Nikola and walked out.

Neither the coppersmith nor the slipper-maker knew the engineer Oleg was looking for. Maybe I'm asking the wrong folks, thought Oleg on his way out. Artisans and engineers—two distinct civilizations.

"I was having difficulty breathing among all the slippers," said Nikola.

"Okay, but roll up your sleeves!"

Nikola thought he'd done just that. He'd been inspecting the surroundings while he waited outside on the cobblestones, so he said, "How about we ask those guys over there?"

There were six or seven men out in front of a convenience store, buttoned up to their chins, passing around a bottle. They shot occasional glances at the newcomers. Above their heads glowed a streetlamp that flickered out every so often.

Oleg walked over, asked about Sobotka, the engineer, and they all started talking at once. Oleg had trouble following what they were saying: a local dialect, or maybe they were just too drunk. After the others quieted down, a lanky guy with a hangdog expression who seemed sober said, "I used to work with him. But I don't know where he lives. Can I bum a smoke?"

Nikola took out a pack and gave them a few cigarettes.

"We're looking for him about business, if you see him," said Oleg.

He thought they might ask him to buy them another bottle, but they didn't.

"Should I have bought them a bottle?" he asked Nikola when they'd moved away.

Nikola shrugged.

Oleg walked back, went into the store, and came out with a bottle that he handed to the guy with the hangdog face. The man looked at him and said nothing but took the bottle.

When he caught up with Nikola again, Oleg said, "Public relations."

Then they ran into an old mailman, a small, skinny man, who talked loudly, enunciating, as if he were presenting a report. He said his name was Youry Šaracen, and that people called him Youry the Mailman, or even Your Mail, which seemed silly. "In short, call me Mr. Mail!" he declared, as if they were on the verge of clinching a deal. He told them they could ask him anything, that he kept track of everything *with an objective eye*, and that he hadn't drunk a drop of alcohol in thirty years, because "the mail's the mail" after all, which they didn't fully understand, and, before they'd had the chance to get a word in edgewise, he asked if letters were ever lost where they were from, or was that only here, and whether illiteracy was making a comeback, or was that only here, and whether the only person who ever received any letters flatly refused to receive them, or was that only here, and whether they had any idea where they were, and did they or did they not have any questions. Nikola stared at him, eyebrows arched, and Oleg finally cut him off and said, "We're looking for an engineer named Sobotka. He used to work at the turbine factory, and we need to see him about an urgent matter!" After hearing the word "urgent," the mailman looked at Oleg as if he'd finally found an interlocutor he could value. He gave them detailed directions, so they did find the engineer, but only after jouncing along a challenging road in the SUV for three or four miles outside the town of N. to a place that included two buildings and a few barracks. The man was sitting in a pub built like a log cabin with a bar that looked like the counter in a store. People were sitting at tables draped with checkered tablecloths, the place smelled like rakija, plum brandy this time, and there were Coke and Fanta cans on the shelf—but more as decorations. The place was lit by a bare light bulb and, surprisingly, there was a Metallica poster on the wall—maybe to give the place a modern feel or to remind them of the failed local industry.

They stood in the doorway and everyone turned to see them. Nikola noticed his shoelace was untied, so he crouched down, which seemed—after everyone was already looking at him—as if he'd sunk. Under all the smoke and white light, the reek of the den gave Oleg a slight shiver of fear: he was overdressed and he'd shaved, though there were painfully dark bags under his eyes and he was a bit puffed up. But he was well-groomed; this was such an unexpected phrase, *well-groomed*. Oh well, it's easy to seem well-groomed around here. But, indeed, he saw that the skin of his face was far too soft for local standards; he felt he was soft, too soft, when faced by their gazes and their dry, bushy beards, so in he stepped, realizing he shouldn't be standing in the doorway as if anxious about something. He had to walk in, walk in like an investor.

Someone should paint the scene, this could be an oil painting

straight out of post-socialist realism—*The Arrival of the Investor*—
he thought as he entered as if stepping up to a podium. In his
knee-length cashmere coat, holding his black scarf and fur hat, he
walked in as if he were entering a property he was planning to purchase, checking to see how the ceiling was faring, peering into the
corners—greasy from all the smoke—and then surveyed the people,
while nodding slightly, as if swaying with a gentle air of approval,
exactly as if he had just walked into the sweaty, smelly locker room of
his home team, with him as the new coach, a miracle worker who'd
turn the sad group of losers into winners, who'd have them up and
playing again; this was how he walked into the place, like an investor,
the sort of mystical figure they were dreaming of, maybe or maybe
not—they probably thought nobody would ever show up. There
certainly hadn't been much hope since the government shut down
the subsidized railway line, and even buses seldom passed through.

"Anybody know Sobotka, the engineer?" said Oleg loudly.

A heavyset, slightly stooped man stood up with no haste and
came over. His hair was already gray, and the ruddy hue of his face
showed he used to be blond.

"Sobotka," he said. "Yes?"

"I hear you used to be the lead engineer at the factory."

"One of the lead engineers," he said. Oleg looked him over.

After all the years of dealing with all brands of liars, he'd developed an eye for human faces: con men wore a protective facial
membrane and a slight cataract over their eyes—theirs were shady
faces, with a gaze that was supposedly directed at you, but which
stayed partly inside, as if already protecting its share in the business.
Another type of people was the kind who evaded looking at you at
all: that type held back from giving you false hope. Only decent
men and murderers looked at you as directly as Sobotka did, but he
didn't have the playful spark Oleg had spotted in murderers.

You could only catch this in the first few seconds—later on it would be less and less evident.

Spoken words obscure the view, he used to say when explaining his philosophy of first impressions.

"We want to restart production at the factory," said Oleg. "We'd like to know if that's possible."

The engineer took a draw on a cigarette, squinted a bit, and peered at Oleg. Open suspicion like his was only purview of old codgers and drunks.

"You must be fuckin' kidding me." The engineer had, apparently, had a lot to drink.

"We didn't come this far to crack jokes," said Oleg.

3

"HOW DID THE factory function?" asked Oleg in the car while plowing through slush.

"Hah, well, we had a market when there were no markets. You know, back in socialism. By the time the markets arrived, we'd lost ours. How do you explain that?"

Oleg waited for the question to evaporate along with the fumes of alcohol. He pressed the button to open the back windows a crack.

"I mean, how did things go organization-wise?" he asked in a voice that showed he knew what he was after.

He'd already thought about this and now he ran through their options again. First, he and Nikola knew nothing about this type of business. Second, they needed to work fast. The two didn't exactly go hand in hand.

But there was a third factor sitting on the back seat: this man knew how everything had functioned. With him, the first and the second factors were both possible. Oleg glanced at him in the rear-view mirror. He opened the back windows a bit wider. The cold smell of evergreen forest wafted in from outside. This is the fragrance I need, thought Oleg.

"Organization-wise? Well, the way all things were back then." Sobotka laughed in the breeze. "Like they used to say: self-management—workers' self-management—that's how they called it in socialism, you know."

"Did any work get done? Or was everything just a complete mess like they're now saying it was?" Oleg asked.

Sobotka was briefly silent, as if taking a deep breath, and then he said, "No, we did our job. Although I don't know how that job is done nowadays, because I haven't worked since then. I mean, not professionally."

"So, my plan is to get the factory up and running as soon as possible, to repair what needs repairing, to procure whatever materials you need, and I need you to spell this all out for me. We'll be manufacturing the same turbines."

The very same ones? While trouncing around in the Japanese SUV, Sobotka began thinking he'd found himself in some kind of time warp with phantoms behind the wheel. He couldn't see Oleg's face from the back seat. The other man had dropped his head, probably dozing. They'd fastened their seat belts, an obvious sign that they weren't from around here.

"So tell me, would you be able to revive production? Pull it all together?"

"Er. Well, if I had everything I needed." While he was breathing in the sobering air, only one thing rang in Sobotka's mind: *the same turbines.* These men were clueless. The technology was outdated. Would he scare them away if he said this aloud? Instead, he just pointed out, cautiously, "But I worked back then, under the old system, the old way."

Oleg almost said, I don't care about systems, but instead he said,

"As far as I'm concerned, do it your way, any old way, any new way, whatever. If you like, you can even self-manage. The finances and the sales are mine. The organization is yours."

He didn't quite hear what I was saying, thought Sobotka.

"It'd be easiest if you organized everything your way. Nikola will be the manager, just so we have some oversight. But we won't interfere much. You will have your freedom. So, self-manage as you please, but the factory must be up and running soon. If not, then we'll do things differently."

Sobotka sighed and said, "You kind of caught me by surprise. But this all sounds good. Look, I'll give this all I've got."

Now you're talking, thought Oleg.

Sobotka watched the two of them up front, then he looked around, searching for a hidden camera. If he were sober, he'd be able to gauge things better. Hang on, they wanted to hire him, and he hadn't worked for twenty years and he'd have serious problems with the modern turbines. Had these guys come from Mars?

Oleg raised the rear window.

"How well is the factory preserved inside?"

"The main things should all be there. Before it was closed there were rumors that the machines might be sold off, so we anchored them."

"What?"

"We buried the footings in concrete."

"Way to go!" Oleg turned slightly toward his passenger. "And nothing happened after that?"

"During the war there was talk that Ragan would be taking it over. He was from another town, a mobster, so people kept their distance. But I guess he didn't know what to do with it. The government made promises, too, but nothing happened."

The silence of two men deep in thought and a third deep asleep filled the SUV.

Sobotka finally said, "So why invest?"

"We have a development plan."

After a pause, Sobotka mustered the courage to say, "Our turbines are, you know … The ones used today are, how should I put it … smaller. Everything needs to be updated. And then you might need someone younger, someone who's better informed."

"Fair enough. But we will be making the same turbines. Type 83-N, right?"

Sobotka paused. "Ah, I see you know turbines." He decided to stop being so cautious, because, though all of this came as a surprise, this last comment surprised him so much that it was as if the things he'd heard before no longer seemed the least bit surprising. Few people still knew about that type of turbine.

The *83-N?* He'd almost forgotten it, himself. They had a nickname for each turbine, they didn't call them by their technical names.

The 83-N. He remembered how at first they'd called it the *osamdeset-troika*, after the number 83, and soon shortened this to the nickname of *ostroika*, like *eightree.* So when Gorbachev introduced perestroika, somebody declared, "He copied us just like Edison copied Tesla!" Maybe this made no sense, but they told and retold the joke.

"Let's visit the plant in the morning. Around ten?"

They dropped Sobotka off at his house.

When Sobotka slammed the back door, Nikola was roused from his slumbers, and as they were turning, the headlights lit incredible creatures in Sobotka's garden.

"What kind of gremlins are these?"

"What?" Oleg had already turned the car.

"You can't see them now."

"Gremlins?"

"Well, not real gremlins. Something weird."

"Okay, back to sleep, Niks."

Sobotka jabbed at the lock several times with his key. When I wake up tomorrow, he thought, I won't remember any of this.

A chilly morning, brisk.

Oleg was smoking out on the terrace, studying the town.

Down on the road, in the fresh snow, there was a man carrying sacks, walking his big black dog on a leash. The man had a lot of sacks and bags of all sizes—too many.

The man with the sacks was talking to his dog as if the dog were a naughty child.

Then, all of a sudden, he hollered something into the air.

After that he started running with the dog, romping, really, with the dog. Though, in fact, there's no telling whether the dog's having fun, thought Oleg. Because the man with the sacks is crazy, but maybe the dog isn't.

Oleg was standing there, smoking, but all he saw were impressions lurking along the edges of language; he could have been said to be *thinking*, or *musing* (if he were, indeed, a character in a novel), but thought is a fickle thing, as are musings, so it takes a little violence for us to work them into sentences, following the convention of subject and predicate, the mechanics of grammar, and they're only tenuously linked to the real world; I don't really think in clear-cut sentences, these are my impressions from the outer edges of language, thought Oleg.

✧　✧　✧

They entered the factory. The smell of dust. Hoots through the broken windows, high above, and then a departing flutter of wings.

There was frozen snow beside the wall, piled up from above. Morning winter light from outside, gloom. Long cobweb threads hung from the ceiling, linked between the pillars, like safety nets for trapeze artists. In the dim light, through the dust floating in the awful cold, Oleg thought he saw the engineer's eyes go glassy with tears. He looked away and held back, letting Sobotka lead the way.

Sobotka would have preferred to be alone: to swear, to shout, to converse with the ghosts. He felt as if he might possibly bump into a younger version of himself—without the gray hair, with the shoulder-length hair and the sideburns; a man cockily driving a Polish Fiat 125 with a beautiful wife and a child who, he believed, would have a better life than he was living, and with the carefree smile of a golden boy who succeeds at everything he touches, a smile some confused with arrogance. While he was clearing away the cobwebs around the machinery they had long ago imported from Japan, and trying to stifle a coughing fit, Sobotka closed his eyes, and even though all he could hear were the sounds of his lungs, he felt as if he could hear the rumble of the machines. And it was as if he could see the people from his past. The hum of the machines vibrated in his inner ear.

He stared at the machinery in front of him and could see old Whiskers, who used to operate the Japanese equipment. Whiskers, who'd taught him once long ago, instructing him in how to do the job: *Take it slow, we're in no rush, doing it right is what matters, not speed.*

He could see Slavko in his blue work smock, a pen and tester in his upper pocket.

Arman, the locksmith, whose curse was *Damn the dirt beneath your feet!*

He saw all the faces at once, frozen in time with the machinery.

He could see his old director, Veber, who often snorted at Sobotka; Veber thought Sobotka was full of himself, he and his whole generation. That man, always in a gray suit—the behind-the-scenes power of the Party, that's how Sobotka saw Veber.

Sobotka remembered that clash he'd had with Veber in the eighties, when he was among those who organized a strike.

The director felt his own children had betrayed him.

"You're turning your backs on me! I was the one who built this factory," he shouted during a workers' assembly.

"But we're facing inflation, and our wages are stagnating!"

"Things start from above. The government has requested help from the IMF. Do you know what that means?"

Sobotka and the others succeeded in persuading the workers' council to vote in favor of a strike. They struck for three weeks; Sobotka encouraged the people and spoke a lot. TV reporters came, and there were reports of the strike on the evening news. He felt like the hero from the Polish trade union, Solidarity. They were his role models: the electrician named Lech Wałęsa with the mustache, the whole lot of them.

At the time, he and his fellow workers were in a strange, euphoric state and didn't sleep much.

Now, he looked toward the door to the section where the offices used to be, and he could see the silhouette of the woman, Zelda, he'd had a thing with during the strike—memory of her thighs came back to him and he suddenly felt a tension in his groin, which threw him off, he almost lost his balance and slowed to a stop.

He looked around.

A flutter of wings above him. One dark bird had been lying low; it flew around in jagged circles and then out through the glassless windows.

Oleg was standing behind him in the open hall, smoking. His assistant—what did he say his name was?—had his hands in his pockets and was looking up. Sobotka knew he shouldn't mention anything about the strike to them. For decades, many had bragged about standing up to socialism, but he'd kept quiet about this for years. All in vain, however—everyone who was supposed to hire him since would ultimately remember that he'd been the head striker, he'd roused the workers. Who needed *that kind* of dissident?

But back in the day they succeeded. Their strike was discussed in parliament, and the government conceded to their demands. He remembered well how the old director called him in to have a word and then—when Sobotka arrived—he stood up and said, "You seem to be doing a better job here than me. Want my job?"

At the time, he told this story many times, it worked well as an anecdote.

But he always skipped the part about how he felt as he left the office after the conversation.

4

WHILE HE WAS waiting, Veber sipped a glass of rakija. Somebody had written *rakija for the soul* with felt-tip pen on the bottle. He was an atheist, he mused, so maybe this was him being teased by the person who'd given him this triangle-shaped bottle with a braid of herbs long ago. He opened it now as if he were celebrating something.

He stared at the paper, still in the typewriter, on which he'd typed out his request for retirement that morning. He looked at the letter as if he were afraid to pull it out of the machine, so he left it there to marinate, like the medicinal herbs soaking in the rakija.

He thought again about their strike. How they'd seen him as someone on the other side. He'd lost his bond with them. In fact, he thought, he'd lost the bond he'd had with himself. With the way he used to see his role, back when he was envisioning his future.

This was the end of the story. The end was written and now was staring him in the face.

He should drink up everything and yank that paper out as if ripping off a bandage.

When Sobotka came in, Veber stood and said, "Nice mustache. Like the Polish guy, right?"

"A mustache like any other."

"Well, you seem to be doing a better job here than me. Want my job?" There was something in his words that made Sobotka smile.

"No. How could I lead a strike then?"

"Yes, that would be tricky! I'm an old revolutionary, you know. And yet, I can't lead a strike."

Veber's demeanor was usually far more formal, so Sobotka knew right away that he'd been drinking.

They sat facing each other.

"What can you do?" continued Veber. "We fought for a workers' state and now we have to lead it."

"I thought you were opposed to the strike."

"I led strikes. Then I went to war and then, goddammit, we won. Victory complicates things, you'll see."

"You came into power after you won. Power doesn't interest me."

"Nice." Sobotka heard the sarcasm and said nothing.

"And that's exactly the problem."

"What?"

"The problem is that you've removed me from power, yet you don't want it. The problem is the people you'll cede the power to!"

"No need to get all agitated."

"Don't you worry. I'm leaving, I'm retiring. Let's drink to that!"

Sobotka suddenly realized he had really taken his director down, and felt a bit sheepish when Veber stood and raised his glass.

"Nothing personal," said Sobotka.

They clinked glasses.

"You managed to fight for higher wages and I didn't. What am I here for? Let me know as soon as you find someone to replace me. I don't want them sending you somebody who doesn't get it."

36

Sobotka felt like the old man was trying to lure him out onto thin ice. *Do you want to take my job . . . ? Let me know . . .* "I'm not a part of the system, you know, I make no decisions," said Sobotka.

"Tough luck, now you have to be responsible. You think somebody at the top will deal with this? You seem to believe in the system more than I do!"

Sobotka grinned with a touch of irony.

"You think: we've raised a ruckus and we're done. Big Daddy will show up and handle everything. But I happen to know there's no one to handle it. Now it's your turn to run the show."

"I'm not interested in power or politics," said Sobotka firmly, meaning he wouldn't join the Party, but there was no need to focus on that.

"Oh, so you don't believe striking is politics? When I led strikes, that wasn't my mind-set."

Veber poured more rakija into both the glasses.

"I ought to get going," Sobotka said.

"Where are you off to now? Do you have a plan? Tell me, what's your plan, Mr. Wałęsa?"

Sobotka lifted his glass and drank it down, then lit a cigarette without asking permission, and said, "Okay, I, too, will be honest. You can't forgive me for the strike and now you're jerking me around."

"I'm just asking for your plan."

"If I had a plan," said Sobotka, "that might mean big trouble for me."

"Hey! We don't lock up workers around here for striking. Luckily this isn't Russia, or Albania."

"But if I had a *plan*, this would be much more serious."

"Oh. You're afraid to say it?" Veber frowned and poured them another round.

"I didn't say that."

"What is it then? You are afraid to even think. So you don't have a plan? Maybe you're waiting to see how this plays out, like all you younger generations do."

"If that's so, then it's your fault!" Sobotka said, even though he knew he was pushing the limits. "Who ever asked my generation anything? You're in charge," his ironic tone got the best of him, "you aging revolutionaries."

"You're right."

Sobotka looked at him—he was nervous because of what he'd blurted out and expected a different answer.

"But things change, as you see," continued Veber, "it's all yours now, so self-manage! Do as you please. I'm sure you'll be better at it."

"We've already gone over this," said Sobotka.

"Okay then, let's drink and be done with it."

The old man went over to the turntable, which Sobotka had spotted just then in the corner of the office, and put on a record. The scratch of the vinyl, classical music, an orchestra. Loud.

Sobotka sipped from his glass.

He looked at Veber, who was raising his glass, as if watching from a great distance.

He hadn't expected Veber to appreciate this kind of music. It was an old dramatic piece, like a voyage on board a ship: strings, trumpets, kettledrums, horns. Veber lit a cigarette.

The smoke spread lazily around the office and the space of the music made the premises seem even bigger, deeper, and, maybe, darker. The old man was glancing over at his typewriter, his face relaxed now. Then he poured them more rakija, and to Sobotka— deafened by the music—it all seemed as if it were happening in slow motion, as if they were underwater.

"*Spartacus.*"

The beat of the music was speeding up and turning into a buoyant dance in which Sobotka imagined only women, nothing but women.

He left the office warmed by the rakija and paced the hallways as if he were Oedipus, thinking: *I ousted him.* He, Sobotka, had done in the old Party honcho who'd seemed untouchable, without hardly lifting a finger.

Fueled by the rakija, instead of just walking by Zelda's office, in he goes. She stands and looks at him in silence, as if afraid of sounds: he shouldn't show up like this, it's not just her office. Luckily, her officemate isn't there. But what is he doing? He's locking the door and coming over: he's moving quickly like an animal, and already he's holding her. They shouldn't be doing this, but he is doing it, and she is looking at him, scared of the imaginary boundaries, but she doesn't protest, she says nothing, and he, too, is quiet—she can only hear his breathing.

She can hear only his breathing while they make love on the floor, and then the phone rings, it rings for a frighteningly long time in her ears, in her whole body; then it stops for a while but starts ringing again, and it echoes—must be the manager, he needs her, only he can be so persistent.

Then silence.

He stopped, then sat on the floor.

She looked at him and said, "What, what?" Then she remembered where they were. When she stood and smoothed her skirt, she said, as if to herself, "Seriously?"

She looked at him: he was still sitting on the floor, his head thrown back, as if he were sitting in the sun, with golden hair and an expression full of an odd blankness.

She went to unlock the door and said, "We are in too deep."

He watched her as he stood up and, for a moment, an odd sentence ran through his mind —*Let us go together to where.*

He knew these weren't quite the right words, but he said them anyway.

Zelda arched her eyebrows and steered him toward the door. When he left the office, she sat down and for a moment repeated to herself, as if somebody older were speaking to her: *Get a grip.*

Her officemate, Hanka, came in and Zelda had the feeling that she knew. Maybe she'd run into Sobotka in the corridor, or maybe she had even tried to come in while the door was locked.

Hanka said, "So, my dear Zelda, what do you think—where is all of this going?"

"Who knows."

"Oh, come on, you're young, you have the good fortune of being able to go wherever you like."

"Where would you go?"

"Me? If I were you: to Hollywood to see Richard Gere."

They both laughed.

Zelda came from the big city; she'd only been here for six months. By having an affair with her, Sobotka stepped into a whole new, unknown world. Everything became so ambiguous, but in an exciting way. Maybe even the fact that he'd become involved so passionately in the strike had to do with her: a new personality was germinating inside him, and this personality wanted to be made known. He'd denied his life so far, and this freed him, like a blast of light. But now, as he left her office, he felt as if he didn't exactly know where he was anymore. Everything was moving so fast, the world was dissolving and purifying momentarily before his eyes, as if a giant snowplow had just passed over it. *What's your plan*, Veber had asked, and the question still rang in his ears, together with the loud music and the image of the swirls of smoke floating around the office, the rakija smell, Zelda's smell, and that feeling that he'd stepped onto an unknown open space and didn't know where to stop.

Later that day when he came home, he made love to his wife Zlata.

He later found out that their youngest daughter was conceived that day, which, in the end, brought him back into the marriage.

He never managed to explain that day to himself.

No, he didn't find anyone to replace Veber. How was he supposed to find a director he'd be prepared to raise another strike against?

He thought about this a lot later on. What should he have done? The old man seemed to be making his final move and exacting his revenge by saddling him with this burden.

Later, he felt weirdly responsible for everything that happened next. Had the workers from Solidarity felt the same way? Sobotka kept up on Lech Wałęsa, afterward; he watched him on TV as the president of Poland and tried to figure out what exactly Wałęsa had done, besides overthrowing their socialism, or communism, or whatever it was.

I did not want to become the director, but he became president, so I guess he knew what he was after, thought Sobotka to himself. However, as time passed, it appeared to Sobotka that Wałęsa did not know what to do, either, just like him, who never in his life had felt better than during their strike, and who had since that time felt progressively smaller and smaller, eventually turning into plankton.

The memory remained that he'd once been part of something big, back then in the factory. But in a way, he could no longer explain the memory.

He often heard people praise him for tearing down communism. During the war this granted him a certain immunity. He would sometimes use it to tell new punks, "Where were you when I was tearing down communism? Where were you when I was a person of interest to the secret police?"

That shut them up.

He was actually called in a couple of times for questioning, but Sobotka was nonchalant and quiet. So they came up with different tactics and started intercepting him at bars, casually showing up right next to him, hoping he'd blurt something out after a couple of beers. They tried to cozy up to him in their characteristically venal way. A particularly clumsy guy—Sobotka called him 'The Log'— was assigned to him.

"You Catholic, Sobotka?"

"By heritage."

"Do you believe?"

"On occasion."

"Ha ha. *On occasion*! Way to go. Why not join the Party then?"

"No rush."

"And your wife is German?"

"Partly."

"German maiden name."

"Wow, you're well informed. Or perhaps it's Jewish?"

"No shit! Really?"

"Look into it."

"Or maybe you are a Catholic Unionist like the Polish guy?"

"My wife is Orthodox, if you must know."

"You're kidding."

"Catholic Unionist? Really? Do you know all about the ethnic makeup of this place?"

"I do actually, which is why I'm surprised."

"I'd be as well."

"There you go . . ."

However, all this dismayed him. He did not like being questioned. His wife Zlata used to say, "the children will pay their debts," because at the time everyone still believed the system would last forever.

A few months after the strike, the new director arrived. A so-called technocrat, supposedly an expert, who did not even bother moving to N., but instead traveled to and fro daily in a company car. Later, the workers went on strike again, but there was probably too much of that going around: strikes were in the news every day, the whole system was on the verge of striking, and the turbine factory was no longer big news.

Not even The Log cared anymore; he and his protegees were dealing with God-knows-what-else by that time.

Sometimes Sobotka would see Veber on the street. They'd usually wave from a distance, but on one occasion, when they almost collided at the door to a bakery, Sobotka had to stop. He already knew the old man was going to lecture him, but he was surprised by the manner in which he did so: "The Party is full of assholes and the workers are fools. But bear in mind, the state still belongs officially to the workers, so take advantage of this. Why don't you take over the factory? They won't know what to do with you."

The old man had a confident ring to his voice that caught Sobotka off guard because they'd never been close. Look at that, he thought, he's a little odd and treating me like his successor.

"All right then, how would you do it?"

"You gather the class-conscious ones and then you move."

Sobotka laughed at the old man's communist rhetoric and said, "Move where, into the woods?"

The old man took offense, and as he was leaving he said, "Laugh all you want. The battle will be fought. The only question is whose side you'll be fighting on."

Sobotka thought about how the old man said whatever he damned well pleased because he had the immunity of an old partisan, while he, Sobotka, could not talk like that.

He followed him.

"What battle?"

The old man turned around and as if chastising a weak student, said, "Don't you know? If workers don't fight for unity among themselves, they'll be turned against each other!"

When Zelda heard that Sobotka's wife was pregnant, she told him, "It's not because you screwed me over, it's because you're a coward."

She left in her orange Citroën Dyane, and he never saw her again.

His world closed in on him once again, but he got through it.

His daughter was born; she kicked her feet a lot. A silly image perhaps, but that was how he remembered her.

With his first daughter, Jasmina, he was serious; with Viktoria, whose name he chose, all he could do was laugh. People said parents are often more relaxed with the second child, and perhaps the laughter was his escape, along with the subtle, habitual smell of alcohol. Zlata was not amused.

When talk began of a 30 percent worker surplus at the factory, nobody wanted to strike any more out of fear of being counted among the surplus, and the anger they felt was diverted to big rallies held under national flags in different parts of the country, covered regularly by the news. There were some people from his company, fellow strikers in fact, who traveled to rallies on pre-arranged buses and returned as a closely knit group. He didn't want to believe this, though he did notice that they kept their distance from him.

Sobotka was no longer the leader of anything.

When the Communist Party announced the first democratic election, and power was divided between the parties of the three ethnic groups, he tried to be as happy as Wałęsa and the other new leaders like him in other countries. But Zlata was worried again because she'd heard that a war might break out, so he shared this happiness only with Viktoria.

Sobotka walked through the cold factory as if walking through a cemetery where nobody remembered the people buried there or what had happened to them.

His forgetting went deeper than the years that had passed; he felt as if there were something like a vacuum inside him. A fissure that reduced his memory to chaos. He realized he'd forgotten what he used to be like then, he'd forgotten the world that once existed.

I am a different person now, he thought, and everyone I know is, now, different. This was the first time he truly understood. Those people from before are gone. The people of today are nothing like the people back then. They've all had their ears boxed and their tails whipped.

Suddenly he thought about the first time he ever heard about snipers. He was flabbergasted. Did this really happen? He'd pictured war as skirmishes on the front lines. But someone picking people off on the street at random with gunfire—this was something he couldn't wrap his mind around. Yet somebody was shooting, a beast, and whoever assigned that person the job was the creator of today's person, thought Sobotka.

This kept him tossing and turning in his restless sleep full of jumbled scenes, disparate images from the life he was living now and his old life, nightmares that left him drenched in sweat—all because of the investor who'd appeared out of the blue to take him back to that world, a world he could no longer imagine. The interloper had lured Sobotka back into this factory, which he had only seen from a distance for years. Yes, he'd seen it, but he'd never really looked at it.

Had Sobotka believed in ghosts, he'd have said the ghosts were here.

Then he thought, What does insanity look like on the *inside*? How and from where did this man *appear*?

He had been drinking for years, as much as he could; the previous night as well, at the tavern where he was to fix the wiring. He wondered, could this be his last hangover? Could what this man is saying be possible? He said we'd do everything the way we used to. Our old turbines, the old way? I guess that is what insanity looks like on the *inside*.

All I need now is a black dog.

Sobotka turned around and looked at Oleg; he was standing outside at the entrance, calmly, watching Sobotka in the dim light, to see if he was real. And again, they were telling him to do it *his way*, like Veber just before leaving. He wanted to shout, *Don't toy with me!* but stopped himself. If he is here to invest, he thought, and I threaten him like that, he's going to think I'm crazy. And if I'm hallucinating, it makes no sense to talk to him, either. What would be the point?

Good, he concluded, his reasoning still functioned.

He walked on to the turbine assembly area. The huge rotor base was still covered, preserved. He remembered how he, Arman, and Slavko had seen to that, at a time when they'd already stopped receiving their salaries.

They'd done it well—you could still tell.

Then he inspected the concrete they'd poured around the base. He smiled wistfully. How did we have the willpower? We really did believe. But he couldn't remember who or what it was they'd believed in. They simply believed it would be insane to just let everything go to ruin. They poured the concrete and were done with it. There.

It was still here. Twenty years later.

Nikola had lit his fourth cigarette. He was feeling chilly.

"How much longer are we going to be here?" he asked Oleg.

"Let the man walk around the whole place."

"It looks more like he is wandering."

"This place is his life story," Oleg said. "He's exactly the guy I need."

"Yeah, you can tell he's the guy," Nikola said. "An old-school loser."

5

"IT'S LIKE THIS, I work as a *plumber*. Below my paygrade, but hey. The money's not bad, and this suits them bigtime: they pay us way less than they pay their own people, and besides we work harder because we know we've got nowhere else to go. The place is a whole little city, there are a couple of camps, and you can hear folks swearing in our language all over the place, just like the old days in our army here, except for the American commanding officers. Okay, I'm kidding, there are others, too, the entire Non-Aligned Movement's over there."

"Go on. I'm not laughing."

"Look, there are tents that accommodate a hundred, but some hold up to three or four hundred! Think about it—four hundred men to a tent. Or a hundred, same thing. And everyone's there: Indians, Filipinos, us, everybody. It stinks like fuck! Who knows who doesn't shower, I don't want to be a racist, there are guys from around here who don't shower, either, and don't forget the boozers, so when the night starts to swelter and they strike up with the snores, it's like a frog-infested swamp in there. And the latrines, what can I say, they make you want to puke. It's a twelve-hour-straight shift, no lunch break, eat out of a can on your feet. Then I was transferred to a small FOB, a forward-operating base, you might call it a camp, and that was less crowded. But every other second you're crouching somewhere in a bunker. There were casualties, all sorts of shit, shell-fire. It's no normal gig—it's stress, you wear a vest and a helmet, and you walk around the place yet you know the place hates you. And now I hear some guys want to go there for peanuts? I mean, I know times are tough, but that's not the way."

"Oh, come on, it all depends on where you land. My neighbor's son is over there, in Jalalabad or whatever it's called. She says there's no action there, her son sleeps like a baby. I mean, his mother ought to know. He goes to the gym and he's bulking up, she showed me a picture. I know the guy, he used to be scrawny, he must be popping those American pills. There's nothing for me here. This recession, it's not getting any better, even abroad, let alone here. And the Americans will always print up more dollars even when they run low."

"First of all, some folks don't read their contracts; everything's there in black and white. Does it say there's a likelihood of hardship? Does it say this is a war zone? Okay, it doesn't spell out the latrines and the snoring, but there you have it. You're grown-ups, literate—some more than others, sure—although the recruiter doesn't care about that. All he cares about is whether you've signed on the dotted line. If you've signed, he figures you've read the small print. I've heard people demand a certain salary, I wouldn't bet on that, speaking from experience, because I saw subcontractors over there, they were brought in by a company and were paid four to six hundred bucks a month, I swear, they're on a two-year contract and given no leave. Not even for funerals. They get food, where to stay, laundry, no expenses, so it's worth it for them because where they're from there's zero standard of living. Keep that in mind, too. The sub-contractors are competing with you. Tell the recruiter whatever you like, but he'll choose. In my experience, the important thing is to get in the door. I used to work in a really fucked-up FOB, so my bio looks way better now, and an American looks at you differently after you've proved yourself and made the rounds. The recruiter even came to me this time."

"I know, man. Tell me, are they paying you to offer folks less or what?"

"Watch it, bud. I find jobs for people, and if you don't want a job, forget it! I'm not here to sweet-talk anyone, all of you have the freedom to choose. This is all about personal choice. Truth is, the salaries are lower now than when we started. But can you bring that much in anywhere else? You know best. You have the information. Nowadays everyone has access to information and there are no secrets here. I've already laid everything out for you, no point in repeating. But I will say: this is not required. It's the Americans and you have the freedom of choice, take it or leave it."

"Hell, I'd go just to get away from here. If it's that bad for you, why don't you come back and leave me your post of, what was that you said? Plummer? I can do plums! You want to talk me out of this, like everything sucks over there, but you've been there for years. There's a sweet Škoda Oktavia in your garage, you've added another floor to your house. Cut the crap!"

"Listen, are we going to discuss how to negotiate the salary tomorrow, or is everyone willing to work for peanuts? That's why they cut the salaries in the first place. Look, there's nowhere to go when you're there, no freedom, you live like a dog. The salary should compensate for that."

"I know, sure, but money is tight everywhere. I'm actually fine with having nowhere to go while I'm there, I'd spend all the money otherwise. This way I know I'll save."

"I fucked up with a bank loan. I have to get out of the red, and when things get tough, you can't be picky. I'd ask for more, but when thousands of people are in trouble like you, they're competition. You can't be picky if they aren't. That's life, what can you do?"

"That's exactly what I am saying. If you aren't picky, you're ruining it for the rest of us. I know, times are tough, but that's exactly how they are trying to get their hands on you dirt cheap. Trust me, they're in no crisis. I say we can get more, I was there, I know, so don't say you'll work for peanuts right away, or you'll screw it up for yourselves and for me!"

"I'm out of options. I am going at all costs. I've made up my mind!"

"At all costs? Why not volunteer then? And don't forget: bring your own food."

"I went to war, and I'm not scared of war or work! It's easy for you to talk! You struck it rich. This is our turn now."

"Go ahead, I'm not standing in your way. But take this friendly piece of advice. The war you already fought in counts as experience. If you volunteered then, don't volunteer now."

"You're getting on my nerves, I swear! Watch it!"

"Temper, temper. Watch your nerves. You'll need them once you find your footing over there."

"I'm not scared of anything."

"Then why go for plumber? Why not apply straightaway to escort convoys, that'll get you the most points. Your bio will be amazing. But don't tell the other guys you're volunteering. They'll shoot you."

"I'm leaving before I punch him."

"Hear that, Erol? He wants to punch me."

"I did."

"You guys! This is not working, let's... So, tomorrow at the hotel, first floor, a lady will be on the right as you come in, give her your passport."

"Fine! But brothers, just remember that we blew this on our own!"

Sobotka, Oleg, and Nikola were sitting in a booth in the corner of the bar, where they could hear this discussion loud and clear.

"Just a moment," said Sobotka. He walked over to their table. They were about to leave.

He patted the stocky young man with short curly hair on the back and the man turned his boxer's mug.

"Erol, off to war again?"

"Well, I don't know, I've heard all kinds of things . . ."

Sobotka used his hand to stop the young man who was championing higher pay, and told him, "I think I know you, too. Your father used to work with me, right?"

"Yes, he did. I'm Branoš."

"Branoš, Arman's son. I remember you hanging around during the strike. You brought us food, played the guitar."

"Yeah, that was awesome hanging out with all of you then."

"I can see some of it rubbed off on you."

"You mean my thinking's from then? Maybe," said Branoš, smiling. "I'd almost forgotten all that."

I, too, used to work at the factory. These days I'm out walking the dog. I walk the dog all the time and I'm fine. Can't complain, there's nobody to complain to because a complaint should be addressed to someone, and if there's no one to hear me out, I can't complain, nor do I care to complain to those who'd like me to, just so they can hear me complaining, because everyone has to complain about something and everybody has to get spat on, because they made us complain so much. I won't, no way will I complain in vain since there's nobody to hear it, so instead I'm cheerful. And I walk the dog, and I run with the dog, and I bound, and I whoop. The dog's happy, I am glad for him, he's genuinely happy, and when I see him happy, I'm happy, too. We're two happy pals.

I often walk the dog around the factory. I dance and bound with my dog, my pal. You can't find a truer pal in this land of bought-and-sold souls, whose lice make my body itch when I feel them all over, they make my ass and my brain itch when I feel them and then I don't feel them; the lice, the souls and the demons of their victory over the other me, whom they routed, unlike the quirky-silly me, itching from their headless lice; I once saw a soldier who had them, the buddy of a dead man who killed himself to avoid the killing; my son, my child once born.

Walking on eggshells around it all, I'm watching; something's swirling and sucking me in; Sobotka is bringing in people, dragging them around, buckling them up; they're huffing and puffing into their hands, they're sudden, it's as if they aren't drunk, or just a little drunk, I don't drink, it's bad for me so I avoid it, only the postman and I don't drink around here, both of us are crazy; he hasn't figured this out yet.

But Sobotka is buckling these people up and delivering them to the factory and it looks like they're doing something that's just plain weird. Maybe they're stealing something or someone, that's what I've been wondering, but they don't strike me as the stealing kind. Stealing has been rare ever since the numbers showed up on the hill, right next to the sacred apparition; I went to see it after the death and there they were, the numbers, on the righthand side, nobody but me saw the numbers, just me, I was the only one who saw the numbers next to the sacred apparition, strange! But from a distance I'm keeping close watch on the men with Sobotka. My sight has become more acute ever since I started talking less, and I can see them clearly. They aren't walking as if they're stealing, they aren't looking back at their souls, they aren't stooped like they've lost their minds, no. They look like they are really doing something, standing tall, calling to each other like workers, clearing out the trash, cleaning up. They're bundled up, wearing big gloves, covered in dust like abandoned cars. They look almost like the old days, which is so weird and makes me feel numb all over, and I don't know why this terrifies me, but it terrifies me and sends me shivering, as if it's summoning me and howling in the distance, calling me to a life so far away that it cracked wide open, a vast yawn, something long gone from the prevailing reality or the map of the world. There's no hole there for shimmying up the rope, up there, down there, in-between, I don't know, to the place where I left everything but myself and the dog. So I stop by the chain-link fence before and behind the world while they're cheering alone in time; and with goose bumps rising like weeds I jut out like a bramble by the fence, and go numb until it's too intense. Then I get up and go, because it's time to walk the dog, that's my job, my rhythm, my song.

Oleg started packing and Nikola perched on the antique settee, the almost-new genuine leather beneath him *squeaking* with his every move. Or was it leatherette, he wondered, his beer resting on a stout-legged coffee table. He was watching the TV in the living room, and he was warm. The cavernous manor, hats off to the landlord, had proper central heating.

After he finished watching a euphoric report on an independent winemaker hoping to export his products to Western markets, Nikola went over to Oleg and asked, "Can you explain to me, one more time, what's up with the self-organization thing? Why run things this way?"

I told you already, thought Oleg, but you were probably buzzed on your pills.

"What do you mean, why? They self-organize! We're clueless. And we can't bring in somebody new to build a 1980s turbine, either. Nobody knows that stuff anymore! We'd have to go to him no matter what. So, this way or that, they're in charge. Look, we're relying on these people. And what did I do?"

Nikola could see on Oleg's face that he was about to come up with the cleverest thing in the world, and maybe the funniest, too.

"I offered it to them as a *privilege*!" he said, throwing up his hands. "*Self-organization!* Freedom. Do it your way. Which means they matter, they'll feel better. Besides, this way, they won't think of me as a tycoon and a usurper."

Oleg was choosing his words. He had to make sure it didn't look as if he'd done this because he felt Nikola was incompetent. Which was mostly true. But he had to look after him.

"Hmm, but what if they start giving us a hard time? He hasn't worked since socialism. He says he only knows the old ways, and if you let him organize according to what he knows..."

"I want him to feel comfortable on his own turf. I told him I'm in charge of the finances. Who cares how they divvy up the work among themselves? They used to have a director and were paid a salary before as well, so they will now again. But get this: they haven't even seen the money yet and they're already cleaning. That's what we're after. If he's motivated, he'll bring in more people. Where would we be without that? Should we keep track of whether they're coming in on time?"

"I'm fine with that. But long-term—"

"Look, I know what I'm up to. If things get messy, we can always fall back on the Labor Law—today's, know what I'm saying? But we need them on our side. We need enthusiastic men to do the job as if this were their own factory. They can think they're managing themselves, whatever, who cares. You just have to supervise them, keep a polite distance, if there's a need to intervene down the line . . . we'll put our heads together."

His idea was to give Nikola more of a sense of security, perhaps even a little élan, because he saw Nikola was feeling more depressed than usual. Oleg wasn't surprised. The town didn't really seem like a barrel of fun.

Nikola hadn't expected he'd be feeling this dismal fear of being alone; something he hadn't felt since childhood. As he watched Oleg's fancy footwork, one part of his brain saw himself take his suitcase, pack to go with Oleg, and tell him, There, fucked up yet again.

But he couldn't do that to Oleg, so, again, he sat down in front of the TV; coming up next was a report from Slobomir, a brand-new town.

The news truck was trundling through the wastelands, its windshield wipers on, and then it pulled up in front of a sign that said *Slobomir.*

"Expatriate Slobodan Milićević, who made his millions as a real estate broker in Chicago, came up with the idea of building a new town in his homeland." At the same time as the voice-over, a man with long gray hair and a shovel laid the cornerstone before a crowd of people.

"This businessman is a prime example of a man who built everything he has with his own two hands. Ten years ago he published his autobiography, *How I Made It.* A sequel, he says, is in the works."

The reporter surveys the people in the crowd for their opinions. Nikola cracked open another beer. Someone in the crowd says, "Slobodan Miličević has already renovated several churches in the area, and we believe . . ."

"Why not build a town here? Everything will be close at hand." Nikola used to work in television, so he knew all about what went on offscreen and with the editing. The reporter is talking to Slobodan Miličević, and his wife is standing next to him in front of the *Slobomir* sign "Slobomir will develop as a private town with a managing director. We're building the first Disneyland east of Paris, the fourth in the world. The creative team in charge of the development plans for Slobomir has sketched a Disneyland theme park with eleven lakes across an area of some twenty-five acres. We're planning to build a huge aquarium, marinas for yachts, and lagoons with magical boats, a zoo with local and wild animals, an array of entertainment rides and heated pools, shopping centers and a private university."

"What will the population of Slobomir be, do you think?" asks the reporter.

"I'm thinking thirty to forty thousand people."

The news truck pulls out of Slobomir, the wipers working while the reporter's voice-over concludes, "As John Fitzgerald Kennedy would say, 'Ask not what your country can do for you, ask what you can do for your country!'"

"It's a shame you missed this report!" Nikola shouted to Oleg. "There are other people with ideas here."

"Hey, Nikola, trust me why don't you!" said Oleg, bringing a bottle of beer for himself. "This is not just an '*idea.*'"

"This guy here is totally in with the times. A private town!" He gave a reluctant laugh. "While we're . . . set in our ways."

"Hey, don't lose faith in me. Let's have one for the road!"

"Let's. And don't forget where you parked me."

"Johnny B. Goode," Oleg laughed, raising his glass, and threw one arm over Nikola's shoulder. "And you will be the leader of a big old band."

"Now you want us to sing, too?" said Nikola in an effort to remain glum.

Too bad the bastard was leaving; he loved this clown.

Sobotka walked out of the store with a bottle of rakija and approached the group that was hopping in the slush with a plastic bottle of wine.

He opened the rakija and took a swig, then offered the bottle to the lanky guy with the hangdog face and the cigarette, who seemed nearly sober.

"Come on, Sken, take one."

Skender took a swig and said, "What's up?"

"You're not going to believe this, but something actually is."

A sturdy guy with a potato-shaped red nose and husky voice joined in: "I've heard rumors, but they don't believe me."

"You've heard right."

"If it ain't a scam," said Skender.

"We'll see about that. I should say right now, we still haven't seen the money. They say it's coming. But we're doing everything our way," Sobotka said. "Why don't you come by?"

"Sounds fishy to me. But I ain't got nothing better to do."

"I could come, too," added the guy with the potato-shaped nose.

"You could, Zulko. Whoever wants to apply should come, and we'll see."

"Check out Mr. Crazy," someone said. "Seems like he's really into marching today."

The man with the dog marched past the slippers shop. When he noticed them, he shifted direction so they were facing his back, and then shouted, as if he were selling something, "Cunt! Libera!"

He could still be heard as he turned the corner.

Gigo was a mid-rank functionary in the county administration. A reasonably cheerful man, if circumstances so dictated he wouldn't hesitate to befriend someone on the spur of the moment. They spent twenty minutes at the desk. Oleg showed him his papers; Gigo invited him to lunch. They went to an old restaurant by a water mill, where they could hear the murmur of the water. Gigo was a regular there.

Oleg slotted him into the category of people who had nothing to hide because they believed in nothing. He knew the type—capable of forgetting what happened one day and treating it as something unrealistic the next.

Gigo was friendly, nodding as if agreeing with every thought Oleg offered.

Ever since he was a small-time Socialist Youth official, through his time as a mid-rank operative for one of the national parties during the war, all the way to his office in the county administration, Gigo followed every going trend as if it were the law. He'd read up on them in the newspapers he checked daily, watch a couple of TV news reports, and then mix it all up.

He was rational; he was said to be savvy about business.

"I've been told the state has plans for the factory," said Oleg.

"I don't know where that's coming from. They're dreaming, someone blurts out something, they wait. You can't explain things to some people. There's no state in the picture. What state? The state can't do anything, that's what the market is for. But people, especially the people here, since they fought in the war and all, think something's here just because there are borders."

"What was the war like around there? Nasty?"

"Not so bad. They've always been somewhat on the sidelines. In fact, that particular municipality, if you ask me . . . Can I be straight with you?"

"Yes, of course."

"If you ask me, people there are a little strange. You'll hear words there you won't hear anywhere else. All sorts ended up hiding out in those mountains. Who knows what's there? I don't even think they do."

"Okay, so there are Muslims, Catholics, Orthodox Christians, a bit of everything, that I do know."

"Yes, but there are also other groups who identify themselves as, um . . . They say some of them have been in the mountains since the Roman Empire."

"The Roman Empire?" This seemed a bit over the top for Oleg.

"I don't know, man, a professor told me about them. I can't even remember everything he said. All sorts seek shelter in the mountains while the new powers or new laws pass through the valleys. When the professor told me this, I remember thinking: I might just retreat to the mountains myself one day," Gigo said with a laugh. "This is off the record, I'm just kidding."

"This stays between us. I'm not one of those Facebook types. But, here, we're setting this thing in motion. So just to be clear: if there's any other policy or plan—"

"Waiting and waiting for investors to appear. No other policy."

"All right, just so I know there's support for this, and that politics won't tangle up our business, right?"

"How could it when there's no policy? Sorry, I'm a joker, as you know."

"Okay," said Oleg. "I'm not interested in ownership, a concession's fine with me."

"Fair enough. I can lobby for that. You can repay me for it but you don't have to, that's just how it is. All I ask from you is to talk to the press. We'll have to sign the papers officially and invite someone from the central government for a splash of publicity. I'm here for you. Well, for people like you, since we're being straight with each other."

After a late lunch, under dim streetlights and through trodden snow, Nikola walked from the Hajduci restaurant to the grocery store. The group out in front of the store was now gone. We must have employed them all, he thought. Pity, he would have loved nothing more than to drink something in the middle of the street. *Yes, you pretend to be a director when you're actually a bum*, he said to himself in a low drone, sounding like the long-since disappointed father talking to the long-since indifferent son.

He sometimes used that voice to speak to himself; it was like malware surfacing in his system. This wasn't his real father's voice. It was the voice of a generic district judge, who had something to do with the way success was defined in his social circle. Yes, while his old friends used their iPhones to check in from ski resorts in the Alps and post pictures on Facebook, it was wiser for him to not get in touch from here because the only thing they could ask him was if he'd gone hiking all by himself like the Yeti.

Luckily, he'd promised to abstain from Facebook. "Forget about posting your location and pictures. That stuff is for suckers," said Oleg.

"Okay."

For some time he'd been feeling like he was merely adapting to resemble something he should have made of himself, something like "the old Nikola," like "he's still holding it together," like a spokesperson.

He bought a six-pack at the store.

He drank at their rented manse, standing in front of the window and gazing out at the gas station, where there was activity in front of the café. He saw young men parking their dilapidated Audis and BMWs, getting out promptly with their hoods on, stretching and rolling their shoulders as if about to perform, and then entering the glass-walled café. From there, they eyed who stopped to fill up and who was passing by.

Then they pulled out of the parking lot, tires screeching, and headed to town, only to return some ten minutes later, having checked to be sure the gas station was the place to be. They got out of their cars again, rolling their shoulders as if about to perform. Sometimes a girl was with them, and Nikola first thought she was being looked after, surrounded by all the young men, and, later he thought she actually wasn't. Because they hugged the girls the same way they rolled their shoulders—as if about to perform on an invisible stage.

He switched on the TV.

He watched a talk show that had the reek of a life lived in a stained sweatshirt worn only at home.

They seemed to be talking about politics.

They were in that limbo of television programs—it was now fifteen years since the war and nothing new had yet begun.

Nikola was on his third beer, when it occurred to him that six beers wouldn't be enough.

Luckily, the gas station was open.

✧ ✧ ✧

Uncle Martin was calling. Unbelievable.

"What's up?"

"My plane lands today," Oleg said into the phone. "You're at the cottage?" There, by the river, he meant. And Oleg could picture him there.

"Yup. Where's Nikola?"

"He's staying over the border for a while."

"What are you good-for-nothings up to over there?" Oleg could picture him saying that.

"We're renovating a factory."

"You?"

"With the workers."

"Really?"

"And . . . And . . . I've scheduled a tennis game with Ajderovitsch on Mrok."

"Can you stomach that?"

"I make sacrifices. We're saving an entire town here. We've given all the rights to the workers."

"Wow! Is your personality actually changing?"

"Take care, Uncle." Oleg meant to hang up.

"Any chance you'll drop by one of these days?"

He hadn't heard this invitation in a very long time. There, by the river.

"Sure."

"Come on then. All that matters is that you're not embroiled with that shady bunch. Remember what I said. I'll be calling you from beyond the grave if you build your fortune on blood."

"You never said that!"

"I'm saying it now."

63

"I didn't, Uncle. I did what I could to survive."

"Drop by."

Wake-up. Cell phone alarm.

Yes, he had a plane to catch. Oh, he'd drunk too much with that Gigo guy.

Was that Uncle Martin on the phone?

Yes, but he's dead.

Right, forget it.

6

NIKOLA SAT IN the director's office, wondering if he ought to be making the rounds of the plant again and whether he looked ridiculous as he nodded sagely.

Then he received Oleg's text: "How's it going? I'm in a cab on my way to Mrok. Keep your fingers crossed that I lose."

Mrok.

Maybe it was because he'd taken his dose of tranquilizers just then, or because he was so far away, but the word stirred images in Nikola's mind that were fragile, almost unreal.

Him and his father. Then: him, his father, and Oleg. Then: just him and Oleg. Then: just Oleg.

Their history in photographs sporting their tennis whites.

He started going there with his old man when he was still a boy, when his dad won an award in Venice and they moved to the verdant part of the city where there weren't so many kids out on the streets, so the tennis club became like a neighborhood playground for him. Back then he didn't know that the people he used to romp around with were the crème de la crème: the directors of companies, bank managers, doctors, lawyers—some of them even dissidents, he later realized. There were a couple of filmmakers like his old man, a few painters, sculptors, actors, television personalities. Only later did he learn who was who. Even today at the occasional reputable watering hole, he'd spot someone he could nod to and, if necessary, remind them—"Son of Martin the filmmaker, you know me from Mrok."

This would always earn him a pat on the back and a sincere smile—the kind reserved for the picture of a child from the past. Apparently, I was a sweet kid, thought Nikola, and I loved throwing them balls as if that were what I was on earth to do.

Yes, he later discovered he had always preferred doing things that weren't his job to things that were. Perhaps this was why a lot of the respectable people, after the sincere pat, had that brief moment of confusion when they wouldn't know what else to say. Maybe they remembered that his business flopped, that he'd sold his father's apartment and moved from the verdant part of town. He thought they'd heard, although maybe they hadn't: maybe they just didn't know what to say to someone who had once been a sweet kid. Or maybe, when they really thought about it, they didn't much care about memories dating back to before the fall of the Berlin Wall.

He thought about that time, when the world was changing like at a magician's show: a man would be sliced up with sabers but come out alive while the audience applauded. That's how, he thought, history is refracted at Mrok in an almost enchanted way. Because, of course, as far as the club was concerned, there was no reason to throw out old members or refuse to accept new ones. And, ultimately, there were new members and a fair number of the old ones, after all the sport in question was gallant, tolerant, gentlemanly; it was not blue or red or black, but white. What mattered were the backhands, forehands, and fairness in judging whether the ball had landed outside the lines; and though they'd come from various backgrounds, Nikola knew that people acquired a certain club identity with time, though ancillary, of course, so ancillary that he never mentioned it on his résumé—but still, if you were a member of Mrok, you were a part of the game; if you were a *Mroker*, you were there, in the changing room, in the heady atmosphere of the club café, always as a hand, either left or right, which mattered less as long as it held a racket.

For Nikola, there was nothing more logical than this quiet, seemingly smooth regime change. To his generation, which had grown up in jeans, this was like reaching the port they'd long been sailing toward. And he continued going to Mrok, of course, just like the other Mrokers of his generation, maybe because, thanks to American movies, they'd always wanted to live in a capitalist society and become capitalists, and it occurred to Nikola that this might possibly have been the mind-set of most of the population living in ex-socialist countries. He thought of how strange it was to think back on this, but most of the people, in his opinion, had been set on becoming capitalists, maybe not consciously, but still . . . nobody was set on becoming an unemployed jerk.

Since this was more or less what happened to him—because without Oleg right now that's exactly what he'd be: an unemployed jerk—his idiocy was, he concluded, even greater than usual, considering that he somehow, almost imperceptibly over time, frittered away all the social capital he'd accrued at Mrok. And Mrok was one of the rare places where the people who'd set their sights on becoming capitalists hadn't been just shooting the breeze—their chances had actually been, let's say, fair. Mrok was frequented by the new powermongers and the old directors and the bankers, all of whom claimed they'd always been technocrats, economics honchos, and the old system had only stymied their ambitions for the market. They all agreed to the necessity of privatizing socialist companies, and after their tennis games they'd often get caught up in very complex discussions about how to take out a mortgage on a property you were purchasing, with frequent mentions of the word "preagreement."

"Preagreement, mortgage, loan, purchase. It's like when you're buying an apartment and you take out a mortgage—you do the same with a company, but somebody has to give you the big loan," explained his friend Hlap.

Later, Nikola did just that.

"If you default on the loan, the bank forecloses on your company just as it would foreclose on your apartment. And presto, bankruptcy. A company, you see, is like property. It's based on property."

"Oh? Meaning—"

"Why wouldn't it be?"

"So it is?"

"Well, every normal socialist company holds property. Companies aren't made of software, are they?"

Nikola also believed in the free market, and it wasn't clear to him at all why, in the end—after having been a viable candidate in the right place at the right time—he hadn't been ushered into the national elite.

He wondered whether his incompetence or a flaw in his character held him back from playing the game as he should have, because he somehow felt that what Hlap said was all wrong, and as a result he spent a long time "searching for himself," thinking that maybe he could make it as a filmmaker, only to finally open a little TV production company following the classic road map: he took out a loan by mortgaging the apartment he'd inherited. When running his company, he turned his nose up at the obligatory sucking up, networking, and deals, which he treated with aristocratic contempt, losing track of the fact that he had no aristocratic castle to fall back on. He thought he'd shine solely on quality—he really thought their productions were good—but the market in his line of work turned out to be an illusion, and the story of quality that would shine on its own became yet another story about justice. A big market functioned differently, he believed, but in this small market made up of public broadcasting and a handful of commercial channels, with only a few players shuffling the cards, Nikola began, as they'd say, *talking shit* about deals, especially when drunk—sometimes so audaciously that, for a while, the ones he'd blustered at thought he had serious backing, after all he was a *Mroker*. But with time they must have seen he was not a serious player; he was an idiot who *got on people's nerves* and spoiled the game, something he was not aware of. He discovered this at an inopportune moment, just when he had, out loud, near the end of a Christmas party, offered *a share in his company,* in passing, as if this were something not to be missed, to the television executive who pulled all the strings in programming, ah yes, that was, indeed, foolhardy, but by then Nikola was already reeling from debt and drink. It was foolish, no doubt, though everybody hated the guy, or so Nikola thought, because the man's backroom dealing was so glaringly obvious, still, he woke up the following morning with a hangover brought on by worry, hoping those last moments of the party wouldn't be counted toward his final score; he tried putting it behind him, but then noticed he'd gotten too few *Happy New Year* text messages, only to realize later that people weren't answering his calls, hardly anybody called him— except for the wonderful people who weren't in the know. His productions weren't being accepted anywhere, he must have been the only fool who had truly believed in the market, and since he was a pain in the neck, everybody had, spontaneously and collectively, *dumped* him.

The question was, he now thought, whether he had ever frankly admitted this to himself. At the time, he had been more focused on his mental state, his sessions with his therapist, his search through his childhood, the talk about his relationships, alcohol, and anxiety attacks.

He moved away and he hadn't been back to Mrok in a long time. I'm probably ashamed of my failure, he thought. Besides, he saw the new car models in front of the club differently now, and he wasn't too eager to meet the people from his old crowd who were *still in the game*, because, even though they greeted each other as if they were friends, he had the impression they were now mere acquaintances.

Since then he'd heard on the Internet that the television executive he'd offended was marched off to prison with a paparazzi escort, though this meant little to Nikola, and nor did the long-overdue texts of support—from the neutral *seen the latest*? to the malicious-yet-supportive *what goes around comes around* to the optimistic *coffee*?—from people who presumably thought he was still active somewhere, lurking on the margins of the business world, poised to jump into the fray, or, they wondered, had Nikola himself been the one to put the crook behind bars? None of them had any idea that Nikola was, in fact, in the town of N., in the middle of Nowheresville, Yeti-land, watching this all from a mind-cooling distance, finally coming to grips with why he was here.

Where I am now, thought Nikola, is the final picture: like when a cuckolded partner finally sees the incriminating photographs, or maybe even a video of the orgy.

For a long time, he thought, I've been nowhere, and now I'm finally also here physically.

He stood in front of the window and looked at the mountains in the mist, the empty road. Then he noticed a man fiddling with a dilapidated sign with only the letters T E BL E LAG O N on it. Some of the letters must have fallen off.

Did I get this from Dad? he wondered. His father hadn't left him his artistic talent, but he had, apparently, left him instead with the irony of his movies and certain character traits.

Old Martin stopped going to the club just when he should have been taking advantage of the way *he'd talked shit about things he shouldn't have* during socialism. He must have believed in the justice of the system, thought Nikola, so he'd paid his dues and could sing the blues. Old Martin could afford to be that way; he'd had his Venice and the festivals, they were his backup.

During the time after the fall of the Berlin Wall, Nikola couldn't fathom what happened to his old man, why he would always say, "I can't," whenever Nikola suggested they go to Mrok. Since everyone had always known that Martin was dancing on the edge, he could have become one of the gray-haired dissidents—there was a shortage of them, anyway. Everybody asked after him.

Sometimes Nikola insisted, because tennis had been their bonding ritual, but his dad wriggled out of it using all sorts of excuses—he'd say tennis was bad for his back, not the game for him anymore.

One time, his old man even gave a problematic interview to a newspaper—luckily, not for a high-circulation paper—resulting in him being dubbed the "old Commie" by Nikola's circle of friends. By then all sorts of people were labeled Commies, and Nikola lost his temper, because his old man had never been in the Party.

"He was exactly the same before, while everyone else kept their mouths shut!" said Nikola, upset by the comment.

Hey, relax, will you look at him, they snickered. They didn't care. Nikola knew that, but still he didn't like hearing the phrase "old Commie." It was not advisable to use it at the club, even as a joke, especially in front of older Mrokers, mostly businessmen who'd actually been Communists—or rather, members of the Party, because none of them were Communists out of conviction, of course, but only out of expedience. In fact, at the end of the day, hardly anyone had ever been a Communist.

Along with the ones who weren't Communists, a certain number of those who weren't Fascists belonged to the club as well. There were doubts about this, especially abroad, but they all agreed that was enemy propaganda. Those who weren't Fascists had mostly moved back from somewhere else, and sometimes, or so it seemed to Nikola, the veins in their neck and the gnashing of their teeth conveyed how they felt about those who weren't Communists.

They didn't seem to believe each other about not being what they claimed not to be. At times an epilogue to World War II seemed to be underway in some magical sense, but that was just an impression—since one group wasn't Fascist and the other wasn't Communist, this was extremely difficult to keep tabs on.

Realistically, there was no quarrel—in the end, everyone would say they supported patriotism, democracy, and market competition. And Prime Minister Izvolski was like a magical bridge between them. He united everything because he had gone through many phases during his long life; historically, he was versatile.

Besides, he was also a neighbor, a member of the club, for whom Nikola had been throwing balls during the man's dissident phase. Nikola hadn't been aware of this at the time, but it was an indisputable fact: Nikola had been helping him when nobody else would. Now there were too many of them eager to throw him balls.

Nikola's personality stopped him from ever telling Prime Minister Izvolski that he had once thrown balls to him, because he thought everybody would think he had an ulterior motive for mentioning it.

Furthermore, he'd liked the man at the time, portly and stern as he was. There were times when Nikola smiled at him, and the man even tried to smile back, looking like a kid, embarrassed about never having learned how to laugh. However, since Nikola was much smaller than he was, the man got over feeling sheepish, and sometimes he'd let out a real laugh, his mouth atwist, which only made this more amusing for both of them. Then they'd both roar with laughter and Nikola was able to see what a funny kid Izvolski must have been, but nobody else was allowed to see.

In a way this was another reason why Nikola couldn't tell Prime Minister Izvolski that he had been the one who threw balls to him—Izvolski was no longer funny, and Nikola didn't want to find him funny, so he felt as if pushing his way through to him and telling him about the balls would instantly falsify the whole memory.

If it came to that he could always tell the prime minister he was the kid he'd laughed with—he'd known even as a child how rare this was for Izvolski—and both at Mrok and in society in general, this card up Nikola's sleeve gave him a sense of security.

Meanwhile, Nikola figured his dad felt this was a new gang hanging out at Mrok now, which must be the reason why his old man didn't go there anymore. Once, he told him who still went there, thinking he'd win him over, but his dad just said, "I can't. I can't look at them."

Yes, that's what I inherited from him, he thought, sitting in the director's office at the old turbine factory. Maybe I really didn't have what it took, but I definitely was not the only one . . . This trait from him—it was my undoing.

Someone knocked at the door.

"Yes?"

Sobotka.

After greeting Nikola, the engineer watched him for a moment as he sat in the director's chair in the empty office. On the floor, next to some scattered papers and binders, lay only a few old phonograph records.

Sobotka gave him a sheet of paper and said, "This is a list of the things we need, in detail."

Then he stared at the records; the top one said *Spartacus*.

"Whose records are these, anyway?" Nikola asked.

"The factory's."

"I'd offer you some coffee, but the renovation of this department is going a bit slower than expected."

"I'm busy anyway... But, yes, well, Hanka, our old secretary, she just asked me... She knows where we used to procure things, and that sort of thing."

"Yes?"

"But... along with her, we need another support person, younger, you know, for work on the computer."

"We'll decide on new hires in a couple of days. Sorry, my phone's ringing."

Sobotka left, and Oleg was already waiting on the line.

"Stuck in traffic?"

"Yes, I'm seriously stu... it's a traffic jam, man... Sitting here in this cab. These things always happen at the worst possible moment!"

"Will you make it for the tennis game?"

"Barely! Like that time before. You know?"

"Right. Make sure that doesn't happen again."

"It won't. How are things going at your end?"

"Don't know. I'm just saying 'You betcha' over and over. I'll email you the new list."

"Hold your horses. I need to take care of this and then we'll be all set."

"Just do it. Hitch a ride with an *ambulance* if you need to."

"Did I ever tell you how I once hitched a ride with a garbage truck?"

"No."

"Get a load of this—a Swiss city, a smaller town in fact, very high-brow, where everything is so expensive, a village actually, and I didn't know there were no cabs around at night. I was freezing in the fog, no idea where I was, when I saw a garbage truck picking up trash. Down the block it had just emptied the trash cans and was coming my way so I stepped into the road and waved with both arms. I asked, 'Do you know where the Ambassador Hotel is?' They stared at me, so I asked, 'Could you take me to the Ambassador Hotel?' I spoke in German, but they looked at me as if I were from another planet, because, you know, I was wearing a suit, tie, what all. A glance at their faces had me thinking that at least one of them could be from back home, so I asked, in our language, *Do you understand?* One of them nodded, so I continued: *I'll stand on the riding steps and hold on. For fifty euros!* And then, you see, the two holding on to the back of the truck gave me some space, laughed, and I stood on the riding steps and held with them on the back. The trash reeked and the driver stepped on it so I had to hold on tight. They left me right smack in front of the Ambassador Hotel, in front of the valets who were standing by the door in their white gloves. The valets couldn't believe their eyes. I entered the hotel, and the receptionist must have seen all this as well. I said, 'Room 512.' He just stared. 'What seems to be the problem, sir?' I asked. And he said, 'Did you just arrive with the garbage?' 'Yes!' I said. 'With the garbage! I came with the garbage!' Then I realized he thought I was in the wrong place; he must have seen me saying goodbye to the garbagemen, we almost embraced—hardly surprising as I'd given them a hundred euros. I was mildly euphoric, you know... So, the receptionist looked me up and down, and I lost it. 'By a garbage truck, sir! There are no cabs! You might consider suggesting to your other customers that they come by garbage truck. Why not give everyone their number!' The receptionist was offended, he was shocked, and this infuriated me even more, so I told him, 'Could you, please, book me a garbage truck for eleven a.m.? I've decided to boycott your cabs and take only garbage trucks!' By then the man was alarmed, as if afraid that one of us had lost his mind, because by then he'd seen that I did have a reservation. This was a fancy hotel, and the man had to be careful. He was already confused, and so he asked me, 'What is the garbagemen's number, sir?' And I said, 'Well, sir, don't you know the number of the garbagemen in your own town?' 'I'm not from here,' he blurted, spreading his arms wide. 'From where, then?' I asked. I was already teasing. Look, we were speaking German until then, but at that point he said—well, muttered actually, because he'd already lost it—in our language, *Why do you give a fuck!* I laughed soooo hard. Then I took the key card and told him, 'Don't worry about the garbagemen, bruder. They're all from back home.'"

Oleg paused for a moment, and then looked at the phone and realized they'd been disconnected while he was busy telling the story.

"Fuck, no signal."

At that, the taxi driver burst out laughing.

Finally, the traffic began moving and the cab turned toward Mrok.

As they were approaching the club, Oleg checked his watch.

His Mrok story was different than Nikola's.

Oleg played tennis there for the first time in the eighties, after moving to the city from his small town to study at the university. Oleg's mother and Nikola's father were siblings. After Oleg's father, who had Ukrainian roots, died in a car crash, Uncle Martin was a second father to Oleg. When he came to study in the city, Oleg lived at his uncle's, so he began to play tennis with Martin and Nikola. He had a natural flair for the game and in just a couple of years he was playing as well as Nikola, and later, even better.

Oleg knew he had to put a bit more effort into providing for himself, and he made sure to earn his own pocket money very early—he became a freelance journalist for a student paper and eventually he became editor of the culture section, which interfered a bit with his studies. His final year became a never-ending slog, and he never completed his degree in English and German. It was his uncle who'd advised him to study the two languages, saying, *You already know Russian, now learn these two and you'll be all set.*

In the late eighties, Oleg moved from the student paper to literary publishing, and was made bookstore manager at a big publishing house which, after the political changes, underwent hasty privatization and gradual liquidation. Most of the company's bookstores soon became prime real estate for new businesses and were transformed into boutiques, shoe stores, and gaming parlors with poker machines. The new owner, who loved national culture, but only if it was more than five hundred years old, undoubtedly repaid the loan in no time, which had enabled him to buy the company, sold the real estate, and had money left over. Only one bookstore was left. The publishing sector was in collapse; the competitors were closing their bookstores, too.

Oleg was out of a job, and so, while still young, he could already feel the spirit of the times running against him, but didn't dare fight back. He was angry at himself for not having gotten the drift of what was underway and for not having tried to privatize the publishing house himself because, he later thought, he could have swung a loan through his Mrok buddies and paid it off later by selling the real estate. Maybe he could have, but he didn't—he was out of a job and had no university degree.

To make matters worse, he was, meanwhile, moving out and set-tling down. He needed his own place even more after his mother found her soul mate, where else but at the spa her doctors had sent her to, where she immediately began feeling better. She remarried, the man moved in, and even though Oleg was no longer living there, he still felt he'd lost his home. This probably also had to do with the fact that, just before he was fired, he'd suddenly fallen in love with Anita and married her; they planned to have at least four or five kids. Anita was a voluptuous poet. He'd met her when she published her first book for the publisher where he was working. He liked the book and liked Anita even more; he loved her aura of ease, which made everything seem right and everybody—good-natured. She relaxed him.

But after he lost his job, he and Anita argued a lot over small things, maybe partly because they were barely able to pay the rent. The aura of ease was gone; their relationship floundered in its encounter with capitalism. She decided to move in with her par-ents, and he, again, with his uncle. This was only supposed to be temporary. But it turned out to be the end of their relationship: their marriage depressed him, and he was in no rush to go back to living with Anita again. Somehow, he could feel in his bones that Anita was not supportive, and he'd find it easier to make it on his own under these new circumstances. He was not conscious of this, but later, when talking to himself in moments of drunken candor, he admitted he was the one who'd given up, not she, though one day she'd told him it was over, she had been dating a clownish literary type who was both poet and critic, who'd written a panegyric for Oleg and Anita's wedding, which they'd read together. The clown bided his time and the romance between the two poets was born; all Oleg had to say was, *I wish you all the best surviving*.

Alone and unemployed, he was humiliated, partly by a feeling he'd never known before, a little like being lost, or maybe shut out—because ethnic origin was, by then, front and center, and, while Nikola cared nothing about his background, Oleg began to ask himself who he was. Moreover, other people would ask him this, too—"Well, who exactly are you?"—because his father was descended from Ukrainian Cossacks who'd fled after joining the White Army following the October Revolution, and then never returned. His surname sounded foreign, and Oleg felt he belonged to *other*s, not exactly one of the enemy against whom the war would soon be fought, but not so far from them, either.

His mother and Uncle Martin always gave him contradictory answers to questions such as, "What was their faith?"

His mother would say, "Catholic."

"Catholic? Cossacks?"

"Yes."

"And they fought for the Russian Tsar?"

"Well, yes, but for themselves, too."

Uncle Martin used to say, "With your grandfather it depended on how much he'd had to drink. When he was relatively sober, they were Greek Catholics. That's what my sister heard, but she doesn't pay much attention to the details."

"When he was relatively sober?"

"Well, yes, but when he was really drunk—they were Orthodox, not exactly like Russians, something all their own. He really wanted them to be different from the Russians. Now, there might have been ulterior motives for that. With Russians you're always part of a bigger story, and you may end up in a dark place."

"My old man still taught me Russian."

"Plenty of the Ukrainians back home speak Russian."

All this was distant for him. Although he was totally assimilated and didn't feel Ukrainian, or Greek Catholic, or Orthodox, this didn't help Oleg, just as those who didn't care about ethnicity and faith still became ideological outcasts, a kind of substitute for Communists, all of whom were gone. There were only leftovers, people like him, who had no new way of identifying themselves. Everybody else was putting real effort into this, and even those who'd left the Communist Party only the day before made up for what they'd missed, going so far as to baptize their adult children. Was there a discount offered for these family ablutions? Oleg couldn't tell for sure, as the arrangements were taken care of in secret and people spoke of them only when drunk.

So Oleg became a collateral victim of the Fall of Communism, a lost character who was shoved aside; the symbolic divisions relegated his identity, against his will, to a drawer, stirring in him a sting of dismay with an occasional episode of depression when he drank too much. At the time he grew closer to his uncle; they sat together like a couple of misfits and conversed about the paradoxes of their family history and history in general. His uncle had a lot to say about this.

"Take, for instance, your great-grandfather, a Cossack, a Ukrainian, a defender of the Russian Tsar, he fought against the Communists and came here after his side lost. Then, your grandfather, who remembered nothing of Ukraine, fought in World War II. I think he was pro-German, because the Germans had something going on with the Ukrainians and Cossacks. He probably hoped he'd march back as a liberator into the homeland he'd never known. Later on, of course, he kept this under wraps. But I have an ear for stories; I notice when details don't cohere. I have the feeling he joined forces with the Cossacks and Cherkess, and later managed to extricate himself. His war stories were on the vague side. Supposedly they moved him around a lot, but I remember once I mentioned a place in the middle of nowhere where I was shooting a film, and he, while drunk, said, 'People lost their souls there.' He said this as if speaking from experience. For a moment, I even thought he, too, had lost his soul there. I'm not likely to miss a sentence like that, I'm a filmmaker after all. So I went to the village and saw a memorial plaque; the SS and Cherkess, and there were Cossacks among them, see . . . They killed three hundred people in one day, even children. Every single person they caught."

"Wait, you think he was with the SS? Are you kidding me? You never told me that!"

"I can't know for sure, but . . . Maybe I wouldn't be telling you this if the system hadn't collapsed. It would've fucked you up before, but these days not so much, I suppose . . . Let me finish. . . . The next time I was going to the village I asked him to come along, to keep me company, but he froze. While he was staring at me I kept thinking about whether he was looking at me as if he knew I knew. 'No can do, bad back,' he said. I said, 'Your back? Bad?' He just kept staring at me. Then I said, 'Hey, I'm not judging, I'm an artist.' It would have made sense for him to ask me what I'd meant by that. But instead he said, 'I had nothing to do with anything, my dear Martin, that was my problem. I thought I was a part of something, but then I realized I had nothing to do with anything.' I wrote his words down later, because I saw a whole movie in it."

"I remember him a little. And my dad, he died too soon," said Oleg.

"I believe your dad knew nothing about this. Later, your grandfather really didn't want to have anything to do with anything. Like a runaway, when you think about it," said Martin.

"So what do you think his story is?"

"He had a secret, that's for sure," said Martin. "I think he joined them, thinking, *I'm one of them, a Cossack*. And let's say he was in that village and saw what he saw ... Then he tried to get away. He said he moved a lot, maybe he meant he ran away. And later, nobody knew where he'd ended up. He was an ordinary citizen, but with a secret. That's how I'd make the movie about him. But who knows, I see things with the eyes of a filmmaker. Still, what he said—that at one time he'd thought he had something to do with something, but then realized he had nothing to do with anything—that sentence didn't come out of nowhere. He was embroiled in something, and then realized it wasn't what he'd thought it would be. Okay, many of us were embroiled in things. From the way he kept his secret, it would seem clear whose side he'd been on. And look, even if that was all true, the fact that he pulled out may mean he had a conscience. This is what I wanted to believe, and after the conversation he didn't open up about it anymore, though we still had a drink together sometimes, but then he'd just sing songs, sad songs, in Russian or Ukrainian, damned if I know which. He'd sing, not as a drunkard, but really nice and soft. Then he'd lose himself in his sorrow, and that probably meant he was not a bad person. That's how I saw him, maybe because I wanted to. If he knew he was guilty, that would mean he wasn't bad. See?"

"I guess."

"After the war," said Martin, "he decided to put all that behind him. Not like a runaway, chances are he was sincere—it had been wrong, he had nothing to tell. Seeing that Grandpa had given up on his background, your dad actually wasn't Ukrainian or anything, and, since he didn't know how to define himself, he became a Communist, although I doubt he'd read Marx. But the Party gave him an identity. What I mean is that, today, maybe he would want to be something else, because he was not a prewar Communist, one who would risk his life for the cause, but a product of the system. All he wanted was a better life. These are two different kinds of men. Should I be frank about your dad?"

"Be frank, we won't lie to each other."

"He was nice, jolly, an *off-we-go-wherever-the-road-takes-us* kind of guy. If he were still alive, who knows what he'd be today. Maybe he'd play tennis."

"But he died. That's the end of the Cossack story."

"See, just when you Cossacks got rid of anti-communism over three generations, it all collapsed."

"Right onto my shoulders," said Oleg.

"You're not keeping up with the course of history," said Martin, laughing.

"And now I should carry this burden of meaninglessness around the world as my heritage?"

They drank quarts of beer while talking; the cans clattered as they tossed them into the trash can. If only I were an American so I could forget about all this, thought Oleg. Why didn't this great-grandfather go to America if he was so anti-communist, dammit!

"I know. It's stupid. But there are ones which are stupider yet. For instance, the island where I was born was occupied by the Fascists, who made our lives a misery for years. After Italy capitulated, the partisans came and took over, and I, a fifteen-year-old kid, hung around them. They made me a sentry but gave me no gun, and then the Germans came, and we had to hide. I moved up to messenger. Then, after the war, they sent us young fighters to school so we wouldn't go wild, and I came here and then later, almost by accident, I found myself in film. The local school of animated film was doing really well. I didn't know how good we were until I won a Grand Prix. A colleague from our group won an Oscar. We were a team with more than one genius. What we did was different, probably because we were from the sticks, we had no traditions, we were open-hearted, doing things our way, and our way was novel. Then I got the chance to make movies. I was included in the regular program at Cannes, and received that little award in Venice. And my movie, when I watch it now, was about the impossibility of socialism, how people don't follow your ideas and you can talk till you're blue in the face but no way will they follow you. The authorities here said the movie was decadent—though they didn't attack me openly because I'd been a partisan—and there was truth in what they said, I was moved by my disappointment. Okay, today others are eager to say they defied the system, but I'd be lying to myself if I said that was what I'd set out to do. Mine was an act of resignation. Here, they considered me a problem; I was a partisan who was not in the Party. Where I'm from, they thought of me as a gentleman who'd moved into the upper classes. The movie was actually a product of all of this. But still, it was a success, so I was given the keys to an apartment by the film company. That's how things worked then: people were given apartments, and after the award my reputation soared. So I, a minor international star, began playing tennis, because there was a tennis court in the neighborhood. I became part of the bourgeoisie in a way, despite the fact that I was making movies about social issues. Looking back on it all now, I can see this puzzled me—I didn't know what to make movies about anymore. I returned to animation, made a short film, dark and absurd, I thought nobody would like it, but the Germans gave me a prize. After that, I made a feature and told myself it was my last, and it was acclaimed abroad as *high modernism*, but here at home nobody watched it, so they told me: you're our film director for festivals. And I thought, No I'm not, and withdrew my registration. All of that was read as defiance of the system, and I saw how, here at the club, both the nationalists and the dissidents greeted me warmly, and so did the bankers and businessmen, because I'm a man of the world. But let's be frank, I, too, was a product of the system. First, if I'd been the son of a peasant in another country, I'd never have thought of making movies. Second, my movies weren't to the taste of the American producers. So I can play stupid, but I know what I know. Now, when I look at them playing stupid, taking what isn't theirs ... The Communist elite was child's play compared to this new elite that has evolved from the new and the old who changed their tune. The elite in the old days were managers without ownership, while the elite today are becoming property owners. Overnight. This is something different, my friend. They'll become owners, and you'll never be able to get rid of them. You can hold elections but you'll never oust the owners. They'll still be the owners, the people in power, no matter who you vote for. It suited the mob of schemers to have one ethnic group pitted against the other while they divvied everything up. They're surprised at me for not wanting to play tennis with them, because only the hard-core Communists aren't playing anymore, and they didn't peg me as one of them. But now as far as they're concerned I am an old Commie, after everything fell apart. But believe me, I cannot go there and play anymore. Bad back, like your Cossack would say. So you see, my story is funny like yours."

Oleg nodded, laughed bitterly, but in his thoughts he was nowhere near Martin's story. He was thinking about how to look after himself amid the chaos, seeing that his Uncle Martin, even though he had a reputation and knew the right people in the new regime, had privatized nothing, and he even bragged about this. Had the old man slowed down a bit and supported the new authorities, who had been, after all, elected by the people, we could have, thought Oleg, arranged for a loan at the club to buy out the film company that had produced his movies and pay off the loan by converting its office space.

He understood his Uncle Martin, but his uncle received a regular pension. Oleg had nothing, he was a proletarian, and he realized there were no proletarians with whom to unite anymore.

No, he would not be making movies about social issues, that's for sure, nor would he feel disappointed while attempting to do so. He had to survive. He was sick of everything. Oleg sat there drinking with his uncle and listened to the damned paradoxes.

At some point after he'd lost his job, Oleg, like his uncle, stopped going to the club, but then, after a bout of depression, worried about his mental health, he shook off his reluctance and started playing tennis with Nikola again. Physical activity did him good; he sweated out the misery and rage. After the match he read the *International Herald Tribune* in the club café—unlike the local papers it was usually free.

He realized that, by some miracle, the fact that he played tennis and read the *Herald* helped him feel a little less miserable.

Since he held only temporary jobs—he occasionally translated something from the English or Russian for pocket money—he had time to play tennis, and Mrok soon became his daily haunt. Many things in his life hadn't worked out, but at least he was still a member there. He could easily beat most of the new members, and those who played the worst tennis readily invited him for a drink, probably because Oleg could hold up his end of a conversation with anybody. The old chief physicians, Nikola's friends from the city, tech managers, people from the sticks, new money, half-assimilated rednecks, thick dolts who always seemed cheery—Oleg could talk to anyone.

Although he could walk there, Oleg would drive to the club in his uncle's old but classy Volvo. He was good at tennis and drank coffee while reading the *Herald*, so the new members thought him one of the old guard, maybe even the old-old, the bourgeois elite—in this context his Ukrainian surname, noble-sounding to some, had altogether different connotations, so when the matter arose, Oleg spoke only vaguely about his origins, and that gave others the impression that his was a long, complicated, slightly decadent Mitteleuropa story.

He made sure not to give the impression of being penniless, because Mrok was no place to mope. Whatever they talked about at Mrok, be it old champagne or a new BMW—which could be armor-plated for a little extra—you never had to say that something was "expensive." Instead, you pretended you were seriously considering whether to buy the thing and were only trying to decide whether you'd get value for your money. Once, after a game he'd won with ease, Oleg eyed a contraption Vili had hauled to the table. It was, as Vili explained, a Motorola. A portable phone.

"Not actually very portable," said Oleg with a smile.

"Seven and a half pounds. But it's fantastic."

"How much?"

"Twelve thousand."

"Twelve thousand whats?"

"Whats? Deutsche Marks, of course."

"Yes, yes," Oleg grimaced, "very nice."

Vili, who obviously really needed the phone, was a muscular guy from the sticks, and sometimes he was ill at ease at Mrok. It was easy to tell he was new to the whole tennis thing. So he liked to sit at Oleg's table, as if they were old friends.

When a friend of Vili's showed up at the table, dressed all in black, and put down an identical Motorola, the waiter, who was just bringing another round of drinks, said, "Gentlemen, make some room. There's nowhere to put the drinks!"

Some of these new members, who were a bit uncomfortable at first, would sometimes dub Oleg Legend when they sat together at the table. He countered by saying, "A friend was telling me about his grandfather who jumbled words. The friend was saying his grandfather leafed through the newspapers, becoming increasingly irate as he read about the thefts and embezzlements, the con men and scammers, so he put down the paper and, referring to these men, said, 'Common legends, every one!'"

They thought of Oleg as having a good sense of humor. A long-time member, never a Communist, well-educated, multilingual, reads the *Herald*, drinks coffee, observes the world.

"You're different from that cousin of yours," said Vili to him once; Nikola usually hung out with his old gang. That's because I don't have an old gang, thought Oleg, but he didn't say so to Vili.

The guy, Vili, whom he'd beat at tennis many times, once asked, begged really, for Oleg to join him at a dinner with some foreigners as Vili was not used to hanging out with world-class people, and he wasn't handy with languages.

The dinner was with two men from Switzerland who actually looked Latino and spoke good English. The dinner proceeded with no business talk, and four women joined their little group. They were obviously paid escorts, and cocaine showed up from somewhere, so Oleg tried the powder for the first time and livened right up, entertained the guests by speaking English, soothed nervous Vili, translated, entertained the women, who were at first awkwardly quiet, and everything went beautifully for him, so in the end the atmosphere was not as grim as it had been at the beginning of the evening.

A couple of days after that, Vili asked, in private, his tone serious, whether Oleg would like to work for him; he said there'd be good money in it. Oleg said he was interested. Vili said that before starting he'd have to go through a detailed background check, a security clearance, which Oleg did. He didn't even leave out his origins: he mentioned his great-grandfather's anti-communism, his grandfather's pro-German stance and shady war history, and also his father's membership in the Communist Party because he figured that Vili and his crew were not people one should lie to.

A few days later, Nikola told Oleg that some men, who did not look altogether harmless, were asking around about him. They were definitely asking around elsewhere, too, and Oleg was ultimately surprised when Vili informed him he'd passed the security check. "I vouched for you," said Vili.

And so began his international career; Vili's job was obtaining weapons during the international embargo. Weapons for the war that was just beginning.

Oleg was paid handsomely and he was also given bonuses, but he never reached the level of making deals independently. They didn't trust him that far; he worked for Vili, shadowed him, handled correspondence, and did what Vili didn't know how to do or could not do.

People were killed, cities fell, news began coming in about massacres; there were not enough weapons for their defense while the other side was well-stocked, and part of Oleg's job was dealing with that. He worked on extremely important, top-secret tasks, enjoying all the privileges high-level security brings. Sometimes what he was involved in and who he interacted with seemed strange even to him. But he felt, at the same time, that he was a full-fledged member of society. Men at the bar clapped him on the shoulders, he was given war commendations and felt like a member of the majority—sometimes even a nationalist—cursing the enemy, their morals and culture. At the time that was normal so somehow it just entered his vocabulary.

"Don't get too comfortable with this," Uncle Martin told him in a conversation that would later haunt him. "Just recently you were whining about your family history and now you're a nationalist? Ridiculous. Your father and grandfather were just like that—whatever it took to fit in. You're like a son to me, you know you are, so this is something I have to say to you."

"But it's how I feel!"

"Like an arms smuggler?"

He flinched. "You think that's easy?" He hated it that he wasn't more eloquent, but he sometimes felt like a little kid in front of Uncle Martin.

"No, I don't. You're part of this because life has pushed you here. The world *mobilized* you, see? Acting like this was your choice, but you had no choice, and I know that. If you'd stayed in your small town you might be fighting for the other side; you're a bare-assed pauper and proletarian—there's no shame in that—but imagine if you'd had to survive there. You'd adapt, because you'd have no choice, and you are the type who adapts. If you were there, you'd also be saying the same sort of thing: That's how you feel. Try to imagine this and you'll realize you lie to yourself quite a lot."

"I'm no longer a bare-assed pauper and proletarian. What makes you think I'd adapt if I were still there? I would not, this is where I belong."

"If it were the other way around you'd belong there."

"I wouldn't. They're the aggressor."

"I know. But I'm saying something else. About who you are. You'd adapt to the aggressor, too, because that's who you are. You don't care about the truth, that's the problem. The problem is you'd buy their story, too, and you'd talk shit over there, too, like an actor who's forgotten he's an actor. See, without concern for the truth, personality can't exist. Be a criminal for all I care, but don't lie to yourself, because in that case I have nobody to talk to."

"What's that supposed to mean? That I don't exist?"

"Wherever you end up, you have to know you're not there of your own free will. That's all there is to it. You were meant to become something completely different, and you know that. In peacetime, in a different situation, you'd have been something else. You wouldn't be drinking with lowlifes who are out to profit on bloodshed. You need to be thinking about what brought you to this, not simply to embrace the role the film directors handed you. You're talking to an old filmmaker. I've seen it all before. Don't be swept up and don't be full of shit."

This hit Oleg like a cold shower; he wasn't about to take it lying down despite everything he owed his uncle. Too many things were said questioning his character. Too many things he didn't want to hear. In fact, he felt the urge to talk back to his uncle, show him he no longer depended on him. He didn't have to take this, he was his own person.

"You don't acknowledge me or what I've accomplished! People respect me. You . . . You don't understand the times! I am more agile than others, successful . . ."

"Successful? What a stupid word."

"Well, your time has passed! You . . . you really are from the . . ." he struggled for words. "You . . . you . . . you really are an old Commie!" As soon as he said this he stopped. He couldn't believe what he'd said.

His uncle looked at him blankly and started in a quiet tone: "Your father was in the Party, not me. And you're neck deep in the system now, not me. The two of you would nominally be on opposite sides, but in fact you're the same. As for me, it's true that I was more interested in social justice than your father was, just like I'm more interested in freedom than you are. Now go! And be careful not to make your fortune on bloodshed."

Oleg left, slamming the door behind him, overwhelmed by the urge to smash something. Eventually he did just that in a café after he got drunk, and everyone eyed him in fear because he let them know what sort of business he'd been involved in. He ended up drinking alone with the bartender, cursing old Commies, and the waiter nodded. In the early morning Oleg paid his tab and left, walking out on the broken glass, still in a bleak mood and—or so he felt—not nearly drunk enough. In the shower he relived the conversation and the cold shower took a long time to take effect. He was furious at Uncle Martin for everything, at times he really hated him, because people were respecting him and Uncle Martin ignored all that. He made Oleg feel like a bare-assed pauper and proletarian all over again and this made him hurl the stupid insults he regretted. But his rage would not go away because he was offended deeper down than he could admit to himself. Who knows when this rage would have left him—maybe never—if his uncle had lived longer and if their quarrel had reached the boiling point of open hostility. But Uncle Martin died of a stroke fifteen days later, while he was at his summer cottage.

That's when his rage toward his uncle evaporated and sadness set in. He even feared that their argument might have helped to bring on Uncle Martin's death and he never told Nikola about the conversation; he realized his uncle hadn't, either. Oleg inferred that the old man thought they'd soon sort things out, so he hadn't bothered to mention it. But they didn't, and Oleg regretted this with a regret he couldn't fix.

Still, the haunting conversation no longer angered him; it helped him calm down and start to see himself differently. It didn't change his personality, but he forever remembered not to lie to himself—only to others.

Yes, arms smuggler, how disturbing that must sound to someone living in a more fortunate country, he thought. Even worse would have been to leave all that behind and then find himself at the front, poorly armed in the chaos and hysteria of the war. He was not short on information about what was happening at the front. At first he was shocked, and then he got used to it. He saw the enemy was pushing hard to the end, but he'd heard enough to realize that there was no lack of revenge on his side, either, most of which harmed those who were vulnerable, isolated families and individuals. He knew he was no superman. He would not be championing order and justice.

By the time the war spilled over into the third country after a year, Oleg, like everyone else, was already inured to the gruesome news. Horror had become part of his world, and he was one of the lucky ones who was part of the horror at a high level. People he met had predatory looks in their eyes, the cynical humor of professionals. He worked with mob bosses, international piranhas, local warlords— the kind of people with whom others didn't dare make eye contact. Oleg needed to present himself as if he were one of them so they wouldn't smell weakness. Cocaine helped. Cocaine became a tool of his trade, and without it he surely could not have ignored all the fear that the people he worked with brought with them. He knew that he, too, had the predatory look and the cynical humor of a professional; he knew he'd crossed his Rubicon, and he'd never be able to return to an unknowing civilian life.

He saw the invoices, bills, and discrepancies.

Actually, no, he didn't see them.

He did not skimp on the cocaine or anything else, he did not rein in his expenses, he did not smuggle on the side, and he did not come out of the war a tycoon as did a few of the people he rubbed elbows with. He was not sorry, because property acquired that way had to be protected from witnesses who blackmailed you unless you destroyed them. So he didn't envy Vili what was ahead of him. Recently he'd seen a story in the paper about Vili's car blowing up and he'd been lucky because he was late, so only his driver was killed.

Oleg smiled grudgingly. Vili was always late. If he hadn't been, he'd never have come to rely on Oleg.

He remembered one of their first business meetings, when Vili clapped him on the shoulder, laughing, and said, "You're okay, we're both forty-five minutes late and we're right on time."

"Yes?"

"We're in sync. Just don't be later than me. Actually, when I'm paying bills you can be even an hour late," he said, still laughing.

No, Oleg never saw any bills. He didn't know anything.

Oleg was surprised when the war really stopped. You get used to it.

You lived, first, in a time of peace. In the beginning you thought, Oh, this can't possibly start. Then you thought: When it starts it will probably last a few more days, and then things will clear up, because everything felt like a bout of bad weather, and bad weather can't last forever. Then there were all the negotiations, the peace talks. They were held often, organized by big, important international players, so he counted on them producing results, eventually. Yes.

But they didn't.

Then, after a year, he started thinking the war would never end, because there was no way for it to stop. So many people died, so much territory was lost, you couldn't stop now, you needed to win it all back for this to make sense. It's like poker, when you lose big and you still have something to play with, because it is inconceivable, he thought later, how there were always more soldiers there to fight. The deeper people are in war, the more normal it becomes for them to take risks, everything becomes normal. Peace becomes increasingly unlikely and every agreement between the warring sides seems senseless. Wait a minute, after all those casualties we're supposed to sign this? Such a despicable compromise. To let them have that city there, and the next one, and the big valley, and the mountain where a schoolmate of mine, whose funeral I attended, was killed, as was another coffee-shop buddy of mine, such a fun bastard to be around. So now we should just let them have it all because the political shit-heads finally reached an agreement?

Hell no! Nobody should sign peace agreements like that, said everyone who was speaking out, as well as the media. Hell no! Anyone who signs this had better not come home.

It was inconceivable to think the war would ever come to an end. Then the Americans managed to maneuver them into an agreement. This miracle confounded Oleg.

He thought about it for a while.

He could consider himself lucky to get out of it all alive and without, like Vili, tormentors who think you owe them something. This way, with his unique business acumen and the connections he'd made, he had the know-how to start up a new business any time. He just needed to step out of the limelight, to slip into oblivion. He needed to try to reposition himself in a more appealing line of work. He remembered everyone he'd met, all he'd heard, how he'd talked about how to pull off various scams at dinners and revelries, and, all things considered, he'd accumulated good insight. He knew about more than just weapons and began to cultivate sidelines. Maybe the other things weren't as lucrative, but they were not as vile. What mattered was who he knew.

Then for years he lurked at the perimeter of international smuggling, as a relatively small fish, working with shady governments, with counterfeit merchandise producers, with tobacco pouring in from legal factories as unmarked surplus, with everyone who had the merchandise but no receipt to show for it, or, for whatever reason, their accounts were blocked. He was guided by the following maxim in his work: cover your tracks, be agile, minimize risk. Most of the time he just connected people, without ever seeing the merchandise. Mostly he communicated over the computer, using encrypted mail from Vienna, Rome, or Berlin, from suppliers in short-term rentals.

The turbine business meant a return to work in the war-torn regions, and this made him edgy; he spent days mulling it over. Still, this was a big deal. This was not just an odd job, he could wrap up his career with this.

He'd been contacted by people working for the Colonel, the leader of a country which had imported technology in the old days. The two countries had been on good terms back then, allies in the international non-aligned movement. The Colonel's country was a little peculiar. Oleg didn't really understand their system, but the international world order didn't like them. They were under an international embargo, accused of fostering terrorism, but, as Oleg saw it, the main thing was the Colonel hadn't adjusted to the new post–Cold War circumstances. Perhaps the Colonel needed to bow his head a bit, but Oleg guessed the man bowed his head only to snort coke.

The Colonel's country was rich in oil, but hadn't been able to modernize its technology for decades due to the embargo, and its power plants still used turbines from the old days. They needed, as soon as possible, a turbine that had been made in N., they informed Oleg. They'd bought turbines from there while the countries were on friendly terms, and their entire system was not equipped to facilitate newer models. They needed one that was exactly the same as the old one they'd had.

They wrote this down for him and underlined it: the 83-N.

"All right, I'll see what we can do, I'll have a look. We can deliver it to the port there." He was referring to a port in a neighboring country. He'd already arranged for the Colonel to purchase a powerful radar apparatus and it had come through there. They'd been pleased.

Straightaway, Oleg sat at his computer and started searching the Internet. But there was not a single word about the turbine factory.

"Wait, it seems the factory no longer exists."

"We think so, too."

He started laughing.

"That's your part," they said. "We buy it, you obtain it for us."

"So, what? You're thinking I should go over there and restart the entire factory for a single turbine?"

"A turbine is no small thing, especially one as unique as this. When we discovered that the factory no longer existed we adjusted the price accordingly."

They told him what they were willing to pay. He was stunned.

"I'll have to look into this some more, but I'm skeptical," he said. He, himself, was not sure whether he was bluffing. Nothing about the proposition seemed doable. But on the other hand, if it were this would be the gig of his life. He could find a place to settle down and start gardening. Change. Maybe even start a family. He had already been haunted by such thoughts.

They conferred quietly among themselves in Arabic. Then they made some calls.

"Look," said the main contact, "we'd buy a second one, we'll need it. Same price. Now go out into the field and investigate the matter."

He thought they must have been prepared for the two-turbine offer from the start.

So, two outdated turbines that are not made anywhere anymore, not even in little out-of-the-way N.

It's incredible what's sought after in the world.

Now he knew, having investigated the matter in the field, that this was technically doable. The factory was surprisingly well-preserved.

They'd protected the machines. Sobotka knew the entire process and could be trusted. If they weren't able to make some of the machines work, Sobotka said, they'd need parts from abroad or produce them themselves. Sobotka gave him detailed instructions, and Oleg made some inquiries. Doable. All in all, it might be even easier that he'd expected.

He just needed a small loan.

He reached the tennis court at the last minute and the game started. He was so relaxed he forgot he should be missing balls. He thought losing would come naturally but it didn't, and by the second set he was so far ahead that it was going to be difficult for him to blow the match with grace. Then he'd have to win and Ajderovitsch would be in a foul mood and pack up his things and say, "Bye-bye."

Once before, at the end of the war, Oleg had screwed up, right after he'd found a connection to bring in some scary rockets, and Prime Minister Izvolski spotted him.

He was asleep in a hotel room at the time after an unplanned night of revelry, and he got a call telling him Izvolski was inviting him for a tennis game, which he, of course, accepted, because being invited was, usually, an invitation to move up through the ranks. But he was hungover and decided to get more sleep first. He did not plan well, and when, upon waking, he saw he might even be late, he decided not to go back to his apartment but to phone his girl-friend at the time and have her hop in a cab and bring his racket and clothes to the club, but she was furious because of his partying and they fought over the phone. By that time it was too late to go out and buy new gear. So he went to the club emptyhanded, furious, and somehow, last minute, he managed to scrounge a pair of sneakers (the rest was easier), and he showed up on the court in ridiculous getup, thirty inexcusable seconds late. He was supposed to be there early and wait. He was so pumped that he beat the prime minister 6–0, 6–0. He'd forgotten they were only to play two sets. When he saw Izvolski look at him while putting down his racket, muttering—only then did he realize the game was over. Four of Izvolski's bodyguards watched Oleg closely, in disbelief, as though he were in such a state that they thought he might do something even more outlandish, like a bona fide assassination.

That was the end of his career in the system.

Now he was playing against a bank director, one from a small Austrian bank with which many things could be arranged, a bank that had developed major business deals on the post-socialist margins, probably because the Austrians did everything differently here than they did at home.

The cost for reopening the factory far outstripped Oleg's resources; he needed the loan, people had already started working, and he was up 4–1.

Bouncing the ball on the court before his serve, he tried to concentrate on close misses, which can be tough to pull off if it's not your lucky day.

He aimed for one a few feet outside the line, swung the racket, hit the ball, and—unbelievably—it ended up in play again, on the very line. Ajderovitsch couldn't catch it, but he did stretch out to try and almost fell.

I hope he doesn't throw out his back, Oleg thought. *Aim for the bottom of the net next time, dumbass!*

7

NIKOLA WATCHED THE people working at the factory, which was no longer blanketed in dust. He saw how Sobotka guided them from one machine to the next and ordered a detailed inspection before the machinery was tested, so decaying or worn or broken parts wouldn't ruin the functioning parts when the machine started up. Everything needed to be carefully disassembled and cleaned or oiled, and everything that looked suspicious had to be thoroughly examined. Sobotka said that replacements might be found because spare-parts storage held generous supplies, and they had left it neat when they left. The only problem was that the spare parts had been kept in an outside storage shed, the roof of which had fallen in under the weight of snow and needed to be cleared, this being the job of what was called the roaming squad, while Sobotka's crew was known as the engineering squad, though not all of them were engineers.

The roaming squad was under Erol's leadership. They had already cleaned the main building and replaced all the broken glass and bad vents. The engineering squad repaired the electrical wiring and

Branoš's facilities squad managed to get the central heating system up and running, so the factory was no longer drafty and Nikola spent more time in the factory hall with the workers, instead of alone in his bare office, where he surfed the Internet using USB Internet sticks, though he was having problems with the mobile wireless connection, which was disrupted by every little puff of wind. The landline was due to be up soon. They just needed to find where the cable was disabled, or whatever the problem was.

At first, once Nikola was left at the factory without Oleg, he'd regularly reached for his Xanax; at times he felt unsafe among these people whose looks lacked the softness he was used to, and whose hands had done who-knows-what during the war. But he did not allow himself to show this. Later, he began feeling that his fears were actually due to his almost childish sense of abandonment, dropped here at the end of the world, where no one from his circle of friends would ever show up. Still, over the last few days, perhaps in part because Oleg managed to secure the loan—with great difficulty, as he said—Nikola felt he was on safer footing, and now that he dropped by the big hall and could understand what Sobotka was saying, they began coordinating the roaming and facilities squad together and he started to follow what they were doing.

"It will take a while, but I don't see any major problems," said Sobotka.

Nikola wrote up a brief daily report, which Oleg expected to receive every afternoon. Nikola knew this was a way to keep him from falling into a rut; he wasn't sure if Oleg was actually reading them.

After he'd sent that day's email, he phoned Branoš to come to his office. Nikola found he was the easiest person to talk to because he'd worked abroad.

When they were done talking business, Branoš said, "I don't

know how much work you have to do, but some of us are going out for a drink after we finish up. The owner of the bar nearby is buying . . . You're free to say no."

Nikola felt a weight settle over him at these words because he didn't know how close he should be getting to the workers. What had Oleg meant when he said "a polite distance"?

Then he thought that, no matter what, drinking in company was healthier.

"All right, and tell me why do they call your team the Plum Boys."

"About something I did in Afghanistan, heh, heh . . . jokers."

"Jokers? They usually seem so serious to me," said Nikola, almost using the word "grim."

"Maybe when you are around, sir. Sorry, Nikola. You know, you're the director."

"I won't dampen the mood at the bar?"

"If you ask me, I think they've accepted you now," smiled Branoš. "But no one wants to seem like they're sucking up."

Oh, so they are afraid of something. Good, Nikola thought.

"That's our rank and file for you," Branoš said. "Know what I mean by *rank and file*?"

"Our crew? Regular folks?"

"Well, yes, but there's more to it. Like, if it turns out someone's been kissing up to the boss, that's a disgrace, and they won't let the person hear the end of it. They also don't like to see anyone putting on airs; they'll make a point of bringing him down a notch or two. They're fools, you know."

Nikola thought this last remark—that they are fools—could be a test. If I agree, he thought, I might come off like a snotty prick.

"It's not like I have so much power. You're doing all the work."

Branoš looked at him and tilted his head. "Well, yes. But no one minds."

"Fine, we'll pick up where we left off at the bar. Where is it?"

"Down the road, the Blue Lagoon," Branoš said and gave a jaunty salute on his way out.

Then Nikola called Oleg.

"How's it going?"

"Branoš was just here, one of the Plum Boys."

"The Plum Boys? What's that?"

"I wondered, too. And it got me thinking."

"About what?"

"Well, look. I wonder if I shouldn't take them out for a drink. Plum brandy for the Plum Boys? Maybe they'd smile more. Can we swing that?"

"Ha ha, Niks, you're perking up, I see."

"No, it's that—it would be a gesture of goodwill. In various ways."

"A gesture of goodwill? Don't lie to me, the fresh air must be doing you good."

"Come here yourself if it's so great."

"Somebody has to travel around looking for markets," Oleg said. "Of course we can swing it. Pocket change. We want the grinning working class on socialist realist posters."

"Fine, cut the crap. I'm off for drinks."

"You don't say! That's great."

Nikola hung up and aped Oleg's voice: "*The Plum Boys? Who are they?*" You'd know if you'd been reading your reports, he thought.

He lay naked under the sheets, happily exhausted in the clean nest of gentle fragrance, listening to the voice coming from the TV in her living room, a report on a business conference where they'd discussed cutting-edge technologies and reached the conclusion that *only new-generation companies would survive the global crisis.*

"And a few old-generation ones!" he shouted, signaling to Lorena that he was up.

Soon she appeared at the door, a brunette with an athletic figure and a symmetrical face, leaning mischievously on the doorframe.

"Hello, renovator," she said, looking at him with a mildly teasing smile. "They haven't a clue that old factories in the godforsaken sticks are actually the latest thing, eh?"

"They're clueless," he said. "Cutting edge? Who knew . . ."

She sat on the bed and then slid down onto her side. She looked at him, lounging on her hip next to his feet, her mane of hair flowing over the sheets.

"Can you explain to me what it is that you do there exactly?"

He knew it. She didn't like the way he'd taken off right when she thought they were getting serious. She wouldn't have liked it even if he'd been part of the NASA space program.

"I mean, why?"

I can't explain, he wanted to say. He didn't want to tell her the whole scheme; it was less risky this way. But he had to say something.

"I'm starting production," he said. "I'm employing people."

"And you said you told them to, how did you call it?"

"Self-organize."

"That sounds almost like self-management. Where did it come from?"

Now he ought to come clean and admit that he and Nikola didn't have a clue about running such a business, that nobody knew how to make obsolete turbines. Then she'd ask him why on earth they were making them.

"They do as they please. They're the most efficient that way."

"Most efficient?"

Efficiency was one of her catchwords so this for her was borderline insulting. She was getting ahead as a manager at a big pharmaceutical company, and they spent a lot of time on efficiency.

"Well, yes. I have workers who are knowledgeable... I trust them."

"Don't fuck with me! You're 'employing people.' You 'trust them'? Are you turning into a patron of the working class now?"

"Ah, 'Don't fuck with me'" he said, quoting her: "So, *how do you see our relationship?*"

"Aw shut up! Those are my lines," she said, grinning. "You're not very bright, are you?"

"Well, look," he said, trying to come up with what to say next, "maybe I have turned into a patron of the working class. And why not?"

He thought he could defuse this with humor, but she planted her chin on her fist and seemed unwilling to relent. "I can't follow what you're saying. Or what you're doing for that matter."

"This is really bugging you, isn't it?"

Her expression was uneasy, and it occurred to him that this might be bothering her because of something going on in her life. She'd often spoken of layoffs at her company, and while she agreed with them, they made her anxious.

"They wanted capitalism. They voted for it, didn't they?"

"Don't worry about it."

"But when you give them capitalism, it's oh poor them, this isn't what they bargained for."

She was struggling with this, he thought, because she felt a little guilty.

He'd been over it all before. He knew where he stood. If they made the turbines and this relationship lasted, if they happened to buy a house, have a garden, a baby, he'd do what he could to explain his thinking to her. For now, there wasn't much point in trying to explain to her how, once the workers' enthusiasm was fully exploited, he'd fire them all at the same time.

Maybe all of this was the reason why he did not really want to go down there.

This job, he thought, is textbook globalization. Capital waltzes in, takes what it needs, and leaves. But here he was compelled to assert the opposite, it just so happened, as if he were a socialist visionary.

"You know, it's an experiment of sorts in business and morality..."

"You're being weird. All I know is that this goes against *everything* I thought of you," she said, staring at him as if he were some kind of poet.

He had the urge to laugh.

He had never thought about this before, but he was slowly realizing that he would have to play a sort of business bohemian, an eccentric dreamer, a social experimenter, an anti-capitalist activist— one of the above. He had not shared the entire business plan with anyone, not even Nikola. Nikola was the only person who knew that the turbines were being built for the Colonel, but not even he knew they'd only be building two of them and then shuttering the factory. Nikola might blurt something after the fifth beer, or his melancholy could take over, and he'd accidentally let the workers know they were going overboard with their enthusiasm.

Of course, the buyer's country was never mentioned anywhere. American intelligence was present all through this area; they had the region in the palm of their hand, and if anyone were to suspect that the turbines were being built for the Colonel, the local politicians would change their tune and the whole thing would be blocked by the invisible hand. The invisible hand of the market—the expression came to him—yes, the invisible hand of the *free market* would definitely come down on his shoulder and say: Wait a minute, bro, the market is not that *free*.

None of this could be leaked to Lorena. She was focused on her own little world and wanted to get through a successful life according to the standards of the confined society to which she belonged. She would gain nothing from the information. Telling her would only lighten the burden on him because he wouldn't be forced to play the part.

This was maddening sometimes: nobody knowing what you were doing, not saying what was on your mind. And if you never spoke of it, maybe it didn't even exist: the idea never came back to you, as if you didn't have a reflection in the mirror of others. He looked at Lorena and thought, Light goes through me, I'm not there in her eyes; what she sees is merely my silhouette.

He was living in such a vacuum. This is why he constantly had to keep his eye on the compass, always to know exactly where he was, always to gauge his position, and this drew him into local and world problems and sometimes he checked over every detail obsessively. A few years ago in Vienna, each time he was on the metro, he would feel out of breath and break out suddenly in a sweat, as if he were afraid of drowning in his own thoughts. He would shoot out of the metro and hungrily gulp in the air. He solved this problem by taking taxis. Considering the expense, he thought, I'd be better off with a good shrink. But would he find a trustworthy one? Perhaps he was reluctant to share his life story with anyone else. When he was in Berlin, he would hang out with buoyant young people, as if he were one of them. Once he was asked why he never used the underground, since they thought taxis were bourgeois, so he just smiled and said, "I have too many acquaintances in the underworld. Maybe some of them are in hell, too. I avoid it."

One woman took him seriously, so he told her: "Just kidding."

"No you're not," she said, and looked at him.

She obviously had unique powers. He usually felt that people's gazes missed him altogether. Like Lorena's today.

She was still reclining at the foot of the bed, her chin propped on her fist, looking at him in a particular way, as if he were a poet who'd suddenly dropped in, uninvited, as the prince of business on his white horse.

"Come on. This goes against *everything* you used to think of me? Well, fine," he said with a grin. "Then do tell what you used to think, now that it's moot."

"Hmm." She was deep in thought. "What I thought?" She looked up at the ceiling, like someone trying to recall something they hadn't studied enough. "Let's say . . . that I thought you were . . . . you were . . . Um . . . A professional!"

Not bad, he thought before saying, "What's that supposed to mean? That all I care about is work and money? Is that what you think?" Now he was really interested in what she'd say next. Because if all he cared about was work, what did she even want with him?

"Yes," she said. "I thought you were utterly alone, hermetically sealed, selfish."

"Is that what you liked about me?"

"Gee, you're really making me think," she said. "I liked the smell of the beast."

Wasn't expecting that, he thought.

She then laughed at the sentence, throwing her head back. She sat up on the bed, took a cigarette from the nightstand, and lit it.

She looked him in the eye, as if trying to reach behind the mask, and said, "I thought you were a beast."

He stared at her breasts, watching them breathe.

"Well, I am," he said in a different voice. "Come here!"

8

NIKOLA WAS SITTING on a barstool in the Blue Lagoon, leaning against the wall at the corner of the bar, thinking about how the place's name contradicted its location in every possible way. This bar, which was closer to the factory than anywhere else, was named—and this was apparent from the framed and very yellowed poster—after a teen movie set somewhere on Fiji, a movie Nikola had seen years before when he belonged to Brooke Shields's target audience. Back then, he wanted a girlfriend who looked like her. Today, he thought, Brooke is full of Botox, and he was sitting here in the Blue Lagoon like nothing had changed, possibly waiting for the love of his life, whoever she was, bewildered while overseeing the renovation of the factory, which, he had to admit, was going miraculously well. Sobotka said yesterday that the repairs were nearly done. This was all being handled without Oleg, the great maestro of the game, who kept saying, "Splendid, I'm handling everything at my end, I'm closing deals," over the phone, but obviously was not inclined to keep Nikola company at the Blue Lagoon. So Nikola was left to brainstorm about God-knows-what in this time capsule of a bar. Why, for example, did the chain-wearing eighties fashion relic, the owner, name a bar next to a factory the Blue Lagoon?

The more Nikola thought about it, the more it made sense in that, as far as he remembered, the whole movie took place after a shipwreck. But back in the eighties, when naming the bar, the owner was not thinking "shipwreck." He was thinking: escape as far away as possible, all the way to the Pacific.

As if the owner had been *wishing* there was no factory, thought Nikola, no industry, probably along with his entire generation. Nikola would not have given the bar in N. such an idiotic name, but, just like the owner, he probably would have done anything to create a different kind of mood. Now, after the owner's business had gone under, he dusted off Brooke Shields, jumped on the wave of factory renovation, and was living off them. What else was he to do?

"Rafo, maybe you could rename the place the 'Blue Collar'?" suggested Nikola. The owner liked to chat with Nikola. From Rafo's perspective, he and Nikola talked to each other like two slightly depressed entrepreneurs stymied by the socialist legacy. Rafo had worked in Germany and had no doubt whatsoever that Nikola shared his opinions, since they were both businessmen.

This was the way the owner understood Nikola's remark about the name of the bar as well, as if they were weighing a business idea as colleagues, an idea which he—for a reason he couldn't quite explain—didn't like.

"Eh, I guess I prefer the Blue Lagoon. From a business point of view, too . . ."

"But can't you see you only get workers here? There aren't any teenage girls," Nikola said, teasing him in a mock-serious tone.

"You never know."

"You have to admit, what matters most in business is to have vision," said Nikola, realizing he was talking like Oleg.

If Oleg were here, he'd take over the conversation with anybody who crossed their path. But Nikola was learning that he, too, was capable of performing in that arena. In a way, he was enjoying Oleg's absence.

True, there were no teenagers around, but Nikola noticed that the Blue Lagoon attracted women who'd been teenagers in Brooke Shields's day, and had aged naturally, no Botox, though that didn't mean they were acting naturally. They were a little stiff, decently done up according to the standards of their small town, and they came in groups of at least three, sometimes four. On Fridays there would be five or six of them, and seemed to be all from an unusual subculture. Their presence was, however, refreshing and even surprising, since most of the town's bars were populated exclusively by men. The factory's workers, Nikola noticed, would instantly perk up when the ladies walked in. Their presence was a kind of compliment to these until-recently unemployed men since, instead of avoiding them, the ladies might be interested in having fun with them again. The women were on the shy side and stuck together, but after a few drinks there was the occasional high-pitched laugh, along with hesitant, playful looks. Nikola noticed, perhaps a bit presumptuously, that he drew these hesitant looks more than the others, always followed, for some reason, by giggles. Since some of the brave women, when they approached the bar, ordered their drinks while standing right next to him, he gradually met all of them and also learned that the crew of teenagers from the time of *The Blue Lagoon* consisted mostly of unmarried public-sector employees who'd continued coming here *because of work. What can you do?* One of them, Tanja, had told him this the other night at the bar. She was, as she said, the director of the town museum, which he should, they agreed, visit as soon as possible: it was a small museum and easy to tour. "Most of the time there isn't anybody there," she'd said to him in a voice with a hint of the sensual. So he imagined himself for a moment at this imaginary museum, clumsily leaning on an exhibit, perhaps a stuffed mammoth (he had no idea where the image was from), or perhaps a priceless stone baptismal font, or under a yellowing imperial charter, stained like an old porn magazine. He imagined himself fucking the museum director in the tense silence, because there'd be no one there, and all of history would be theirs, hot, wet, and lustful. Lust and the museum. That was what he thought this Brooke Shields with a few wrinkles smelled like. *No, she really isn't ugly*, he thought, *she's attractive in a way.*

"It's not far from here," she said coyly.

"Yes, yes, I should stop by. I love history," he said.

"*Historia magistra vitae est*," she added. He thought of Pompeii and the eruption of Vesuvius, of all the apocalyptic sex. He had to admit it now—he'd really been in a dry spell. Besides the museum director, the group also numbered the head of the town library, an attorney working at the town hall (he had heard someone call her "the head honcho"), an English teacher at the primary school who was also a poet ("no, really," he'd been told), a veterinarian, who joined the group when she was not out in the field, and a dentist, who had maybe even brought them there in the first place, since she'd been seeing more patients since the factory started working again. This was the female intellectual elite of the town, he realized, a mighty group that the men from the factory were hesitantly eyeing. All the directors, the libraries and the museums, the town hall, the poetry, and the dentist's chair—they probably intimidated the local men merely by their positions, which was probably why they were still single into their thirties and forties. The English teacher-poet was the youngest, in her mid-thirties, and the veterinarian was in her mid-forties but very athletic, so much so he'd thought there must be a gym hidden away somewhere in town. She was the only one dressed casually, while the others preferred to wear plain woolen jackets and suits under their fur coats—because it was still fucking cold—along with boots with kitten heels, like careful politicians touring mountain municipalities.

Nikola watched them every time, trying to decide which to focus on, though none of them genuinely appealed to him, but as a group, except for the plump attorney from the town hall whom he dismissed out of hand, they all intrigued him, each in her way, so he eyed them now and then as a group, creating, he sensed, added tension because they must have felt he couldn't decide which one to choose. He thought this was why each of them—as she was approaching the bar or going to the bathroom—moved as though in slow motion, or in a reality TV show. Each one of them had her own style and her own idea of femininity, too pronounced perhaps, with a flair for spontaneous acting, playful elegance, a few dainty steps, a shy lack of confidence, and other signs that depressed him. The veterinarian was the only one who strode along as if she didn't care. Despite her athletic build, the expression of her face was tough: more like Clint Eastwood than Brooke Shields. But, he thought, as the years passed, these differences cease to matter.

He found them attractive as a group but not as individuals, and he was torn. If he offered them group sex, he thought, he'd surely provoke a scandal that would be talked about for centuries. Besides, he wouldn't know what to do with them anyway. But, on which one should he focus? And, should he even involve himself with any of them at all, because he had the feeling he wouldn't fall in love, he didn't know if, realistically speaking, sex was possible here without emotional entanglements.

Maybe the veterinarian after all?

Maybe, but . . . He'd visited the town museum earlier today, and now he wondered if he'd already made a mess of things.

Tanja, the director, was of course already there and was very flustered when he appeared, as if her house were a mess, and the museum was of course deadly quiet and immaculate, and there really was nobody there—where were these people she was in charge of, he wondered—so he had the privilege of being expertly guided through local history. There'd been all sorts of things in the jumble of history, the West, the East, the middle, the Celts had mined ore here in primeval times, the ancient Romanized tribes had disappeared leaving a few traces, a handful of words and names were left, said the director breathlessly, the Bogomils were buried under standing stones, and there were many more, she said, many people who'd been persecuted and sought refuge in these mountains because the hordes and armies thundered through the valleys and raised hell, and the governing was done in the valleys, and the hordes and armies couldn't penetrate the mountains quite as easily, so many people who wanted to hide from the world, the army, the government wandered through them, and they lived in seclusion as they pleased, and this is a strange region, strange, she said, "you'll see, sir, or maybe you won't because it can't all be taken in at first glance."

"Tanja, may I call you by your first name?"

"Well, I guess." She blushed again, feeling she'd misread his intentions, and he didn't know what to say or do to put her at her ease, and her edginess was infectious: he thought how he should have gone for a drink or two beforehand and then come, but he'd been more focused on taking a shower and, foolishly, showed up sober, and he was much more susceptible, sober, to the museum's atmosphere where their steps creaked and he could even hear her breathing, but not in a sexy way. More asthmatic. Maybe she really was asthmatic.

Maybe she was ashamed of taking out the spray and inhaling it? Or maybe she thought she wasn't dressed as nicely as she'd like? Who knows what kind of fuss was going through her mind, he thought, so he decided to give her some time. "Where's the gents?" he said.

She waved her hand in the general direction, as if she'd been given a reprieve, and he went into the bathroom and decided to stay there a little longer. He messaged Oleg: "How's it going with buying the parts and materials? Hurry. We'll need them soon. I'm in the town museum washroom waiting for nothing in particular. Sincerely yours, Niks." He also messaged his childhood friend Vito, who was in Washington, where he'd escaped from the crowds of New York. They messaged back and forth on a quarterly basis: "I'm up in the mountains where many shady characters hide out. Don't fire at us from there."

When he came out Tanja was a bit more relaxed and seemed more like a director who had things under control. Who knows what had been wrong before, he thought, but never mind, she was now giving him a look, bottled-up yet erotic. He knew he could, that he should, that "it was expected of him" to embrace the erotic charge crammed under the armor of civilization, which was in a way more present here, at the end of the world, than off in the crowds of Paris or New York. There, no doubt, he would have fucked the museum director in MoMA, he thought, if it were this empty, even with Marina Abramović watching, but here, in this touching provincial museum, his dick was completely absent and he had to force himself to think of Eros, not to forget it all, and this turned it into a strenuous sort of task, and all the while he couldn't guess what would happen next even if they eventually got to sex. All these thoughts gave him a mild anxiety attack, but he had already gone to the gents and could not go back to take a Xanax. And what for, anyway? What kind of sex would that be, why go through all the trouble? It was easier to be alone and avoid it all, he thought, and suddenly—he was definitely the one who looked asthmatic to her now—as if he were out of breath, he said the museum was interesting, he should see it again sometime. This maybe sounded promising, so before he left, without knowing why, exactly—maybe it was a way of consoling her, because she had a look which said that she thought this was her fault—he kissed the director on the cheek and said, "You are wonderful."

Now, he knew he shouldn't have done that, although he was, in fact, being honest, because there was something wonderful about her; even so, he hadn't meant it to sound *as serious* as he saw reflected in her eyes, which followed him out, he noticed, as if he were an officer and a gentleman. So he blew it, and they hadn't even fucked. Damn.

Oleg was right when he called me a romantic, he thought. He didn't get what was so romantic about all this, but the truth was that this would never have happened to Oleg. After visiting the town museum, he went to the factory, but he didn't stay there long, he needed a drink, besides, everything was going along smoothly without him anyway: Hanka the secretary, whom Sobotka had rehired, was keeping the paperwork under control, yes, they'd also hired a younger woman who was handling the computer, and Sobotka was supervising the process in the workshop, so Nikola didn't quite understand what he was supposed to be doing, except pretending to be a manager, which was maybe, he thought, the essence of being a manager.

He was brought back from his thoughts when the doors of the Blue Lagoon opened. For a moment his stomach clenched—please don't let it be the museum director—but it was just Erol, Branoš, Sobotka, and a young woman.

Sobotka had run into Šeila, the woman they came in with. She'd once been best friends with his older daughter, Jasmina; she used to come by their house often and he was glad to see her, almost as if she were his daughter, though he hadn't seen her for years. When they ran into each other in front of the bar, she asked, as always, after Jasmina. She used to really miss Jasmina, he thought, but now the questions were more her way of not forgetting their friendship. She asked about Jasmina as if she were asking about a person who was lost, someone she was not sure still existed, because Jasmina had left at the beginning of the war when she was fifteen, and ever since she'd lived in a different world, in the north. The way in which she asked after Jasmina was like the way Sobotka felt, as if he had a hole inside of him.

✦ ✦ ✦

Sobotka's life was clearly splitting into two very different halves.

In the mid-seventies he came to N. as a newlywed engineer, he was awarded an apartment by the factory, and apart from the strike-related episode, he led a life typical of the socialist middle class: he had his job, his family, his strolls through town most eve-nings with a drink or two; he went on the occasional outing to a restaurant with Zlata and friends, there were holiday visits to his folks in the village or her folks in a bigger city, and three weeks spent amid the heady scents of the Mediterranean in summer. Some of their vacations were spent at the factory resort, and some came out of his own pocket; he loved to travel and discover islands and always slept at campgrounds in tents he pitched skillfully with the not-so-skillful assistance of his two daughters. He remembered that he, both in the village and in the city, had often been crudely asked about whether he intended "to keep going," meaning would he and Zlata go for a son. Questions like that felt like an insult to his girls. "Go where?" he'd say.

The nineties snapped him in half. The factory finally went bankrupt in the melee of the collapse of the old system and the state, followed shortly thereafter by the war.

As Sobotka refused to believe the war was coming, it happened that—when it did come—there was barely enough time for Zlata and the girls to pack their things. They managed to get out of the region on the last convoy, and their town soon fell into several years of isolation.

The convoy was pulled over in several places; they were taken off the bus and questioned, and all the money that was found was confiscated—the girls complained to him later, their voices despondent when they called him from the coast, newly in a different country—and soon after, when the accounts of rape began appearing on television, he was stricken by dread at the thought that, on their trip, something might have happened to Zlata and possibly Jasmina, who was fifteen, something they were reluctant to tell him, though he found roundabout ways to ask them many times. Jasmina always sounded sulky, not at all talkative, while Zlata sounded high-strung, speaking without much tenderness, though, truth be told, their bickering had already worsened during the time when the factory was going bankrupt; she nagged him about his drinking and his lack of ambition, which was why they stayed in the small town on the other side of the mountain when she was itching to move to a bigger city.

"We did well, we had a good life," he used to say to her, but over time she grew bitter about the past. When she called from the coast where the former factory vacation resort had been transformed into a refugee center, she said they were sleeping in miserable conditions in overcrowded rooms, the locals were now treating them differently, the former hospitality was gone, everything was rigged, she'd never come back, she wanted to get as far away as possible. "When you were a tourist once in a place, and then you come back there as a refugee, you see everything with new eyes," she said over the phone. "You see what your bond with the place really was. There was no bond, honey. I don't exist. And worse, honey." She said *honey* in a tone that implied he might be to blame for all of it.

He was sorry that even the good memories of the summer vacations he had taken the girls on would be soured for them. He talked to them, discouraged by the thought that there was nothing he could do, feeling he'd failed as a father and a protector because he hadn't predicted what would happen. Why hadn't he known what was coming? Because he was gullible, brought up in a culture of peace, and he started to beat himself up over this and loathe everything he'd believed until then, because all of it had betrayed him, cheated him, and was the reason his girls were now sleeping at a refugee center with no money and no father. He sensed they felt abandoned and harbored a silent hatred toward him which, Sobotka sensed, Zlata was encouraging. She soon started to blame him for the fact that he, too, hadn't left town—this was when he started thinking she didn't love him—having literally said on one occasion that he should have seen into the future, so, for a moment, he pictured himself poised on the prow of the family, in charge of gazing into the distance, no land in sight. She'd *felt it coming*, she said, while he said *that's not how it was*. At the time she'd thought, He's a man, he knows. "Ah," she laughed sharply, "I thought men understood politics. No, you believe, you root for your team, you run, you're . . . I won't say what. Never again will I believe, never," she said.

The question, he reasoned, was how he'd have fared had he been on their convoy. Maybe he'd be in a concentration camp today. At the time he thought it made sense to stay and guard the apartment, their only property; besides, he was liable for military service and had been told he couldn't leave. But her accusations ate away at him; he knew he'd failed to protect his family. They were the ones on their own out in the cruel world, and he was here, in his slippers by the phone, trapped in his apartment and his misery, in a town where cigarettes and food were running low.

"It was all a lie, honey," she said over the telephone. "Maybe everything had to fall to pieces so I'd see the truth. But the truth is useless, honey. I'm taking the kids and leaving so I can go to a place where people still lie to each other. I'll have to figure out where, exactly. A place where lies are stable. That's the place to be."

"Zlata, what's happening now is not the truth. It has all been twisted," he wanted to console her, though he himself didn't believe this anymore. "See, you'd like to go to a place where the lies are stable. But then they become the truth even there. Why not? Everything's not quite so grim. This is all just a hiccup."

"I can't get past the hiccup."

"We move forward."

"Maybe I'll forget if I can get away. If I forget everything."

"Everything?"

He was already indifferent by the time he was called up by the army, demoralized by the emptiness of the apartment, the lack of work, the powerless anxiety. The news was horrifying, and Sobotka could see that one ethnic group was more prepared for war than the others; the leaders of that ethnic group were deliberate in their brutality; and their militia members—obviously following a premeditated plan—were driving out and killing people of other faiths, opening concentration camps, and perpetrating mass rapes. The other groups were not merely standing by, arms crossed, because, as Sobotka saw, evil spread like a virus among the warring parties. The tide of evil swept away before it all previous experience and made the world a different, unrecognizable place, very much like hell. This was the world where Sobotka was now living. Apart from that, Sobotka had been newly anointed as a member of an ethnic minority in N. Fortunately for him, his situation was not as bad as it might have been because the other two ethnic groups were the ones at war with each other in the region; if his compatriots had been over on the other side of the mountain he was aware that he'd have fared far worse. He knew people who'd fought against their own relatives to defend the town, yet, nevertheless, they were still mistrusted by others in the community. That would push you right over the edge, he thought.

Occasionally he'd hear that N. had been spared the worst, because it was so remote that it wasn't worth fighting over. "You have no idea," said a man, Berin was his name, who'd come on foot to the town—he had relatives there—after his rural unit fell apart and his village was torched; he'd made his way across the mountain with a hunting rifle and boots which he literally swore on—"I swear by my boots!" he said—because he knew all about edible plants, and he'd also killed a vulture along the way.

"A vulture?"

"A griffon vulture, a rare bird, but what can you do. It was flying in from somewhere, low to the ground, as if overfed."

"You ate it along the way?"

"You have no idea, I'm telling you," said Berin, which was supposed to mean they'd had it easy; they weren't pleased about this—that they were clueless—and Berin, with people swarming around him at the bar, kept ordering drinks and asking others what they'd have.

When the bar owner requested that he settle the tab after last call, Berin said, "I haven't got any money. I'm flat broke!"

He took out a frayed document with the stamp of a local, no-longer-existing community government, which confirmed that he was, indeed, Berin and had his own gun.

"Write it down, I'll pay. I swear on these here boots."

The bar owner pondered what to do with the man, he had men who dealt with people like this, but Berin flung wide his arms, repentant, and said, "Fuck it, I made it here alive, the drinks are on me."

"So, roll up your sleeves . . ."

When he was called up, and they were being transported to more distant positions, Sobotka saw that things really did look worse everywhere else—all it took was stopping to take a piss and you immediately felt it in the air. There were cattle wandering aimlessly until somebody caught them. There were dogs on the loose. An evil wind.

He was not especially afraid of death. He moved zombie-like around the combat positions, but he functioned—an autopilot of sorts nudged him to react; he shot when necessary, ran at the last minute. The autopilot shielded him from depression, kept him from dwelling too much on his family. Animal-like he sharpened his focus on the here and now, because the here and now was so potent, so physically present, and everything else felt distant in space and time, so distant that making contact seemed hardly possible. He did call whenever he could find a working phone; he called the coastal resort, and sometimes he'd get through, but then he'd be reticent, bumbling, rattled, like somebody communicating with the other side and invoking spirits. Numb, as if anesthetized, at times he'd be surprised when his familial, prewar personality surfaced mid-conversation, as if he were split in two. He was afraid he'd start crying, sobbing in front of his daughters, so he avoided emotional language—he was only tender with his youngest, Viktoria, and then his throat clenched and he'd cover the phone with his hand, and she told her mother she couldn't hear Dad anymore and handed the phone back. During their last conversation from the factory resort, Zlata told him she'd be granted asylum in a northern country that was accepting refugees, she said this would definitely be a step up from where they were now, and he agreed, though he'd never been there, but, yes, undoubtedly things would be better there.

The telephone in his—formerly their—apartment, to which he sometimes returned from combat, no longer worked. He rarely spoke to them over the next three years, and even when he did find a functioning phone, he had to brace mentally for their conversations, because, in a way, he couldn't explain anything anymore. He had to speak as if they were still in the same world, as if they still spoke the same language, yet they no longer were in the same world, nor did they speak the same language. So they adjusted to one another with hollow words patching up the silences. He felt no better after those conversations. They reminded him of a time with his commander, the man's name was Tihan—they were forming the engineering technical unit at the time and had a bit to drink at the headquarters; Tihan wanted to pick Sobotka's brain about several things as he was planning to promote him and pull him off active duty. Tihan, who said he wished his family had left, too, told him countless times, "Call them from here," and Sobotka would say, "Thanks, I will, I'll call the girls. You know what they're like? Not just because they're mine, but . . . Beauty. Soul and beauty."

"Feel free."

"I will, I haven't heard from them in ages."

He kept saying the words, but didn't dial the number. He'd pour himself another drink while Tihan sat and watched him, already half-drunk, talk about his daughters, Zlata—such a beauty! "Both of us are blond, you know, and people often thought us foreigners. What a woman. You'd think she had to be from somewhere abroad."

When the war ended, Zlata said she had no plans to return for now, she'd started a new life, the girls were in school, bringing them back would be a sin to the ruins and rubble where, if there ever would be a real peace, the hatred of war would linger until God-knows-when. He asked whether her new life meant she had somebody else, and she told him it was not about having someone, she had her own life, she was independent and still young for her age, forty-two. This stayed with him because he himself was forty-six, yet he felt old. He really thought of himself as an old man, and he was surprised to hear her say that. He and his wife, they'd been separated in time, he thought—he was in a place where time beat faster.

Half a year after the war ended, once he'd taken care of the paperwork, he went to see them, there, in the northern land; he arrived and felt out-of-place: father, husband, guest. He could tell Zlata didn't love him anymore; she saw him only as a reminder of a kind of dread. She'd invited him out of a feeling of obligation, for the girls, but she avoided him—a burden from the past. They didn't sleep together.

He was out of his element there; he had no idea what he was doing or even how to do anything. They knew everything better than he did. He had to ask them how everything worked, like a grown-up child. He didn't even know what to tell them—to poison the girls' minds with the war, with what he'd been through, the horrible stories about what people can become, people you once knew—to poison them with those stories just because he could? He'd begin a story and then drop it, sinking into the silence of someone superfluous. As their father he asked about their lives, but everything sounded empty, a hollow shell, as if coming from a person who hardly knew them, asking how they were doing. Still, he completely embraced the role, adopting a fatherly tone, and they accepted this even though all of it seemed irksome and awkward to him. Zlata acted as if this was nothing but routine, as if she didn't see problems in it. She even yelled at her daughters, "Answer your father's question!" This only made things worse.

One of these days there when they found themselves alone in the apartment, he tried to stir Zlata's memories by talking about the old days.

She listened to him, smoking nervously at the kitchen table, and then at one moment she interrupted him: "I know you cheated on me!"

His jaw dropped; for a moment he couldn't remember what her words were referring to. He'd been through the war and everything, and now she was talking about something that happened during the strike? As if that still meant anything?

What is the statute of limitations on infidelity, anyway?

"You know when I found out? Down there at the resort, when we were refugees. That you had a whore at the factory. Just so you know—finding that out . . . That was just what I needed then."

He wanted to tell her it didn't matter, he wasn't that man anymore; time had passed.

But he said something stupid, something that had meaning only for him: "That . . . That was before the war."

"So what?" she said, getting up from the table and looking at him as if everything was now settled.

She stood there, leaning against the sink, her arms crossed, her expression stern, staring beyond him.

That was before the war, he repeated to himself, and then realized that everything he was looking for here was from before the war.

"You're right," he said. "Everything has already happened."

Not for me, she thought. For you maybe, but not me. She didn't want to be cruel; she knew there was no point in saying that. But she knew exactly what she wanted just then—she wanted him to leave. He'd cheated on her. He deserved it. She had every reason to start over.

She had dreamed several times how he'd come and how she'd have to tell him that, and then fear would swamp her in her sleep, fear of the fact that she was not a good wife, fear she'd betrayed him, fear of everything going on back there, in the country from which the fears came in her dreams. She was afraid to declare everything over. He still lived there and was clutching at her heel like a zombie.

But now she knew.

"You cheated on me," she repeated; this repetition seemed redundant to him.

"Tell me," he said, looking at her, "is this just an excuse? Did you ever love me before that?"

She frowned and looked down, staring, as if asking herself whether she owed him an answer, and said, "Truth be told, I can no longer remember how it was. I loved you at first, sure, but afterward . . . That was the world we lived in and I respected it. That world was . . . set that way by default. I can't remember now how it felt . . . I was inside it. I never thought about being different."

She paused and lit a fresh cigarette.

"When I heard you'd cheated on me—down there of all places, a woman told me at the refugee center, there, where I'd seen what our world had come to—I could finally say my goodbyes to our world. If you hadn't cheated on me, I wouldn't have. But, there, that may have been what saved me. I no longer cared about looking back."

She glanced at him, he at her, and in a way he appreciated her for being so frank, for telling it how it was, and then he realized she really was a different woman sitting there across from him. She was no longer the same Zlata—she was someone else who, it just so happened, was talking about how he'd cheated on her. "Don't think that . . . " she continued, "It's not that I didn't care what happened to you. But . . . with every day everything grew farther and farther from me and . . . I said to myself: I have to raise these children. I have to make myself different. And there it is. I'm not going back. If that's what you came here for, it's over . . . Our world has evaporated, it's gone."

"I'm glad you said that," he said, hunched over in the chair. He thought of adding how grim his days had been here, in their house. For him, he wanted to say, those days had been even worse than the war itself; only now did he see that there was nothing left for him. But, instead, he just stared.

"Ah, Zlata, my Zlata," he said. "I think I'll go now."

Slowly, like an old man afraid to make a wrong move, he stood.

"I wasn't going to tell you to go," she said, and as if something had moved her, she put a hand to her mouth and took a step back toward the window. She didn't know where this was coming from. She'd been waiting a long time for this final tie to be sundered, but now that it was happening, she felt a faraway pang.

"It's difficult for me to be here. I need to leave now."

"Won't you wait for the girls? I mean . . . I didn't . . . Not without saying goodbye, for their sake," she said, her voice breaking.

"Right now. I can't be here anymore."

She saw in his eyes that he couldn't; she could still read his face.

"Tell them to come whenever they want," he said. "My home is their home."

It didn't take him long to pack. When he emerged from the room with his bag he stood in the kitchen doorway and said, "I'll sell the apartment. It's too big and empty for me. I'll send you half of the money."

"No need," she said without a second thought. "Leave something for the girls and give it to them later."

"I'm sending you half, it's yours."

She stared straight ahead, trying to focus on this. Maybe because of the guilt she was feeling, or because she'd crossed out all that had happened down there, almost stuttering, she said, "You needn't . . . What you can get for it won't go far here . . . but it could be a help for you."

He gazed briefly into her eyes and for a moment she seemed like the old Zlata.

If only she hadn't said that.

He left.

She watched him through the window as he was walking away down the empty street and silent tears ran down her face.

Big and stocky and slow as he was, he floated down the street.

And then, though she knew she shouldn't, she thought about how she'd loved him once, how he'd seemed sturdy and strong, how proud she'd been of him, and then she remembered herself, herself from that life, her first pregnancy when they listened to the baby— Jasmina—kicking inside her belly. Why was she remembering that now, where were these images coming from?

She shook her head.

Then she started to shake. She wasn't crying, just shaking. He moved out of sight, she couldn't see him for the hedge.

He was gone. Everything was gone. She was alone now, outside it all.

But I've known this for a long time, she said to herself, shaking, I've known this for a long time, it's nothing new . . . *Calm down.*

She couldn't stop shaking, like someone naked in the wind.

She reached for her cell phone and, barely hitting the keys, called the man she was in a relationship with; she hadn't told Sobotka about him. He answered the phone in their language; she was at a loss for words.

He asked, in their language, "Is everything all right? Say something! Hello? Is that you?"

She wanted to say, "He's gone," but her words made no sense.

"Did he do something to you?" he shouted, agitated, at the other end of the line.

Yes, she thought. But that wasn't what she needed to say. She was on the edge of what was real, by the window, staring at the shaking empty street. She'd pull herself together, now she'd pull herself together and see what was real and what she should be feeling.

"Hello? Zlata! Did he do something to you? Zlata?"

9

LIGHT SNOW SWIRLED gently, swept up from the ground by a quiet force from above. The day would be clear, dry, one that would sober you up as soon as you stepped outside.

The mountains were sharply visible. Black forests with patches of snow. He knew they were green, but from here they looked like a moth-eaten wool sweater on the body of a big black woman. Like the black forest of Germany, he thought. Whoever came up with that name must have seen forests like these from afar.

Was anybody there? If so, they certainly had quite a view. He would be very calm, he felt, if he were up there, watching.

He looked toward the road.

The mailman had encountered a man with a dog; they were all standing by the side of the road while the dog was bounding around the mailman's feet, apparently trying to play. But the mailman didn't even look at the dog; he just stood there like a soldier frozen at attention.

The mailman looked as if he wanted to hand something to the

man with the dog. The man with the dog raised his hands as if he were encountering a glass barrier.

The mailman was holding something; an envelope, or was it a package, or a bomb, and the man with the dog stepped away, hands raised.

Now the dog was barking at the mailman, you could hear it through the double-paned glass.

Then the man went his own way with the dog, while the mailman stood there, his head slightly tipped.

Nikola watched all of this from his window.

A cutting north wind quietly swirled the dry powdery snow that had fallen during the night.

Gone... Gone...

The thought, *gone*, wouldn't leave him.

He thought about Šeila. He wondered if the miracle was starting, when your spirit is charged with blood and you're so physical yet virtual, so much a part of life. Was this what he was leaving for the younger generation?

The first night he met her they barely spoke—Erol hovered around her, and from the sidelines, Nikola watched Erol mark a space around the young woman with his body, tell her something with his lively face and laughing eyes—he was clearly trying his luck with jokes—by speaking close to her ear, and how in time he went from enthusiasm to more insecurity, until he eventually gave up, though she didn't move away from him and she smiled, but apparently not in the right places. He watched the slow crumbling of an alpha male's performance through the eyes of another alpha male, without a trace of solidarity. Erol's face cooled, he scratched himself behind the ears, and then, after a time, he stopped fencing her in, so even Branoš was within reach, while Erol moved away to the bar as if he needed to catch his breath, not far from Nikola, who said, "Beautiful, huh?"

"Yes," said Erol. "But not for me."

Nikola looked at him, and even felt sorry for having rooted against him.

"How can you tell?"

"I just can . . . You know when a burly boxer like me spars with a person who has long arms and fancy footwork," said Erol, scratching himself behind the ear.

"Wha?"

"You end up missing a lot is all."

Nikola had no chance to talk to Šeila that night because while Branoš was trying his luck, the museum director showed up at the Blue Lagoon bar with her taut face and a look that said she was afraid she'd left something behind on her way out the door. She planted herself right next to Nikola and soon he had to think of ways to cool her mood, because she tended to turn any inkling of mutual understanding into *ha ha* euphoria. It's awkward when your mission is to sour someone's mood. It usually takes a while—until the other side decides you're a bore, but the road there is a long one, especially when you're dealing with skittish yet persistent women who, like the museum director, at one point say, "Oh, I see I'm boring you."

They came to this, however, only after the conversation turned to the local chess club. Earlier, he'd tried with local soccer, more specifically by talking about the local team, known as the Turbines. But when Šeila was on her way out, his sad gaze followed her.

"Damn, what were we talking about?" he said just then.

"Ha ha, you sure are distracted! The Turbines are in the third league, as far as I know," said the museum director.

The conversation went on.

He handled the subject well because people from the club had already hit him up for money, no doubt since the soccer club had been named after the factory. So Oleg shelled out for the sponsorship and Nikola was invited to a game where, standing next to the club president, he witnessed awful soccer. Even the whiskered president shot occasional glances at Nikola, arching his eyebrows and gesturing in despair. *What can you do . . . The coach . . .* Embarrassed, maybe a little overdoing it, the president shrugged as if seeing all this for the first time.

What can you do . . . All my life, I've . . . I've worked. But the entire system—the players . . . and the coach . . . and even the league— it can't be done. No way . . . Impossible, trust me . . . When you think about it, where has my life gone? For what?

Nikola consoled the gentleman.

He noticed, however, that, despite everything, the club had a surprisingly large group of supporters known as the Turbos who mixed turbo-folk culture with hometown pride, creating an inextricable amalgam of depression and the waving of arms in the air. At one moment he thought he'd misjudged them because they came alive when they sang a song in which seven shots of Jäger were mentioned multiple times, and the chorus was—*If my daddy could see me nowww . . .*

"Is this an anthem of some sort?"

"Nah," said the club president, before yelling, "Where are you going . . . Where?"

> *If my daddy could see me nowww . . . If my daddy could see me nowww . . .*
> *Getting wasted, getting wasted . . . Seven shots of Jäger . . .*

There was also a marginal group watching it all from their own corner, gathered around a band called Turban-Rap. When one of them heard Nikola's question they explained how the chant had been taken from a viral Internet video of a young woman explaining how she celebrated the holiday of Bairam by drinking. Later they gave Nikola an MP3 of the song and asked for his sponsorship, so Oleg gave them some money. He listened to it and memorized the chorus:

> *Wound, salt, corrida, bull,*
> *My team'll never get a goal.*

He mentioned some of this during his reluctant conversation with the museum director and asked impersonal questions about the club, keeping the conversation as far from their personal lives as possible, hoping he'd seem boring. But Tanja the director turned out to be a steadfast fan of the Turbines; she even knew that the *seven shots of Jäger* and the chorus with daddy came from the viral video.

"From her statement?"

"Yup. In a survey."

"The song comes from a response to a survey?"

"Yes, yes," laughed the director.

This even sounded interesting, but as he had to prove to the museum director that he was boring, he instantly switched to chess.

Because, apart from the disaster that was the local soccer club, an incomparably better chess club had also survived in the small town. Yes, Oleg sponsored them as well; chess was widely played, maybe because the game was suitable for long stretches of unemployment. People were training their minds and maintaining their self-esteem, and there were men in town who looked like bums but sported the title of Candidate Master.

Clarifying this with Tanja and apathetically gazing at the bar, Nikola talked about the sudden drop in interest in chess after the Cold War, about this being the game of a bipolar world, about the absurdity of the black and white pieces, the inertia of the king, the pointlessness of chess in the digital age, and pointlessness in general. He mentioned the twilit showdown between the computer and Kasparov, thinking this would bore the director to no end and she'd finally decide to talk to Erol, for instance, or maybe the entrepreneurial owner, Rafo, who was also there.

But then she said the infamous, "Oh, I see I'm boring you." With a question mark.

"Oh, no you're not. I'm boring you," he said.

"I am. I'm boring you."

"Look, I'm boring you!" he said a little sharply.

"What was that?" she asked with an intent look.

"Nothing, I feel kind of . . . lousy."

"Just relax," she said.

He felt a little foolish having the museum director tell him to relax.

Then he asked himself, All right, all right, what do I owe her? There's nothing between us, nothing, zilch. I just thought about sex out of desperation, but then I changed my mind and gave up.

We could have a normal conversation if only she'd stop staring at me like that. This isn't just a crush. It's a full-fledged infatuation . . .

It's a relationship.

When someone has a crush on you yet you had nothing to do with it, that's a special feeling. And when someone looks at you like this, with a crush, you're ripe for Xanax.

What would have happened if we'd actually hooked up?

"I'm sorry. . . . Don't be angry, I'm not in the mood for conversation today."

She looked at him and said, "What does that mean?"

He looked at her, wondering what does she mean by, "What does that mean?"

"Well, it means that . . ." he started, but stopped. No, he couldn't say something and then explain what it means. This could go on ad infinitum.

He wasn't lying when he said, "I'm feeling irritable." She looked at him intently. Then, to ease things, he said, "But it has nothing to do with you."

After a pause, he added, "Other stuff. My bad."

"Hmph, *my bad*." She found his slang irritating.

"Pardon me, apologies, I'm sorry—whatever," he said, thinking about how poisonous his irony was.

"All right, see you tomorrow," she said, pursing her lips and picking up her handbag.

See you tomorrow. That actually surprised him.

Erol was laughing at him, he thought.

Nikola exhaled deeply and looked around to make sure the room was still there.

Then, he remembered that the interesting young woman had left and they hadn't even had a chance to talk. He consoled himself by thinking she was too young anyway—still in her twenties.

He asked Sobotka, "How old is the woman you introduced me to?"

"Šeila?" Sobotka was trying to gauge how old his Jasmina was and was a little shocked by what he came up with. Jasmina had started school a little earlier, so Šeila could be "around thirty-three, thirty-four."

The next day, Nikola talked with Branoš at the Lagoon about reorganizing tasks once the repair stage was finished. In various meetings over recent days Nikola mainly nodded sagely, while Sobotka proposed old experienced workers as managers of the production departments. The department teams were formed and the suggestions Sobotka made were readily accepted, with some reassigning here and there. For a few younger and more capable people like Branoš, a special department was established, and Sobotka filled them in on the engineering details. There was also something they called the "plant commission," whose members were elected and whose function was to oversee "everything."

Nikola formally rubber-stamped all of it, but, in truth, he'd be lying if he said he knew how it all operated on the inside. He thought to himself that it was all a jumble, but he didn't want to interfere too much, nor did he have anything constructive to say. They all knew each other, and they knew the substance at hand better.

"All right, so if Sobotka were to catch the flu tomorrow, is there anyone who could control the process instead?" Nikola asked Branoš.

"It wouldn't be easy, but we'd manage," said Branoš. Then, what Nikola feared most happened: Tanja, the museum director, walked in and parked herself beside him at the bar. Branoš, considerate gentleman that he was, immediately moved away, thinking Nikola and the museum director should be left alone.

She smiled like the six o'clock news anchor and said, "How are you today?"

Nikola rose to his feet and said, "Busy, gotta go!"

He felt both miserable and furious for having to evade the museum director, but he had already tried the boredom ploy and felt that every counterattack would lead to complications in their *relationship*.

Fleeing was the only option. She sighed, "Where are you going?"

"Busy."

As he walked away, he imagined himself in a brief flash of self-pity as a cartoon character running from a boot with kitten heels.

On his way out, he heard her saying, "Now that is not gentlemanly."

As soon as he set foot on the street, his mind was singing the song: *If my daddy could see me nowww ... If my daddy could see me noww ...* He couldn't get it out of his ear. He strode along, slightly shaking his head. *Getting wasted, getting wasted ... Seven shots of Jäger ...*

He bought six beers on his way home, sat in his rented living room, drank in silence, and mournfully checked Facebook. He realized that, since he'd stopped posting, he felt like those people who go out but don't drink: you just watch everyone else drinking and having fun while mildly embarrassing themselves.

He turned on the TV.

He caught a report about the oldest resident of this or the neighboring county, he didn't quite understand. "Old Hajra is one hundred and three years old, she had ten children and a total of ninety-three direct descendants," he heard.

He still had the "TV professional" disorder, so an image of the tedious office meeting where this report was approved came to mind for a moment.

He watched: a village, a cottage, a meadow, and all the living relatives gathered for the shoot. They were standing like a huge team in front of a shanty, with Old Hajra in the middle.

Old Hajra had a wizened face and sunken mouth, and couldn't have been taller than five feet. She said something into the outstretched microphone, but Nikola couldn't catch it, so he thought he must already be drunk. Still, he doubted he'd understand her even if he were sober, which gave him enough reason to frown and protest the reporting technique. "Everyone says Old Hajra was never a woman of many words, but she has great results under her belt," said the reporter. The camera pulled back and the assemblage of offspring stood in front of the cottage. Old Hajra moved forward toward the meadow, closer to the camera, she slowly sank to her knees and Nikola thought she might be about to strike a yoga pose.

The moment felt as if there'd be an unexpected outcome.

"And even at one hundred and three years of age," concluded the reporter, "Old Hajra prostrates herself in prayer with ease!"

Nikola was finishing his fourth beer and the remaining two seemed less than enough. He thought he definitely wouldn't live to be Old Hajra's age.

Then he imagined what that would be like—to bury his whole generation and a few of the younger ones? How lonely.

We're all going to die soon, he thought.

But then, getting his fifth beer from the fridge, he thought how, in a way, he had so far lived his life as though he'd live forever.

What am I doing?

Luckily, the gas station was open. Suddenly, Nikola wanted to drink Jäger.

He sank into a depression for the next few days. He avoided the Blue Lagoon, going only to the factory, where trucks full of parts and materials, which Oleg was sending to them according to Sobotka's instructions, frequently arrived.

When he entered the Lagoon for the first time in ten days, he expected to see the museum director parked and waiting for him, but Šeila was standing in the very same spot by the bar.

Delighted, he approached her directly and said, "Now this really is a pleasant surprise!"

Then, he realized she couldn't have followed his train of thought and he might've been approaching her too aggressively.

For a second, she seemed to be staring at him as if seeing him for the first time. Still, she answered with a smile, "Nice."

He realized this made him look more relaxed than he really was. Sometimes people perceive you as more relaxed than you really are and that's a help: the whole thing starts running more smoothly. He was asking ordinary questions and getting ordinary answers ("Waiting for someone?"—"No," etc.) but there was something in the overall tone of the answers that made him feel so alive, as if he had a reason to be there. He looked at her and thought that she shone.

Shining, something he hadn't hoped to find here. "Now, everything looks better," he said after a pause that wasn't awkward.

"What?" Again, she was sizing him up as if she weren't quite sure what she was looking at.

"You know, like with TV back in the old days. When you moved something and the reception improved."

"Oh," she smiled, "you're looking for an antenna."

"Don't move."

He watched Šeila sleep on the sofa bed in his house. This town looked better covered in fine snow, he thought, maybe the last snow before spring.

They hadn't made love. As the saying goes, "nothing happened."

He'd asked her to come over for a nightcap that night, and she did, with no sexual drama, the usual test signals, the hemming and hawing, with no fear of him, she just said, "Okay, we'll talk and that's all." It wasn't exactly clear what Šeila did for a living. She'd tried her hand at all sorts of things, she said. She had even been a manager once, but in an illusion, which sounded like thinking back on failure. She didn't say any more about that, so he realized she was still looking for her place under the sun. It hit him that he might have gotten slightly carried away. Maybe he said too much about himself, maybe he should have painted a better picture and not talked about how he was riding on Oleg's coattails, even though he tried to pass this off as a joke. Never mind. He would have told the story differently in his hometown; he would have played the game and tried to cover his position. He would've circled, twisted everything around until eventually even he wouldn't know what he was talking about or who he was representing—himself or a version of himself for public consumption. As if you're fulfilling other people's expectations of who you're supposed to be until, he thought, even you yourself don't know who you are: you're only throwing yourself into the web we weave for each other. Why continue the charade in front of this woman who shines, he thought, here at the end of the world? Why not just talk, and then even caught himself off guard with what he was saying; exploring a whole new story, the world created when two people really talk.

She seemed to feel the same way about talking with him because, laughing, she said, "I had a love affair that, you know, disoriented me. After that I didn't know who I was anymore, or who I was when I was in love, I didn't know who I was, see? I'm still not sure, but maybe I was what people call a gold digger."

When he heard this he realized she wasn't afraid to talk.

"It's the relationship, I realize, the 'who are you' stuff... It's not just you. It's many relationships. But there's always one that stands out, something always stands out and takes you far away. And if that something abandons you, you're disoriented like a soldier after a war."

"Damn it if this country doesn't look as if the war abandoned it," he said, half-drunk.

"But even you don't know what to grab on to. I see you don't like being at home. Look, here you can become someone else." She laughed.

"And who might I become?"

"Well—you!" she said, through her laughter.

"Ah, my *you*," he said, using a local phrase he'd picked up, and they both laughed even more than the humor deserved. The way a man and a woman laugh, using the excuse of a joke.

He thought about the conversation.

Through the window he watched the postman striding along officially from front gate to front gate. The man walked as if he were at the center of the world, the deputy of the state: the postman, who still believed—you could see this on his face—that somewhere there, at the center, the system was up and running.

10

ONCE, WHEN SHE was still sitting next to Jasmina at school, Šeila won the district chemistry contest: the formulas came together in her head as if she could see them, and she scored a perfect 100 percent. The runner-up had a score of 41 percent. They called her a genius and took pride in her at school and at family gatherings, but then the war started and lasted until the end of her high school years. If what passed for school during the war could even be called school. When it ended, she wanted to enroll in the university in the capital city, but her parents, once in the middle class, were now poor. Her father lost his job; her mother worked as an accountant at the water utility, with a salary that would barely have covered the cost of the student dorm and cafeteria along with their own living expenses. "And what about the books, the living allowance, the clothes. You're not going to walk around naked," they said.

She would talk about how brilliant she was at chemistry, especially in the company of guests and relatives because she realized her parents were the most vulnerable to criticism then. She harped on chemistry even though she didn't care about it anymore. During the war, she'd joined a drama club, dabbled in writing, and dreamed of the wide world. "Your head is in the clouds," said her mother. They didn't let her leave during the first year after the war ended. Maybe they weren't sure it was really over. But someone soon told them that Šeila was starting to hang out with the town's weed-smoking "druggies." So, to stop Šeila from throwing the year away with the space cadets, they allowed her to go to the capital city, as long as she promised to stick with chemistry. They weren't going to scrimp and save so she could squander the year. Microbiology would do. They'd asked around and heard that microbiology would give her a firm footing, and later she could work for the water utility or possibly handle blood samples in a lab. There will always be a need for that, they said. So she enrolled in a degree program in microbiology, hoping that something would happen in the meantime, and maybe she'd meet a stranger who'd save her from this world.

After the war, there were foreigners in the capital city engaged in calming the situation down, involved with humanitarian work, establishing order. So she and her friend Alma, a student who was a year older than she and who knew her way around the city, went to the places where the foreigners hung out and ordered Coca-Colas. They spent their weekend nights at this one basement club, actually, and didn't drink only Coca-Cola. They were invited to parties where there would also sometimes be coke, which Šeila was afraid of, while Alma wasn't so cautious. Šeila saw how men acted freely around Alma. So Šeila would sometimes have to wait for Alma, who slipped out for a while. Whenever Šeila tried to talk about this with Alma, her reply was, "It's not like that." Still, Alma seemed to be the one who was getting invited everywhere while people tolerated Šeila. Something like: she's pretty, let her sit here; she'll probably relax sooner or later.

She had a knack for the microbiology thing, however, because she somehow made it into second year. Alma said, "You have it easy, you've never fallen in love." Alma failed the year because, in her words, unfortunately she was in love with a Spaniard who worked for the United Nations. He did not join his life with Alma's. Instead, one day he told her he'd been transferred and he'd call her, maybe even have her join him after he'd had a look at the situation there. He never called. Yes, that's how things stood.

Back then, Šeila began thinking she should stop hanging out with Alma because everything in Alma's life seemed to be headed in the wrong direction and she'd end up with anyone who had a little cocaine in his pocket. Yet all the while, Alma was feeling unhappy and neglected. You couldn't focus on one thing at a time when talking with her; their conversations ranged across a hundred topics and everything was scrambled together. This rattled Šeila's logical mind. There were always men at the parties who hit on Šeila, and once she even gave in to an Italian who seemed harmless enough because she wanted to lose her virginity to a man like that. But she didn't fall in love with him. His name was Marcello, and he didn't fall in love with her, either, possibly because he, too, didn't enjoy the sex, which they'd only barely managed. Still, he wanted to continue seeing her; he must have figured she owed him for all the hassle, though he used nicer words. They saw each other a few more times; she was out to learn something about sex. When Marcello told her, after a few months, that he was leaving for another country, she didn't expect he'd let her know what the situation there was like. This surprised Alma, but Šeila said to her, "He was only a lover to me."

"Look at you, everyone thinks you're a nerd, but look! I can't believe it! Only a lover?"

Alma was shocked by Šeila's response, though Šeila couldn't understand why, given that Alma'd been with many more lovers than she. The difference was that Alma was always hoping they'd be boyfriends, too. Although, at least from Šeila's perspective, they, obviously, were just lovers. Šeila even thought this had something to do with intelligence, that Alma was unable to put two and two together because of the chaos in her mind. But when Alma said, "Well! I'm impressed, but I could never do that," Šeila was shocked and came to realize this wasn't a question of intelligence: Alma was resisting putting two and two together. She wanted to believe in her image of herself as a good girl who'd unfortunately fallen in love over and over again because she wasn't born under a lucky star. Šeila saw that Alma desperately wanted to lie to herself. Šeila then told her, "Do what you want, but I'm emancipated," without even knowing where she'd picked up the word.

Sometimes, when out with friends, Alma teased Šeila for her use of the word: "Šeila will tell you. She's emancipated." Šeila couldn't figure out why Alma was clinging to this, why she thought it was funny. If there was a local wiseass present, he'd invariably ask, "And what are you emancipated from, for God's sake?"

From you and your questions, she longed to say more than once. But she was afraid of making trouble, so she answered, "Legends."

"Hear that? Legends?" they laughed. "What does that mean?"

"Just kidding."

"Old stories, you mean?"

She kept her mouth shut, but she didn't like the way most of the local men talked with her, their bossy tone, how they saw themselves, because most of them were *legends*. And those who weren't, wished they were.

She would have loved to laugh about this with someone. But she didn't have anyone for that. She found things easier with foreigners, almost like living abroad: nobody ever preached at you or scolded you. This was why she put up with Alma, while waiting for something to happen. And happen it did. He was not only an American but—and this came as another shock for Alma—an African American. In fact, Michael was not an average African American: his mother was black, and his father Taiwanese. If you looked at him closely (which she most certainly did), you could see his slightly slanting eyes and his smooth, soft skin. Simply put, he was beautiful to her, and quiet and unobtrusive, too, maybe even a little sad because Alma and the other women who hung out with them didn't really talk with Michael: they didn't actually see him. Because if you're having sex with a white man who buys you presents and pays your rent (as in Alma's case), nobody notices. But if the man is black, people probably do notice. She'd never thought people there were racists because nobody ever spoke of themselves as racists; still, people often asked her, "Really?" Then they eyed her to see if one of her legs was shorter or she had some other defect.

"Really."

Michael had just turned thirty. He worked for an agency that promoted the free market. She fell in love with him and he with her, or so it seemed. No, actually—and to this day she was certain—it didn't just seem. He was genuinely in love, but their relationship became burdened with drama because he was married, a fact he'd initially kept from her and only later confessed. He confessed and wept. Wept because he was in love. He was miserable because he was in love. She didn't know something like this could happen, and she liked him even more in his misery and felt sorry for the American man who was suffering: his life had come undone, despite being so smoothly organized. He'd married right before coming here to prove to his American girlfriend, whom he'd been dating for years, that nothing would get in their way.

Now he told Šeila he could no longer lie to his wife over the phone, he was finding this unbearable and he was going crazy, he must get a divorce. While he was telling her this he had the look of someone who was trapped. He felt incredibly guilty for what he'd done to his wife.

Michael no longer knew who he was. He'd managed to surprise himself. He used to think he was different, yet now here he was in a world where he no longer recognized himself. So he drank heavily, but didn't hold his liquor well. During his hangovers he explained that he lacked a certain enzyme, probably having to do with his Taiwanese genes. Nevertheless he drank, and often wept. Their relationship was beautiful in a certain melodramatic way, however, because, when he wasn't thinking about everything, he was lovingly tender and would stare into her eyes as if into the abyss into which the world was disappearing. She hadn't known that making love could be so beautiful. It was as if they were in this totally alone, outside of the world, on the edge of the vast space between the past and the future, just the two of them, holding each other tight. And she gave in to it as if every moment they spent together would be their last.

She comforted him and never demanded that he get a divorce; she didn't ask for anything—that was how sorry she felt for him—even though Alma told her she shouldn't trust him, she'd heard lies like this only too often.

Then one day he told her he'd called his wife and admitted he was in love with another woman.

He said it softly. He also said she'd been shocked and yelled at him through her tears, and then—after he'd wanted to say more but couldn't think what—she hung up.

It was strange to hear all this, because deep down it made Šeila happy, but she knew the situation involved another person's grief. Michael was shaken, trembling like a person who'd just run over someone on the road. She saw he was suffering because of the woman he'd betrayed, and this was why—even though there was something in this which might bother her—she loved him even more deeply. Ten days later, one evening while they were lying naked, watching *Frances*, starring Jessica Lange (a movie she would finish watching only much later in life), the phone rang next to the bed. Michael answered and then cupped the receiver with his hand and asked Šeila, with a look of unease, if she could leave the room.

Michael's apartment was spacious. She was there all the time and had almost forgotten what it was like to live in a dorm. Now she was sitting in the other room, in a bathrobe—what's more, she'd forgotten to grab her cigarettes—and this was the first time she'd felt that this other woman really did exist. Suddenly, she felt as if she were nobody. A stupid little kid who'd been sent to her room while the two of them talked, sitting there, smelling of sex with another woman's husband. I deserve this, she thought. This woman does exist. What was I thinking—that she was only a name?

She looked out the window at the city. It was wounded, real, poor. They were still receiving donations from abroad, which were helping them survive.

Almost an hour later Michael opened the bedroom door, holding her cigarettes. She was lying on the couch, staring at the window.

"Sorry," he said, sounding drained as he brought two bottles of beer from the kitchen.

She lit a cigarette. The flame shook.

"What did your wife say?"

"She wants me to go back to the States to work things out."

"And?"

"I'm going. To work it out."

"What's your wife like?"

"She's . . . okay. I haven't a bad thing to say about her."

"Is she pretty?"

"Well . . . I was in love with her."

"Does she still love you?"

"Unfortunately, she probably does."

"Tell me more about her."

She'd been careful not to say "about the two of you."

He sighed with a look as if apologizing to someone far away, and started talking about his wife, about her journey from a bad neighborhood in a lousy city, about the struggle of an African American girl to attend college, and then (smiling sadly) about how they'd met, how great things were at the beginning, how he'd sneak into the women-only dorm on campus and stay the night, how with her he started feeling as if he had someone he could rely on, how they started living together, how for years they helped each other become more successful, and how, somehow, without him even noticing, it all started to fade—which he could see now—even though they didn't admit this to themselves and believed everything was fine. They truly loved each other, maybe just at a lower intensity. But when he was given an offer to work abroad, he felt he wanted it. He married her to convince her he was not running away, because he honestly didn't believe that things . . . could end like this. He finished his beer and looked at her, his eyes brimming with tears.

"So, what are you going to do now?"

"I'll have to divorce her."

"Are you going to change your mind when you get there?"

He sucked on his empty bottle before saying, "No, I won't."

"I . . . I should go . . . Could you please call me a cab?"

As she said the words he saw her lost look, so he hugged her and whispered, "Don't, please. Stay here while I'm gone. Everything's going to be okay."

"You told her the same thing, Michael."

"Yes," he said, and sighed. "There's really no need to bring that up."

"Okay."

"I'll be back."

They made love again. Tenderness mingled with sadness and then the body, filled with wild desire, turned that all to dust.

Michael left. He was supposed to come back after two weeks, but he called to say he'd stay another week.

She stayed at his place the whole time he was gone. She couldn't go back to her dorm room, which she shared with a first-year student from a small town; she felt centuries older than the girl, the two were worlds apart. If she were to lie there on the bed, just steps from the quiet girl's bed, she believed she'd slip away into a crack somewhere in between, a world that didn't exist.

She could barely make herself eat. She couldn't think straight. There were times when she was certain Michael was coming back because *he sounded so convincing over the phone*. The next instant she was sure he'd never come back because *he hadn't sounded so convincing over the phone*. Staying at his apartment felt like floating on an iceberg that was nearing the *Titanic* through the mists. But the people on board, would they be saved?

If they were saved—she might go mad.

Michael did come back. When she saw him at the airport she screamed with joy. Now she was able to bounce back from a fear she'd felt for the first time: the fear of losing everything. He'd done what he promised and they were free. Now they had all the time in the world. Their story was no longer shimmering on the verge of the real. *The fear took its toll on me*, she thought later. At one point, she became aware of something: a blurry and ominous presence in the distance—a distance that quickly shrank.

Five months later, Michael told her he'd be transferred to Georgia and, seeing her shudder, asked her immediately if she wanted to go with him. Despite her parents' wishes, she moved with him to Tbilisi. It was a big city in a state of ruin, yet beautiful. And the Georgians were pleasant, unaware of a racism that was complicated by their love for Americans, which they felt as strongly as their lack of love for Russians. With Michael she perfected her English, and with time, she noticed that people treated her as if she were an American, a white woman. Indeed, she walked around like an American there, liberal enough to be dating an African American, and only at fancy dinner parties was she asked where she was from exactly. When she said she was from N., in the country they saw on the news, all of a sudden there would be an unexpected sorrowful silence, because all the things that had happened there, when considered together, or even separately, were inexplicable.

Sometimes, the wives of other foreigners would ask her, "But why?"

They were referring to the war and all the horrible things.

They believed there ought to be a handy answer, an answer Šeila should provide them to satisfy their wish for the world to be explained and accountable.

She tried, but the nice ladies were never satisfied.

"Yes, but why?"

It was then that she realized she'd stepped out of her language and that everything about where she'd come from and her life were inscrutable in the English language, which she had perfected.

She began to realize that so far she'd lived in a world that was drawn into itself and her life was maybe a little odder than normal, as she'd been used to thinking of it. She also noticed that when they talked about life under communism, the Georgians talked about something different from what she remembered and what her parents had told her. "Yes, it was much harder for you," she often had to say. She began to realize she'd been born in an unusual, enigmatic place, because not only was she unable to explain—to the Georgians or the Westerners—what had happened during the war, but also how things had been earlier.

She had no one in Tbilisi but Michael, and she didn't know what to do except with him. She was forever waiting for him, and she started fearing she was being a bore. She told herself they had all the time in the world. So maybe that was why he was no longer running toward her. Maybe he started frowning when she told him she was eager for him to come home because that sounded as if she were complaining about being lonely, and he came home tired and sometimes couldn't concentrate on what she was saying. She understood him. She knew very well that she had almost nothing interesting to say, seeing as nothing special was happening to her, so she spent her time thinking about how to reignite the spark. She struggled through preparing dinners with candles and wine, and asked him gently how his day had gone. It was only then that she started to be more interested in what he did, realizing they mustn't lose contact. She didn't really understand, though, the promotion of the free market or what his agency was up to, but she hoped to learn something or maybe even—she thought optimistically—become involved somehow. It would be great to do something, to contribute. Talking to him she learned that his work was about the promotion of privatization; Michael supervised marketing campaigns, organized expert symposiums, brought in lecturers who explained the procedures to local people, and provided advice to government agencies. At the time, for example, he advised them on amendments to the privatization law, which (he explained to her) meant introducing auctions without minimum bids, a concept which she barely knew how to translate into her own language.

"So there's such a thing as an auction with no minimum for the starting bid?"

"Yes, this makes things significantly easier."

He told her that the government finally decided to privatize the energy sector, and this was the main thing he was monitoring.

"Michael, does this mean, for example, that the water utility should be privatized?" she asked during one of their dinners. She had made them a few French dishes and was surprised by how delicious they'd turned out.

"It's not part of the plans yet . . . But why not?"

She found this odd, probably because her mother worked for the water utility and she wasn't able to picture the building where her mother worked as a private company. Her mother hoped Šeila could get a job there and replace the old microbiologist who was in charge of monitoring water quality—as far as she knew her mother kept track of such things—and no one else from their town, except Alma, had studied microbiology. Šeila's mother was counting on Alma not to earn her degree, and Šeila was embarrassed that her mother was thrilled to hear how Alma flunked out of first year. Now in Tbilisi, she remembered all this and thought how funny it was, so she retold the story to Michael. He, too, found it funny, and she was pleased to find she could make him laugh.

She sighed when these things came back to her. They seemed so far away.

"But, say, for example," she asked Michael, "I get a job as a microbiologist at the water utility and I'm supposed to monitor water quality. It would be a little different if the utility were privatized. I might be scared to say the water's bad if it ruins my boss's chance for profit. I mean, I'm not stupid. I know what he wants from me."

By asking this question, she actually wanted to show Michael how smart she was and how easily she could analyze a problem. She wanted them to talk to each other like adults, sipping fine Georgian wine, enjoying their romantic candlelit dinner and the view of the city lights.

"Sure, but there is a system of controls."

"I know. And I would be that system."

She wanted to compete with him because sometimes she thought of herself as stupid when she was just saying "uh-huh."

"You'd be protected. There are rules."

"You mean there would be rules."

"Yes."

"Hmm. Say the boss at the water utility decided I was the type to dig in my heels and might cause trouble. Maybe he wouldn't even hire me. Maybe he'd hire someone else, a person he knew was more flexible."

She felt she'd cornered him, and she relished this like she'd relish a passionate courtship. She could feel herself becoming aroused and wanted to make love.

"I don't think you should worry so much about whether they'll hire you as a microbiologist. As far as I know, unfortunately you dropped out of school."

Not only did his words sting, but suddenly the whole evening took an entirely different tack. The flickering candles reflected on their faces. Darkness all around. She knew this was a mistake. The whole conversation was a mistake. Yet, still . . . *Unfortunately.*

"Unfortunately?" she repeated. "I did come here with you."

He touched her hand, which was on the table. "Sorry. Slip of the tongue."

"It's my fault. I shouldn't have started—"

"No, everything's fine. It's just, you . . . you're holding on to the vestiges of a socialist mind-set. Like these people here," he told her, looking at her as if he understood and held no grudges.

"You think so? I don't know . . ."

She'd tried so hard, yet everything came out wrong. She puzzled over what kind of socialist mind-set she'd been holding on to. I spend my time only with foreigners, she thought. Socialism collapsed when I was a teenager. Did he want to say I was still acting like a teenager? That I pointlessly protest and rebel? These thoughts crossed her mind, but there was no use, no conclusion, so this reminded her of Alma. What's going on with her, anyway? Šeila wondered.

And what about me?

He saw her mood shift to gloom, and he felt sorry for her. But he was also very tired. He had worked the whole day, unlike her. "Okay. Sorry. Just please don't get depressed," he said.

They went to bed, and he quickly fell asleep. She, however, didn't fall asleep till dawn.

She tried to forget that night, the moment at the table when the darkness around them seemed to gain a dimension of depth. She remembered this only much later, when she read somewhere that the Italians were opposing the privatization of the water utility and how—the same article said—there had been opposition in England to the privatization of the energy sector. She asked herself: Why would he tell me I was holding on to vestiges of a socialist mind-set? Do the people there cling to socialist mind-sets as well? But they never mentioned the conversation again.

She tried to forget his use of the word *unfortunately*. She must have really annoyed him, and what they talked about must have mattered a lot to him. She wanted to forget about it, and she did.

She tried hard with those dinners and all sorts of other things, struggling to keep everything together, because the way they were in love with each other in the beginning was worth something. That was why she was still in love with him, in a different way, though, as if she were constantly recalling those moments, the Michael from before, the sad and melodramatic Michael, drinking and weeping (he no longer drank or wept), the beautiful misery of his when she consoled him, not thinking of herself or what was going to happen to her when he left the city where she was a black man's mistress. She didn't worry about it in the least, and she loved this version of herself much more than who she was in Tbilisi, where he no longer looked deeply into her eyes as if this were their last moment together, where everything could be on hold, where he worked while she sat in their beautiful apartment with nothing to think about, where he was an older, grown-up man and she an immature and spoiled pretty young woman, turning into a Stepford wife and whining about being lonely, as if that were the world's biggest problem.

She felt as if all their differences had become more glaring than they used to be. In her country, they'd been nearly invisible—he being the foreigner and she always knowing where she was, and always having something to explain to him. But now he seemed irritated with her, so she was becoming irritated, too. "We used to function as lovers, but this, this is not working for us," he told her at one point, staring at the ceiling. She knew he was right, but she no longer knew how to picture her life without him in it or where to go back to. If only he'd married her, if only she'd gotten their papers so she could travel without a visa, she thought, knowing how horrible this would sound if she actually said it.

Tbilisi turned into torture, because he knew—and she could see it—how much she would lose if they separated and he felt sorry for her. If he hadn't, maybe they would have already parted ways, she thought. But she could see he was angry both at himself and at her. Even though he said nothing, he was bitter because he'd divorced naively and abruptly due to their relationship. Although she wasn't quite sure why, she felt she'd ruined everything. She felt like a burden, like a poor woman clinging to a spent love she kept hoping to revive.

The ordeal even made her ugly. She gained weight, and the walks she took around Tbilisi did not help. She felt she was supposed to walk, so she went shopping and visited stores in order to look like a woman with a purpose. Luckily, there were few things she liked in the stores so he never had to complain about her spending too much. But, boy, did Georgians know how to make baklava. With a guilty conscience she would visit the pastry shops with the plain windows on Rustaveli Avenue. She couldn't stop herself. Those were the most exquisite moments of her days. One day he asked her, "Have you ever been to Istanbul? It is quite close."

To him everything was close.

"You know I have hardly been anywhere."

"Let's go. Seven days," he said.

"Let's," she said, hoping their story would take a twist.

"And then I'll spend a month in D.C. attending a training program," he added.

He said that in the singular. The trip to Istanbul felt about them saying their goodbyes, but she said nothing.

"Sure. I'll visit my parents after Istanbul. I haven't seen them in a while."

Istanbul, Constantinople, was so magnificent, but in a dark way, as if overcast by a shadow, obscuring access. They used to rule over her people from there, her family's blood was part of the ramparts, she thought as she looked out over the gracious, ancient city full of both legible and illegible traces of culture, upheaval, and cruelty. She'd read somewhere that the city was besieged by the Turks for roughly a hundred years; they advanced toward the center of Europe before conquering Constantinople, the "second Rome," which, after the fall of the "first Rome," held out for a thousand years. Now she was there with Michael, an American who'd never heard a single epic song sung about Stamboul and who would return to his capital, which fancied itself as eternal, while she went back to her small town at the old outer verge of the empire. They walked the cobblestone streets, their love dragging behind them like a stray dog. Everything turned into backward glances, distance-gazing, and there at the Galata Bridge—where people were fishing as if idling away their days, old Turks, their faces furrowed with wrinkles, fishhooks in hand, straddling two worlds—an elderly, melancholy fisherman snapped a picture with Michael's camera of them, hugging. Today, she sometimes looks at the picture and can still feel the impasse, the vestige of love dying with them, afraid to look each other in the eye.

He'd insisted on buying her things in Istanbul, as if outfitting her for her future life. She tried on dresses, she tried on bathing suits, she came out of the changing rooms to ask, "How do I look?"

There was so much between them that could no longer be put into words.

What gave weight to every breath was the love that was shifting to a memory before their very eyes, a sadness they could share with nobody; because lovers cannot console each other as they fall away—they can only avert their eyes and stare into the distance: ships navigating slowly through the reflection of the Bosporus. She sensed he was impatient to leave. He seemed guilt-ridden, like the old days, but this time they couldn't talk. He'd only be able to talk, she thought, with a lover, or a whore, in Washington. He'd drink and weep, like he had with her. He'd be sweet with the lover, or the whore, while he spoke about her, a woman he used to love from a tragic country. He could no longer talk to her—that's what he'd probably say to the new woman, while drinking with her— because lovers cannot talk about falling away. And that is why we ultimately grow apart. She'd like to see him, she thought, with this new woman as he drank and wept. Šeila would like to see how their story sounded when he told it to the third woman, she'd like to see his eyes. She'd like to see herself in his story, this leftover of what had been great, and if he never told their story, if he never drank and wept, it would be as if she'd never existed.

"Michael, tell me about this," she told him in the quiet of a restaurant.

"About what?"

"Tell me the story, as if I were another woman. Like back then."

"I don't understand, Sheila. What am I supposed to tell?"

"About me."

She did not want to say "us."

He looked helpless.

"Imagine you're in America. Or, imagine it's been five, ten years, and you're talking about me."

He gazed briefly into her eyes, then shook his head as if he didn't get it, and turned his eyes to the windowpane, to the mute hue of the street.

"Michael, tell me, because I don't know . . . as if I were another woman. Tell me what this all meant."

He looked down to the left, as if he were trying to see into himself.

"It was beautiful, so much so that it erased itself," he finally said. "We erased an entire world, Sheila, but never made a new one."

Later, they made love in their hotel room, the windows open to the sky. Michael seemed his old self again, with his sadness and tenderness, but he lacked courage in the way he touched her body, how they made love, as if he feared he was taking advantage of her.

She watched Michael, asleep beside her. She turned over onto her side and surveyed their clothes scattered on the floor and her naked reflection in the big mirror.

They parted at the airport: his plane was to leave first. He wore a helpless expression, his eyes wandered. Then he arched his eyebrows and looked at her with a child's gaze, and they hugged each other, tightly, so she could hear his heart pounding, she pressed her lips to his and said, "Take care, Michael. . . . Be safe, kid."

He murmured, "I'll call you." He spun around, headed for the international security check—his back in a dark blue suit. With his head bowed, he waved over his shoulder a few times. At the barriers he turned around once more, unexpectedly, stopping for a moment, like a sad clown, then disappeared.

I want you to know that I loved you. She wanted to shout to him this desperate, stupid sentence—but she couldn't speak, like in one of those dreams when you are unable to do things you normally do.

Then she sat down and slumped over—her hands in her hair—on one of those rows of chairs. Her plane wouldn't be leaving for another two hours. Arriving at the boarding gate, she grabbed a free newspaper, opened it, and stared at it so nobody could see her eyes.

It was the *Turkish Daily*, a newspaper in English. At first she just held it open, but then she noticed a headline about the sale of a Georgian electric power company: "75% of Company Sold to US Corporation SAE for Equivalent of US$25.5 Million via International Tender."

When they were kids, she and Jasmina loved to watch jet planes flying across the sky—their contrails, those white lines melting into the blue, were poetry to them, although they didn't know the word contrails then.

They couldn't imagine those planes as anything but tiny objects in the sky leaving behind them a fragile trace, and yet they'd been told by the grown-ups that people were sitting inside those planes, and that those people could see them from up there.

And someone once said—one of the other kids—that the people were called Americans, the teeny-tiny people in the airplanes.

Just like that, Michael was now shrinking, becoming smaller and smaller, and she was returning to the country from which she used to gaze up at the sky.

I I

I CHANGED AT one point when I saw how everybody else had
changed. I changed, miraculously, into nothing, became indescrib-
able, and, in this state I moved among people who no longer exist,
because they'd been taking blows morning till night to the head and
ears, they'd been flexed like a muscle and stretched, curled, stooped
and furled, pounded into the dirt, dredged, and tilled with a pick,
until up they sprouted anew, fertilized and slightly artificial. Though
they looked real they were all cultivated, raised in a greenhouse like
a celestial television, and now they're limping around with their new
gadgets, I see, they're all in constant contact, all day long they're
walking around like they're embroidering and stitching needle-
point, talking to themselves out on the street, and I'm crazy? Me, the
crazy one? Because I yell? They're the ones talking to themselves on
the street as they walk, with wires hanging from their ears or little
boxes in their pockets or their hands, and it won't be long before
they start talking at a run, because they'd love to talk and run, obviously, but you can't pull that off physically, until a species capable

of such things evolves, and they have nothing to chase, otherwise they'd be running, obviously, otherwise they'd run and chase and words would spew out as they pant, and they're catching something ahead of them, which they can't yet see, but I see it, numbers, like the numbers on a cake, sugary numbers in all colors like ones for children, and abacuses for counters, and soot.

And two parallel lines that will never intersect even unto infinity, I see, two parallel lines, up close, but doomed never to intersect, I see, two parallel lines, and because they will never intersect, this is death.

I am not blind, yet.

Once he'd faced that his family was gone, Sobotka moved into a cottage with a yard. He had no reason to keep the three-bedroom apartment, or his absent family's clothing, the children's bedroom furniture, the toys, frozen time, his queen-sized bed with the built-in radio, the wardrobes from the late 1970s—all of it resembled a form of death.

In that apartment he left behind Zlata's version of good taste, which, in the old days, Sobotka would quietly support in furniture stores selling merchandise produced domestically, but with foreign labels. The apartment still contained their living-room wall unit with built-in mirrors and internal lighting, lights which soon stopped working and he insisted they couldn't be fixed, when in fact he was concerned that they were a fire hazard. He recalled the name of their bedroom set made of oak from a town on the plains. Ophelia, which sounded posh to him at first, but then someone told him it was a bit odd as a name for a master bedroom and suggested he reread *Hamlet*.

"Reread?"

Zlata's taste, he noticed while visiting them up north, had meanwhile changed; her furnishings now had simpler shapes, she no longer felt the need to "make every inch count," and she spoke of her bedroom as feng shui.

He ultimately stopped believing in "a woman's touch," or in the notion that their apartment was attractive. He'd rather have rearranged it to his own liking, turned it into a combination of garage and factory, but he didn't know what to do with the children's bedroom furniture.

He needed to get away, and the people with whom he traded houses were convinced they'd got the better part of the trade—they moved into a nice apartment building with wooden floors and central heating, while Sobotka moved into a cottage. Not a terribly old cottage, but one built in the style of the old-fashioned rural houses in an area on the periphery of N. where there used to be a village. Soon enough, the town encroached upon the village with several small apartment buildings, but the town was now retreating again, so to speak. Around him lived people with last names that were traditional in these parts, and some of them had never stopped farming the fields around the town. But there were also newcomers who moved there to till the land. After the country's industrial base collapsed, a return to the old ways was all the rage. Once socialism fell, traditions resurfaced in all realms, though family farms were not what most had in mind: they wanted the spirituality of the land, but a return is a return.

Sobotka himself kept a few beds of cabbages and onions in his garden, but most of the yard was given over to the metal sculptures he had been obsessively welding. There was nothing traditional about them. He welded scrap metal to car headlights. The sculptures looked like weird fantasy vehicles.

His avocation began for Sobotka when he participated in sculpture workshops the factory used to organize. Professional sculptors, even famous ones, did what they could to convince the workers—some successfully, some less so—that they, too, could become artists. Sobotka maintained that these artists said such things because they'd been told to. He couldn't care less if he was called an artist or not—*better not*, he thought—but the beauty in this for him was the discovery of something he'd never had as an engineer: he could work on something without knowing the direction it would take, or how it would turn out. When asked, he'd say it relaxed him, although he felt he needed a better word. He found a certain pleasure in sculpting he'd never found elsewhere. There were no guidelines. If he wanted to, he could make something "wrong," he could make *anything*.

So one time, while having a drink with a sculptor who was running a workshop—a melancholy older fellow whose last name began, he recalled, with the letter *R*—Sobotka told him what he enjoyed about the craft. The fact that he could create *anything*.

"Well that settles it then! You're an artist."

"I am no artist. Heck no!"

"Why?" asked the sculptor, taken aback.

"Look, I like doing this, but I'd rather not be called an artist. Why would I want to be an artist?"

"Wait a minute, are you saying being called an artist is a sort of insult?"

"Er," Sobotka took a moment. "This is a little *risky* for me. . . . If the guys at the factory start calling me an artist, I'd be better off having stayed out of it."

The old sculptor laughed heartily. "That's right! So for you being called an artist is an insult!"

"No, it's not that," Sobotka said, trying to explain. "It's just that if I consider myself an artist, I'd have responsibility. You know, art, quality, all that jazz. But I couldn't care less! I can do things the wrong way if I feel like it. See?"

The sculptor's face turned serious.

"And I want the freedom to not give a shit!"

"You're right," said the sculptor. "You've reminded me of something I'd forgotten."

"What's that?"

"I've been an artist for a long time. . . . But you're right, I need to forget I'm an artist!"

Sobotka found this perplexing, but in a way it made sense.

"Look, I don't know if you can forget you're an artist. . . . But, yes, I do forget I'm an engineer."

The old sculptor looked at him, made a toast, and emptied his glass.

"I must forget I'm an artist and then I'll be free again!"

"You—do whatever suits you," said Sobotka, feeling a bit uneasy. The artist was thinking he was smart, and he didn't want to say something stupid to spoil his image.

This sculptor, whose last name always eluded him, though Sobotka thought it began with an *R*, poured him another drink and said, "Well, thank you!"

This funny conversation would sometimes pop up in Sobotka's mind, especially when he saw certain artists—there were several in his small town—and noticed they seemed unhappy. Their art must have become a burden. One of them who had an academic degree in painting—or something like that—would always say he was "living in the wrong place," and a young sculptor would say he had "nobody to work for here." The young man stepped into Sobotka's yard once, looked around, and said, "Interesting, interesting." He looked washed out, smoked quite a lot, and probably drank a lot, too. Sobotka asked him what he did.

The guy said he hadn't sculpted for two years now. He was done. He had to get out of this place.

"You would like to be somebody in this world?" Sobotka asked, feeling sorry for him.

The youngster just looked at him. He left. Sobotka hadn't seen him since.

During his years of unemployment, Sobotka pretty much cluttered up his garden and yard with what he called his "ironware." He began to wonder where to put all his sculptures. He thought about asking Nikola if he could place some of them around the factory, but he felt a bit uncomfortable suggesting it. Not so much because of having to ask Nikola, but because of the workers.

He noticed that his neighbors had begun to see his garden as somewhat alarming. Had Sobotka not been such a good handyman—"Hands of gold," they said—they would not have respected him much.

In any case, they didn't visit often.

Sobotka thought about this while he shaved—an old morning habit he'd returned to since returning to his old job, after years of neglect.

He heard a knock at the door.

Half-shaven, with shaving cream all over his face, he opened the door.

Before him stood the man with the dog.

Sobotka looked at him as if examining wreckage that had suddenly washed up on shore. He stood speechless, the shaving cream still smeared over his face.

No, this visitor he had never expected. He knew the man's story well and had tried many times to approach him, but stopped trying ages ago because the man with the dog never wished to talk to Sobotka; in fact the man shunned him, as if Sobotka were a stalker.

And as he was running away he flailed his arms, raising them to the skies like a person making an announcement, or perhaps protesting—it was hard to tell the difference—and yelled out his mantras: "This dog has no master, ha ha ha!"; "Liberty! Cunt! Ha ha!"; "We are the best! Ha ha ha ha! Eat it!"

"Slavko," said Sobotka.

The man with the dog kept blinking and staring, as if frozen, with flakes of dandruff in his graying black beard. The dog was just as calm. Sobotka felt an eerie atmosphere arising from the silence coming his way in place of a reply: the man's eyes looked as if they were staring from behind bushes.

The primeval fear of unfamiliar beasts.

But it's still Slavko, I can't pretend it isn't. Maybe I shouldn't call him by name, maybe that bothers him, he thought.

"Come in?" said Sobotka, stepping aside.

The man with the dog observed him, as if he were so far away that recognizing faces was a struggle.

He just stood there, as if watching the scene from a hill, only to finally enter the house, dog by his side, passing Sobotka, who, for a moment, felt a chill again. Not because he feared the man with the dog—he'd overcome his animal instinct—but because the past had just stepped into his cottage: Slavko, his companion, his disfigured past that no longer responded when you called its name, who wandered around like a haunted ghost. Slavko—his best man, his scarecrow, his mirror.

Everything Slavko was now, he, too, could have become. Sobotka knew this. The only difference was that Slavko had had a little less luck: he'd had a son who wasn't allowed to leave town like Sobotka's daughters had, a son who'd turned eighteen. Slavko's wife and daughter left on the same bus with his girls, and ended up, according to what Sobotka had heard, in a different northern country.

He remembered how their womenfolk had waved to them, him and Slavko, standing there watching the bus pull away. Slavko was a different man then, still they waved at their families together, went for drinks, and sat in silence for a long time. He remembered Slavko saying, "The world is going to hell, and we're just sitting here."

Sobotka didn't remember whether he answered. That could very well have been the last sentence he'd heard from Slavko, not counting the shouts in the streets.

The man with the dog sat down at the kitchen table and exhaled wearily, as if this were just another visit and they were neighbors who had talked for so long that they'd run out of what to say to each other. The dog sat at his master's feet.

Sobotka looked at him and said, "I'll go make us some coffee."

He found a clean dish towel and used it to wipe off the remainder of the shaving cream. He thought he probably looked like a madman himself with only half his face shaved, but never mind.

Then he said, "How nice of you to come by . . ." He looked over at Slavko and had no idea what to say next. "Right."

As he poured the water for the coffee he kept thinking, What should I say? How should I talk?

He'd already had coffee and felt like he could go for some rakija— but he didn't want to offer any to Slavko—so he took cover behind the pantry door and poured himself a shot glass. He soon concluded that this was stupid, so he went over to the table and set down his glass. "I'll have a sip of rakija with mine. I'm not offering because . . . well, I hear you don't drink." Then he gestured sharply with his forefinger in the air and said, "And that's wise!"

The man with the dog looked around with no particular curiosity. As if counting something.

Sobotka drank down half his glass, lit a cigarette, and, with nothing better to do, said, "I don't know if you've heard, but I'm working again."

He did not say *at the factory* because he thought that might be the wrong thing to say to Slavko, as if saying *at the factory* would be like asking, "Where have you been?"

"We're starting to get some work done, nothing much, it's mostly for the fun of it," Sobotka said. "I had this idea, why not clean it up a bit . . . Touch things up . . ."

"Yup," said Slavko, nodding grimly, looking straight ahead.

Sobotka threw him a look you give someone you'd thought was dead: was this him *coming back*?

Even before this, Sobotka sometimes mused, Slavko couldn't be completely mad or he wouldn't have survived. He knew where he was living. Sobotka knew that during the war Slavko took in refugees, relatives from the village. Sobotka knew that later—after Slavko's son died when the man lost his grip—those same relatives took over his entire house, and now he lived in a tool-shed, a garage, or whatever the little shack was. He didn't know if they fed him. Guess they must have—they probably decided they wouldn't kill him; they probably needed him for something. Word on the street was that he'd never signed his property over to them, so they'd have trouble when Slavko died because his daughter was still alive somewhere. There was talk that Slavko's wife had died, but nobody knew where the daughter was, and there was nobody to ask about her. Slavko had refused to communicate with anyone in any way since his son died, and these relatives of his were not exactly a reliable source.

The water came to a boil and Sobotka brewed the coffee.

He'd given a lot of thought to how to help Slavko, after numerous unsuccessful attempts at approaching him. Those scenes horrified him. He watched Slavko escape while roaring "THIS DOG HAS

NO MASTER, HA HA HA!" because Slavko had probably been using noise to keep his demons at bay; at least that's how it seemed to Sobotka.

A long time ago, in the village where he was from, Sobotka's grandmother had told him that demons could be chased away with noise. "Just shout! And shout joyfully!" she used to say, wishing to protect her grandson from demons and all manner of evil spirits whose existence she never doubted, having encountered them herself. Sobotka recognized the same exuberant warding off of demons in Slavko whenever he'd tried to approach him. Each time this happened, Sobotka felt the need to get drunk, and he usually succeeded. *What to do about Slavko?* he'd muse, at a moment when his conscience troubled him, one of many at that time. The only thing he could do, thought Sobotka, was to have him hospitalized. But what would become of him in an asylum, in this society that didn't even care for the sane? Would that be better than letting him roam free with his dog? He felt Slavko was better off free, out in the open air.

And so Slavko roamed through most of the war, and had his son not died, as everybody knew, someone probably would have gunned him down, maybe as a joke, maybe irritated by his yelling, from which he seemed to be suggesting that his son had killed himself, though the boy—Tren was his name—had died heroically in an attack on enemy positions, as had many, indeed, at the time, so people were jarred by Slavko yelling, "My boy did himself in! Charge-charge!"

Sobotka was there once when a young man said, "I could pick him off right now," and Sobotka asked, "Who?"

"The yeller. He's so fucking annoying!"

"He's not here," Sobotka told him. "He's a ghost. Understand?"

"Not here, you say?" The boy threw him a menacing look.

At the time, Sobotka was armed, so when he said, "Whoever touches him is a dead man," he meant it.

Sobotka set the coffee cup down in front of Slavko.

They were silent for a while, because Sobotka was trying to figure out what to say. He didn't know a lingo for lunatics.

Finally, he chose to speak. "So . . . little by little, day by day, we've cleared up the mess, cleaned . . . I've examined the machines, we tweaked a few things here and there. . . . The spare-parts shed roof collapsed, but we cleared that out and I found all sorts of material. So now we're starting to work, we're almost set."

"Yup," nodded Slavko, his eyes fixed on the dog on the floor, as if he'd already talked this over with it and was asserting that he'd been right—Slavko, not the dog.

"Two guys showed up out of nowhere. Do your thing like back then, they said, build the exact same turbines. . . . One of them, the one who stayed here, he's acting like he's the boss. He wants to be asked about things. It's like he doesn't want us to forget he's in charge. But in fact he's always the one doing the asking. He's completely clueless. I could give him the runaround tomorrow. But why would I? The paychecks keep coming. You wouldn't believe it, we have everything neatly organized, we don't need any outside help."

"Yup," said Slavko, nodding again.

Then, tucking his lower lip under the upper one, he looked at Sobotka, like a person who'd taken offense, and then he slowly averted his gaze and stared at a corner of the ceiling.

"Come, too, if you like."

Slavko shot him a quick glance, then looked at the window. Abruptly he stood.

"Or stop by again for coffee."

Slavko was already on his way to the door, leaving his cup

untouched. The dog, as if stupefied by the heat, rose slowly and trotted after him.

They left without a backward glance.

Sobotka stared as they walked away, until Slavko disappeared around the corner.

He went back to his shaving but was so distracted that all he could do was stare blankly at the mirror for a while. Images flashed through his mind—he and Slavko as young engineers, proving their worth, snapshots from parties. The Municipality of N. Award Slavko received in 1984, when Sobotka thought perhaps he'd deserved it as well; he figured Slavko was given it was because he, Sobotka, wasn't politically suitable, otherwise it would have been his.

Ah, the award; at the time he thought all that meant something to him. Yes, he, too, used to be vain, once upon a time, how strange to remember. Then he caught his reflection in the mirror.

He soaped up his face again.

12

THE DINNER WAS complicated, cutting-edge; Lorena's acquaintances were open to everything new. So open to everything new, in fact, that they were a bit weak on memory. Lorena introduced Oleg as a Viennese entrepreneur, and they all shook hands. For a moment he was going to tell them he remembered them from the old days. But as they showed no signs of recognizing him, he let it go.

He and she arrived late to the culinary festivities, so the animated hosts summarized what they'd prepared, having already provided the other guests, apparently, with a longer disquisition. Oleg made no effort to remember any of it; his eye was caught only by oranges where he wouldn't have expected to see them. But he did realize all this was fairly important; he'd been noticing how cooking was becoming the cultural medium for a new class. A new bourgeoisie had risen out of the counterculture and asserted itself in the kitchen, he felt, and alternative cuisine was playing a role in fusing the alternative and the bourgeois.

The food was decent; the portions, modest.

He observed them. The host used to be a guitarist in a quirky demo band—*did they ever release a record?* he couldn't remember—and now he produced commercials and collaborated with Lorena, or with her company. The guitarist's wife, well, she was an ex-metalhead and used to be charmingly depressed, but these days—to Oleg's surprise—she happened to be working in public relations at the same bank where he'd taken out his loan, after only just managing to lose the tennis game and clinch the deal with Ajderovitsch, to whom he'd paid a small commission.

Oleg remembered them from a time when he himself used to be a different person, namely, the late eighties, when they listened to gloomy alt-rock, full of painful resignation, because, as he read somewhere later, it had lost its belief in its own liberating force. Even drugs no longer opened the doors of perception, but instead sucked them in. Theirs wasn't a joyful youth, they'd left the joy to the country hicks, which surprised him in hindsight: he always remembered his youth as a time of happiness, but that must have been his stereotypical memory. Now, meeting these people, he couldn't say they'd been happy then. They even *longed* to be fucked up like Nick Cave—and they were reasonably good at that—and they'd come out on the dance floor for the local hit "You Are All My Pain." They really did feel all the pain. No longer. As if they'd been anesthetized.

I probably look even more anesthetized than they do, he thought. At first he didn't say much over dinner, but his brain was busy.

Images flashed through his mind of the cheap rock clubs of his youth, and how his generation hadn't put up much of a fight when they were shut down. He assumed that, like him, they were in post-socialist shock and, like him, they'd made their peace with it, had become part of the shock, thinking now only about themselves and nothing else. Exactly, just like me, they had to find a new place under the sun.

Cooking seemed to be the only thing they did now. This focus on cooking, he thought, was in some way a continuation of thinking only about yourself, in a more relaxed and sophisticated manner. Still, if I were in their place, I wouldn't know what else to do, either. He watched this from a distance, because, despite all the shit he was caught up in, or precisely because of it, he lived differently. The fact that Lorena saw him as a kind of bohemian businessman actually made some sense to him.

Undead, undead, undead . . . —was quietly playing in the background.

Lately he had been thinking about what settling down would be like. At moments, this seemed like exactly what he wanted, yet, soaking up the atmosphere at this gathering, he wasn't so sure.

He couldn't decide what he really wanted, so maybe this, he thought, was the reason he gambled so much.

He observed this generation of his, who, *after all they'd been through*, said they were keen to lead a normal life. During the war, as he recalled, they'd developed a nationalist, even radical nationalist, bent and given him a thumbs-up, knowing something of the circles he ran in, but now they seemed to have forgotten all that and realigned as bland urban liberals, at least for the time being, until the next wave hit.

They surfed the waves just as he did, yet somehow differently, he thought, more safely, nearer the shore, whereas he rode waves somewhat farther out to sea, and so they hadn't seen much of each other over the last fifteen years. This was how they now seemed new. He examined the new images they'd nestled into, and found it interesting to see how the waves were ridden here; just like surfers, each merged with their wave, and within each there was a precursor or two, who proved the authenticity of the path they were on.

The former guitarist was now talking about his great-grandfather who used to be a judge back before the war. But the archives had been torched somewhere in the tri-border area. Because everything there was periodically torched, especially the archives. All that was left were the stories of the fires, joked the former guitarist and current commercials producer, a witty guy, who was, perhaps, the offspring of a family of aristocrats, or of a family of arsonists, thought Oleg on his way out of the bathroom. This is when he finally noticed that the former guitarist was wearing a T-shirt with a print of something or someone resembling Che Guevara—the design was a slightly psychedelic visual game, containing elements of Che's famous portrait, which is why he didn't catch on right away.

Lorena wasn't saying much, either, Oleg noticed, and she was more high-flung in her choice of words than usual when she did talk. She must be distracted, he thought, and her jaw showed a certain clench, possibly from the coke he'd given her.

The wine was good, too.

Apart from the hosts, a newspaper editor and a theater studies scholar were also guests. The newspaper editor kept dropping the names of ambassadors from important countries, making it more than obvious that he rubbed elbows with them, while the academic intimately mentioned a renowned theater director who was working on a production of a piece by one of our greatest writers, about whom the newspaper editor knowingly said that he was in fact "our most bourgeois writer." His tone, when he said this, was as if he just happened to pick this tidbit up today while at his editorial desk, so he was in the know. In fact, he even added that the renowned director had said as much in an interview which the editor had proofed that very morning, and he himself concurred, as did the drama doctor, who nodded.

Oleg found all of this amusing, or—a better way to say it—he thought it could lead to some amusement. So he asked the experts: didn't this great writer of ours—apparently, as of today, the most bourgeois—write about the bourgeoisie with a healthy dose of irony, or did Oleg only think so because he was already high on pot when he read him? Now he was worried. Was it possible that Sid Vicious, too, was a bourgeois artist? Because the entire period during which he smoked pot was hazy for him. He couldn't tell anymore if his memory was playing tricks on him, or had he remembered everything wrong. On the other hand, there was also the possibility that this great writer had written everything just so it would be staged in a lavish production by the national theater and he could show the world that we had a highly civilized culture. Although he wanted to go on, Oleg started laughing.

For some reason, he thought these people would have a sense of humor and only needed to be prodded a bit, but he must have said something off-color, because everybody stopped eating and started squinting at him, as if somebody had taken their picture at a bad moment.

Only a few minutes had passed since he'd come out of the bathroom, and at the peak of his high he saw them all in sharp focus.

"Hey, I meant that in the most bourgeois possible way," he said cheerfully, thinking this would lift their spirits.

Still under the influence of the coke he'd given her, Lorena swept her hair off her neck and then jumped in as if about to sweep everything under the rug, saying, "You know, Oleg is an entrepreneur currently renovating a factory and he's granted autonomy to the workers. It's almost like workers' self-management, heh-heh. . . . Until you get to know him, please, don't take him too seriously!" She laughed as if with this she'd solved everything.

Oleg knew she only meant to brighten the mood, and she actually did: everybody stared at him like he was a freak, and he shook his head in a silly way and everything went slightly askew. Fine. But though he'd told her his past and future businesses were not for public consumption, she'd mentioned the factory, which she shouldn't have under any circumstances. Didn't she know the factory was a risky venture? Or was this her subconscious speaking, because something was bothering her? In any case, he set out to distract them. Before the dinner, he'd asked Lorena how they felt about cocaine. She knew the former guitarist was fine with it, as was the newspaper editor and probably the academic as well. But she didn't know about the evening's hostess, because obviously, as far as he could tell, Lorena knew the husband better than the wife. Since arriving Oleg had been sensing some strain between Lorena and the hostess, and he noticed that when touching him Lorena was sending the signal that she and Oleg were a couple, which helped the hostess relax. He also observed the former guitarist. Every time Lorena touched Oleg, the host looked away; he was noticeably absent. I'll think about this later, if I don't forget, thought Oleg. However, most important now was to take the quantum leap, but before he did, he needed to identify the hostess's position on coke, which is why he asked in a clownish manner, "Miss Vlatka, if I told you I was under the influence of strong drugs, would you hold that against me or for me?"

"Ha ha ha . . . Miss? Why so formal?"

"I'm sorry, I was carried away by an urge for elegance."

"I'd say: for you," said Vlatka.

He placed the coke on the table. Each of them snorted a line, they started talking more, and then the dessert came, and some wine, and some beer, followed by more snorting. Their eyes sparkled.

The newspaper editor asked derisively, "Wait, what sort of workers' self-management are you up to?"

Whoa! She's really landed me in it this time, thought Oleg. He could see why the newspaper editor would be intrigued. Instantly he became aware that everything came across differently here than it would at a dinner party in Vienna, where people would bat their eyelashes with curiosity and think it amusing. But he felt he was merely reminding the newspaper editor of the past. Damn, I'm going to have to explain the inexplicable again, he thought.

"No, it's not self-management. The workers just organize what they have to do on their own. Meaning: self-organization."

"And what's that?"

Oleg smiled and said, "A bourgeois form of organizing, maybe the most bourgeois form."

He hoped they'd find this amusing, but they didn't.

"Where's the difference?"

You really won't let it go, thought Oleg. He stopped to think.

"Well, I'm not really an expert. This is a case of sheer practicality. If this were self-management, wouldn't they be co-owners?"

"In theory, yes. Workers' self-management is simply the way the company is managed. How this goes down in practice is something else, but in theory it is management of revenue," said Vlatka's husband lightly.

"Now that's not part of my plan, not even in theory," said Oleg. Vlatka smiled. Oleg wondered if she was being friendlier because she thought her husband had screwed Lorena and was figuring out how to get back at him and Lorena in one fell swoop.

"It's simple: the owners decide where the profit goes—into paychecks, reinvestments, or the owners' pockets. If someone else is the owner, how could you self-manage?" went on the former guitarist, today's commercial producer, knowingly. He'd said he had a master's degree in sociology. Oleg understood he was dealing with an expert, albeit a failed one. "This means that self-management is possible in cooperatives or companies where workers own most of the shares, but that isn't the case here, if I understood you correctly."

"Now you've explained it all," said Oleg.

"It's interesting, nevertheless," continued the editor, who would not leave the topic alone—Oleg believed on purpose—having sensed it was making him skittish. "What prompted you to allow them to organize themselves this way?"

Oleg spread his hands righteously and said, "Well, it's so much better than having me organize them!"

Finally. They found this funny.

"Isn't it much better that those who aren't using coke do the organizing?"

They laughed, just like in school when you're not supposed to but you laugh anyway. They have a sense of humor after all, when you shake them up a little bit, thought Oleg.

"You know, Lorena was a bit worried about this. But it's all rational. The people who have coke should provide the initiative and the people without the coke should do the organizing."

They laughed as if his joke had a good punch line.

The next time Šeila went to Nikola's rented manse they ate a dinner Nikola prepared. He was not a good cook, and he apologized too much for everything.

He was not relaxed. Over the last few days he'd been thinking too much about her, and all of this created a parallel world in his head. In this world, in his mind, he came across as easygoing, witty, and charming; in his mind, he and Šeila would spontaneously end up in bed and make love. But now the mood was different than it had been in his mind, because he was in no way the guy he'd fantasized about. He was not the master of ceremonies, the man for atmosphere, the person suavely steering the mood toward intimacy, leading to a touch, the touch so achingly desired, and so forth. His mind was on his management responsibilities, and this was apparent. It was apparent that he had images in mind and was jutting from them like somebody snared in a self-made cage. He felt that the essence of a man was to take matters into his own hands, to fashion the mood, to shape the world, and this weighed on him, but he believed this was his task.

Šeila didn't think much about such things. She only saw how anxious and tense he was. He was funny in the cute little role he thought he had to play. She'd seen this many times. She had watched countless men try out this kind of magic on a woman, which was supposed to lead to sex (they were always, anew, so full of hope). There was something amusing about watching men attempt to play at being the director, while invariably tripping themselves up in the process, since all these unfortunate wretches might as well be one and the same, so similar were they in how they acted. She watched men struggle with this ambivalence. The coarser specimens couldn't handle it, so they'd "get down to business" in a hurry and had to be stopped. The ones who were this type had to be identified before finding herself alone with them in a room. The only ones who were worthy of any consideration were those who could mentally endure the tension and didn't rush things as much.

These men were more skilled, tried telling racy stories, broached the touch barrier almost imperceptibly through jokes, and put off any kind of action until the woman gave them a sign—recognized by such men through steadily held eye contact with the woman. But the problem with these womanizers was exactly the fact that they were so intent. This fascinated Šeila in earlier years, but, with time she realized these men were cold as ice and taxidermically stuffed with experience. No, they were not bumbly like Nikola, who was so completely wrapped up in his own thoughts that he hadn't even caught her responses (he even avoided touching her, probably fearing he'd come off too strong). He clearly wasn't noticing anything. Apparently he was unable to read body language at all. He couldn't interpret what was hiding behind her smiles, her squirming legs, or how she nudged her chin ever so slightly toward her bare shoulder in response to the music he put on.

Thinking this was all up to him, he sank completely into the isolation of his own thoughts.

His eyes fixed downward and to the side (what was he looking at?), he started confessing about his love life.

Holy shit, thought Šeila, but nevertheless she smiled.

And he talked. He told a long story about an ex. It might be deemed sad. A story that said a lot about him. He was a fool. He said so himself.

"Why say you're a fool?" said Šeila.

"Because I am."

"No," she said, though she wasn't so sure now.

"What am I then?"

"Well, you are . . ."

She really did want to say "a fool." Instead, she laughed. She laughed at her train of thought, and he glanced at her, anxious.

Nikola knew he shouldn't be rehashing his sad love story. He himself didn't know why he was doing it, but he was already talking about how long he'd dated Mirna, how the relationship became a drain, how he met her parents and felt like their confidant (the word made her laugh), how he had dinners at their house, how the plates clinked; how he became absent, officially present, but absent in spirit, as if he had a doppelgänger who was involved in the game; and how the love faded away. But despite that, he didn't give up. So it goes, he thought. After all, he was not so young anymore, and it was about time he accepted life, life as it is, that is just how life is, that's life. (Šeila was really annoyed by his repetitions.)

After years of indecisiveness, he and Mirna finally stopped "saving themselves," because this was her last chance, and they actually didn't know why they'd been putting all this off. Then she got pregnant, and he—anxious. However, he didn't attribute his anxiety (which was why he started taking the pills in the first place) to her pregnancy because that would have upset her. Then what happened happened. Mirna miscarried, and he was maybe even a little relieved. This was, nonetheless, awful. They wept, she was desperate, and he did what he could to console her. Everything was so terribly sad. He felt guilty. He felt everything happened because he hadn't wanted the baby enough. Had he, deep in his subconscious, even willed the miscarriage? All of this created even more tension between them. He felt guilty, and his anxiety levels shot up, but he didn't want to be a pig and leave Mirna after everything, which is why they were preparing to give it another go, but while they were preparing, while they were "working on it," she found another man out of the blue.

This surprised him so much that he didn't know where he was, and he couldn't believe it was happening, so he behaved like a lunatic for a while and made Mirna's new life a living hell. But he heard she was pregnant and he stopped—he didn't want to be at fault again if something bad were to happen. Recently, Mirna had given birth to a baby boy, and he still couldn't believe all of this had happened in less than a year. He even thought the baby might be his. He thought maybe she'd lied about how far along she was so she could take his baby from him—he did not know why, but suddenly he wanted the baby to be his, perhaps so he wouldn't have to face complete defeat. Or maybe because, while, imagining all of this, he started feeling it might be much easier to have a child with Mirna now that they didn't have to live together.

He thought about what he'd do if he heard the baby was born prematurely, because that would mean all this had been a lie and he'd have to nose around the maternity ward (he went so far as to consider the necessary strings to pull to get the right information). He waited, asked around among their mutual friends, kept his ears open, and carefully analyzed everything he heard or got wind of.

When all was said and done, the child was born two months too late to be his. And this is how his final hopes were dashed for staying at least partly in the life he'd been leading for years. He was left utterly alone—and this was his situation when he arrived in the small town of N. where his loneliness took a physical form. It was as if he had been kicked out of his world, so he drank loads of beer every evening, often chased with pills, until the image faded away.

He looked at Šeila (because until now he'd been staring down-ward to the side). She looked at him, anxious.

Now he realized—he continued—while thinking about it in retrospect, and while telling her (because there was, after all, a good reason for telling her), that he'd actually left Mirna before she left him. His rage, his inability to accept it all, making her new relation-ship a living hell—all this was just his delusion. And he couldn't face the defeat of his delusions, delusions about what life should be like, delusions about the life Mirna saved him from; because if they'd stayed together, they'd have blamed each other forever for their life together and yet would have felt obliged to act as if they were a per-fectly happy couple, which they might have been once, but stopped being somewhere along the way, after all they'd been through. Yes, he had left her even before she left him, he left her for real, because he really didn't want to be involved in it anymore—he was only there because he thought he needed to be. And then, luckily, she left him officially and saved him.

"She really is a decent woman," he said, finishing his story.

He also added that, now that it was all over and done with, when he thought about it, he was glad he was in N. because, in some way, he really couldn't have figured all of this out back home, maybe because he'd had nobody to confide in the way he'd just confided in Šeila. Why? Because he was ashamed and probably would have become the grist of the rumor mill. It's weird how you cannot trust people you've known your whole life, but can trust someone you've just met.

"All right. Yes, you are a fool," said Šeila, like this was sort of funny, a comforting compliment. "But hey, if you are interested in having a baby with someone you are not going to live with, I should tell you, I've been thinking about the same thing."

This told Nikola that perhaps sex might be an option after all, which made him realize he should snap out of the glum mood that had taken over while he was telling his story. He considered flashing a devilish smile like Oleg would have done, and half-tried it, but felt it was too obvious and a cheap gesture. This attempt (to smile devilishly) looked more like a sort of apology for wrongdoing he hadn't committed yet.

She thought about telling him he was cute. Yes, she'd thought he was handsome from the get-go. But for some reason, men don't really know how to act when they're told they're cute. It throws them off, and the poor guys don't know whose line it was (weren't they supposed to be saying that?). She'd noticed this a long time ago, and, considering that this guy didn't know what to do anyway, maybe it was best not to confuse him any further.

Besides, she badly needed to use the bathroom. She had been thinking about this for some time during his confession. Dammit, she needed to take a shit. She wondered if he'd hear her or if he had to use the bathroom after her and would smell the stink she left behind. She felt like laughing aloud because of what she was worrying about, but then again, she thought, No, I mustn't go take a crap now, it'll totally kill the mood.

She did laugh aloud, and Nikola didn't know what she was laughing about.

She stood up and said, "Sorry, I have to go home."

"Because of me talking that way?"

"No," she said. "No, really, it's not that."

She was at the door, and he stood there before her like a rejected child, so she hugged him and then suddenly kissed him on the lips.

"See you."

Nikola was baffled. Touched by the soft kiss, he couldn't interpret the jumble of signals. Had he driven her away? Why did he speak of Mirna? He must have made himself sound like a complete lunatic, thinking another man's baby was his.

Instead of making a fool of himself in the end, this time he did so right at the beginning. That's all the progress he'd made.

He stood by the window and watched her walk away down the road; he thought of how, in this small town, others might also be watching, and how they must already have declared her his mistress.

She, on the other hand, was walking and thinking about the unearthly woman, about the taboo of the body, about how she couldn't reveal herself in her corporality; she mulled over the aesthetics of the feminine, which was unearthly, which drove women into using cosmetics and into faking their bodies, into wearing corsets and telling lies; she thought about how she was afraid to use the bathroom. Is this normal? She felt she wasn't going to make it home with the pressure in her gut, and began looking around. Luckily, street lighting was not a top priority in the depressed town.

Nikola sat by the coffee table and turned on the TV. After drinking wine with dinner, and later switching to beer, he now poured himself a scotch. There were efforts to reach an agreement on whether to help Greece. The Europeans will manage somehow, they must know what they're doing, thought Nikola. He figured the crisis would soon end.

There was talk of a lack of investment, of fear. "Oh I see, now all the investors have crept into their mouseholes," he said out loud. "Right . . . Look at the collective fear! Where's your individualism? Where are the challenges? Where are you, pussies? Oleg and I are the only ones riding through the wasteland!"

While billions of euros and words like *bailout*, IMF, and José Manuel Barroso echoed from the TV, he poured himself another scotch. He wanted to reach proper drunkenness and dissolve in it.

"Very well, Manuel," he said to the TV screen.

Then he heard the doorbell. He went there thinking it was, who knows, maybe Oleg. He opened the door.

It was Šeila, with an odd look in her eyes that seemed to last as long as a free dive.

Then she stepped inside and kissed him.

Their tongues entwined like eels; he finally wrapped his arms around her body, felt her thighs in his hands and his erection, which painfully sought its way. They staggered off to the couch. He noticed the front door was still open, fresh air flowing in from outside; the TV creaked, the voice was reporting on riots in Kyrgyzstan, the sound faded into the background. The couch was like the frothing sea during southern gales and she was so supple, her vagina so thick, the opposition was, apparently, taking over the government in Kyrgyzstan. Their bodies writhed as if fighting something from within. President Kurmanbek Bakiyev, they said, flew in from Bishkek. She found this hilarious, he yelled—What?—she answered—*Come on, come on, keep going!* The TV crackled; the head of the opposition, Roza Otunbayeva, formed a provisional government, waves were lifting her, he kissed her as if he were going somewhere; then, later, the couch subsided, the fresh air flowed in from outside.

13

EROL FOLLOWED SOBOTKA'S instructions to the letter while they spent two days preparing the base—after they'd checked and oiled everything and replaced the decayed paneling—for the rotor installation, along with four other workers. Erol had a flair for mechanics and tried very hard, but at times he lost the thread; he'd never been to a university and, unlike Branoš, couldn't understand everything Sobotka said. Sometimes he felt as if he'd be able to do it by himself next time, but today must have been one of those days. A feeling of dejection took hold of him. At the moment, it hit Erol that he would never make it as far as Sobotka had, that he couldn't keep up with Branoš. He felt as if he were missing vital parts.

He went outside and lit a cigarette.

He told himself, Okay, you should be satisfied even with this. You're working, in your hometown, people respect you. Just this past summer, in the scorching heat, you labored up north in the big city on rutted streets, amid the pounding of compressors, down in the dust, practically invisible, next to the pipelines and the gas fittings, getting the job done, while the city's residents were off, floating on air mattresses on their vacations (that's how he imagined them).

From that partly enclosed ditch, bare-chested and scorched by the sun, he'd watch women in summer dresses walk down the sidewalk. If one of them noticed him, she quickly looked away and hurried off, as if faced by a threat from below, even though he didn't glower at them in a threatening manner, but was more like a troubadour under a balcony. But he was no troubadour, nor was he under a balcony. He was a grunt in a ditch, and they, who were walking down the street in their summer dresses, avoided exchanging glances. Maybe this was because he was bare-chested, strong, and tanned. But wasn't that the reason nice guys went to the beach and to the gym?

Maybe, but there was that barrier of dust, of yellowish dirt hiding under the sidewalk, there was the rung on the class ladder, and Erol knew this without thinking about it. He was down in the ditch, and his gazes from below seemed more brazen than normal, almost as though they were from a wartime trench.

Erol had been in the trenches as well and he could compare the two, indeed the two began to merge for him under the sun, in the dizziness under the sun, with the constant bursts of clatter of the heavy drilling machines pulverizing the dark tarmac. Back in the trenches, he thought then, always the dirty mission, the body at work, while others walk around up there and run superior errands. And that's how it'll be for you until you kick the bucket, because you have no education, and you don't have it because you were in the trenches, because they handed you a weapon and you took it, just like you're taking these tools.

He was a hard worker, but Erol had been considered a lazy bum at school. He was one of those *problems* the professors took a shine to, a student they tested with a smile, keen to give him a passing grade. But he enjoyed being the *problem*; it was part of his image and, come to think of it, that was what led him to run away from school at the age of seventeen, and the excitement he felt at holding a Kalashnikov for the first time. He felt like a king; because before that he hadn't been accepted into the regular unit, but then Ragan and his unit showed up in another town. Military or paramilitary, Erol didn't care, as long as they let him join and didn't ask about his age; he was already one of the bigger troublemakers in town—before the war, he'd resold tickets for *The Silence of the Lambs* and *Terminator 2*—and he realized that, once the war started, this was the game he'd have to get into if he wanted to maintain his status. It was impossible to remain both a hotshot and a civilian, he understood that.

There was no other choice—no better choice—than Ragan, who had come to the region from somewhere else, where he had, according to rumors, shot a high-ranking commander who'd wanted to "straighten out" his unit. Erol really liked the sound of this, although Ragan himself told him later he hadn't wanted to shoot the commander, but to shoot over his head. But he forgot he had fragmenting munitions in his grenade launcher, and that's what took the guy out.

Ragan was about forty. Before the war he'd done time in five different European countries, so he spoke foreign languages; he was muscular and had long black hair like a rock star. Erol thought of him as a man of the world.

When he arrived—on a motor scooter with a friend from school who quickly drove back—at the hotel above the ski resort where they'd installed themselves, Ragan looked Erol over for a while, patted him gently on the cheek, and said, "Kid, you'll be here and I'll look after you." This made Ragan's crew laugh, and Erol didn't know whether they were laughing at him or their leader's humor. Doesn't matter, he thought, I'll show them.

On another occasion, Ragan said to Erol—he remembered the exact words—"Kid, I've got your back, but you watch mine, too: when I want to eat, drink, or fuck something, it'll be up to you to fetch it." That made everyone laugh, which wasn't comfortable for Erol, but he felt Ragan actually was watching his back; even guys like Ragan had paternal instincts. This didn't help Erol much in the end, however; he kept his mouth shut, rolled his eyes, and scowled quietly to show his disapproval of what had been going on at Ragan's hotel, things he hadn't expected; he'd imagined war as battles and gunfights when courage would be on display. When Ragan was slapping around a girl they'd brought in from the checkpoint, Erol sighed darkly and said, "Gotta go out." He left, walked around the ditches, smoked, and came back, never asking a single question. If he hadn't been a minor, they probably wouldn't have let him get away with that, either, he later thought; he was expected to be with them throughout. This way, he was Ragan's pet, *uncorrupted*, which in a way pleased Ragan, so he came up with a clumsy rhyme he repeated when drunk: "Erol's such a goodie-goodie, hasn't fucked, nor ever will he."

Erol had grown up without a father, so everything about his relationship with Ragan touched a part of him he'd never known existed. He wanted to prove himself to Ragan. But he also had sympathy for unprotected women; he'd assumed the role of his mother's protector as a child and understood a woman's position in a deeper way, as her ally. This was not a clear attitude but more of a feeling, never voiced clearly because it wasn't something to brag about to tough guys. Even in peacetime a line was drawn between the worlds; nothing feminine was allowed among men, as if the polarizing war had begun years before. Since he never articulated his alliance with women, he himself wasn't fully aware of it. But after what happened to the girl, who he thought was pretty and whose documents he later found, soaking wet, by the junkyard, he became numb and distant, then restless again and prone to risk-taking. That was the only form of rebellion he knew: to not look after himself, as if secretly trying to get himself killed. He didn't even know where it came from, he just felt torn between two desires.

One of the desires was—like a comic-book superhero—to protect women in distress. Here, however, this was tantamount to suicide and undoable because it would lead him to a clash with the group he wanted to be a part of. They'd accepted him as one of their own, even though some of the fellows told him he didn't belong there. This showed that maybe they, too, belonged somewhere else, but like Erol, here they were.

This was how he realized he was no righteous hero; he suppressed these thoughts, which is why he wanted to prove himself even more by acting fearless in the face of the enemy. One day, from his window Ragan saw Erol in full gear heading for the woods, planning to cross the hill and get behind enemy lines. He pointed his gun at him: "Report to me at once!"

He arrived to find Ragan sitting in his apartment with a bottle of whisky. Ragan said: "You're not easy to keep track of."

"What can you do . . ." said Erol with a hint of pride.

"Don't go there!"

"I was just reconnoitering . . ."

Ragan saw the kid loved him but didn't fear him. "Don't go there, I tell you! You'll foul up a major deal!"

Erol now thought Ragan had had too much to drink. His eyes looked drunk, though his speech wasn't slurred.

"What are you going there for?" Ragan had said. "I do business with them, for God's sake."

"Aren't we at war with them?"

"Not right now. From here on out ask who you should attack. I've got business deals, understand?"

"Yup."

"I'm a businessman, you know. Not just a bonehead."

Erol stared at the floor. Ragan kept looking from the muted TV to Erol. Then he told him to bring himself a beer from the cooler and have a seat, which made Erol feel important. Not many people drank with Ragan in his apartment.

"How do you think this war will end? Who'll win?"

"I hope it's us."

"I'll win," said Ragan. "And you won't."

Erol didn't see where this conversation was heading, so he kept quiet.

"You know why?"

"Why?"

"Because you're good," Ragan said, laughing at him.

Erol, for some reason, felt ashamed, and Ragan looked at him as if wondering what to do with the kid.

"You remind me of someone. This is what saved your ass."

"Of whom?"

"Someone I owed something to. It's not yours to know. It was a long time ago, even before you were born. When exactly were you born?"

Erol told him, and Ragan leaned back on his sofa and stared at the ceiling.

Then a folk singer appeared on the screen, a blonde, and Ragan grabbed the remote and turned up the volume.

"See her? She's my bride-to-be."

"Really? Gee, I didn't know."

"Neither does she."

"Yeah?"

"Where are your folks from, Erol?"

Erol said where his mother was from.

"What about your father?"

"I use my mother's last name," muttered Erol.

"Is that so?" Ragan said, looking at him as if seeing him for the first time.

"He ran off somewhere, never heard from him again."

"Where'd he go?"

"West."

"Don't you know his name?"

"I do."

Erol said the name he didn't love.

Ragan stared at the screen, at the singer he intended to marry, and said, "Incredible. Such beauty."

Then he asked, still watching the TV, "So, what happened to him?"

"I don't know."

He turned to Erol and said, "You're free to go."

When Erol left, Ragan poured himself a scotch and stared at the chair Erol had been sitting in.

"Unbelievable!" he shouted at the chair.

A moment later he added, "I thought it was some kind of joke from the above when he showed up. And I look at him. He wants to be bad, with all his might he wants to be bad, but he's good. I'm thinking, a joke sent from above because I couldn't tell from his last name. And now ... ha ha, this is unbelievable! How'd you find me? What is it that draws you people to me?"

Ragan was talking to the chair as if it were actually listening to him. He lit a cigarette.

"It's true, my friend, I owe you. You took me with you out there and I thought, You're a scoundrel. Not me, but you. I saw you have a heart and you're not afraid. I even envied you. Oof," he shook his head.

He poured himself more scotch.

"But heart and balls are not the same thing, my friend. When

196

we started pimping whores I could tell you didn't have the balls for it. Only your stupid heart. Not the way to run a business like this, my friend, you can't.... To lift a hand against me, pal, for some beaten-up whore who didn't make it. If only you'd picked up a gun, maybe you'd be here now. But to lift a hand against me, that boxing hand of yours, ah, ah, how foolish."

He stopped, deep in thought.

"It wasn't for you, and yet you pushed your way in. Just like this schmuck of yours wormed his way into my good graces, unbelievable. Same hand, same fool! He, too, wants to be bad and good. Why me? Is this a sign or what? What do I do with him now that I know who he is? Do I keep him or kill him? Tell me.

"Can you kill the same guy twice? I mean, I can, but since he doesn't know anything, this is between me and you.

"He hates you. And I'm indebted to you for taking me on when I hadn't yet become me. You created me.

"You created me—you, who wanted to be good and bad. But you can't do that, pal, you're either here or there. Suckers who join the bad guys get fucked in the end. What can you do? I'd really like to know if you, with that attitude of yours, are in hell or in heaven. About me there's no doubt, I guess. Although, you know, it makes me want to play a combination, like in sports betting: 1/2. Not a draw, a draw is for you. And I'm thinking, if we're not just fighting the enemy in this war, but also for God and our faith, as some say, will that earn me points? What would you say?

"I'm thinking, since I've always been a betting man, I'm thinking about the odds, so let's say, given that there are three faiths at play here, if, let's say, everybody's playing for their own god, and if there's only one god, I mean, there can't be three, one of them must be the right one... Then each has a 33.3 percent chance that they've bet on the right one, and it's 66.6 percent that they've bet on the wrong one. Bad odds. For those who root for their own and bet on who they root for. Not for serious players. Now look: even if I put my money on the right one, is my god gonna like what I've done? Let's say—and this would be pretty optimistic for me—I've got a 50 percent chance, which breaks the 33.3 in half, which means I've got 16 or 17 percent from the get-go. For me that's weak. And if any of these other gods exist, I'm sure they won't like what I've done, so I'd be in for a pretty nasty treatment. In any case, the odds of me profiting in this are weak.

"And if there's only one god for everyone, and he doesn't care who's who, he'll just hold this against me. What would you say the odds are that there's just one god and he doesn't care who's who? In any case, this just lowers my odds.

"So I have little chance for this to improve my end score. Which is why I'm running my little business on the side, I'm not one of those who are in the fight to the core.

"There's no denying it: my deeds are my deeds. And you know, I feel I don't owe anybody anything. I can murder and torch things . . . Even those who were only born yesterday can murder and torch things now. It's weird to see how the fear has melted away. That's starting to worry me, purely for technical reasons. Because, you know we used to build our image on those things. Even you could pretend. Now I have to become worse—I don't enjoy it, believe me—so these amateurs don't think they've reached my level. Why I feel indebted to you, I don't know. Is it because these feelings are from the old me, before I became this man? For you, honestly, I felt bad because it wasn't just you I was saying goodbye to. There weren't many after you who loved me and didn't fear me at the same time. But when I got rid of you, I became me, Ragan."

After leaving Ragan's apartment Erol fell into a glum mood, and later, when he tried to fall asleep, he started from his half-sleep with sudden concern about his mother, which haunted him all night.

When he ran away to join Ragan's unit, Erol hadn't wanted to call his mother at first because he was afraid to talk to her, and then the phone lines were down for a while. The day after his conversation with Ragan he finally managed to get through to her on a borrowed Motorola, and he was shocked by her quavering voice; she told him she was ill, the doctors believed she had cancer, there was no one to bring her food; they lived on the fourth floor and she said the elevator had been broken for over a month. He immediately left for N. without telling anyone. When he got there, he found his mother standing on her own two feet, and he was overjoyed. But then she told him she'd pulled some strings to have an ultrasound that morning. She had uterine cancer and she didn't have much longer to live. She told him to put the Kalashnikov in the pantry so that she wouldn't have to look at the damned thing, and have a seat and eat a little something. Later, when he went to his room, stretched out on the bed, and dozed off, he heard a click in the lock, but slept on, unable to face what this meant through his sleep.

She'd locked him in, he realized this later.

She locked him in, and when he woke and started pounding on the door, she tongue-lashed him with insults, the way only she could, while he, inside, screamed at the top of his lungs for her to let him out. He soon realized she'd pushed a chest, and probably many other things, up against the door, and all he could do was listen to her tirade. "You ungrateful dumbass! You ungrateful worthless shitface! You dipshit! Shame on you for abandoning your mother during the war! You piece of shit! Did I raise you for Ragan? I'm gonna shoot that son of a bitch with your gun! Just let them come looking for you! I'm gonna fucking kill that worthless piece of shit, who is he to take my son?"

He was trying to say something...

"And as for you, asshole, shut up in there! Shut up, I don't want to hear a word from you! And don't even think about smashing down my door!"

He pounded on the door with his fists and head. Apparently she'd piled things up on top of the chest, too, he could tell by the sound. At one point, he broke down and started howling like a baby, at first because he was miserable for being locked in, and then the misery took hold of him and he sobbed for everything he'd seen, because of what he'd known and hadn't known. He put his head under the pillow and wailed in his bed. Then fear gripped him, fear of the fact that, if they came looking for him, his embarrassment would come to light—that his mother had locked him in—and then he remembered what she said, that she would face off against them with the gun, and he began being dead scared for her.

"Mom!"

"What is it?"

"Let me out, I won't go anywhere."

"Shut up, asshole! Shut up and lie there!"

After a while, he shouted, "Mom!"

"What is it?"

"I'm hungry."

Now I'll get her, he thought. She can't stand the idea of me being hungry.

But she didn't answer.

After a while, he heard something at the door and she said, "I talked to Sobotka upstairs and explained everything to him. He's tying a tray for you right now. A smart man, he comes up with everything. He took a drawer from a shelf and we'll pass you the food on it from Sobotka's apartment using ropes. We'll have two drawers, he said, because he has to make you a tray for the chamber pot so we don't put shit and food on the same tray. Hands of gold, that Sobotka."

He listened to her, stunned before shouting desperately, "Tell him not to breathe a word of this to anybody! They'll rib me in town forever!"

"I'll tell him," she said. "But if you shout and bang, you'll tell 'em yourself! And I could spread it around town myself if you drive me up the wall!"

"Mom!" he shouted the next day around lunchtime, after the food delivery was already becoming routine.

"What is it?"

"Tell Sobotka to send some sports news, or a newspaper, for me to read, will you? I'll go crazy like this."

"There are no newspapers, son. Where have you been? They don't sell them anymore."

Right. He'd completely forgotten. He'd thought everything would be the same as it used to be now that he was back home.

"Tell him then to send me a book."

"Oh? A book?" she laughed. "Well, I'll be damned. . . . Should've locked you up sooner!"

Sobotka didn't have many to choose from. Two books were inscribed, meaning he had received them from the factory as prizes for his years of service. The third he must have bought, himself, since there was no inscription and the cover only said *Hamlet*. The first two were the novel *On the Edge of Reason* by a Croatian author, Miroslav Krleža, and a book by Engels, Marx's thinner-bearded companion.

"Oh, man, don't you have anything better?" Erol asked Sobotka through the window early in the morning, because he'd insisted that deliveries be done at dawn, so nobody would see.

"Nope! I only have books on engineering and sculpture."

"Engineering and . . . what?"

"Sculpture!"

"Aw, come on!"

Hamlet was the shortest one, so that's what he read first. He read it twice in three days, and it made him restless, so he took a break from reading and had nightmares in which everyone killed each other, like at the end of *Hamlet*. His dreams took place in Ragan's hotel—Erol was shooting everywhere, and everyone ended up dead, including him. As a disembodied spirit he could still see his mother, carrying his light, soulless body to a distant grave, where she laid him to rest next to the girl who was raped, whose name was Ophelia in his dream.

Then, just to move on, he started reading *On the Edge of Reason*. He read it over a few days and had no idea an author could write such a book, let alone the man in the picture, who looked like such a complete bore.

After pessimistically staring at the book cover, he eventually started reading Engels as well. Engels was a mystery to him—everyone knew Marx was the man in charge, but nobody knew who Engels was or how he came to be on the bulletin board at Erol's school. He seemed like someone who'd shown up to a party uninvited, yet he'd always been there.

Erol thought he wouldn't understand a thing, but his own cleverness surprised him. He would have liked to look up some of the words but, all in all, the book was as readable as a newspaper, albeit an old one. In fact these were, indeed, newspaper articles describing events of one hundred and fifty years ago from old American newspapers, which surprised him—the fact that Engels had written for American papers. How was that possible? Those must have been some other Americans.

Once he'd read that one as well, it was clear he had to do something, so he stood by the door and tried to persuade his mother to let him out.

"Come on, let me out, I'm not going back there, no way, this Engels guy explained it all."

"Liar!" she yelled.

"May I drop dead if I'm lying!"

"You've read it, my ass! Not the Englishman."

"I have so read it!"

"How do you know English?"

"It's not in English. Engels is his name. It's in our language!"

"An Englishman writing in our language? Yeah right!"

"He's not English."

"Then what is he?"

"He's German. I didn't know that, either."

"The Englishman is German? Then what's Marx? A Kraut, too?" she said, laughing at him from the hallway.

"I don't know about him, but you can let me out. I'm not going anywhere!"

She didn't believe him. Luckily, the war was getting complicated, so Ragan's boys no longer had the time to come to N. to look for him. He warned his mother that they should return the Kalashnikov to Ragan's crew so it wouldn't look as if he'd stolen it, and she claimed that had all been taken care of, Sobotka had sent it to them.

Later, he found out that Ragan and his unit had moved to a different region altogether, where—Sobotka informed him from the window—a new conflict had erupted.

"They probably went to stir things up," said Sobotka.

"Ragan's not such a bad guy," Erol said, feeling obligated to defend him in front of others, if only to justify his own actions.

"Come now," Sobotka shot back. "Luckily, you were with them when they weren't doing anything serious here."

Erol had plenty of time to think while in his mother's makeshift prison. He knew he wouldn't have restrained himself had he stayed with them. Eventually, he would have mustered the courage to prove he was not a mama's boy, that he had the guts to do the nastiest things. But somehow he knew that wasn't who he was. The same thing could happen to anyone caught up by a wave during which he couldn't turn around and save the girl he found pretty, the girl who became prettier every day in his memory, and he thought that in a strange way he'd fallen in love.

Later he thought that he wasn't so afraid of death—because if he'd needed to go behind enemy lines, that would be easier—but he felt it impossible to turn against the people he ate, drank, and slept in the same room with. That's why the desire to save her manifested itself as weakness, trembling, like clenching his jaw, a fuzzy headache and throbbing in his temples, like fear at his own thoughts, so he said, "Gotta go out!" and he walked through the ditches there, and smoked, Hamlet-like.

Many more things could have befallen him had his mother not rescued him.

Yes, he thought, all of that could have happened to anyone who had no one to protect them from evil.

This was the worst thing he learned in the war.

Years later, he thought of this often, and he explained it to himself in his own particular way: as a fight for his soul between God and the Devil. When he drank, he'd explain what he called his fate to anyone willing to listen.

"You see, God loved me, but the Devil loved me, too. I loved God, but I also loved the Devil. I loved God more, but the Devil impressed me. Besides, the Devil was stronger. God was weaker.

I loved him more, but I didn't appreciate him. I didn't appreciate him, and I suffered for it, and I'm suffering for it now, because my soul is heavy. It's not light. Because this is not about who you love, but... Do you appreciate the good one or the evil one more? That's what I'm asking. Do you appreciate a good man more than one who squashes a good man like an ant? Who do you appreciate more? God is weaker, I'm telling you. If God were stronger, it would be easy to be good. Right. It would be easy to be on the right side, but I'm telling you, this is not easy."

A couple of Ragan's boys turned up after his mother had already let him out of the room. They found him in town and told him Ragan had said he was never to talk about them. They told him he was lucky.

"Ragan let you go, and you should be grateful," one of them said, his name was Kardan. Then he added, "I wouldn't have let you walk like that. But there you have it."

When he was eighteen, he was drafted, but Sobotka had already arranged for Erol to join the engineering-technical platoon. Sobotka took care of him, and under his wing, Erol lived to see the end of the war. They were in plenty of combat, but even there they were mostly fixing things—because electricity was essential even during the war. He learned a lot, even though that would never make up for his lack of schooling. He was thinking about this today when he came out of the factory, smoking and looking at the distant mountaintops, where the snow still gleamed and reflected the sunlight.

Just then he noticed a man with a dog standing by the factory gate. He'd seen the nutcase around town, and now the man was trying enter the factory grounds. The watchman had stopped him and was saying something to him.

Erol went over to them, and just as he reached them and opened his mouth to shoo away the man with the dog, the man suddenly made a run for it, weaving around him, heading for the main building. The dog ran with him.

"What's going on?" Erol asked the watchman. "Did you let him in?"

"No!"

Erol chased after the man and the dog.

By the time the man with the dog entered the building, Erol had caught up and grabbed the man by the scruff of the neck with his huge hand, holding him like prey, while the dog growled and sunk his teeth into Erol's work boot.

"Let him go!" thundered Sobotka's voice from across the hall.

Erol let go and the man shot him a sideways look, full of melancholy disapproval, as if Erol were an annoying fly.

Sobotka ran over and shouted joyfully, surprising Erol, "This is Slavko! He used to work with us."

Erol had let go, but the dog still hadn't released Erol's heavy boot, so he considered his options—clearly he shouldn't kick the dog. He heard Sobotka shout, "And he will again if he wants to."

Nikola saw everything just as he was entering the building from the other side where the offices were, and he didn't like what he was hearing.

The nutcase is going to work in the factory? Isn't Sobotka going a little far?

Nikola waited for everyone to quiet down and then said, calmly but loudly, "I don't think that depends solely on him."

Nikola soon realized this was the wrong place for a discussion, and he and Sobotka should have dealt with this alone, in private. As it was, things took a different turn. Sobotka's reaction must have been due to feelings he had from the past, or because Erol had been holding the guy by the neck like a sparrow.

At any rate, Sobotka yelled at Nikola, "Fine! It's not just up to him, we'll all take a vote!"

Sensing the situation turning confrontational, Nikola went over to Sobotka and said, "Wait!"

But Sobotka went on so everybody could hear him. Sounding a little bitter he declared, "When we started this thing, you told us we could do things our way. This man was one of the best engineers we had. Actually, he was the best. I'm saying this even though he was my rival. We should give him a chance. Where's the problem, why not put it to a vote?"

Nikola felt his whole bloodstream vibrating. He had to think fast. What was the problem? Sobotka had been the one in charge of hiring people from the beginning. So what was it then? The problem is that my authority is slipping, that he didn't ask me, that Oleg is the owner, that he and I didn't think about the consequences of our promises, and I overreacted instead of working this out with Sobotka, that's the problem. Nikola caught Branoš's fixed gaze, and thought this was not a gaze of support. If he now confronted Sobotka and the workers, he'd gain nothing. He had to extricate himself from this without appearing to be backing out.

Nikola stood next to Sobotka and turned to the hall, saying, "You may stop working for a moment."

Everyone was already looking at them anyway.

"It's true, that's what we said when we started this, and that is how it's going to be. We won't enforce anything. That's why I said it's not up to one person. Everyone needs to have a say. But we haven't created procedures," Nikola said, facing Sobotka. "Tell me, what exactly do you propose?"

After a short pause, Sobotka said, "I never worried about that, either... Everything was spontaneous, and maybe we should have decided on procedure. But I'm proposing we take a vote. And if there's a tie, we'll ask the watchman's opinion."

At this point, Slavko giggled.

Sobotka and Nikola looked at him, and he said, "The dog has no boss!" He laughed more.

"Okay, we need to know if this man wants to work," Nikola said, "and then we have to check to see if he can work, if he's capable."

"I want to," said the man with the dog.

Sobotka realized this was the first sane thing he'd heard from Slavko in many years, and looking at him, he noticed that Slavko had shaved his beard. There were small cuts all over his face, which didn't leave the best impression, but still: he spoke, he shaved, he came.

Nikola said, "I think it would be good to vote on whether to take him for a one-month trial period, and then make a final decision. But first, let's listen to why Sobotka supports him."

Sobotka knew he ought to introduce Slavko, so he told them Slavko's story, focusing on his work at the factory and his competence. He emphasized the award he'd received from the town of N. in 1984, but he didn't mention the death of his son, to avoid upsetting the man. Instead, he said that Slavko had "suffered hard blows during the war and it had taken him a long time to recover."

Slavko knew his turn was now. Frowning and looking up, he started talking in a rusty voice. "I want to work . . . I have walked the dog for a long time . . ." Somebody laughed at this, but Slavko went on. "I had nothing to do. . . . There was nothing there . . . just emptiness and numbers. . . . Then I saw you were working. . . . I know the factory and the machines. . . . I know all of it, it's all familiar to me."

Nikola was listening and thinking, What will Oleg say when I tell him we're hiring raving lunatics?

The workers voted: most of them seemed to be in favor of hiring Slavko. Nikola had meant to abstain, but then he raised his hand, too—let the man work.

In the end, Erol wanted to add something, so he raised his hand slowly and said, "Can someone get the mutt off my boot?"

14

OLEG'S MOBILE WAS RINGING out in the hallway, somewhere among his clothes.

He stepped out of the bathroom naked after a long shower, which was supposed to wash away his hangover. He shook his head as if trying to stretch a stiff tendon in his neck; his hair was still wet, and one eye was very red, probably from the shampoo. He stood in front of the mirror in the hall and picked up the phone, which had, meantime, stopped ringing. He returned the call while studying himself in the mirror. I'm so hideous, look how my fucking gut has swelled. Why did I drink so much last night? He'd had a meeting with an emissary of the Colonel and told the man that everything was going according to plan. The dinner had been great. And there had been no way around all the drinking. He felt as if he were going to burst into flames on the inside if he didn't drink, if he didn't quench it with alcohol. He tried to do his liver a favor by mostly sticking to beer. Wine only with meals and hard liquor only sometimes. Beer is for marathon runners, someone once told him. His apartment was full of bottles. That morning he thought he ought to start taking care of himself. This was a big game and was stressed and afraid, which he hadn't acknowledged.

When Nikola said a journalist had stopped by, Oleg asked, "A local one?"

"No. He traveled here."

"Wait a minute..."

He put on a bathrobe, went to the living room, and through the window watched a barge float lazily along a Viennese Danubian canal.

"Damned babbling," he muttered.

"The watchman put him on the phone," Nikola continued. "Apparently the guy had heard that the factory was being renovated and he's interested. He wants to talk with me and the workers. Writing a small article, he says."

"Even if it's just publicity, media attention is a potential problem. It could lead to further digging."

"So I shouldn't let him in?"

Oleg immediately knew this was happening because of the dinner party. So there, he had created the problem, not Nikola, as he had feared. He'd allowed himself a few minutes of the utmost bourgeois irony, and yes, as soon as Lorena mentioned the factory in front of the newspaper editor, he knew the genie was out of the bottle. Damned parties! The fact that a factory was being renovated was already bizarre, but one in which the workers weren't bullied was highly unusual news, and this didn't escape the attention of the post-socialist editor.

Dammit, Oleg thought, when he started this thing he didn't count on all the historical aspects, and when he realized his mistake that night he moved to befriend the editor; he started talking to him about wines, hinted they could take a road trip to the Gorizia

Hills, those sunny Slovenian slopes where you could see the lights of Udine at night, where a friend of Oleg's lived, a famous winemaker whose pinot gris was *quite something*. After hearing this, the editor was all ears, and they started an almost poetic conversation about wines. Oleg was on his own turf here, because he'd been sipping wine for two decades, over dinners with people he didn't know and who didn't know him, with people who didn't need to know him better, or he them, and wine was always a safe topic of conversation, certainly better than the weather, as there was always somebody to bring up aching joints, while when talking about wines the tongue savored its own enjoyment. You can't have an anxious conversation about wine, and there is no better small talk at critical moments, and, generally, in times of crisis. Talking with the editor about wines, Oleg was sending him clear signals that they were both members of the same class, they were equally refined snobs. He was trying to tell him that he, Oleg, was not some equality ideologue, because a man who knows this much about fine wines has to believe in hierarchy. He'd thought the conversation was going fine, and there was that really first-rate cocaine—about which, although Oleg did know a lot, one couldn't properly converse, because the poor cocaine producers, unlike winemakers, couldn't have clearly marked labels, so Oleg had another small monologue that evening. "If they only had a simple label, we could differentiate among the many different kinds of coke, but as long as it's like this, everything stays hazy . . . Just, like, hazy . . . Imagine if the wine label didn't say whether the wine was excellent or superior, or who made it, or anything. No reviews, no magazines, everything hazy . . . There's no way to determine true quality, and basically, the market cannot function properly. . . . Because the state is standing in the way, and if the state stepped aside, man, you would know who produced what, and you wouldn't have to think every time about whether you're getting value for your money. As it is, we're groping in the dark, but I've developed a vocabulary of my own, so for this coke, I would say it has a particularly strong but supple body. . . . We have the aroma and tang of berries and mint . . . mixing with a strong accent of bitter chocolate and traces of coffee. . . ." He paused for laughter. "The texture is especially fascinating: it's smooth, luxuriously rich, quietly glazing the cartilage of the septum and melting on the gums. . . . The *aftertaste* is tropical, bitter, and long. . . . And you see, if the state weren't meddling in the market, I'd be sitting on juries as a *connoisseur*, attending festivals called 'Poetry and Coke'—actually no, 'The Stock Market and Coke,' where we would confer international awards, medals for quality, and such, and there I would also offer my marketing services. This one I would dub Paloma Blanca and charge a fee for the name, so I earn something, too. But as things now stand, dammit . . ."

They were laughing, nodding, and clapping him on the shoulder; everybody seemed to be having a jolly time and he was convinced that the questions about the factory had been forgotten. But no, now some jerk was asking questions about the reactivation of the factory, coming from who knows where to see the miracle in the shithole.

"Hold him off for a few minutes so I can think this over," said Oleg. "Be polite, go easy. I'll call you soon."

Apparently, the whole Paloma Blanca act had been in vain. Plus, the editor hadn't called him or asked any questions. He just sent a reporter. Not at all friendly. He probably woke up the next morning and thought that Oleg, to put it in the most bourgeois way possible, had been laying on the charm a bit too thick.

There's no mercy for an overzealous showman.

So—he thought—the editor probably instructed his reporter to Google Oleg. The politicians in N. had bragged and had him pose with them for pictures. Damned Internet, everything is there.

Admittedly, there wasn't much on the Internet except that the factory was being renovated. Nothing about their labor organization. Still, Oleg knew how newspapers worked. The journalist had been assigned to unearth something. The editor was already working on a headline. Otherwise, they wouldn't be sending a journalist out to the sticks in these hard times. So, if he came looking for something, it would be stupid if he didn't find it, because his editors would tell him he was incompetent, or even redundant staff.

Oleg hoped the topic of the article could simply be their unusual system of organization. The fact that they were building obsolete turbines would lead to further amazement, maybe even questions about the buyer. If the tip came from the dinner party, the journalist knew nothing.

So: damage control. Why did he let the workers do such a thing? What should he say? That all this was fake? A practical joke? No, then the guy wouldn't have a topic but he would have an enigma: What were they hiding? He'd need to beef up the cover story. Maybe call it a labor-social experiment, something almost artistic. Let their minds boggle, just keep them off the subject of turbines. He'd have to create a smokescreen, he thought, even if it made him look like a fanatic of workers' democracy, or a visionary of a new form of efficiency, just in case they gave it a positive spin, which he found unlikely. The story would probably end up sounding bizarre.

Waiting for Oleg to call back, Nikola looked out the window.

The reporter was walking around with a photographer. They were taking pictures of the factory from the street. He imagined what the shot would look like. He thought the camera angle would make it appear as if something clandestine was underway here.

He didn't want to wait any longer, so he phoned Oleg again.

"I think we should either get rid of him or let him in right now.

He'll wonder why we're being so evasive. He might get the idea that we're making an atomic bomb, and are stalling him so we can hide it."

"Let me call you back in a second," said Oleg.

He called him from another phone.

"Don't say those words on the phone! There's software that captures them," he told Nikola.

"Which words?"

"What you said before. Never mind now. Tell him you'll see him in an hour, during the break. As in he can't come in while people are working. Just keep it cool, don't let him see you're nervous. Until then you'll gather the workers and tell them a few things. Go and call him right now, and then we'll talk."

Oleg's phone rang two minutes later.

"I told him. He said no problem, he's heading for the Blue Lagoon."

"Where?"

"To a nearby bar."

"All right. A couple of important things. I'll speak slowly so you can take notes . . . First of all, I doubt this journalist has a clue about the technology. He probably can't tell the difference between the turbines from the Titanic and those from 1983. But in case he does ask questions, tell the workers, make sure they understand that they mustn't say anything about us working with old technology. Tell them it would be bad for the factory, its image, and future business. If he asks you or the engineers, the answer is that we're in the process of an accelerated modernization. If by any chance he asks about the market, the buyers—you're the only one he can ask about that— make something up, Tajikistan, whatever. Actually no, no Muslims. Say China! China is huge, he won't be able to Google that. If he asks more questions, say it's an energy company. Don't tell him anything else, that's our business prerogative. I assume he's come because of something else, but these are the most important things to remember. Have you written all that down?"

"I've taken notes. Got it."

"If he has come to see this miraculous system of organization, well, in that case, he can write whatever the hell he wants. Tell him we've allowed a form of self-organization because these people know each other well, and they know the work process. If he continues to press, tell him we first wanted to see how it would go and we've actually started a little experiment, which, for now, is going well. We had confidence in them and they haven't disappointed us, and so on. . . . So everything is cool, rational, you have nothing to hide. And if he still asks why, which is not unlikely, because "rational" may not be enough for him, and he may find it boring, then blame it all on me. You don't know a thing. But with me—and he'll never be able to reach me over the phone— that's a different story. Tell him that because of some health issues, I've become a vegetarian and a visionary who for no particular reason has decided to study Robert Owen and Prudhomme. Also tell him that I listen only to Lennon in case he hasn't heard of the other two. . . . Feel free to complain about me. Say that I used to be normal, but when I began having these health problems and became a vegetarian that's when it all started, as if I'm searching for redemption of some kind. They love psychological portraits. Anyway, stick to the worker miracle. I think that's why he's come and it has to do with, well, with some stories . . . I mean, I'm just guessing. . . . Yes, probably with stories about direct democracy and all that stuff, so now they want to fuck around with us. Let him wonder. Keep giving him something to think about for as long as he's asking penetrating questions, and when he stops, tell him to visit the Haiduci restaurant and advise him in a friendly manner not to order the fish but the meat. That way he'll see you're reliable. If you're in the mood, go to lunch with him, you know. But then again, I know you and your bribing abilities. . . . In short, just don't let them think about the turbines. If you give him other things to think about, he'll come to his own conclusions. And make sure the workers understand the technology part. As for the rest, since he's already there, let him do what he has to so he goes home happy."

Sobotka sat at home drinking beer, thinking about the journalist who was at the factory today and his questions. He had been among the first to talk with the man and he'd expected more questions about life here, about how they'd started production, what the factory used to be, what all of this meant for them. He didn't know what he'd been hoping for, but he'd expected something from the journalist. When a journalist comes to your town, and on top of that he's coming from far away, you think to yourself, this is important, the world should know about all of this, we have an opportunity.

But this journalist's voice had a somewhat capricious tone, and, to Sobotka, he seemed to be a joker, fine, he liked jokers—but for some reason he'd expected a different kind of journalist, a serious one, one who was what Sobotka had imagined a journalist would be like. Perhaps he'd carried this image since the days when reporters approached them during the strike, or during the war, when a journalist had occasionally managed to fight his way through to them. Those journalists had always been serious, maybe because the times were serious, he thought. So this, this must be the time for jokers, because everything was resolved, everything was clear. Except this self-organization, which was a curious problem, because the guy kept asking about it, although—it seemed to Sobotka—it was as if he had been asking questions about a children's game that would end as soon as the parents came home. Sobotka understood the journalist's perspective because he'd thought of this in a similar way ever since the two oddballs arrived. There was something off about this. Nikola was a fine young man; he was trying hard to be strong. The other one, Oleg, he was the shady character, there was something elusive in his eyes, like a sculptor who'd been here years ago, whose name was Nandor. He'd seemed to be a cheerful sort, and then one morning they found him hanging in the factory.

But Sobotka believed things were going well now, there was serious work underway, so what did the journalist find so funny about it? The fact that they'd voted to hire Slavko? The others had told him about this and the journalist had nodded three times, as if he really liked the idea. He'd stepped aside because the journalist seemed more interested in the others, and Sobotka couldn't imagine why the journalist should have liked this idea so much.

"I see this is a true workers' democracy," he said, and the workers nodded somewhat proudly.

Then the journalist asked those gathered around Erol, the ones he was talking to in a mocking tone, "Tell me, do you address each other as 'comrade'?"

"You mean like we used to? No."

"Only from time to time. You know, 'How's it going, comrade, haven't seen you in a while.'"

"As a matter of fact, since the war I haven't seen any journalists in a while," Erol said, teasing back.

"How's it going, comrade journalist, haven't seen you in a while," said Skender to show he, too, was a joker.

Even the journalist seemed to be joining in. He looked toward the mountains with a smile on his face, trying to come up with another question, and then said, "What about Marxism and stuff? Are you familiar with that?"

"Well, we used to have it in school, but that didn't go so well."

"What are you talking about? No one ever failed Marxism." They were trying to be funny.

"Well, have you read Marx and all?" the journalist asked, and everyone shook their heads.

"I've read Engels," bragged Erol suddenly to show they were not so uneducated.

"You? You've read Engels?" said Skender in disbelief.

"Yes, I have."

"Way to go," said the journalist. "What did you study?"

Sobotka noticed the journalist had taken up a more informal tone.

Erol said, "I didn't even make it through high school. What can you do, the war and all."

"So Engels is readable?" the journalist asked as if he wanted to give it a try.

"Well sure, if you have the time . . . I sure did," said Erol, laughing about something only he understood.

"He's just fucking with us. Where would he get Engels from?" Skender butted in.

"Where'd I get it from?" Erol puffed up his chest and glanced over at Sobotka. He thought of his late mother, remembered his captivity as if this was a happy memory, and said with a dreamy smile, "Well, that I won't tell you!"

"A secret connection?" joked the journalist.

"Not important," said Erol, noticing Sobotka frowning and thought something was wrong.

Then the journalist turned to Sobotka and asked him, "Are you in charge here?"

"Nah," Sobotka said in a tone that deviated from the humorous atmosphere. "I'm just an old engineer."

"So who's in charge then?"

"Dunno. Nobody," said Sobotka reluctantly.

"Is something bothering you, Mr. Engineer?" asked the journalist.

"To be honest... I've been listening to you, and I don't really know what you'll write."

"That's for me to worry about."

"I know, but at least tell me, are you on the side of the workers?"

"What do you mean?"

"You know—"

"Look, I'm not on anyone's side. I write objectively."

"Is that so?"

"Yes. That's journalism."

"So what do you think of us, objectively?"

The journalist looked somewhere above him and said, "It's very nice, all of this." But you could still see that smile at the corners of his mouth. Then he asked Sobotka, "Do you think this is some kind of revival of workers' self-management?"

"Mr. Journalist, you may be interested in labels. But I'm not. What I care about is the town, the people. I thought we might talk about that. I was working—and striking—during self-management, and I can tell you this: That was not the same. Everything was different. I have to go now. Goodbye."

When Sobotka left, the others also seemed to lose the will to talk, so they started dispersing. Then the journalist went to talk with Nikola in his office.

Now Sobotka was mulling over everything. Come to think of it, the journalist reminded him of an anchorperson on a TV show who did nothing but report on stupid people. He regretted talking to the journalist. We'll come off as gullible again, he thought, and he'd promised himself never again to come off as gullible.

This felt like taking a makeup exam.

Twice, he thought, he'd been offered to do things his way. Perhaps he should have accepted the first time, but back then he didn't know what Veber knew—that the system was in collapse. The signs were there, he thought, but they'd had the habit of waiting, an incomprehensible belief that someone else would sort things out. Perhaps he should have taken over the factory with the workers during the mayhem between the two systems, but such a thing was alien to him. Why, he wondered. On the one hand I believed in the old system and waited, he thought, and on the other I believed that once capitalism came, it would look like it does in the West, with certain standards, progress. . . . Between these two beliefs there was nothing to do but to wait.

And now? Oleg has the money and he's the boss, but we are the ones pulling all the strings production-wise, and we could blackmail him if he turns against us. He knows this, that's why the work pays so well.

Sobotka had expected Oleg would bring his own men to run things, maybe create a top-down sort of union to divide the workers if they started complaining; as things stood Oleg was completely dependent on them. Not only was the way they were now working more agreeable, but this was their strength, he'd explained to Branoš the other day. The truth is Oleg hadn't gone back on his word, he was just traveling so he could locate a market and partners, and Nikola was easy to handle. It was as if this capitalism—in which he'd already lost hope—was working for them in some unbelievable way. This time, he thought, he would be extra careful that nobody turned the workers against each other and nothing was mishandled.

We'll see what happens if he finds a partner for modernization, he thought. Whoever gets involved will have to be tough, because we do what we have to do.

He waited for Slavko.

Now that Slavko wasn't running away from him anymore, Sobotka had invited him to sleep at his cottage. Once he'd recovered, Slavko might possibly start fighting with those relatives of his who'd taken over his house. He wasn't yet strong enough.

Slavko was still immersed in his own thoughts and gave terse answers, but he did communicate and he actually began coming across as normal. As if the normal people here were more normal than he was, thought Sobotka. At the factory he worked like a clock, absolutely focused and precise. People even started admiring him: crazy, yet working.

Admittedly, he'd still sometimes go off for a few hours—Sobotka had to discuss this with Nikola; he told him they needed Slavko, which was true. It was as if his memory had stayed frozen all those years, as if he hadn't received any new data to overwrite the old. He remembered every detail as if he'd been doing it only the day before. Sobotka, on the other hand, did need to search his memory in order to remember everything.

He opened a new beer. Now that he was eating normally, he felt he could drink almost infinite quantities of the local beer. It did make him a little dizzy in the evening, just enough to help him fall asleep, but at least he didn't need sleeping pills anymore.

He began staring at the telephone on the small table and suddenly realized he did have something to talk about now, he wouldn't sound apathetic and empty anymore. So he carried the chair to the table and dialed a long number.

Viktoria picked up the phone.

"Hey, what made you think of us?" she said, surprised.

"I'm always thinking of you," he answered in a choked voice as a wash of sorrow came over him. "I'm your father."

"Yes, I know."

"So how is everything going? How are you?"

"It's fine. Me and Mom are here, but she's outside right now. Jasmina is all right, but she's not here. She lives with her boyfriend, you know."

"I know. What about you? Have anybody?"

"I do, but I still live at home."

"How are your classes at the university?"

"Fine, but I'm also working, so I'll need more time."

"Really? What are you doing?"

"I'm a waitress."

"Oh," he said, not so happy to hear that. "That's not easy work."

"I work at an alternative bar. It's not bad. How are you?"

"Fine, I'm working again."

"Really? What are you doing?"

"The same as before, we're making the old turbines in the old factory," he laughed. "Same target, same distance. We're organizing ourselves."

"You're kidding! All on your own?"

"Well, there is an investor. But we're running everything ourselves."

"That's wonderful," she said in a tone that surprised him.

"You think?"

"Of course I do."

"I'm glad to hear that—not everyone finds it normal."

"So how does it work?"

"We do what we think is best. We run it ourselves, because the investors don't know anything—the two oddballs who showed up here.... And there's an oddball living in my place as well. Slavko, remember him?"

"Slavko? I'm not sure who ..."

"It doesn't matter. Is there anything else new?"

"Oh, yes—Jasmina's pregnant."

"Really? Wow! With that boyfriend of hers? Will there be a wedding?"

"I don't know."

"Wow! Tell her I'm happy for her.... If you want to.... Does she ever mention me?"

"Not really."

"She's angry at me, right?" He stopped for a moment. "What about you?"

"Me? Well ... Right now, I'm glad you called."

"You can come here whenever you want. I'd be thrilled."

"I'll think about it. You don't plan on coming here?"

"Not right now. I don't know. I don't think ... I don't think I should."

"Oh. I see. Keep in touch."

When he hung up, he felt as if he'd gotten someone back. Viktoria. He barely knew the child, and they talked more like equals. And her voice ... He'd just realized—so like his mother's. Do people inherit voices? He'd never thought about that before.

But that name of hers—Viktoria—it was so serious. Yes, he was the one who'd wanted the name, after he'd beaten Veber.

Maybe I should have given her a different name, he thought. Something gentler, a name that fit her better. And that victory of mine turned out strangely in the end.

Slavko entered the house as if someone were after him, slammed the door shut, muttering "What a lunatic!," and stomped off to his room.

Sobotka went to the door and opened it. There was Youry the Mailman.

Youry the Mailman said, "What a lunatic!"

"What's going on?"

"I'm trying to give him his mail. He won't let me. But I'm persistent."

"I know," said Sobotka.

"The mail is the mail. The mail is the state. I don't care if everything around me goes to ruin, I will not allow this. Order is order."

"And Your Mail is Your Mail," said Sobotka. He enjoyed Youry the Mailman's circuitous sentences. Talking to Viktoria had buoyed Sobotka's mood.

"Can you bring him in so I can give him his mail?"

"Doubt it. Slavko is Slavko. He's weird."

"I asked the police if it was possible to bring in someone to make him take his mail—they said not unless it's a police summons. There you have it. The police are the police. They won't protect me. I'm left to do this on my own."

"You're right. The police are the police. Everything is exactly what it's called."

"And now I have to deal with this lunatic!"

"Have you been chasing Slavko for a long time?"

"Don't get me started! There isn't a corner in and around this town where I haven't searched for him. But he doesn't want to receive his mail. He's persistent as hell! I, too, am persistent. I say—you can be as crazy as you want, but as long as you're that guy, as long as that's your name, I'm not leaving you alone. Work is work."

"So what's in this mail of his?"

"There's a whole pile of letters. I carry his burden every day."

"Oh," Sobotka became serious. "Real letters? Not bills?"

"Letters are letters, don't you think I know what letters are?"

"All right, just asking."

"You think I'd give bills to an idiot who wouldn't pay them? I'm not crazy! Bills are bills, you can give them to a subletter as well."

"You said it!"

"I keep track of everything, don't you worry. So are you his guardian now?"

"Um, yes."

"You have papers?"

"These are ordinary letters," said Sobotka. "There's nothing to sign here for them, right?"

"Ordinary letters are ordinary letters. You can't just give them to anybody. This isn't even his address. It doesn't work that way."

"But maybe they're important?"

"They're definitely important. But work is work, as I said before. Bring him in so I can give the letters to him."

Sobotka thought about this. Slavko obviously didn't want to receive his letters. He was still unstable, and Sobotka was afraid this could worsen his state of mind. Who knew what was in those letters?

"I'll talk to him, but let's take it slowly. Why don't you come by in a few days?"

"Look, you're not the one who decides when the mail is delivered."

Sobotka scratched the back of his head and said, "You're right."

"You betcha."

He tried to talk to Slavko about the mail, but didn't even get that far—starting with the mailman—because Slavko immediately jerked his head, meaning he was switching off.

Sobotka had begun to consider him a normal person, so he was irritated that the man was able to switch on his madness whenever he felt like it—or so it seemed to Sobotka.

"But Slavko, someone is sending you letters. You know what that means."

"I can't read," Slavko told him.

This confused Sobotka.

"I can't read what others think. What others think are their wishes," Slavko continued. "I don't know who's behind the words. I don't know them anymore. I can't read!"

Sobotka had not heard such a stream of words from Slavko since the eighties.

"No letters, no goddamn letters," Slavko shouted as if the words hurt him in some way.

To reassure him, Sobotka, said, "I don't know. Maybe this is all a mistake."

"A mistake," Slavko repeated, twisting his mouth. "Of course it's a mistake! It's an absolute mistake! It's all a mistake!"

Sobotka didn't know what to say. He just watched Slavko pacing frantically around the kitchen, reminded, once again, of a real lunatic.

"Adam and Eve—a mistake! They say it's a sin, a sin . . . but it's not a sin, it's a mistake! It's all a mistake! A mistake since the beginning! You can't correct a mistake! The numbers don't add up, there's no way! You can't solve it, there's no solution! Everything's set in stone! All wrong!"

Slavko glared at Sobotka as if he were the enemy and left. The dog followed him.

15

THE DINNER BECAUSE of which he'd had to travel, where Oleg and Lorena met the editor, was wonderful. Oleg was wonderful, the fact that he'd heard nothing about the turbines was wonderful. Everything was wonderful. Everything but the journalist, who, as the editor put it, always brought a touch of irony to his work. He was just that kind of guy; he couldn't write anything without a little teasing note, most likely so as not to lose his critical distance. This is what the editor said of the journalist, in a somewhat ironic voice. "What can you do? He is that way. I can't interfere with his article unless something is clearly wrong because that would be violating the freedom of the press." But all right, he said, he, the editor, would take a look at the piece's layout. Titles and subtitles went with the editorial remit, so he would. He'd take a look. Then he looked over at Oleg as if they were old friends, actually new friends, but as if Oleg were an old friend because the editor drew no big distinction between old and new friends.

Now Oleg understood: he had dispatched a journalist who

couldn't write without a little provocation, who had scribbled God-knows-what, and heaven forbid he'd interfere with the freedom of the press. However, Oleg felt that freedom of the press began before the article was written, as soon as you decided to send a guy like that off on such an assignment. And then you even wink to him. Surely, at that point, you already know what the freedom will be like. But things were not so bad. They weren't interested in the turbines. Given the circumstances, things could not have turned out any better. This was actually great, and the dinner was delicious—was there anything better? Anything more dinner-like?

Oleg drank some more and also snorted a couple of lines. He realized this business was very unhealthy for him. But all this would pass, let them have their fun. What mattered was they had no interest in the turbines whatsoever, for the editor showed no sign of having smelled a bigger story than that Oleg was a slightly oddball bohemian businessman. Therefore, he could continue acting like this. Just avoid major outbursts—he kept saying to himself—avoid major outbursts.

Oddball yet no major outbursts—he had to find this middle ground.

Nikola saw Šeila talking to a man in the town square. He was walking toward them when—and this happened in a split second—because of the way she looked at him, maybe just a tiny twitch of her facial muscles, he decided she was not glad to see him. He slowed down and, not knowing what to do, stopped in front of a dusty shop window, and then, realizing it was empty, he went to a neighboring kiosk and asked for a packet of tissues.

The vendor with thick glasses said to him, "It says in *Novi dan* that the main actor in the TV series *Triumph of Love* was lucky to escape death in a plane crash."

"Why tell me this?"

"I have to tell everyone."

"Oh really?"

Nikola's confusion seemed to encourage the vendor, who said, "So you tell me—is this normal?"

"What?"

"The new directives."

"What?" said Nikola, turning around.

Šeila and the man were just saying goodbye, and Nikola thought he heard the man speaking English.

She approached him, now with a smile, and said, "It sure is small, this town."

"A very small town," he said.

"It's a village," she said. "There's no getting around it."

"I was about to grab something to eat at Haiduci. Do you want to join me?"

"Sure."

"You forgot your tissues," said the vendor.

Nikola dismissed this with a wave, and Šeila smiled.

While they were walking, Nikola couldn't help but ask, "So who was that?"

"Just a friend."

"A foreigner?"

"Yes." Then she added, "A business friend."

When they arrived, they took a seat at a table and ordered. Nikola began listening to the silence around them. Actually, it was not really silence—you could just barely hear the song "Unde-s haiduci" coming from the loudspeakers, which he had gradually realized was something like the restaurant's anthem.

Nikola thought she'd say something else about her friend, but she didn't, so he said, "I didn't know there were other foreign business-people in town besides me."

"You'll find the occasional one."

"Where does he come from?"

"Is this an interrogation?"

"I just asked where he's from."

"He's American. But let's stop the interrogation, all right?" she said.

His next question, though, had already slipped out of his mouth, "What's a Yank doing here?"

He could hear the lyrics which he knew by heart, although he didn't understand them: "*Să ia toți banii pentru țăranii . . . Pentru sărmanii plini de nevoi . . .*"

"He's on a business trip," she said with a sigh. "I'm not having an affair with him. Can we stop?"

"All right. But . . . what's he doing here?"

He could see her hands fidgeting. The waiter brought their food, and she kept looking around, as if she regretted coming to the restaurant.

What is an American doing in this nowhere town, where we are coincidentally making turbines for the embargoed Colonel? When did he get here? What exactly does she do?

Yes, she had told him something vague about an occasional job—some kind of outsourcing—but she'd just waved it off, he remembered, as if she found the topic distasteful. He remembered from her stories that she'd worked at a variety of different jobs before coming to N. and the jobs that sounded the best were the most bogus—this was what she used to say. You know, the more fictional the job description, the better its title, she'd say. She had mentioned associations and projects, named names she'd worked with as if they were well known—but when she realized he hadn't heard of them, she said it was better that way.

He never realized until now that she was working on something *here*, he thought she conducted her business over the Internet.

Nikola had many questions even though the interrogation was over.

"Wait a second, you're doing something *here*?"

She gave him a piercing look, saying nothing. Maybe an extorted *yes*.

"Šeila, what are you doing? Hey, you really should tell me."

She stared at him. The fact that she had told him the interrogation was over meant nothing? She hated this behavior, his complete disregard, which surfaced so spontaneously. Now she was looking at him and thought, *Here's the boss.* This thought dismayed her. As if she were being attacked in a space she'd thought was safe.

"I should tell you? Who do you think I am? Your *wife*? Let's say I have a contract that doesn't allow me to talk about it. There's nothing for you to worry about."

Where does her coldness come from, he thought. I shouldn't worry about it? We are making turbines for a man whose country is under American sanctions. Of course, he hadn't told her about that, so she had no idea why he should care. Hmm, no, he couldn't tell her why he was asking questions. He stopped talking. He was hungry, but he hadn't started eating. Then the thought hit him: he should find out what the Yank was doing here, and what she was doing with the Americans. Thoughts welled up and roiled in his head.

"Wait, I can't know what you do?"

"Not necessary."

"Like, like you're some kind of secret agent?"

He appeared a bit frantic to her, and in that instant she felt she didn't know who he was.

"And who are you?" she said, smiling caustically. "The Service for the Protection of the Constitutional Order?"

He fell silent, swallowed some of his food. Meat. She tried to eat, too, but then she realized she couldn't. She had to tell him some things now.

"Well, I didn't know what my partner was doing, either, and we lived together.... I don't even know what you do, you and your cousin.... So what's the problem? A woman shouldn't be able to do the same? You have to know everything about a woman? Oversee everything?"

"No, but I should know some things. Is what you do secret?"

"I'm telling you, I have a contract that says I can't talk about it. I shouldn't even have said that much."

"Well, what kind of job is it? Here? What could it be?"

"Are you deaf? I told you I'm not allowed to discuss it. Your questioning is getting on my nerves. This is beyond me.... You want to know my every step? You see ... this is all about the ancient fear that the woman will get pregnant with another man. That's why the Taliban keep their women at home. C'mon, think about what you're saying before you open your mouth again, because if you don't stop, I'll get up from the table and you'll never see me again."

"Wait, you say you don't know what I do? I go to the factory every day."

"No one here knows who you are and how this is possible. Why was the factory brought back into production so suddenly? Why are the workers voting on who they'll accept? What are you? Businessmen, hippies, lunatics? Nobody knows. But, you see, that's not a problem for me."

Lunatics, yes, we are lunatics, he wanted to tell her, but this was not the moment for that conversation, so he just said, "It's about self-organization."

"Self what?"

"Self-organization."

"Well, my business is also self-organization."

Now she's laughing at me, he thought, and said, "I've heard a lot of things from you now, but not what you do."

"That's my own fucking business! Can't you understand that?" she raised her voice.

The bartender glanced over at them and then acted again as if they weren't there.

Then, more quietly, she said "Look—no matter what we are, I don't have to answer to you."

"I just asked one thing."

"You really don't give up," she said, wondering why she was still sitting there. Hadn't she just told him she'd leave?

"It's important to me. I just need to know what you do."

"Well you can't! Not like this. No! Not now! It's like you suddenly became a different person," she said, withdrawing deeper into her chair.

"I'm a different person? You can't tell me what you do for a living. Who's a different person?"

She wondered what kept her from walking out. The fact that she'd already formed a picture of him in her mind, a completely different picture, and the picture still had a hold on her? She gave him a long look, as if this were the last thing she was going to say.

"Look . . . I organize some things for them in the field. Technical. Okay?"

And what do they do, those you do the organizing for? He wanted to know, but he obviously wasn't going to find out.

"If I hadn't seen you with that American guy, you would've continued talking about it as outsourcing and stuff, right?"

He really is acting like a cop, thought Šeila.

"That's what I said, 'outsourcing' . . . That's what it is. I'm not a regular employee."

Yeah, I bet they formally hired you at the CIA, he thought. Then he asked himself—Wait, is this paranoia? I must be paranoid. . . . She can't be an agent, can she? But then he thought about how they'd met. Whose initiative was that? Hmm, she showed up at the Blue Lagoon, Erol and Branoš were hitting on her, and then a couple of days later she was sitting there alone. She went to my place that same night. . . . She even initiated the sex. . . . Could it be? I've made an idiot of myself again. . . . No, no, can't be.

He fell silent, ate his meat, and she thought he'd somehow taken what she'd been saying on board. But the conversation, the restaurant with the stuffed deer head on the wall—like the one time in Tbilisi, everything assumed a somber tone.

Nikola was now thinking about something else: Where did the journalist even come from? Was Oleg the one who messed up, or was he, Nikola, the patsy?

"That—what you do . . . This information, you must understand, it's really necessary for me," he said while leaning toward her, knife and fork in hand. He said this in a voice that sounded to her as if it were trembling with a strange fever.

She studied him a bit more as he leaned over the table like that, and thought he might be insane. Then she shuddered, remembering how he'd been convinced that his ex was carrying his child. She got up without a word, fearing he might come after her.

He didn't—she saw when she looked around—he remained seated, with his silverware in his hands and his mouth slightly agape like a person who'd suddenly died.

The article was published with the title "Self-Management Beyond Seven Mountains"—and now the journalist's purpose was clear to Sobotka. He'd already known that the people living beyond seven mountains in a godforsaken place were funny and ridiculous, like dwarves who sang as they worked. Nice people, generally, but in one part, right before the end, the article became serious, creating the impression that these workers were not just reviving self-management in their own spontaneous, idiosyncratic way, but were taking it a step further by reading Engels, though they'd been reluctant to talk about this. One of them had blurted something and then fell silent after exchanging glances with a stern leader, a certain engineer named Sobotka, who was of course an opponent of free speech and even tried to give the journalist lectures in politics ("That is when everything stopped being funny"), which he, the journalist, managed successfully to resist, because he was in fact apolitical—and to him this had been an interesting experience of "a confrontation with atavism in a remote town where time stood still." In addition, the journalist, Miho was his name, casually pointed out that he'd experienced other pressures regarding this article. Is he referring to the editor, my new buddy, wondered Oleg while reading. At that point he noticed that there was no mention of him. Had the editor left that out like a real buddy, or did he just realize that the story about Oleg was unbelievable?

At the same time, Sobotka, reading aloud, said in front of the other workers, "Look, they pressured him. He's probably already in Siberia!"

People laughed, although some didn't quite understand all of it.

One man said, "Just so we're clear, I don't read those books. You asked me to come and I'm working. . . . I don't know what you're up to."

"Well, we're planning a coup d'état, don't you see?" Sobotka said.

The guy gaped at him. Sobotka added, "Any day now we'll be in power."

"He's just fucking with you, man," Erol said to the man, who was on his crew.

"And what are the newspapers saying?" said the man defensively.

"They are saying what they want. I was the one who said the thing about Engels," said Erol. "I really am a fool."

"Don't you be calling me a fool," said the man. "Just so you know. I am no Communist."

After that word there was, as usual, a brief hush.

"Hmm . . . Should we exclude him from the Party?" said Sobotka, winking at Erol.

"I'm not in any kind of party," shouted the man, whose name was Ćamil.

Sobotka looked at him and thought, and this is who I'm working with.

Another one, however, raised his hand and said, "By God! I'm for exclusion!"

"It's all good," said Oleg in his bathrobe after he'd showered and was recovering from his hangover; he flicked his wet hair and both his eyes were red, probably from the stupid shampoo.

"Look," he said to Nikola on the phone, "it turned out well considering how things could have gone. . . . What matters is they didn't mention you-know-what. What matters is they don't look in that direction, and I don't give a fuck about the ideology, let them mock and laugh. That's their democratic right."

"Sure, fine, I agree, but the workers are upset. They're pissed off. It's kind of a different situation here. You should come. They might really organize themselves into something—I don't know what," said Nikola, using the situation, because he wanted Oleg there. He was feeling depressed again after what had happened with Šeila.

"Them? What could they do?"

"I don't know, all of this is so strange. They've realized now that the public is not on their side, it's like they've seen that they're on their own and no one has their back."

"Well, tell them we have their back," said Oleg, bothered.

"What do you mean, 'we'?"

"I intervened, man. I take shit every night from some pretty fucked-up motherfuckers."

"Yes, but the workers have forgotten about you. You are like an enigma to them. You should come here, let the people get a sense of you."

"Damn, better not."

16

THE IMAGE OF the man she was falling in love with had evaporated. He wasn't who she'd thought he was. In the beginning you imagine the man, and the man imagines the woman. The images fall in love with each other, the images make love and only argue when they bump into the fissures of reality.

The desire for the image comes from the entire body: sex *desires* beauty; yes, sex desires beauty; sex without beauty is a failure of human illusion. Because sex desires beauty—those who fall in love are artists at that moment, a moment which is the very essence of the human desire for the illusion with which they are copulating. This is why everyone knows what art is, and what poetry is, and what painting is: they are all the same. Everyone knows that, even when they despise it, when they despise infatuation and art, and that's most of the time.

This time, the image needed to be discarded, it had collapsed. Maybe better that this happened now, at the beginning, rather than later when she would've been so used to the illusion of him that she wouldn't be able to discard it so easily. She'd try to patch up the image. Yes, it's better this way, she thought.

Still, she had just begun to fall in love—Oh, don't make less of it, she thought. I've already fallen in love. That's why this is rocking me like an early, terribly early, morning wakening after a night of drinking. All the desires of the body are on the other side, and any wakening simply hurts. You put your head back on the pillow and something from the outside is rocking you again, shouting from reality, the reality itself is shouting, poking into the dream. No, let me sleep! Let me dream! Why couldn't you leave me alone?

She was angry, thinking about everything. She was angry because she didn't understand the seam, the crack in the image: What had actually happened? Was this mere jealousy? A yen for power? He didn't seem the type. How could she have been so wrong? Was it possible that he was unhinged? Why did he need to know what she did? Nobody was supposed to know; she'd promised.

But yes, she might have told him if he hadn't been so obsessive about it. Goddammit, why? She wouldn't have been so obsessive. A woman would never be so obsessive. Many women barely know what their husbands do, but she can get over it, to her this can feel normal; it can even be sexy—the ignorance, the opacity, the secrecy. But to him, this was an insurmountable problem; he couldn't bear not knowing everything about her.

What a stupid illusion, she thought, to know everything!

They want to know everything because they know nothing about women. That explains the panic.

Like you're a secret agent, he'd said. A woman whose job is opaque to a man, a woman he doesn't control, is instantly a Mata Hari, a security threat. This rude awakening hurt.

With Michael she'd felt like a trinket, and that killed their relationship; she'd sworn then that she wouldn't do that again. She wanted to have her own life, she'd fought her way through these backwaters, but there simply were no more men for her, there'd been none for a long time, and then one showed up, and soon after that, he burst like a balloon.

They were driving on a heavily rutted road up a hill, Šeila, Lauš, and Alex, clumsy Alex, the American who'd caused her relationship with Nikola to burst.

The road looked like it was leading them away from the world, and that suited her fine. It felt good to gaze at all the greenery in this little valley between the mountain peaks. These paths could only be traveled starting in late spring.

But the path, which more or less resembled a road, was now narrowing and disappearing. The SUV with huge tires they'd rented could pass through all kinds of trackless countryside, but now there was simply no more space.

They climbed out of the car.

"The pass is up here, we'll have to go on foot," said Old Lauš.

He was Šeila's distant cousin, and she'd brought him along as their guide.

They set off with backpacks. They left some of their equipment in the SUV. If everything went according to plan they'd return for the rest of their things the next day.

They walked for a long time, making their way through the pass to a sunlit plateau on which there were scattered a dozen stone monoliths.

Alex walked through the grass and started to examine them and run his hands over them. Some were in the shape of little roofed dwellings and ornaments carved in the stone.

"What is this?" he asked.

"Large stone suitcases."

"You're joking."

"They're tombstones," said Šeila. Alex flinched, as if he were unsure of where next to tread, so she went on to say: "Don't worry, they've stood here for centuries."

"Hmm . . . I've never seen graves like these."

"They can only be found here, for a radius of a few hundred miles. Thousands of them."

Alex looked around, lost in thought, and proceeded to sit down in the grass, as if he'd forgotten he had company.

All right then, this is a nice place to rest, thought Šeila.

She lay down on the grass.

A brisk breeze and quiet sunlight on her skin.

They'd chosen a good spot, she thought.

Colorful imagery behind closed eyelids.

She imagined death now as a pleasant experience and the thought made her open her eyes.

Half an hour later the village came into view. Dwellings of stone and wood blended with the landscape so you could barely make them out; they were cut into the rock that was towering over the small village almost like a cave opening toward the sun. Was anyone still living there? Mists lay above the village like an army that could descend at any moment.

As they approached the village, a long-haired yellowish dog appeared in front of Šeila, barking loudly.

Another dog they couldn't see barked back.

They stopped, and the dog eyed them.

It was the village where her grandmother, Drita, was born. She knew some vague stories about her family and this place: this area had been their summer pastures and, once, during a war that thundered through the valleys, they chose to stay here. In her childhood she hadn't been interested in what her grandmother was saying. No one cared about it, and Grandma didn't talk much. But Šeila had listened enough to know one important thing.

She'd told Michael about it.

When he recently called her, the voice she heard wasn't the old Michael's anymore, he reminded her of what she'd told him about the village.

"I'm sorry I never called," said the new Michael. "It just turned out that way.... You know ... I'm calling you now because ... I'm onto something new. I remember, it is etched in my memory, how you mentioned that there were no bald people in the village your grandmother comes from."

Šeila laughed, realizing that the Yank, who she thought had forgotten her, remembered her genetic predispositions.

Back then he must have been thinking about them having children after all.

"Did I really tell you about that?" she said, laughter rippling through her instead of sadness. Yes, she'd often imagined a conversation with Michael back in those days, but he never called, nor did he respond to the few calls she made, and by now, by the time he finally did call, everything she'd wanted to tell him had evaporated, as well as what she thought he'd say—because she'd imagined so many versions of the conversation.

But her versions had been serious, not like this.

"You see, I did everything to win you over," she said to Michael.

"Wait, did you make that up?"

"C'mon, tell me, please, did you like that, picturing your sons protected from baldness because your wife had such unique genes?"

"Well ... maybe."

She laughed again. "This conversation is terrific."

"Don't hang up now," Michael said. "Seriously—did you make that up? This is important."

"Important? That?"

"Oh, fuck ... okay! Things didn't work out between us. You know that. What was the point. I was supposed to call and say what you already knew?"

She was silent for a time, and then she said, "I didn't make it up. My grandma used to say there were no bald people in her village. She saw a bald man for the first time when she came down into the valley. The baldness took her by surprise, I don't know, like seeing a black man for the first time.... Sorry, Michael. It completely slipped my mind that you're black.... It's amazing, the things a person forgets."

"Sheila ... I'm sorry if this call upsets you. Do you want me to call tomorrow?"

"No, no, everything's fine. I'm just ... uninhibited ... I speak what comes to mind, see? We know each other; I can speak freely, right?"

"Of course," he said. "I'll stick to the point. Do you think the story about the village is true? Have you been there?"

"Only once, as a child. It's way up there. My father was born in the valley."

"Do you believe it's true?"

"I don't know. Wait. Yes. I did believe Grandma."

"Why?"

"She would always open her eyes wide when she came to that part in the story, when she saw a bald man for the first time. What had happened to him? That's how she told it. Convincingly. That amused me, so she repeated it."

"And in your family, are there any bald people?"

She pondered for a moment before saying, "As far as I know, no. Tell me, what's this about?"

"Biotech. You know, there are some people who would like to look into this."

"Really?"

"You could be their fixer and a guide for a researcher, maybe even a whole team."

"You're offering me a job?"

"Yes."

"How nice, thank you. . . . I am broke."

"But don't think like that. Charge for it. Not by your rates but ours."

The advice was unexpected. It was as if Michael were speaking as his old self, the self she'd once loved.

"Also, you should get a small percentage in the project, if it comes to something. It probably won't, but if it does, that would be huge."

"Oh yeah?"

"These are serious matters."

What a conversation, she thought, before saying, "I don't even have a lawyer, Michael. How am I supposed to negotiate?"

"My lawyer will take care of your contract. Do you trust me?"

She paused for a moment, thinking, *What else can I do*? And then she said, "I will trust you on this."

"Think of it like this—if I wanted to screw you over, I could've just told you about the fieldwork and you'd have agreed. They will be researching genetic material, as well as the environment. They'll try to figure this out. After they've found the location, they won't need you anymore. They'd pay you like the Sherpa guides who take people up Mount Everest. And you would be okay with that, right?"

"Probably," she said, disheartened. In his hands again. "Okay, Michael, so why are you doing this?"

She said this quietly, as if she were talking to the Michael of the past.

"I am also on contract with them. I have half of the information, I lead them to you, and you have the other half.... Maybe I screwed you over once.... I don't know.... That was difficult for me, because ... well, it was how things were. If I were to trick you now, that wouldn't be right. Sorry, you said we should talk freely."

"Fine," she said.

"Besides.... I don't like them very much," he said.

"Really?"

"Simple as that. I don't want them to use you."

"All right, tell me everything now."

"I've only been in this for a short time. Some things have surprised me. Honestly, Sheila, I don't really like all of it."

"What, exactly?"

"They can patent genetic material. You are a microbiologist, after all, you know what that means."

"I never became a microbiologist, my dear."

"No? What have you been doing?"

"All sorts of things. Mostly worked for NGOs on peace, culture issues.... Projects. Fictions of all sorts. Even an art manager. Nonsense."

"Art manager?" he repeated like he found this impressive

"Ha ha ha, sorry," she laughed. "That only sounds serious. You know how things work here. *Auctions without minimum bids....* And I didn't get the job at the water utility. There's nothing tying me down business-wise, if that's what you're asking. Go on."

After a brief silence and something resembling a sigh, he continued: "Right.... They can patent it. As a discovery. Even though it's something that exists in nature. That's the law, and I ... I don't like it. I've been thinking about where this all leads. But that's the state of affairs. If there is something there, they'll patent it."

"And then it's theirs?"

"Yes. There's a huge battle underway. Companies like theirs will patent anything showing potential for profit. Everything. So much is already under patent. Life itself will have an owner."

"Michael, you are telling me this now, after you've told me to work for them."

"Yes. I don't tell this to everyone. . . . Fuck, I haven't told anyone."
He sounded like a man who was struggling.

"Michael. . . . This is weird."

"Yes. But I'm in."

"Why are you in?"

"I don't know. I guess I don't know what else to do. . . . I don't know. . . . It's all pretty much the same. Besides, I've got some ideas."

"Wait, you want to be fair with me? Or share your burden with me?"

"This is my thinking: If such a thing exists they'll find it, no matter where. Okay, that would only be the cure for baldness. Nothing bad. But if by some chance I were to earn a lot of money off this, I could stop working, and then I'd join the fight against the laws that allow the patenting."

Now he really sounded like someone who wasn't feeling well.

"First we make money off it, and then we fight against it?"

"I will," he said, the tone of his voice rising quite high. "It bothers me. . . . Designer babies, cloning. I don't like the idea of cloning."

"What?"

"Cloning. These are private companies. I work with them, I know them. Sooner or later they'll try everything. Who will monitor what they are doing? It should all be regulated. . . . Maybe, maybe it shouldn't even be private. But that's business for you."

"Michael, has something changed you?"

There was a long pause.

"Maybe it's the fact that I have kids," he sighed, knowing this

wasn't merely a piece of information. "There have to be limits. . . .
This is a Pandora's box. I don't know what to think. . . . But it is realistic. The laws are on the books. This will happen with or without
our help."

"I understand."

"Think about everything."

"Michael, this is a really weird conversation."

"I know."

"So, you have kids?"

"Two."

"Happy marriage?"

"Yes."

"Take care, Michael."

"Bye, Sheila."

"You ask me what sets us apart. We were Bogomils, we sought shelter
here, in the highlands. That's what my relatives used to say, that we
were Bogomils, but others prevailed. I don't know what to tell you.
We're not anything anymore. We forgot, and we dispersed. My
grandfather used to say that his grandfather still knew everything.
But that man disappeared when he was young, they say. He went
down once to trade and never came back: he was enlisted, mustered
into an army. Never to return. My grandfather used to tell me this.
After that, they lost the knowledge. Since then, we've remained as
you find us. Some say this; some say that, but nobody really knows
for sure. Everyone worshipped as they knew how and as they said it
should be. I, for example, call our god Godling, as if he were small.
And that is how I pray to him. I say a prayer that is mine only. Some
men used to say years ago that this was wrong, Godling. They said

that's womantalk. But older women called on God that way, and I liked it. That's how I say it. That's how I like it. This other woman in my village, Irva, she says it differently. But none of this matters any more. Our church no longer exists, anyway. It was, my folks used to say, a people's church, but our community was isolated and small. So I believe my god to be small, too. Smaller and smaller. We're gone. The folks from here all moved down into the valley. Only she and I are left. Her son visits her sometimes, almost never, in fact, and nobody visits me. I never had any kids of my own, there. The last of my kin, those who still used to visit, went off to faraway lands during the war, if they're even alive. I know nothing of them.

"Since when have we been here? I don't know exactly. A long time, child. We were attacked, or so my folks used to say, even before the Turks came. People slaughtered each other here before the Turks came. That's what they told me. Over religion. And probably over money, because you had to give the church its due. Our folks refused. They persecuted and killed us Bogomils, and I guess we did the same to them. Then we took refuge in the mountains. One elder of ours, Dragodid, led us to the mountains so they wouldn't kill us and we wouldn't kill others. Later, when they finished killing each other down there, the Turks came with their religion. Our people used to say this was the reason why the Turks came here in the first place, which is something I've never heard about over the radio, I don't know if you have. I never went so far down the mountain, but I did get a battery-powered radio, and I can hear how, whenever a shot is fired somewhere, someone arrives afterward. I don't know who they are.

"This used to be Bogomil country, that's what they told me. Then the country changed, and now no one dares say that their family were Bogomils, because they've become something else. What're you going to do? The people change their ways, and then they're embarrassed to know they used to be something else. That's the way it goes. I ain't one to complain. The Bogomils, after all, came after someone else, it's not like they were the first.

"The way we disappeared, I've made my peace with that. We've always known—even when I was a child, we knew we'd disappear. We weren't a people anymore but something on the margins. And we were always sad about that, about the fact that we were gone and our folks forgot about their ancestors. The standing stones are everywhere . . . everywhere there are monuments to what our forefathers used to be; it's just that folks turn strange when the tide turns: when that happens, they say, *I don't know, I don't know what this stone's all about, I don't know what things used to be like*, and then they say, *It's always been like this, and nothing's ever existed except for us*, even though all kinds of things did exist before, and everything used to be different. Then it disappeared, just like this here will disappear one day, and no one'll remember, because everyone'll be embarrassed to remember that they used to be someone else, that someone's grandfather fought for something different, that someone's father changed his faith with tears in his eyes, that he was humiliated in this faith. But that's how things've always worked, they say, everywhere. Who knows who chose whose faith? I respect every person who chooses beliefs on their own terms and immerses themself deeply in it. More power to them. But a lot of people, my folks would tell me, changed their faith with a sword hanging over their heads, and that's why their faith's restless; it's not peaceable and it doesn't live inside them but is external like flimsy armor, it's linked to the sword, it thinks about the sword and follows the sword. . . . Then they start killing each other again, one side led by one sword, the other side by another, the third by yet another, because they confused the sword with God. It's the same everywhere, I hear, because I've got a radio, and sometimes I listen to it in the dark, and I can hear they're killing each other here and there, just like they were once trying to kill us and we were trying to kill them. Dragodid brought us to the mountains to stop us from killing each other and so we could disappear in peace and quiet, dwindle in peace and quiet, and forget in peace and quiet. That's why my faith's small but peaceable, and my small god, Godling, is by my side. There. And this friend of yours who doesn't understand what I'm saying, where's he from?"

"From America."

"Right."

"That country is far away."

"I know. You can only come from away. And what does he want?"

"He'd like to stay here for a while. He's a doctor."

"Oh, he cures illnesses?"

"Yes, if there's a need."

"And he just does that for free."

"Yes."

"Right. You're lying about something."

"Why do you say that?"

"I see it in your eyes."

"What do my eyes say?"

"Nothing. Your mouth talks, but your eyes keep quiet. Like they're ashamed."

"Fine. He is a doctor and he's got different kinds of medicines. But there's one more thing. He'd like to know if any bald person has ever lived in this village."

"They've already asked about that."

"They've already been here?"

"Yes."

"When were they here?"

"A long time ago. Communists."

"Really?"

"They were here and asked about that."

"And?"

"They took some blood from us."

"And after that?"

"After that, they disappeared as well."

"I see.... And you and the other old lady are the only ones who are still here, you say?"

"That's right."

"And her son visits her, you say?"

"Let me tell you right away—we don't speak to each other."

"Really? Awkward. You're the only ones here."

"What can you do?"

"Ma'am, have you ever seen a bald person in this village?"

"Never seen one until during this last war, when they came here."

"Who?"

"They came here looking for shelter, four or five of them. They ran away from the war down there. Didn't want to join the army. Sometimes they come back. They linger, repair things. They say they're going to move here."

"She didn't tell us anything about that."

"She wouldn't. Because they're hers."

"Hers?"

"A sect. She's filled their heads with rubbish."

"What kind of sect?"

"A sect based on her nonsense. She says we used to be Bogomils.... These are her stories. Her grandfather told her about it, she says. She doesn't know anything. It's true we used to be a special breed back in the day: a tribe who knew some things, but I've

251

no idea where from. We used to be miners in the old days. We had a mine right here."

"My grandma told me you used to be shepherds. That your summer pastures were here, so you stayed."

"Your grandma didn't know anything. They had livestock, of course, they had to for food. But they had a mine, too."

"Which ore was mined? *Did all the men work in the mine?* My friend here is asking."

"Ore? They used to call it *cone*. The men worked there, who else... But that was before. The mine shut down years ago. The supports fell in when folks started to leave. There was no one left to maintain them. They fell in while I was still a child, but I didn't know about that at the time. Maybe we were running out of the *cone*, I don't know for sure. They said there was less of it than before. I don't know if that was the reason why folks left or if they just got bored with life here. But, yes, it was the men who went into the mine, not the women. The mine was farther up the mountain. They built their houses here because the shelter was better. The material extracted from the mine was in small amounts, I know that because the elders would carry it to places far away to sell. They were able to carry it far away because there wasn't a lot of it. They didn't want to sell it close by so no one would find out we had something here of value. They took livestock with them and pretended to sell the cattle, but they were really selling the *cone*. Being just kids and all, we didn't know anything about it because they were afraid the kids would eventually leave and go to the valley and spill the beans. And the kids did go. Only those who stayed to have their children here found out about the mine. The parents knew about it, but their children didn't. That was the rule. That's why she doesn't know anything about it. Ask her about the *cone*. She won't know a thing. She couldn't have children, so the older folks didn't tell her about it. They stuck to the rule even when the mine fell in. They did it because they thought the mine could be brought back and because that was the nature of our rule. She believes in fairy tales, the things they'd tell the kids. Sometime later, I once told her this has nothing to do with faith, because it didn't even matter anymore and because I was tired of her stories. Everything was over by then anyway. But she wouldn't hear of it. She says I betrayed our old faith. This ain't about faith! There used to be old faith in these parts that nobody knows much about anymore, whether it was Bogomils or just the folks believing in something they'd made up so they wouldn't have to give money to the collection plate. I heard both versions and nobody now knows for sure, least of all her. Only thing folks knew was that there was something and there was trouble with it, folks being persecuted on all sides, and then it was gone and nobody talked about it much. You could just keep quiet and pretend like you knew, which is what our folks did. They went out into the world, silent about their ways, and I really mean that—they kept to the shadows, silent, letting people think whatever they wanted. But our folks had something else in mind. Our folks would act strange when they went down among the rest of the people, so no one would think of them as their own. Our folks would say: Stay out of our business, don't marry us, don't talk to us more than necessary, stay away.... That was our forefathers' wish. That no one would want to have anything to do with us and no one would come up here out of fear of devilry. And everybody would think we were living up here because we're strange, and not because of the mine. And they'd return from faraway places carrying coins, loaded with all kinds of things, but cautious and following their own paths. And life was good here. And they were clever."

17

SOBOTKA CAME UP with a simple solution: he added Slavko's name to his mailbox and the door.

Sure enough, the next day Youry the Mailman appeared at Sobotka's door and said, "Okay, I can see this is where he lives."

"So the name was the only problem?" said Sobotka.

"A different address is written on the letters, but I can see that this is where he lives. I've been keeping track," Youry the Mailman explained.

He handed over a sizable bundle to Sobotka and said, "You give it to him, you're his housemate, it's not registered mail."

Out of curiosity, Sobotka asked, "How come you didn't give these letters to those relatives of his? They're also his housemates, aren't they?"

Youry the Mailman gave him a meaningful look and said, "First of all, they don't seem like such a reliable bunch. Second, and most important, they're not his housemates. That's not their address. They've never registered as living there. They have no documents on them. I asked them, they don't have anything. I reported them to the police."

"What did the police say?"

"Nothing. I don't get their logic. The only thing I can do is work alone. I've done my part."

"Yes, you have," said Sobotka.

"You betcha," he said. He had started to turn around when he decided to say, "You know, Mr. Engineer, people send so few letters these days that they have to be delivered. To tell you the truth, he's the only one who receives them, and he doesn't even want them. Get it? Like someone's playing a joke on me. He almost brought me to rock bottom, to tell you the truth. I've started pondering the meaninglessness. If I weren't so tough, I'd wonder… I'd wonder whether I should even exist. If I don't deliver everything that's been sent, where has this world gone? I don't know what's happened with letters. What do people do?"

"I don't know, either. But if there's one thing that works properly in this town, it's the mail," said Sobotka to soothe him.

"I work. I deliver bills. But nobody waits for the postman anymore, Mr. Engineer. I've always comported myself professionally, but I've also always been glad to see someone waiting for their mail. But now it's like I'm a parasite, like the bank's sending me. This has to stay between us because I'm a civil servant. I don't want it to seem like the state's whining and doesn't know what to do and ponders its meaninglessness. I usually don't talk like this, but I can't help it. Because I think I'll never deliver this many letters ever again. I have given you these letters because I'm compelled to, just so there's some meaning left. Now it's up to you. And what I told you, that should stay between us."

"It will. I promise."

"There you go. And I'm glad about the factory," said Youry the Mailman, and left.

Sobotka entered the house and opened the most recent letter, sent two months earlier:

I'm the only person who still writes letters. I don't know anyone else who does. I write them since you have no email address. I don't know if you have any address at all; actually, I don't know if you even exist anymore. I never hear from you, but you should write, fathers usually do, at least as a function—you are a function I imagine as a living body, but the function is actually more important than the body, at least to me, because I can't even remember what you look like anymore, I'm not sure I do. The images of people have all jumbled in my mind and we didn't bring any pictures with us in our hurry. Mom thought we'd be back in fifteen days. I only remember you waving there by the bus, a man in a trench coat, waving, a sad man in a sad trench coat, yellowish like a leaf on the ground. You are the man in the trench coat, faces change; I remember when the face of the man in the trench coat started to fade. Every time I'd see a man in a trench coat that was yellowish like a leaf on the ground, his face would appear later in my dreams and memories instead of yours, the face of a random passerby, the face of a dismal man leering at me with lust on the street, like he's leering at a high school girl who's staring at him. One of them fucked me once in a public bathroom, I let him. It was disgustingly exciting.

Oh no, this one's as crazy as her old man, thought Sobotka. He grabbed a beer from the fridge and lit a cigarette. Now what? It would be better for Slavko not to read this. He must have felt something, not accepting his mail. Sobotka kept on:

I wonder why I'm writing. I'm writing because I know you won't read it, so I can tell you everything. You don't exist, you're like God. You're only an address, tucked away on a geographical map in a territory jotted with tiny borders. Nothing but an address, you're a father, a shell, an empty place where letters are transmitted, an address, an enigma, a father, a real one, not like these fake fathers I fuck by accident. Oh, don't worry, I've learned how to use condoms, it's just that sometimes . . . never mind. But let me tell you about my studies—surely that's what you're most anxious to hear about—they're coming along, they're coming along just fine, don't you worry, Dad, both of my majors, our language and theirs. I'm all about languages, what else? There are no solid points in my life, I think that's definitive for me. I have no property, and I think that when you've got no property, you can't work with math, although I used to be really good at it. Mom used to say, you got that from him. I really hated it when she said that, you're so disgusting with your math. Mom used to brag about the math; I guess she thought it was the same as being smart, but when you've got nothing, there's no point to working with numbers, you should understand that—maybe you don't because you're a mathematician. You used to own something, I guess, so this principle is instilled in your mind, you must be counting into the void, you probably don't even read. I've thought about mathematicians, I've studied that particular species, fucked them, they were pitifully grateful, but I'm all about languages. You know, they can't believe I'm real, I'm celestial to them, that's a good thing; I'll marry a mathematician when I no longer have a place to go, before I kill myself or simply walk away, so make sure I'm not there and that I'm not out of order.

"Damn, she's completely insane, even more than he is," said Sobotka aloud.

He stood up and looked out the window at nothing in particular. He was disturbed, he thought of his daughters and all that had happened. He went to the pantry and poured himself rakija.

He returned to the table, and the letter:

Once, when I was at the hospital, okay, to be frank, in an asylum...

"There she goes," said Sobotka. "For fuck's sake!"

... I was with a mathematician. What a relationship, see-through, made of nothing, ah, he even fell in love with nothing, I felt so sorry for him. The guy was into higher math, loved zero, my zero, a quasi-zero that multiplies by zero. He loved, a strange young man, actually

an old man . . . he was young but old, which really is the worst part. But this guy had an excuse, a genetic one, he was going extinct like Leopardi, getting old a little bit faster, living in faster time. You're not interested in this? But hey, I can write whatever I please, Daddy-O, because you don't exist, although I learned to write with you, by writing to you, that is, to me inside of you, Daddy-O. And I learned there's no sentence without me, there is no book without me, because you know I enrolled at this university to write. I was planning on writing poetry, only poetry, and it turns out I'm writing letters, letters to you, you who have been fucking me up for years now. And you're not there, you're so poetic, like a trench coat, like bus windows, like dirty plush seats, my darling, I love you so much, Daddy-O.

"This is fucking awful," muttered Sobotka.

You're so wonderful, wonderful. You're wonderful like failure, like the most wonderful failure, like the pleasure of failing, like a model, like nothing. You are my style, there's a song that goes something like that, of course, what else are songs supposed to be about if not you, my dad. Oh, I can't live without you, ah, help me, help me, you old function, don't stagger, don't limp, don't screw around, be it, Daddy-O, don't fuck around, be it, untouchable, be it, be it, at least feign, reign, you feigning godhead. Fatherhead, that's you. Is that a word? Fatherhead. I've never heard it before. A fake godhead. It places you right where you are and shouldn't exist. There is no fatherhead. But there is fatherhead. He's the only one, as far as I could see. My daddy. My fatherhead. What else should I tell you? You're the reason for my rapture, you might not even know. How could you, when you don't read? But my book was published, a book-book. Do you know what a book is, you goddamn mathematician? My book was published and it happens to be about you, about me and the leftover of leftovers. Critics-critics write about it and they nicely praise-praise it. I've become a waitress, an exposer and blamer, that's the news, the book-book. I should've started the letter with it but I didn't because I'm a waitress, ha ha, who's not out from the order, you motherfucker!

The letter ended there. It was signed: *Nedra*.

18

HE DIDN'T RECOGNIZE them until he got closer to the entrance and heard Kardan's voice. He needed a little time to catch his breath. There were three other guys with Kardan. A black Audi was parked on the side of the road.

"These men want to talk to the director with no appointment," said the watchman in alarm.

"Whoa! Wait, we know each other," said Kardan. "What's new with you, kid?"

Erol was thrown off balance for a second; voices from his past had the power to bring everything back. He nearly fell for it and was a *kid again*.

"What do you want?" asked Erol sharply.

"Oh, come on, you're not even gonna say hi? Did all this self-management go to your head?" said Kardan, slapping Erol arrogantly on the back.

Erol felt cold inside and his shivering turned into a strong desire to punch Kardan in his leering face. But they were definitely armed, he knew.

"You read the newspapers too much," said Erol through clenched teeth.

"We read too much? You got a lot of likes so we thought we'd come take a look."

"So what do you want?"

"You do know that this factory was supposed to be Ragan's?"

"No, I didn't," said Erol.

"First of all, it would've been polite to ask. Second of all, you bringing communism back to this place is something we can't let happen as a matter of principle."

"And a matter of money," added one of Kardan's pals, setting off laughter.

"What communism? We're restoring the factory, what's wrong with that?" said Erol.

"No entrance fee. That's what's wrong."

Sobotka also appeared at the gate just then, along with a few workers.

"Something going on here?" asked Sobotka.

"No, we're just seeing how everything's coming along."

Sobotka looked at Erol.

"They're Ragan's men," Erol said.

The workers standing next to Sobotka seemed to move away slightly.

"What do you want?" said Sobotka.

Kardan lit a cigarette and said, "To talk to Mr. Manager. Just to make his acquaintance."

"He's not here."

"An old trick."

"This won't get you inside," said Sobotka.

Erol thought what a weighty sentence this was, but he couldn't come up with a lighter one. He looked around. The workers around

Sobotka—four of them—now seemed to be standing firmly again. He looked at Kardan and his men. What were they going to do?

Kardan was silent for a moment before saying, "Protecting your little Mr. Manager?"

"This is the factory entrance. This is where the workers enter," said Sobotka.

Kardan laughed forcibly. "The workers, eh? A force to be reckoned with." He studied Sobotka for a while before studying all of them. "Full of yourselves? We'll sweep the floor with you."

Then he turned and headed to the car, his shoulders twitching as if his trench coat were uncomfortable.

Erol was standing in a room where folk music was streaming around him. Actually, he'd just entered. He somehow found himself there— at least, that was how he felt, as if he'd dropped into the scene. A man with a patch over one eye told him, "Your father's in there." He was referring to the next room, where the music was coming from. Erol walked in the way a movie camera would enter, he surveyed everything like the Terminator. And then, in this hall, at the table on a raised platform, the same one where the bride, the groom, the best man, and the maid of honor usually sit, he saw his mother, who looked tired, as if she really was really sleepy. Next to her sat Ragan, who looked at him like the most obliging waiter and told him, "My son, my boy, my scion, my child."

Erol took a step back, as if trying to avoid a stench coming his way.

"I'm glad you came. As well you should have," said Ragan. "I'm your father, and it's not every day that your father dies."

He said this and then started dying, with pathos, as if imitating paintings depicting Christ. He pretended being feeble, the victim; he was dying while trying to compel Erol to show his love. And Erol did show it by leaning over the dying man, at one horrible moment, and receiving a kiss on the lips.

Erol woke up trying to catch his breath. He felt as if he were choking, as if his lungs were filled with smoke, his mind racing the whole time, You are not my father, you are not my father.

Then he got up, went to the bathroom, and washed his face. He examined his face in the mirror.

"Hey, these guys are armed," said Nikola.

"Okay, I'm on my way," said Oleg. "I'll find men for that."

"It's not just them," said Nikola. "Our guys are, too."

"Ours?"

"The workers."

"Really?"

"Sobotka's and Erol's men, they went home to grab their guns. Apparently they have them. No idea where they got them from—the war, I guess."

"Right, been there, done that. Did you give them permission?"

"Yes. I mean, if they'd asked I would have. But this was their initiative. What was I to say? If they'd let the men in, the thugs would have humiliated me or blackmailed me or whatever. This way, the bad guys are gone. But I don't think they, the bad guys, can give way, either, now. They have their reputation to consider."

"Okay, I'm on my way."

After this conversation, Nikola fidgeted with his phone and came across Šeila's number again. What am I doing? he said to himself. She's the last person I need now.

He hadn't mentioned anything about her to Oleg. He kept this story for himself, although he felt a bit guilty for not mentioning the American to Oleg.

Why? he wondered. Am I protecting her, or what?

Sobotka was sitting at a table. On it lay a gun and a sheet of paper. He stared at the paper, edging closer to it, leaning over it like he was about to pounce on an enemy. The paper had "Dear daughter" written on it, and more was needed.

Dear daughter,
I've been crazy, all these years.
That's why I haven't answered your letters or read them.
I

Sobotka knew it was no good, so he crumpled the paper, got up, and brought over more paper.

Dear daughter,
I've been having some psychological problems, for quite a few years now, I don't know if you've heard. Maybe you shouldn't insult me like you did. I know you are angry, but I haven't had things easy, either.

Sobotka looked at what he'd written. What he wanted to do was pacify the situation so she could respond with a normal letter that he could then read to Slavko. Sobotka had to admit to himself, however, that the whole plan was somewhat dizzying. But what else could he have come up with? There was no point in showing Slavko the letters, but if he received a nicer one, could he perhaps read it to him in a soothing voice?

He was hoping Youry the Mailman would not run into Slavko and ask him if he'd received the letters. In that case, he'd have to calm them both down separately. Slavko would be furious and Youry the Mailman would probably want his letters back.

For a second, he thought about how this would look from an outside perspective: a man sitting at the table, writing a letter to someone else's daughter, afraid of the mailman. Ugh, he thought, it's as if all of these lunatics have pulled me into their madness.

But he needed to do something. He couldn't just read the letters and put them away in a drawer. This daughter of Slavko's was not doing well, she might even kill herself. If she only realized what kind of psychological state her father was in, maybe then she wouldn't feel so bad or hate him so much.

Maybe.

Sobotka stared straight ahead. He could not believe he hadn't thought of this years ago.

He grabbed some beer from the fridge and drank down the whole glass, slowly.

My dear daughter,

I don't know why I haven't written to you sooner. That time when I visited you, everything was wrong; I couldn't talk to you at all, nothing felt right, not who I was or who your mom was, or who we all were. I came home a man crushed, I almost really did kill myself, that's how terrifying everything was. Then somehow I decided to forget about it, that seemed the only way to keep myself in one piece. Okay, maybe not in one piece, because I blotted you out of my mind; that isn't being in one piece, that's like when you turn off the light in one part of your house and then it stays dark. I'm saying, not in one piece, but at least alive. That was my way of keeping myself sane, I realize this now. I realize it now because there is an even tougher case in front of me. It's Slavko, you may remember him. You weren't as small as Viktoria then. You probably remember a lot more; you're probably more upset and in more pain, so that's why you resent me more. There, so you know that's how it happened, that I put things out of my mind just to survive. It wasn't a decision, at least not a conscious one, things simply happened that way, like a sort of necessity, as if the brain had a mind of its own and blew a few fuses, like when a system overloads. My explanation is very technical. Don't hold that against me, but that's how I see it—as if I overloaded and my brain shut down certain parts to prevent everything from going up in flames. Now I see what this was like for Slavko—he blew even more fuses, probably one of the main ones. But okay, that's not important. Please don't hold this digression against me, but it's a way I'm able to explain things to myself, too; until now I, myself, hadn't understood why I haven't been writing to you, everything was in the dark for me, and only now did I see this when I told his daughter. . . . Okay, that's not important, this is difficult to explain, but in a nut-shell—his daughter is very angry with him, so somehow I realized you could be angry, and how that would look, sure, she's headstrong just like him, but, to keep this short, I realize now that I'm not so very different, even for me, who thought I was so normal. But everyone blew a fuse, everyone has a few rooms still in the dark, we're all a bit crazy from what happened yet never passed. Just because something happened doesn't mean it is over. Time goes on, they say, but what's time got to do with the fact that some things are stuck, frozen, it's only us who leave, move on through time, but the things remain, they stay stuck, and you have to go back to the past, like in a dream, to touch them, to unfreeze them like the machines in the factory. Some things work themselves out, but those are the things of forgetting, the ones you're able to forget. How can I possibly forget you or you forget me? No way. I want to reach back and touch you at that moment in the past when we went our separate ways, where you stand at a crossroads, frozen, so that you can begin moving forward, because I've begun to move, and I'd like to be alive again for you.

Dearest daughter, don't think I'm lying or that I'm making excuses.

I've realized this now and I want to fix things. I don't know how. I don't know any other way than to tell it to you straight, by writing this letter. We all have defects, and everyone has their own things they don't have a place for, so they leave them in the dark, in those dark rooms. There, that's what I wanted to say. I could talk more about this, but not right now, this took a lot out of me. Viktoria told me you're pregnant, maybe even close to your due date, and I'd like, just so you know, I'd like to wish you every happiness, whether you're angry with me or not. That's all.

Best of luck!

Dad

He looked over the letter again. There was a lump in his throat. He felt he had a daughter again, that he was talking with her, that something lost was being forged anew. He could thank Nedra, Slavko's oddball, for that.

Yes, she cleared a path for me to be so honest with Jasmina. How strange, thought Sobotka. Now I'm in her debt. He should have written a letter to her as well. But how? That letter would be even more complicated than this one. Or would it be simpler?

He decided to think about this some more. Maybe in the next few days. Now he had to catch his breath. He folded the letter for Jasmina and slipped it into the envelope he'd bought for Slavko's daughter.

He gazed at the envelope: what a swap!

He realized how happy he was about all this. He took a sip of beer, lit a cigarette.

He sat there, looking at the envelope. Everything is evolving now, he thought. Everything being rebuilt.

He looked at that gun on the table.

Who cares—let them come, he thought.

19

AFTER THEY'D INVENTORIED the new shipment of material in the storage shed, Branoš and Erol sat in the sun on the front steps with beers, looking out at the mountains. Branoš wanted to find out as much as possible about Ragan's gang, which prompted Erol to tell his story, and while he was telling it he stopped at one part, then continued, only to return to the same moment again.

"There was something in the conversation with Ragan in the apartment. When he said I reminded him of someone and then, the way he looked at me when I said I had my mother's last name. . . . The way he asked about my father. . . . I can't figure him out."

"You can't figure him out?"

"It has nothing to do with this situation. But there was something about that conversation, something unclear, which keeps bugging me. Later, when I was reading the play, *Hamlet*, that feeling kept coming back. I have that book, Sobotka gave it to me. I've read it every now and then ever since."

"*Hamlet*, eh?"

Erol nodded and drank his beer.

Branoš looked at him sideways and shook his head. "You should have told that to the reporter. I wonder what he would have written then."

"Please tell me, how did you manage to get your university degree?" Erol asked Branoš, as if he'd always wanted to ask him that. "How come the war didn't get in the way?"

"Long story."

"So, brother, shorten it."

Then they noticed the watchman circling the factory's grounds. He yelled, "Aren't you two leaving?"

"Want to grab another beer at the Lagoon?" said Branoš.

"Let's go," said Erol.

"My old man, Arman, he was against the war, but he wasn't like all those others who didn't see it coming," Branoš said as they settled onto the barstools. "He used to say, ever since the war began up north: this disturbance is moving toward us. That's how he used to talk, he didn't say 'war,' but 'disturbance,' because the only evening news he followed closely was the weather report—we had to keep the noise down for that part. Oh yes, I remember now, he also favored the phrase 'major disturbance,' like when they say, 'Later this evening a major frontal disturbance will move across the region.' He would, supposedly by chance, watch the political parts of the news as well and say, 'There, you can see what a major disturbance is. . . . Soon it will be frontal.' Those last days before the war, he said to me, 'Go pack your things, son, say your goodbyes, I worked it out with our cousins up north.' I protested, the war wasn't at its worst at that point, just a few skirmishes. Everyone else thought the same until the last second, and he told me, 'Don't think this shit will pass just because you want it to.' That's my last memory of him.

"And so, okay, I go to my cousins in a town, not a city, not a village, in the plains. The war is partway there, but the major frontal disturbance has already passed them by, and my cousins take me in as their own; they take care of me, and they enroll me in school as a refugee, and one way or another I finish my senior year of high school, and then comes summer. I start thinking what I'll do now, because the war is in full swing here, so I couldn't come home. Then one day they tell me, 'Cousin Benjo's building a new house and we'll be lending a hand.' So I tag along and they work all day, and so do I, of course. I work hard, because my cousins are all I have and I want to show them I'm part of the team.... I didn't even know Benjo before this, because he was my cousins' cousin, and I'm feeling good about how my network's expanding, this helps me feel safer. Benjo slaps me on the back, he likes me, and when the time comes to leave, my cousins say, 'Why not stay at Benjo's tonight?' What could I say? 'Sure, I guess.'"

"I figure I've overstayed my welcome. But Benjo is glad to let me stay.

"I already know the work on the house will continue at Benjo's. And so it does the next day, and the day after, and the day after that, because it's a sizable house he's building. He'd slap me on the back, tell me he doesn't know what he'd do without me. My mother's cousins' cousin, Benjo offers me food and drink, and so we work in the heat every day like two friends, like father and son, only his son is over the border, working, and I'm not his friend or his son. I'm just there. So Benjo sends me here and sends me there, do this, and this and this, then we eat and drink, and Benjo marvels at how strong I've become while helping him. No wonder, I bust my ass all day long, and those cousins of mine never show their faces again. I understand that I'm Benjo's project now, and Benjo is in charge of me. That's why Benjo sometimes gets mad if I rest a bit too long, and the house is getting built too slowly. We work from one day to the next. This could go on for a year, I figure. This is the summer when I turn eighteen; then, luckily, one day Benjo says we'll stop for a bit, because he doesn't have the money for building material, I hang out there in the plains for a few days, because Benjo has given me a little pocket change, but only when I ask him for it—because he's short of cash. I spend it all in a flash, although I manage to save a bit. I just lie around in the plains, don't have money even for coffee, much less to go out with a girl. No money, no nothing. I become quieter without money or anything of my own, and one day one of Benjo's neighbors comes over and asks Benjo, 'Can you lend him to me tomorrow?'

"He doesn't ask me, he asks Benjo, and Benjo stands there for a moment, looks at me, and ways, 'No can do, let him rest.'

I see on Benjo's face that he thinks he's being gracious, such a big man. He looks over at me as though I should be thanking him. But I just look at him from my body like a cat. I want to call my mom and dad and cry, but I know the phone lines are down. Then I realize my dad will say the disturbance won't pass if I just wait, so I pack my things and leave Benjo's that night. He would later say how he was absolutely baffled that I'd left without a goodbye.... That's what my cousins told me when I called them later from a refugee center, which took me a day and a night to reach on foot. They were disappointed with my behavior, too, and they'd been worried about where I could have gotten to and said, 'Okay, that's your choice, if you prefer living at the refugee center over being with us.' I'd offended them, but their door was still open to me.... This was all very upsetting, and I even thought about going back, but something stopped me: the image of the man asking Benjo if he could borrow me, and me being afraid Benjo might just say yes—and that little spark in my brain, my little spark of rebellion—because things around you are lining up, so it looks as if your rebellion will come across like a slap in the face and bad behavior, because your servitude is now somehow normal, and inch by inch, you've gone along with it, and you've fallen into an altogether different logic and status, you must be living with a different status if someone can ask your host to borrow you. If you were to stand up at that point and say, 'What the fuck is this?' you'd be starting a small revolution, but you can't be so rude, and especially if you've been good and silent and obedient till then, this would be a little impolite.

"So that's how it went down, and when I hear someone's a slave or a servant somewhere, I know how these things go.

"But never mind, I had a little of the spark left in me, so I fled to the refugee center, although things weren't coming up roses there, either. They made me work there, too, unloading this or that. I carried my fair share of coffins as well, because every time a grandmother died in the camp, they'd grab me and three Gypsies to carry the old woman and lower her into the ground. We became something of a team for that, so even now, when I see a death notice for a grandmother taped to a streetlamp today, it gets to me, and at night I dream they want me to carry the coffin and I'm back in that life as if nothing ever happened after that. In short, I was at the cemetery a lot. I noticed bands at other funerals, and I started to go to the funerals on my own, silently singing along with them until I learned the songs. Then I came with a guitar once, which I'd borrowed from someone, and I told them, 'I know the songs and I can play the guitar.' Because I'd had a band in high school, a punk band, the metal kids got on our nerves, but fuck it, it was the times. . . . One of the graveyard singers told me, 'Good, we thought you were from the tax ministry, checking up on how much we earn, or that you were a disgruntled customer for whom we didn't sing nicely enough.' They were regular jokers—because when you're at the cemetery all the time, you have to joke around. So they told me they'd call me if one of them couldn't make it. And, it just so happened they were a man short. Little by little, I began to sing with them—I was paid less than they were, but that was fine, too. First, I sang with them for a year, I bought a guitar, and then I made some connections and went to the big city, figuring that there had to be more customers there. I was right, although there were also more singers, but I continued to put in the effort, got books and sheet music, learned some old songs, not many folks made such an effort, so I really was sought after and popular. A year or two passed. . . . Those cousins of mine helped as well with some paperwork. They were glad I'd made it, and when Benjo died of a stroke just after having finished the house, they called me to sing for him."

"Really? Did they pay you?"

"You can't ask your cousins to pay!"

"Ha ha, but wait, I asked you about the university."

"Well, those were my preparations for the university, Erol. First, I had to not become a slave, and then I had to realize I didn't want to sing in graveyards all my life. Only then did I enroll in engineering school, while working. I was still preparing for my last exams before graduation when I worked in Afghanistan."

20

OLEG PARKED IN front of the vast house. Nikola was surprised to see he wasn't alone.

Oleg hugged him and said, "This is Lipša."

"Glad to see you again," she said.

Nikola had heard the name before, her face was familiar, but he couldn't place it.

Oleg added, "She worked in that café where we stopped on our way here. She just quit."

"Oh," said Nikola.

"Let's have a drink!" said Oleg.

After they sat down, Oleg announced, "I've hired Lipša as my personal assistant!"

Then he laughed, and Lipša looked at him and rolled her eyes at Nikola.

She said, "Don't ask me. It's his idea."

Oleg got a bit more serious and added, "I need a secretary here, and we need someone who'll sniff around town to find out about these gangsters and things. She's from around here, and she knows people there as well, from their town. She used to work there."

Oh, it's important that she has hands-on experience, Nikola almost said. It was pretty clear to him that Oleg had offered the job to Lipša so they could fuck, which, he wagered, they'd already done.

Thinly veiled prostitution, he thought. It was clear to him that Oleg was in drinking mode again. He probably wasn't carrying drugs on him. But, thought Nikola, his new secretary could surely get them for him. She knows people.

"Okay," he said to Oleg. "You're the boss."

"She's not just a bartender. She studied law," said Oleg, as if reading his mind.

"I kind of dropped that, fuck it," she added, looking at Nikola. "I'd really like to clear the air right away. This is his idea. He said he needed a secretary. The part he said afterward, he added that later. I don't want that."

"Fine, relax," said Oleg. "You work as a secretary and I'll explain what that entails."

"You're a bonehead," she said, shaking her head with a half-smile.

Nikola watched them and didn't know what to say.

"Can't you see she's a real firecracker? She's just what we need," said Oleg, turning to her. "It's no big deal. I'll just be asking you what you've heard. You tell me, as my secretary, in passing, over coffee. A simple conversation."

"That ain't simple," she said, lighting a cigarette.

"Okay, it's a business meeting. Business communication."

"Wow, look at me now, business communication." she said and turned to Nikola: "Are you following this?"

"A little," said Nikola once he realized she'd been talking to him, and smiled.

"Fine. Now it's settled," said Oleg. "I wanted to introduce you two. Lipša will go home now, on foot. She says it's better if I don't drive her there."

"Yes, it's better this way. People will say I'm whoring myself out," she said. "Which isn't so far from the truth."

"She's a bit crazy," Oleg said to Nikola.

"Well, see you later, alligators!" said Lipša, and she left.

Oleg saw her out.

Coming back to the table, Oleg said, "Okay, I know what you're thinking. So we fucked—it happened. One salary here or there doesn't matter. But she could really be useful. And even if she isn't, let her do some communicating for me. I think she's good enough to scare people off over the phone. She'll also be useful breaking the ice when we're dining with morons. You see how ditzy she is. That relaxes people. I'll really have to do my fair share of communicating. We have to deal with this Ragan without conflict. That's the last thing we need. We don't want to draw any more attention to ourselves."

"Okay," said Nikola.

"Really," Oleg continued. "That's how I started out: some guy asked me to break the ice at a dinner as well. It's important."

"You don't have to explain," said Nikola. "I get it."

"What do you do for fun around here? Got anyone?" said Oleg.

"Hmm," Nikola choked briefly, "there was something . . . But not anymore."

"Hey, come on, what happened?"

"Something with a woman here, but then we had a fight."

"About what, man?" said Oleg, laughing. "What did you talk about?"

"Oh, nothing."

"Are you sad about it?"

"Nah."

"You don't fool me. Go ahead, call her now. Ask her out to dinner."

Nikola shook his head and said, "Sobotka's coming over. We have to talk with him. By the way, what does this Lipša know?"

"Nothing. We've reopened the factory, the mobsters want protection money. End of story. She doesn't care about the details."

Sobotka arrived shortly after that and Oleg found out all about how things were going with the turbine construction, and they discussed the realities of completing the first turbine by the end of the year.

"We'll do everything we can to make the deadline. You betcha, as Youry the Mailman would say."

Oleg kept an eye on Sobotka—the man seemed stable, a far cry from the wreck he'd met in the dive. Oleg also noticed how Sobotka was quite comfortable around Nikola, but not sure how to act around him.

When they came to the topic of Ragan, Sobotka said, "A lot has changed, the whole situation. Truth be told, I've changed, too. I've come to my senses and I can thank you for that. Just so you know, we're ready to defend the factory. We weren't ready when the system was changing, but we'll defend it this time around."

Oleg nodded and said, "Glad to hear it"—although there was something about Sobotka's tone he didn't like: as if it really was their factory, not his.

He decided not to give this any more thought. It was to his benefit that they were so gung-ho. He only had to deliver the two turbines. After that he'd pull out. Manufacturing made no sense. Dammit, it'll be difficult to explain this to them, he thought.

He obviously seemed worried, so Sobotka said, "You have no idea how popular you are around here. If those dirtbags show up, the workers will defend you."

"Really?"

"One kid, Erol, is in charge of defense. He'll look after you whenever necessary."

"And I thought I'd have to organize this, but you beat me to the punch," smiled Oleg. "Still, do you need more people at the factory?"

"Well, ten to fifteen more wouldn't hurt."

"Fifteen. We'll put out an ad right away."

When Sobotka left, Oleg told Nikola, "It's not that I mind, but it seems as if we're unnecessary here."

"Look, I told you over the phone", said Nikola. "Stop them if you want."

Oleg thought for a bit, and then said, "It's easier this way."

"Self-organizing," said Nikola.

"Right."

"You thought this would be a joke?"

Well it is, thought Oleg, but he kept that to himself. Instead, he said, "Got any hard stuff? Beer sometimes makes me depressed."

"Only Jäger."

Although he didn't know why, the last conversation he'd had with Veber played back in Sobotka's head as he walked home, about the time he pulled the old man out of a makeshift prison during the war. Veber had been held there for no reason, which was worse than actually being arrested. If Sobotka hadn't heard about it, those young men might have executed him purely out of spite, as an old Commie. But they released him after Sobotka pulled rank and they saw he was with two others.

Emaciated and limping, the old man invited him home for a drink. As they were coming in, Sobotka noticed bullet holes in the walls, although the house was far away from the front.

"Who did this?" he asked.

"I don't know them. Young. Probably thought I screwed up their lives."

They entered the cold house.

"You probably thought the same once, too," said Veber. "The strike leader sticking up for the old director, who'd have thought, eh?"

"I had nothing against you. It was the times."

"You don't have a mustache like that Pole anymore—fed up?"

"Are you pulling my leg?"

"Laughing is all we've got left. I was serious my entire life, but there's no reason for this anymore. I'm a wanderer like our Slavko, just in a different way."

Veber then added that his son, luckily, had left ages ago. "He couldn't bear being in my shadow," as he put it, and Veber's wife ended up with his son when the war started. "She's there now, so we'll die apart," he said.

"My family left, too," said Sobotka.

"Ha, me and Wałęsa. . . . We've stayed to ponder."

It was odd for Sobotka to see Veber laugh. He was a completely different man. Without the status that had been an integral part of his persona, he was just a man from a bygone time.

But his eyes were more alive, intimate, without the shadow he used to have in his gaze, the shadow of everything he represented. It was as if for all those years his gaze was not his own, but the gaze of what he represented. Sobotka thought he'd known this man, but now someone different was before him, as if the snow had melted away, and the sun was scorching his bare head.

Am I like that as well? Sobotka asked himself. I'm without what I was before as well—naked—maybe that's why the old man is laughing at me.

Veber took out a bottle of cognac, unopened, because, as he said, he never drank alone.

Sobotka then took out a bag and started to roll a joint. Veber asked, "What in the world is that?"

"Pot, Comrade Director," said Sobotka.

"You've started doing drugs, Wałęsa?"

"The younger guys give it to me. It relieves stress. They grow it."

"What sort of a war are you waging!" declared Veber. "We were more serious once."

"Revolutionaries. Not that you've laughed much since."

"True," said the old man, "I missed my chance. Can't make up for that now."

"That's life."

"Can you believe," said the old man, "that for some twenty-odd years I didn't drink? Not a drop. Hey, twenty years. Sober as a church mouse. How to make up for that? You can't! You can't make up for that!"

Sobotka laughed while smoking the joint. "That's what you think about?"

"A man would live differently if he knew the future. Especially if he knew there was no future. In the times when I had a reason, I wasn't happy. I was a sourpuss, worrying about things that might go wrong, as if I could prevent that by keeping a straight face."

"You're not happy with what you did?"

"I was a soldier of life. I could have done all that without being a soldier of life. I had some valid excuses, excuses that would allow me to withdraw into myself, to disappear into the system, to stop existing."

"I thought we were going to talk about politics. About what's happening now."

"Well, this here is not politics, it's just a mess. When you were on strike, it had already become a mess. We could do nothing more, and you had no politics of your own. Do you remember, Wałęsa?"

"We had nowhere to go."

"You had no politics. Then along came these things—nation and religion, but that's also not politics, man. How can it be politics if it's given to you by birth? That's biology."

"I guess I don't understand politics."

"Bah, this has nothing to do with politics!"

"You still think you were right?"

"I'm not saying who's right or not. But we're the ones who industrialized this country. It used to be a wasteland. And it will be one again."

"What about political freedom? How were we ever supposed to become something when you treated us like children? You can't do this, you can't do that—"

"Well, fuck it, we didn't know any better. We gave the people some freedom, more than any other socialist system ever did, but you're right. I still have no idea what we were supposed to do, but something should've been done differently. This way, you were completely gullible, like children. Living in a bubble. Then you go outside and believe anything any bastard says. They fuck you from behind like an idiot."

Sobotka laughed. Before the war, he'd never tried weed and would never have thought this possible—he was high and talking to Veber, who also seemed relaxed in his own way.

"Have you ever tried weed, Director?"

The old man shook his head and carried on, saying, "My Wałęsa, it's not so much that you saved me, it's that, as I see it, you're the only one left. Well done, you did it again—you've given me something to think about. You didn't want to join the Party, I remember that, and there were so many who were willing to. What did we do to lose you?"

"It's because you guys couldn't call strikes."

"You were right to call the strike. Just so you know."

"I'm an engineer, Director. It's all over now. When the war ends, I'll leave."

"I'll leave, and you'll stay," said Veber.

A few months later Sobotka attended the old man's very, very modest funeral.

Dear Nedra,

I've been thinking about what to do for a long time now. First of all, I would like to apologize for reading your letters addressed to my friend Slavko. It was a matter of circumstance, since he is not able to read. And since he is living with me, I've been taking the mail delivered to him. Trust me, it was impossible for him to read the letters, because psychologically he is in a very peculiar state and was in even worse shape before. He walked around town for years with his dog, never communicating with anyone, not even with me. People thought he was crazy, which is sort of true.

I know you are angry at him, and you think he is selfish and that he didn't think about you at all. Maybe it was selfish of him to lose his mind, but he had no other way out. He is much better now, but still in his own world. He built a wall and only allows a few things in. I will try and talk to him about you when I see him doing better. I don't know if that brings you any comfort or what it will mean to you. I couldn't show him your letters or talk to him about them, because they are not fit for those purposes. I'm not saying you should do this or that or anything, it's just that if you could send a letter that's more normal, or maybe a postcard, it would be easier for me to show him something like that. I don't know if he is the one you need, because he isn't someone who would be able to behave like a father should. If anything, he is more the one who needs taking care of. Yes, he has started to work at the factory again, and he is doing all sorts of things. He cleans up after himself and everything, but I still can't tell what exactly is going on in his mind. He's been living at my place for a while, and some cousins of yours are at his house, cousins who have not been kind to him and took over the whole house for themselves. I'm writing you this so you know of the situation, because that house is yours, too, and you are, except him, the sole heir. In one of your letters, you wrote that you have nothing, so, you see, that's not the case after all. Maybe it is not worth much in terms of money, but still, the house exists. Keep this in mind.

*   That's all from me.*

*   Sincerely,*

*   Sobotka*

21

THEY WERE SITTING at the bar in the Blue Lagoon. Branoš was telling Sobotka a story but then realized his companion was paying no attention. Sobotka was smiling dreamily, nodding and drinking. He seemed like he was gazing into himself with an odd glow, like a poignant child.

Nikola also noticed this and whispered to Branoš, "What's up with him?"

Branoš shrugged, turned toward Sobotka, and said, for the sake of saying something, "This rakija of his is not bad."

He was referring to the homemade plum brandy that the owner, Rafo, had been bragging about, calling it his weekend special. Sobotka only nodded in return.

Rafo was bragging about the marketing strategies he'd learned in Germany.

"You always have to have an *Angebot*, a special offer," he said.

"Yeah, that's right, nothing without an *Angebot*."

"No. Without an *Angebot*, you're an amateur. I see them, opening bars and—"

At that moment, Sobotka exclaimed, "A round for everyone. On me!"

"You celebrating?" Nikola said.

"Yes!" said Sobotka sharply.

He did not feel like explaining that he'd become a grandfather. This was sort of an odd thing for him to say out loud. Or it just seemed that it meant he would then have to tell a really long story.

Earlier, Viktoria had sent him a text: "Another girl in the family. Jasmina is doing well. We've been swimming, although the sea's still cold. But we're used to it. Christina sends her regards."

This Christina kept sending her regards, which confused him, but he decided not to dwell on it.

He called Jasmina's cell. She didn't pick up. He thought she must have been exhausted from the birthing so he sent her a congratulatory text.

He had just received an answer: "Thank you. Jasmina."

Before the text's arrival, it felt hypocritical to celebrate, as if he'd be celebrating something he was only imagining was his to celebrate, something that didn't acknowledge him as being a part of it. You can't have a granddaughter if you don't have a daughter, he'd thought. But now it felt right for him to buy everyone drinks.

He clinked glasses with Nikola, Branoš, Oleg, Lipša, Erol—everyone within reach.

"Friends, I'm happy! If I die tomorrow, I will die a happy man!" he said, without explanation.

"C'mon, stop fucking around!" Oleg said. "You can't die tomorrow. That's not what the plan says."

They toasted.

Everybody loved Oleg, maybe even more than they loved Nikola. Perhaps because he drank with more fervor and eloquence. He kept buying everyone drinks and every day was like a holiday with him, so much so that Nikola had to keep prodding him to cool it.

The previous night, back at their apartment, Nikola had said, "You can't keep getting them drunk, they have to work tomorrow."

"But they do work. Even harder than we deserve."

"Okay, but don't say that in front of them. They'll start slacking off."

"Ha ha. Them, slacking off? They're working as if they were the owners. I was right, wasn't I?" said Oleg drunkenly. "The country's in crisis, yet we're working. You have to celebrate that!"

"Yes, yes," said Nikola quietly. "But we mustn't mess things up now with all this drinking."

"Too bad I can't give them everything," Oleg whispered, as if bad luck were preventing him from doing so. "But I'm going to, someday."

"What are you going to give them?"

"Everything!" said Oleg drunkenly. "You've seen how much they love me. And I don't deserve it at all. . . . Fuck."

"You know," Nikola said, looking at Oleg, "sometimes I really don't get you."

"Like that would be of much use to you."

People thought of Oleg as a bit mysterious, a well-respected oddball, and Nikola was concerned about him. At times he appeared to be bright and cheerful, his eyes shining as if there was no tomorrow, and then he would look as if there were something chasing after him.

In any case, Oleg had completely disregarded his instructions about "moderate intimacy" and "keeping a polite distance." When Nikola warned him, which happened mostly when he was already drunk, Oleg answered, "The organizer reserves the right to make changes to the event program."

Now, talking loudly so the whole bar could hear, Oleg declared, "We're drinking, but we're not slacking off!"

The drinks Sobotka had bought were now in everyone's hands. At least the weekend began tomorrow. Nikola didn't care. Let them drink. Then Nikola noticed Šeila come in. She was not alone. There was a man with her, and Nikola knew right away that this was the same guy, the American.

Sobotka also noticed Šeila and started to wave to her as if seeing a member of his own family. She seemed hesitant for a moment, because she'd noticed Nikola, but then she came over.

"Šeila!" Sobotka said. "It's as if you knew!"

"What?" she said.

"Our Jasmina had a baby today!"

Sobotka hugged her as if she were Jasmina, or at least his connection to Jasmina. She suddenly found herself in the center of all his joy. She was also glad to hear this news from afar, this virtual bond with the past.

"What are you having, Šeila? You and your friend," asked Sobotka.

Šeila explained to Alex that this was the father of her childhood best friend, and her friend now lived far away and had just had a baby.

Alex congratulated Sobotka and Sobotka realized he had to announce the news to everyone else as well. "Hey everyone, I'm a grandfather!"

"Wow!" shouted Oleg, clinking glasses with Sobotka again, then with the American and with Šeila.

Nikola was looking at Šeila over Sobotka's back. She nodded to him.

Oleg said to Alex, "And who are you, my friend?"

"Don't understand," he responded in English.

"Oleg. Nice to meet you," said Oleg, also in English.

"Alex. Glad to meet you, too."

"We're having a party tonight, so you should be prepared for anything."

"I see," Alex said with a laugh.

Then Oleg went over to Nikola.

"This guy's American," he said as if he'd sobered up a bit.

"I know," said Nikola.

"You do?"

"Yeah."

"What is a Yank doing here?"

"That I don't know."

"Well, shit," said Oleg. "We'll have to get him drunk and find out."

"You think?"

"If I can't get him drunk, that means we have a problem."

Nikola wanted to give him more information, but Oleg was already standing next to Alex, raising his glass.

Šeila walked over to Nikola.

"Hey."

"Hey," he said.

He looked as if he were still upset. She said, "So you still can't get over not knowing what I do for a living?"

Nikola dropped his head. He knew she was out to provoke him, but he couldn't gauge how much. If the Yank was here to keep an eye on him and Oleg, Šeila was being really provocative.

"Well, you know, sort of," he said.

"That's just unbelievable!" she said bitterly, as if continuing an old family fight.

Standing at the bar, he rested his forehead on his index finger and thumb, and started moving them around as if massaging. What was he supposed to answer? Until he found out what her job was, he didn't know what answer he was supposed to give. If he told her that, she'd go crazy. And she'd think he was crazy. *Dammit, just say what you're doing with the American!* The words hovered on the tip of his tongue.

"You find it unbelievable. I don't. We obviously don't understand each other."

"But why?"

Because we are making goddamn turbines for a country under international embargo, for the enemies of America, and you're here with a Yank, and they don't come here on vacation. That's what he thought about saying to her. It would have been lovely if he'd blurted it out before discovering what she was up to with this American guy. He was getting really fucking furious as he thought about this.

"You don't trust me," he said. "There are certain things you don't want to tell me. Okay."

"And?"

"And nothing."

"It's unbelievable how you just cut through everything," she said, shaking her head.

He was fuming. He thought he could see her soul, but he still didn't know who she was. She was so sexy, but he couldn't reach her.

"Look, it's just that one thing," he said abruptly.

"But this one thing means everything. I've been going against this my entire life. Avoiding boss types."

"Are you trying to say I'm sexist?"

"I'm a bit angry. Never mind . . . I did care about you, you know."

"I cared about you, too," he said stiffly, frowning at her.

"Fine. I can tell," she said, making to turn around.

He used his hand to stop her and pleaded, with a grimace, "Tell me what you do. That's all I'm asking!"

"You're crazy. Honestly," she said, looking at him in disbelief. "No. That's not how it works!"

She moved away from him and left him staring at the drink in front of him on the bar. He wanted to smash his head into the glass.

But he couldn't do that here in front of the workers, Sobotka, Oleg. He couldn't do anything.

He finished his drink and ordered another round. He could see that Šeila hadn't left, but was standing near Sobotka and the American. But what could he do with that?

At that moment, Lipša, who'd been mingling, emerged in front of him.

"Look," she said. "Don't stare, be subtle ... I think there are three of Ragan's guys here. Over there, at the table in the corner."

Nikola glanced over. He hadn't even noticed the three before with all the smoke and people milling about. He shifted position so he could take a better look at them. They were dressed in sports clothes. Yes, they did seem somewhat apart from everyone else, alone.

"I remember faces, and I used to work there," she said. "I'd say they're his men."

"They're just what I needed. I could kill someone tonight, really."

"Hey, what's up with you? Oleg is clearly not himself, but I'd thought you'd be acting more normal."

"You'd think."

"You're running a factory here! Have you all gone nuts or what? Four beers and that's it—crazy? C'mon, I've seen my fair share of crazy! For God's sake, remember what you're supposed to be doing here!"

Nikola looked at her ... and thought how she'd just earned her paycheck.

"Okay," he said.

He sent a text to Erol: "Come over here, but make it casual."

Lipša was still standing next to him. "Has Šeila been giving you the runaround?"

"No, no."

"Sure she hasn't."

"You know her?"

"Sort of. Nerd."

"Really? You know why she is in town, what she does?"

"Nope, I didn't even know she was here. She was gone for a while. She was supposed to marry some American guy, that's what they used to say. Who knows, maybe that's the guy."

"I see."

"On second thought, it can't be," she said. "I think her guy was black."

With that, Lipša left.

Erol leaned over to Nikola at the bar. Nikola explained the problem.

Erol eyed the guys in the corner and said, "I don't know them. They're not from the war."

"What do you suggest?" Nikola asked.

Erol thought hard.

Nikola added, "How many men do you have here? If we're going after them, I'm coming with you."

Erol sized Nikola up and concluded that he was quite drunk. Still, it was nice to hear this from the boss.

"You've become a real man of the people," he told him.

Nikola sighed and said, "Ah, I don't even know anymore...."

"Look, they're not doing anything. If we make a fuss we'll be asking for trouble."

"They're sitting very close. Breathing down our necks. That's what they're trying to tell us."

"Me and the guys will go and stand closer to them, just so they understand we're not scared of them. You stay out of it, whatever happens."

"Do you think they're armed?"

"So are we. We'll see how well informed they are," he said.

Just then live music struck up, coming from young men who'd walked in with their instruments.

Those from here who've gone away
I used to see them in my dreams
I don't believe they'd lie to me
It's better for them there, they say.

The band of four had with them small drums, a concertina, a saxophone, and an acoustic guitar.

"Who are they?"

"This is a band called Turban-Rap. I have no idea what they're doing here," said Erol.

Oleg was meanwhile toasting Sobotka with his glass raised high.

Nikola was watching the musicians and the rollicking hubbub, while stealing glances at Ragan's men, who were busy looking at each other around their table. They seemed to be the only ones who were not taking part in the festivities. Then one of them moved his head so as to signal something, and they started to rise. Nikola's eyes followed them as they walked out.

Look, the music made them leave, he thought.

At that moment, Oleg came over to Nikola and said, "I told Lipša to get some music for Sobotka, and she got these reggae-rappers.... Crazy woman!"

Sobotka was waving his arms in the air.

"He seems to like it," said Nikola.

Oleg was looking at Sobotka as the man was standing with his arms outstretched, immersed in the reggae-rap-sevdah music. Then he said into Nikola's ear, "I don't think the Yank's a problem."

"How do you know?"

"He seems to be some kind of scientist."

"A scientist?"

"Yes. I kept calling him 'captain,' so he got tired of it. He told me he was a scientist."

"You believe him?"

"Well, yeah. . . . I mean, when he said 'scientist' he looked at me, like, as if he were apologizing for not being a captain. And he didn't tell me what kind of scientist, he went all quiet, like it was something secret."

"And that doesn't sound suspicious to you?"

Oleg looked at Nikola like a drunken professor planning to give one of his last lectures. "It sounds suspicious to you, Nikola, not to me. You should know that's not how a spy acts. The guy is totally confused . . . I know spies. If he were a spy, he'd know I was checking on him. I mean, if he were a spy, he'd tell me what kind of scientist he was, he'd have a perfect cover story in case anyone asked him something, you know? He wouldn't just say scientist and then shut up and raise his eyebrows, as if he wants to say, I'm not saying another word. Remember, I have training. For fuck's sake, those stories were a part of my training. I always knew exactly what to say."

"You weren't a spy!"

"I wasn't a spy, Nikola, goddammit, I was smuggling arms! You can't say you're smuggling arms. When you can't say something, they make up a detailed, logical story for you. You don't say you're a scientist when you're in some fucking godforsaken place and then clam up. You don't do that. You know? That's suspicious."

Nikola was already slow from all the booze. He also wanted to make sure, because of Šeila. "So it is suspicious, but it's not suspicious?"

"Yes! It's suspicious to you. It's suspicious to amateurs, not to me. See?"

"All right, I'm an amateur."

"That's fine. You're better off."

Nikola took a sip, lost in his thoughts, and then he started laughing. "A scientist?"

Oleg liked seeing Nikola laugh; he had looked very glum the entire evening—in fact, for some time now.

"A scientist!" Nikola couldn't stop laughing.

"Yeah, I know!" Oleg was also laughing now. "He came here to study us, I guess."

"Holy shit!"

The rappers were getting silly:

The old poet's dead now, and so is Emina
All that's left for us are turbine machines
The poet's returned, a baby for Jasmina
The craft of the turbine will never leave us . . .

Sobotka was dancing, waving his arms.

Nikola headed over to Šeila.

22

DEAR SIR,

You, who are reading the letters I'm writing to Pops, you're just one instance . . . an unexpected parapaternal formation . . . micro papa, para-papa, paraphernalia . . . truly, the missing link between . . . between me and . . . between us . . . and you say, "The house exists." This caused in me an incredible laugh that has been here for days and because of which I have resorted to trying out some pills, because it is pretty awkward, you must admit, when you are walking down the street laughing because a house exists. And the house exists and you can't stem the laughter, you can't do anything about it, the house exists, there it is, I got what I wanted, you fucked up my conception of everything and the immaculate conception of my mind, because the house exists. It's not true that I don't have anything, a father exists, a crazy one, he doesn't know about me, that is who he is, it's a tragedy, and a house exists, a normal one, a brick house, not crazy, but a normal house, mine, it's just that it is occupied, so I'm here, preparing for battle, armoring myself with armor, picturing the battle, the battle where

I'm coming to throw all of you down there out of the house, my mouse house, which exists.

Dear sir, you gave me this gift, as heavy as a house, and now I'm like a snail with a hallucinatory shell, a ridiculous snail, a little snail that is creeping, creeping slowly down the street against time. Is there an animal more beautiful and more ridiculous than the snail, I ask myself while I'm laughing because the house exists. What should I do now, sir? Should I come home? Should I return to take care of my father-father? Ah, such a fucking ridiculous feeling of anxiety has been produced in me because the house exists, such a ridiculous crisis; just a crisis, they tell me "it's just a crisis," but still, I had to take shelter here again because the house exists, fuck, the house exists, the house is looming over me like the shadow of a mother, of a megamother, and my mother, mommy. Do you know how my mother died, do you know how those with cancer who have no house die, even though the house exists? Ah, it was so beautiful, in a hospital, a white one, I came to visit, always wanting to escape and always wanting to stay, to stay with her and to escape, to be with her and to . . . The fear of death is life itself, it is not actually fear, it is the deepest urge to escape, into the vastness of pure animalistic life. Imagine me running, sir, you who are reading these letters, you who were, until now, missing, imagine me running across a great vastness, a vastness as green and gleaming as happiness, imagine, because I am imagining, too: it never looked like that, although that is the image, the real image. The reality, which is a disturbance, made it all take place in concrete. The coming and going, from my mother—yes, she was mine, as opposed to the house, she was mine, it's you who made me say that, well done, she was mine, although she was so, so hard to handle, so unbearable that it still makes me sad, it was so hard to deal with her misery, which dribbled about endlessly like a leaking bag. There is something in that leaking bag, and I'm a child-child and don't know what it is, because there is nothing left that would tell me, nothing but a language with no background, distorted stories, stories distorted by silence, because she wanted to stay silent, because she didn't know how to talk about it, how to say it all, I mean, she talked, but she didn't know how to say what kind of life this was, I mean, she spoke, but then you could tell she didn't know how to create a story out of it, she would keep saying, you just can't imagine it, that was her saying, you just can't imagine it, because she couldn't explain what that world was like, I mean, she could and she couldn't, she had a couple of stories of hers, but she couldn't, couldn't explain what that world was like and what the death of her son down there, in that world, was like. She couldn't talk about that world, she could not, nor could she talk to our people here, we would avoid them, but she would say to me "they should be making movies about it." Movies, what kind, about what, who would explain it, sir, do you understand, movies, movies I haven't seen—and that haven't even been made yet, as far as I know? That's what it's all about, an empty tape, about the fact that I'm a foreigner making guesses about that fog, that white, even though the house exists, as you said, and my father exists, kinship, blood, similar head shape, long limbs, short body, all that biology inherited from the Fatherhead.

Ah, sir, you're so damn real it is unbearable, you really do exist, and that's the fucking problem, and all that does exist, with you as the ambassador of existence, the existence of the house, the house my cousins have occupied, my cousins, evil puppets.

Oh, sir, thank you for taking care of my father-father, you are truly a great man-man. I must confer upon you a medal, I mean, I'm actually awarding you one right now as we speak. You must be a good person, you're from that world I'm unfamiliar with, which I thought didn't exist, because these relatives of mine don't surprise me, evil clowns, I reckon that's normal, everything I hear and read leads me to the thought, evil clowns, but you're something else, you've fucked me up on all counts, I can hardly be ironic with you, it's so wonderful of you to take care of my father-father whom, now that you've told me of his existence, I don't know what to feel or say about, since he exists. How am I supposed to address him now that he exists? The fact that he's crazy makes the whole thing easier, the fact that he doesn't read the letters helps only seemingly, because you do the reading instead of him, you crawled in here in order to be and said the house existed, but you can't fix all that, you sir, as far as I can see, think that you can undo the harm, you are trying really hard, but maybe you need a bit more power, a bit more power to patch up and refill this hole that's been opened. You, sir, resemble a character from those stories about good old folks of ours, which my mother used to tell me, unable to explain in what way exactly they were better or how they became bad, you probably know all these secrets, but I don't. I don't know what to do with you now that you've contacted me from this world of yours. Have I already told you that I imagine your world as hell? Maybe I have, but this has nothing to do, you know, with art and such imaginings, the thing is that I thought I came from hell, you understand, there was plenty of evidence for that, there is no need to tell you about all the crap we heard from survivors at the court hearings I attended, and which those evil clowns on your TV channels deny and don't deny at the same time: I mean, they deny, but they don't really deny. By winking, winking devilishly. My house is over there, the house that exists.

You'll have to send me a photo, of the house, I mean. You'll have to, there's no other way now. Because the house is what I remember, although no other part of it more vividly than its interior. I've always remembered the house from the inside, in my dreams I've remembered the house that you say exists.

23

I KNOW, YOUR FRIEND TOLD ME.

I know, nothing is easier than going crazy, I know that, I know. It's not like I'm ignorant of these things. It's difficult at first, actually the hardest part is when you're crazy, but not officially crazy yet, and you know the feeling when you're still behaving as if everything is perfectly normal, but are at the same time slightly afraid because you know you've gone crazy, you have to stop participating, because it's easier that way, much easier than listening to all the idiots and their meaningless words. It is a living hell you simply have to shrug off, nothing is easier than going crazy, but then again, I know, I know that it's not really so easy at first, you're struggling to hear them, to assign a certain meaning to them, to the words uttered by the fools of the world, to their constant prattle, those untruths they keep forming, sealing, and perpetuating, those untruths they impose and make binding upon others, those untruths they repeat and repeat, repetition is the worst part, everything they say is repeated, and they keep saying the same things all the time, for heaven's sake, they keep saying the same things over and over again, they establish those untruths as binding and you start feeling bound by them, it's not just like that, you feel bound by those untruths, by the reality that actually isn't real, because you're not in it, which means it isn't real, for if it were real you would be in it and wouldn't be sticking out like a firearm from a shelter, you wouldn't be peeking into the hole and into the sky, you wouldn't have to be so silent in that language, if that were the reality. But this is just a veneer, just a coating sweetened to the point of bitterness, in its thinness, just a coating of words selected to describe that two-millimeter-thin world in a proper manner, as is appropriate, no word is more abominable than propriety, it means that something is appropriate, it isn't proper on its own, it is appropriated in a way, it is just an appropriety, what a disgusting word this propriety. It could be also called pouriety, it could be called changiety as well, this is enough to drive you crazy, and I completely understand you, I know quite a lot about going crazy, you know, so I could clearly see you going crazy after your son died. You wouldn't if it were me who got killed, you've completely forgotten about me, but you're not to blame, he was your son after all, the designator, the propagator of your name. Because you're primitive, you old mathematician, I have to tell you that, although not as primitive as the normal people, because craziness does spiritualize a little after all, you probably conceive of yourself as a spiritualized person with a predilection for the sky and the stars, and the reason you've forgotten about me is that I've never been part of your idea of lineage, the extension of your being into biological eternity by means of posterity, which is what every animal craves, and the only one who actually existed in your primitive vision was your son, as the heir to the lineage, as the propagator of our glorious name and integrity, of which not a vestige has remained, may its memory live forever, and as for me, why even bother giving a fuck about me? It was obvious from the get-go that sooner or later someone would fuck me, wasn't it, so I simply wouldn't be able to preserve the intactness of our family name, nor the integrity of my body, as if this being fucked meant I was multiplied by zero in your mathematician head that had been seized by language, name, symbol, rather than numbers. Not those numbers you swear by, but language, language is the reason you've gone crazy, your son's death seen as the death of your name is what has driven you off the deep end, because if biology and mathematics were the only things that mattered you would remember me as well, I'm a number myself, but I wasn't a name to you, I wasn't a designator in your primitive head, despite the fact that my books are published under your surname. But this means nothing to you since they are about that downfall of yours, that fucking of mine, as well as the body of our lineage irrevocably lost, the body without a cock which you regard as the beginning of mathematics, this is that prime number, Daddy's son and his weenie, there's nothing mathematical about a pussy, wouldn't you agree, you old reckoner? A father and his son are what count, everything else equals zero, that's why you've forgotten about me, and now I'm supposed to take care of you in your own fear of hollow language, in your act of taking refuge in the void. I tell you, nothing is easier than going crazy. I completely understand you, swallowing pills won't help you, only my slapping can, incessant slapping until you finally notice me, until you start noticing the rest of the world outside the tin can you crammed yourself into like a dead sardine, and you've always been in a can, you've spent your entire lifetime in a can, you've seen nothing of the world apart from the little part of it you've managed to see since you went crazy, you're nothing but a canned fish needing to be fed, what a scoundrel, you're exactly what I thought you'd be, the only good thing is that you're crazy, because if you were normal, it wouldn't even be possible to talk with you, if that were the case, you'd be the only one talking and would hear no one but yourself, and this way you're silenced with contentment, a madman. But this isn't really madness, you just keep yourself aloof, waiting to be activated, because you don't know what to plug yourself into in the empty world replete with words that pinch, upset, babble, everyone keeps babbling about themselves, all those castles in the air, those pathetic identities and self-persuasion, all those people, incomplete in every aspect, perpetually roiled around by the sea, the sea one hundred times more powerful than they are, so they make up their spurious stories about the subject, saying one thing one day and another the next, depending on where the waves carried them, always cursing yesterday's delusion, that nonexistence remaining hysterically unacknowledged, which tells more blatant lies each time, which wounds and kills, which murdered your son and my brother, who died for an illusion and in this illusion your name is inscribed, I can see that from here, I don't know what it's like up close, but I know, nothing is easier than going crazy, it is easier than watching all of it, being in it with words and participating with words in the humiliation of everything, even of death itself, which they'll still be lying about tomorrow, and the day after tomorrow they won't even remember what happened, why it happened, who fired at whom and why, just as they don't remember the past, destroying their own monuments, because they say those monuments aren't theirs, so they'll eventually begin destroying these things as well, because they aren't theirs, they'll say.... When the wind starts blowing from the east, west, north, or south, when a powerful gale starts blowing, everything will be reversed, as it's always been with the clowns who destroy and don't remember, as you know so well, for you lived in the period which nobody seems to be able to explain to me, in the peace that can't be explained, so you can't even explain yourself. The only way you can explain yourself is by lying, so everything tends to be explained by recourse to lying, and everything is actually explained by lying in the end. I'm aware of that, and everything is a phantasm, everything that was and everything that is, and nothing is easier than going crazy, stepping aside and saying nothing, walking your dog and walking yourself, being walked, nothing is better than walking. I used to walk through cities, I would walk all the time, we homeless walk like that, and I try to stay away from those who don't walk, those who keep looking down from their windows and from the embrasures, those who glue themselves to their observatories and who hate walkers, us, me and you, you old lunatic, we have common suffocators, those observers from windows, which I can sense every small town abounds in, there you have to resort to madness in order to go for a walk because it is well known that one shouldn't walk aimlessly, diagonally or sideways, and purposeless walking is forbidden except for strangers. And lunatics are also strangers, a lunatic is nothing but a local stranger, someone who grew up here but walks like a stranger and no one knows what he thinks and talks about, this is the reason why it pays to be crazy. You know what I'm talking about, because it's easier to go crazy than stay attached, attached to the language of those endless greetings, the only thing they do is greet one another, saying, "I'm here, I'm here," "Here I am," but you're not here, are you? You're not here at all, and your greetings are deceitful, your existence is deceitful in this language you're attached to, and you have to flee to a foreign land. It's difficult only in the beginning, because going crazy is a disgrace, we both know this, not a small disgrace but a vast one indeed, everyone is wondering, everyone is looking for you, and you're not there, and that's a disgrace, but you have to disgrace yourself, there is no other way, this disgrace becomes freedom, it becomes freedom and a stamp, it means you're getting erased from registers and records, erased from accounts, and this disgrace comes as a huge relief, just like when a boy and a girl finally undress each other and have sex for the first time, when they forget about shame and decency, when they fuck themselves lewdly with language. With the exception that you're all alone in this, once you go crazy, you wouldn't go crazy in the first place if you weren't alone, never has a person who had the society of a few friends, who had someone to share language with, gone crazy, but you couldn't stay in language. I respect that, you didn't slog in the mud of language, although, following the death of your son, you could have accepted that role, embraced the language of great sacrifice and gained the admiration of others, greeted and been greeted with great respect, but you stayed silent, which is more sacred, more honest, but you didn't see me, you didn't even notice you'd forgotten me, and I have nothing for you from this oblivion but slaps that won't wake you anyway, it's only my hand smacking in a void as if slapping, this story is only mine because we don't keep each other company, you can't keep company with anyone in that deceitful language you're hiding from, unable to hear anything, and each of us is alone, without truth.

24

MAYBE IT WAS because of all the bright northern African sunshine around him, or maybe it was the clamor of the city streets here on the Mediterranean's southern shores as he hurried back to the apartment, but he bought her roses. He suddenly felt a longing for something like love, so he whispered to her, there on the terrace of the penthouse, "Tell me, how much do you love me?"

An agitated crowd was thronging below.

She gazed into his eyes, which he found arousing.

"What? We fuck, but no mind-fucks," she said. "The gentleman would like proof of my love? Do I bare my heart? Why not give those flowers to that little girl of yours, your manager who believes in a better world? Where the two of you will be in charge together, welcoming guests to your dinner parties, right?"

She laughed in his face, then went inside. He followed her, an erection bulging in his pants. He didn't understand the logic behind these erections, but they kept coming—they simply kept coming.

He seized her around the waist and spun her around toward him, grabbing her ass with one hand. He wanted to kiss her.

"No way, no sex for you today," she said. "Stay in the realm of love today."

He released her.

"You started so nice and look at you now."

She entered her room, closed the door, and turned the key.

I hate her, he thought. The woman was making him feel like a beggar, a beggar for something, he didn't know for what—since he was actually the one paying her.

A beggar for truth, he thought. I need some truth to hang on to in this whole lie. I got what I wanted. This is what she has to offer—a damned mirror. She is a criminal. Oh yessiree a criminal. He didn't know why these words seemed so compelling to him, but he kept repeating them, like an inebriating explanation.

He felt as if she were the one in charge here, even though he couldn't find a rational explanation for the feeling, since, realistically speaking, he was making all the decisions. He had decided to take her with him, he was the one in the know. She was just traveling with him, going along like a suitcase. Where did the absurd feeling come from that she was the one in charge?

He turned on the TV and flipped to CNN.

He had leased this huge apartment in the center of the city because he was trying to avoid hotels and security cameras. Here he had everything he needed, no surplus.

Lipša lay on her back, smoking a cigarette.

She was having a conversation with herself in her head; she had practiced this to perfection as a kind of therapy.

"What is he thinking? That I've never had a guy like him before? As if all those other bosses were easy to deal with."

"You're right, don't let him draw you in. You're not stupid. Once was enough."

For her, this was a way of staying in touch with herself, she engaged in her dialogues, sometimes even out loud, as if talking to a friend, the savvy friend she didn't have.

"All right, so you trade something, sacrifice a piece or two, give pussy from time to time, but that way—give your pussy voluntarily, and not unwillingly as if it's being taken from you. I've been telling you this all along."

"When I'm giving, I am giving, or at least I'm acting that way, I'm not suffering, I don't fuck with suffering."

"You must understand, to suffer means to admit defeat, to recognize their authority."

"I'm not suffering."

"You're really not suffering?"

"No," she said, "I'm not going to suffer. Where would I be if I gave in to suffering? I would be constantly suffering. I'd already have dropped dead."

"Your lack of suffering seems to bother him. You're giving the impression of being undefeated, and he doesn't like that."

"I know. It's his vanity. Asshole. He'd like to pull me in. If I allow myself to fall in love with him just for a second, if I begin hoping for his love, I'll immediately begin to suffer. Then he'll be satisfied. Then he'll know I've fallen under his sway, he'll know he mattered."

"He doesn't matter."

"He must keep not mattering."

"He's not the man for you."

"And who is?"

"You haven't met that man yet."

"I certainly haven't."

"Are you waiting for him?"

"Not really sure."

"And why should you? Let him find you."

"Where would I wait, anyway?"

"This is what it is."

"No way am I going to suffer because of this, I decided that a long time ago."

"And who should you be suffering for?"

"Probably for myself. I don't know."

"Why should you be suffering for yourself? To make your own life miserable? And all that for yourself?"

"Why do others suffer without love?"

"They have ideas about how their lives should be, so they suffer. They think everything's lost because they failed to meet the bar they set. You used to have such ideas."

"Luckily, I no longer have any ideas about what my life should be like."

"You're free as a bird. You've already ascended to a higher level."

Oleg really had no interest whatsoever in the ordinary women who embraced suffering, thinking of it as a currency they could use to endear themselves to him, and, eventually, in their dreams and maybe even permanently, bind him to them. He was fed up with these maneuvers, which, after all, completely spoiled the pleasure for him and also evoked a feeling of guilt, the archetypal guilt—*alas, I made her miserable*—and the class guilt, which washed over him every time he hooked up with an impoverished woman, who would then start hoping her relationship with this promising gentleman might become something more than a one-night stand.

These women simply wanted to leave their lives behind, lives they found even more unbearable after they'd had a taste of something else, he knew this full well, damn it, and while he felt pity for some of them, he couldn't rescue them one by one—you can rescue only one, no more—and every single time this led to the tears of a penniless woman who couldn't bear feeling like a whore, but he made her feel that way, of course, which was terrible, terrible. All of this was horrible, he'd been horrible throughout the affair, and eventually, their sex would also be horrible. Sometimes, truth be told, it was from the very start.

If you imagine me with no money, exactly as I am—you'll see that I'm not a good man, nor am I handsome. Why suffer over me? He said this once over the phone to the physiotherapist he'd tangled with at a wellness center—where she was employed, and lived nearby as well—a tryst that soon became a steamy adventure at the hot springs.

He thought maybe this way of thinking would make everything easier for her.

Yet she claimed she loved him and sobbed over the phone.

Now that woman wasn't actually poor, though when he thought about her "poor" was the word that sprang to mind. No, he thought, hers isn't real poverty. It is the ordinary average poverty of those who watch TV and read the trashy magazines, of those who follow what celebrities do and where they spend their summer holidays, thus becoming poor from all the things they desire. They are poorer than the poor; those paupers of television and tabloids, they are the poorest, their poverty is in images, in the luxury of yachts and flashy cars, in high-fashion clothing brands and fantasies about tourist destinations. Their poverty is thorough and complete, with no pride or rebellion, for they keep hoping, they project themselves into images, they save up and buy one of the things they desire, something similar to what they've seen in the images—they *indulge* themselves in something, and, I should say, deservedly enjoy it, but then have to pay it off and go on fading in front of their TVs and those sleazy magazines. Such paupers were incredibly common—they seemed to constitute the majority of the population. The poverty of the people who obsess about wealth is vast—and he could feel this emptiness on the skin of young women, even in their sorrows, in those misfortunes of love he *indulged* them in, because he was a swine.

"Then why such suffering over me?" he asked her.

"You got under my skin."

He realized there was nothing to be done here. If they conceived of me as a door to a better world, then it's useless to think afterward that I'm someone else. If they, to lay everything bare, were involved with me because they saw me as a source of money and a pathway to a better world, then they are in the whorish game from the get-go, but they can't face thinking of it that way so they fall in love, they deny it all by falling in love: falling in love is a form of lying in this case, and I'm expected to sweep the game under the carpet—and turn it into love—otherwise, everything is just terrible. . . . But yes, it is, indeed, terrible.

There was no need to explain this to Lipša. She didn't come from the class of the miserable consumers of images. She gave pussy differently—even though even she wouldn't be willing to fuck me were I not seen as *money-work-world*—she wouldn't, but this whore wasn't unable to face the air of whorishness, she was insolent in all of that, as if she were telling a truth, an insolent fucker, she'd screw when and how she wanted. He appreciated her as one appreciates those self-made gangsters arrogantly clawing their way up from the very bottom, and he was in a way becoming a little crazy over her, her sexy provocations, those looks she gave him, the paradoxical rela-tionship between them, in which certain strange feelings of respect, companionship, and affection had begun slowly sneaking in—he was hoping these feelings would soon disappear—for this could lead nowhere, no way.

He knew there was no reason to trust her, and she certainly hadn't asked him to.

As he was buying her flowers, he was thinking of them as a childish prank, he hoped they'd pretend to be in love on this trip, far away from the world that defined them. But the prank was rejected.

"Shit," he said.

The city they were in had just shown up on CNN.

Oleg went out onto the terrace with a beer in his hand and looked down from the sixth floor. Down there on the street, people were walking hurriedly, maybe nervously, now and then a group of young men could be seen walking at a faster pace than the rest. The crowd from before was not there anymore. He lit a cigarette. He'd taken a couple of drags when he heard the door on the right opening—each of them had their own entrance to the terrace. Lipša appeared.

"Oh, what are you doing out here?" she said, sleepily.

"Passing through," he said.

Watching her stretch brought a smile to his face.

"Do you have any plans for today?" he asked.

"I really don't know. I should probably eat something. To spend these wages my company's paid me."

Oh great, now I'm a *company*, thought Oleg.

"You know, I was watching CNN earlier, that's one of those American—"

"I know what CNN is."

"Anyway, protests have, apparently, started here. I noticed today things weren't quite normal, but I figured who knows what this is about. Then I heard on CNN that some guy set fire to himself in the marketplace, or something like that, and now everyone's lost their minds."

"He set himself on fire?"

"The government was putting pressure on him or something, I don't know exactly. Poor living conditions."

"I could've done that myself a hundred times."

"Yeah. You do look flammable."

"Are you hitting on me?"

"Absolutely not. We are talking politics here."

"You say he set himself on fire? Good luck to him."

"This is no joke. This shit is becoming serious."

"Finally, at least something. If you set yourself on fire back home, you'd burn up and that would be that."

They were quiet for a while.

Then Oleg sighed and said, "Why now? Just when I have to move this turbine!"

"Where is it supposed to go, anyway?"

"To a place not far from here. The ship arrives tonight. Then the turbine goes its own way."

"Where, to the desert?"

"Don't worry. You won't be going there. We're leaving this place as soon as they pay."

Lipša watched the city from the terrace. The street below was pulsing with rage; she didn't have to understand the language to know that. Oleg was somewhere out there again. They'd been there nine days already and the turbine still hadn't left the port. Supposedly, the ship unloaded it hastily two days ago, even though the port workers were on strike. Unloaded it and left. If ships were leaving, they should have packed their bags and gotten the hell out of there, too. She'd already said so to him. But he thought he could take care of this amid all the damned chaos. It was out of the question for them to leave until they'd taken care of this. In fact, if she wanted to, she was free to go, he said. She could leave. I can still leave, she thought. He said some people, skilled people from another foreign country, were helping him, but nothing here seemed to function anymore. He had the best connections, but now, all connections had been severed. "I can't find the damned turbine in the port," he said with a laugh. This was a huge port and nobody was working there anymore. Everyone was out on the streets, picking fights with the police. And they had to find it, they had to transport it, a special truck for special cargo was waiting outside the port, waiting to go somewhere over there, through the desert, and people around the special truck were shouting because they thought it was some military vehicle. "Which it may be," said Oleg with a laugh, "only not theirs." Every time he came back to the apartment he brought with him tote bags full of beer—he always managed to procure it somewhere—and he looked odd because he kept slathering on the self-tanning lotion so he wouldn't stick out as a foreigner. "We have to pull the turbine out of this damned chaos," he kept saying. "Otherwise all is lost. They've got to pay me. But how are they supposed to pay me the damned money when they haven't seen the damned turbine? If they don't pay me the damned money, this is the end of me. I can go down here or at home, it doesn't matter." *Oh fuck, why set yourself on fire now, my fine friend*, he'd shouted from the balcony the night before while even louder shouts could be heard coming from the city. This morning, as he was preparing to go out into the city, he left three thousand euros on the table. *Just in case, if I happen to stay longer in town*, he'd scribbled.

She was drinking the beer. He'd brought so much alcohol into the apartment that it was as if he were preparing for a blockade that would last several months. She sat on the terrace, under the mellow winter Maghreb sun. The sounds of sirens came from below. She peered over the railing. An armored police van raced down the street. Some people threw themselves to the side, while others hurled whatever they could grab at it. She felt the urge to go outside and fling something at the vehicle.

"I feel like going out. I'll go crazy in this apartment," she said to herself.

Is that necessary?—that's what the savvier friend in her head would say.

No, but I feel like it.

And then what?

I'd like to throw something at the vans. They can't drive through people like that.

Do you really need to?

No, I don't.

Okay, don't.

But I'd like to.

Are you talking about a kind of sex?

I don't know what it is, but people are down there. And I see the people aren't attacking each other. They're attacking the ones who are running them over. Got to respect that!

And now you want to go down, too?

That's what I'd like most. I feel like I belong down there.

But you're a foreigner here.

I know.

You don't know who they are, and they don't know who you are. That's why I'm sitting here all the time.

You don't know this part of the world, you don't know what could happen to you. You're a foreigner, a woman. All sorts of nasty things happen on those streets.

I know, goddammit.

"I really like you, you know," said Oleg, his eyes closed.

The city was humming beneath them, like a ship engine that's about to fail. He imagined for a moment that they were on deck, sailing above the turmoil below. He thought the passengers aboard the *Titanic* had probably felt the same way.

Whatever, right now he could only drink beer, wait, and soak up the sun. It was the perfect time for romance.

"Imagine we're on the *Titanic*," he said.

"Why the *Titanic*?" she asked lazily, reclining on the other deck chair with a beer in hand, wearing only dark sunglasses and her panties and bra. Of course she hadn't remembered to bring a bathing suit. She couldn't even remember if she had one. But she had watched *Titanic*.

"Well, you know, everything's sinking, but a love story is developing. It doesn't matter whether you're rich or poor. Class differences are overcome."

"Oh yeah? And where do you see this love story?"

"You and me. We're the real *Titanic*," he laughed.

This actually sounded plausible to her, but she didn't want to laugh.

"It's just that you're a bit uglier than DiCaprio."

"And you're a bit underdressed. Is your costume designer on sick leave or what?"

"Never mind the costumes. I can't remember the last time I was at sea."

He laughed. "I really like you. Really."

"Why do you like me?"

He thought about it.

"Maybe because we don't fuck anymore."

"Yeah, a sexual dry spell makes everyone attractive."

"Ever since I mentioned love, we haven't had sex. Way to go. That's usually my line."

"I can see it has fucked with you."

"Other things are fucking with me. But yeah, it's weird when someone behaves the way I'm supposed to behave. What should I be doing then?"

"The usual, behaving like an idiot."

"You're really insulting me," he said, even though he didn't mind at all.

"Such are the times."

"You mean the revolution?"

"Uh-huh."

"So how was it down there?"

"Brilliant."

"Did you fight or just shout?"

"I wasn't sure what to shout, so I came up with something of my own."

"Did they watch you?"

"Yes and no."

"Was it dangerous?"

"A little."

"Hey, Lipša, I really love you," he said with his eyes closed, behind a pair of sunglasses, on that deck chair, on their *Titanic*.

"Right. Am I supposed to say thanks?"

"Kissy, kissy."

"Whatever rocks your boat."

"Lipša?"

"Yeah?"

"Let's fuck."

"Uh-huh, as soon as I fall in love."

"Let's do it."

"As soon as I think about marrying you and spending our lives together, I'll immediately feel like I want to fuck. You know how it goes."

"No, seriously," he said, his eyes closed.

"I'm totally serious."

"Okay, look. I'll leave you everything even though you don't love me, how's that?"

"Deal. Now that's real love."

"I'll leave you the account number where the money comes in. I mean the card. In case something happens to me or you kill me."

"Uh-huh."

"I'll leave you the card and the instructions. You'll need to take the money to the losers in the factory, if it ever comes . . . unless you keep everything for yourself."

"Uh-huh."

"I mean, you can take a part for yourself. I mean, it'd be fair if you took a smaller part and gave them the rest."

"But of course."

"What do you mean, 'But of course'?"

"Oh come on, let it go. You were talking about romance."

"I have to go with these guys around the neighborhood. Talk to their boss face-to-face. He'll judge whether to pay me or not when he sees me. That's what he said. He's a madman, by the way."

"But they haven't received the turbine."

"I explained that we don't have enough money to continue. We can build them a new one if we continue working, and hopefully, they'll find this one at some point. It's in the harbor somewhere. It was unloaded. They'll find it once the chaos dies down, when they start working again. They have to start working again at some point, they won't strike and revolt forever."

"And?"

"I'll go there with them. And you demonstrate over here until it stops. Then go home."

"You're really like my father."

"You think so?"

"Sort of."

"What happened to him? You've never mentioned him."

"You never asked."

"I'm asking now."

"He was killed on the way to a prison camp."

"Really? I'm sorry."

"Uh-huh."

"Let's move on to a lighter subject."

"Yes, let's."

"Does it annoy you if we talk about sex?"

"Uh-huh."

"But it's silly to avoid sex. So philistine."

"What can you do, I come from a philistine town. And you?"

"Me too. But I've broadened my horizons."

"Why didn't you become gay then?"

"I just didn't."

"Shame."

"Hey, Lipša, I'm serious.... When are we going to fuck if not now?"

"Probably never."

"This might be our last chance."

"The chance of a lifetime."

"Just imagine we're on the *Titanic*."

"That's the easiest thing for me."

"Tomorrow I have to travel through this country gone berserk and into another one, where the boss is batshit crazy."

"Are there riots?"

"No."

"So you're going someplace safe?"

"Look, you don't know where I'm going. Remember, you shouldn't even tell anyone we were here. If you come back first, act as if you have no idea where I've gone."

"At least I don't have to memorize anything."

"The card has a code, by the way."

"And?"

"I've been thinking. I know you're a decent person, but Nikola will have the code so you don't get tempted. I'm leaving you the card, and he knows the code. Just so I don't create any confusion in your mind."

"Hey, thanks for that."

He got up from the deck chair. There was an explosion of voices from below. He peered over the railing. People were rushing toward a square several hundred yards away. Some of them were shouting. The status quo.

"You remember the first time we met?"

"Vaguely."

"Could you have imagined you'd be traveling the world with me, taking part in a revolution, and sending me off into the unknown like a hero?"

"Why of course, but I did expect you'd be riding on a white horse."

He crouched next to her legs and started to kiss her calf.

"What are you doing?"

He raised his head.

"You have such nice legs, the best I've ever seen."

"Why not browse the Internet?"

"You know, I thought about sex as soon as I saw you."

"Oh, really? Why didn't you say so?"

"I just didn't."

"I know why. Because then you'd have to do that all the time, walk around telling women, 'Sex, sex, hey, I thought about sex...' Who knows if you'd say anything else."

"Yeah?"

"Your vocabulary would shrivel and die."

At this point he was becoming depressed. "So you're really turning me down?"

"Yeah."

"Wow!" he said, and stood up.

The world suddenly looked very gloomy, too realistic.

He went inside for another beer.

The TV was on. The announcer said the American military had denied it was holding Bradley Manning in solitary confinement. He took a beer from the fridge and sat down on the absurdly large bed. He opened a new pack of cigarettes and lit one; then he picked up some kind of saucer as an ashtray. Who's Bradley Manning, he tried to recall. He knew he'd known this before, but not anymore. As soon as a name wasn't mentioned for a while, he would forget it. The media functioned as his external memory. He himself didn't retain anything anymore. Things would go in one ear and out the other.

He remembered who Manning was when they mentioned WikiLeaks. Dammit, he thought, you'd think I could have remembered the name.

Other news followed. Secretary of State Hillary Clinton was on a five-day tour of the Middle East.

He looked toward the terrace door.

Lipša stood there in her tall black boots, naked. She had a cigarette between her teeth, and held her arms crossed underneath her small breasts.

"Any good news?" she asked him.

"Excellent," he said.

With a few strides she reached the bed and lay down near its edge, on her side. She was watching him.

"You're looking despondent, hero."

"So-so."

"What is Clinton saying?"

"Something vague."

"Would you fuck her if she were your boss and if you were a little secretary?"

He was looking at her body. "Are you comparing me to Clinton?"

"No, the other one."

He thought about what to say.

"I'd fuck her."

"You'd be her . . . what was her name again?"

"I would."

"Go on, show me how you'd fuck your boss, little secretary!"

He put on a slightly hurt expression as he looked at her.

"The boss is horny." She took his hand and put it between her legs. "Gently, please. Respectfully."

He wanted to say something, but she put a finger on his mouth and said, "No noise, please. I want to hear the newscast as well."

In her other hand she held a cigarette, which she then placed on a saucer, next to his. She was excited and bent over by the edge of the bed. He came from behind. From outside came warm air and shouts from the street that now sounded like calls of joy. The bed was squeaking like an old boat, while he, Oleg the little secretary, was losing himself inside her. His dick throbbed as if it had a heart of its own, her pussy contracted thickly, the TV blared, the government in Tunisia seemed to be changing. She was being raised in waves and she caught sight of their cigarettes rolling out of the saucer, falling onto the blanket, burning through it. She tried to reach them without going far from his dick. *If we set ourselves on fire, she thought, set ourselves on fire, ah, we'll burn and that will be that.* President Ben Ali had flown out of the country, announced the TV. It was extraordinary news, but she found it a bit funny.

"What did they say?" he shouted.

"Yes! Yes! Yes!" He was cumming, cumming in his boss, no respect. She moved forward a bit, took the saucer and started hitting the spot where smoke was rising from. She was shaking; her body was aglow, glowing, fading, and she put it out, lay on it.

"Secretary," she said.

"Yes, ma'am?"

"Do you have any idea where you're going?"

"Barely."

"Well, do you have to go?"

"I'm always going like that, ma'am."

"You're not a bad guy, you know, although you are horrible."

"That doesn't make sense, ma'am."

"Fuck sense, secretary. I actually love you a little, even though I hate you."

"Why do you hate me?"

"If I loved you, you'd screw me over immediately. You know that."

"Perhaps I wouldn't, ma'am."

"You'd crush me like a worm."

"Perhaps I would, ma'am."

"I love it when you don't lie, it's almost like love."

"I also love you a little, without hating you at all."

"That's because you have no reason to hate me."

"And you do?"

"Yeah."

"Why?"

"Because you're the boss."

"Is that the only reason?"

"You're paying."

"That's the only reason?"

"It's not so simple."

"How come?"

"Because you wouldn't love me if I loved you. Because you're the boss."

"Uh-huh."

"That's where we differ."

All these exchanges were made without eye contact. She way lying on her stomach, looking at the TV, and he was looking at the ceiling while President Ben Ali's escape from the country was being retold on the news.

"Lipša," he said, not moving. "You're a fine piece of ass."

"Is that a compliment?" she said, not moving.

"Yes."

"Thanks, then."

"It doesn't sound so good if I say you're a fine piece of dick."

"No. Come up with something better."

"You're not bad."

"Thanks."

"Maybe you don't have to go?"

"I have to go to the desert. There's no other way."

25

I FLEW ON the plane, which I'm not afraid of at all, because I'm only afraid of silly things, not things like flights—so we don't crash, eh—I'm afraid of walking over land that's crisscrossed by human fences where their stale souls have their seats, penned up in drawers they sometimes emerge from as enraged lions prancing, leaping toward the enemy, because the enemy releases them from airlessness, the enemy opens the way out into an open field, a field of revenge due to musty misery, a petty fear changed by the enemy into pleasure, so the enemy is drier than bread, he is like a father to them whom they kill in their dreams, screaming from the little fences they carry with them. When they introduce themselves, they describe nothing but the little fences. They always introduce themselves and because of this you cannot walk the land and always listen to them introducing themselves, greeting them all the time and constantly establishing and glorifying the little fences and fixing them with every greeting. You have to find measure, act in a measured manner, measured according to weight and leg-length, and moderate, psychologically and sexually, moderation is the worst because it retracts, and you have to walk like that on land. That's what I'm afraid of, not planes, but greeting little fences and moderation. I'm afraid of the glorification of the misfire of everything, because then I don't know where I am, and what's the use of this labyrinth of words, shining and sparkling armor within which I tread like a burglar, going through the holes of the earth like a fugitive who hasn't yet been found but who needs to be found, so they find him in me, the alleged me, even though I neglected the little fence, set it awry, left it like that because it was leaning anyway. This was a problem for me until I saw there is no problem, I'm not interested in the little fence. Then I received news of a house, a house that exists, and the house wants me to make it mine, it is calling me from within, it wants me to introduce myself and enter, almost like in a story I once read—my suffering countrymen told me the story is so nice, a children's tale about a hedgehog's home—in which a little home is glorified, certainly glorified.

And I flew over, I can't say I wanted to, but I had to see it. The fine gentleman who read my letters greeted me and I could tell he was a little uncomfortable what with knowing me too well yet not at all. Through the dark we reached his little house, entered the garden through a little fence. . . . The sound of a swinging bat could be heard, then a hard smash, and shadows disappeared, quick and rustling.

Two of them disappeared, I think, I couldn't see them clearly.

This man, I could see, had enemies, and they attacked him just as I came. Am I to blame? It can't have anything to do with me, I think, while I hear my shriek, still in the air ever since that blow.

"They've killed him!" I scream.

The door to his house opens and someone appears in the light of the doorway. A man in a sad trench coat, only without the coat, staring into the garden. It is Pops, an old apparition walking through my shriek, he walks up to his friend covered in blood. We look at his eyes and at his eyebrows covered in blood, his eyes appear to apologize for summoning me, for claiming that things are different now.

Father jumps around him flapping his elbows like a scrawny bird that can't fly, and then he props the man under his neck and lifts his head, and I tell him clearly, I can unexpectedly hear myself saying: "Lay him on his side."

At this point, shadows start coming in, their horrific faces appearing, questioning and exclamatory, because they heard a scream they say, pull out their phones and call—ambulance, ambulance—and I am standing there a stranger, and my father crying like a child. Me looking down at him, standing next to him, standing on the same spot for a long, long time, looking at my hands that appear to be typing midair, as if typing a letter on a ghastly keyboard, shocked as always, a shock that has been going on for years and has had its ups and downs, and this is, indeed, one of the ups, in that yard, close to the house that does and doesn't exist, mid-return, in a front yard where I spend time studying a creature made of metal with headlights instead of eyes, a sculpture of sorts, and I silently understand it.

The ambulance sounds like an alarm from a pillaged house, nothing unusual, it sounds like this all the time in the body, it sounds as soon as it is woken, this is what's hidden inside me, I thought, an alarm ringing and nobody turns it off.

The ambulance parks, the door opens, the belly, and people in white approach, walking, weary of compassion, not at all surprised at how life is so painful, they—I know them—have perfected their gait by everyday walks to this painful place. I know them. I've fucked them. Only one of them, admittedly, one, who needed to fuck in the neighborhood of death, that's what he said. In a body that might scatter at any time, or so he'd say. His eyes were full of sexual fear, as if there were no tomorrow, eyes fighting for life. We fucked multiple times, in the restroom and in other white rooms, everything over there was as white as a restroom. They thought they could fool somebody with the whiteness, because it would be so painfully clear if they had red lab coats. If they had red walls, it would have been hellish, as, in fact, it was. That was where we fucked, in a whitewashed hell, it was always hot there, warmly frightening, and I fucked him in the restroom and other white rooms, while he was always saying we were out of time.

They dragged Sobotka into the belly of the vehicle, switched on all their equipment, and disappeared with a *weoo-weoo*, while the father, still crouching, was now holding onto my calf, tears streaming. I patted him on the head and he yelped down there like a lost dog, or, I look, is this the black dog yelping I hadn't noticed before, or both? Then I took him under my arm and stood him up— he was smaller than me, smaller than my famous slimness—what a surprise, I'd always thought he was taller. He hugged me around the waist and sobbed on my bosom as if I were his mother; he wasn't acting the father, a relief. He was a son, I thought, somebody's son who couldn't be a father after he'd failed once, he deleted that function, mounted a plaster cast over the fracture, never to be removed. And I, I thought, might have wanted to be the son, to take the place of the dead brother from the stories, not embracing the life of a woman, not looking to get anything from this, but scattering it as if it were someone else's.

And the neighboring faces near us, questioning and exclamatory, I see they don't know what they want, they want to go and not go, and they start to move and not move, they look at us and ask who the attackers were, they asked me suspiciously who I am, *who do you belong to*? One of them asks me like that—*Whose are you?*—so I say,

I'm Slavko's daughter, and there is a murmur of great surprise, and the woman who asked told me she'd seen, she'd recognized me, her sister used to babysit me and I'd played over there, she was glad she'd recognized me so easily, and everything was flickering, everything was full of the sweat of the fear we'd released into the air in that place, the stench of a vengeful desire quickly worm-eaten, the bitter spit and epileptic clarity when I said—*Let's go to my house!*—as if it were obvious they'd follow me, and this was obvious, because they would have followed me even if I hadn't invited them along, just so they could see it all, my return from oblivion, the searching for the house. So they walked with me down the road, and I knew the way, there was no need to ask where we were, but, like a cat returning from far away, I walked in the dark. A car approached, its siren wailing, it was the police, late. They rolled down their windows, they came to investigate, says one of them tired or tipsy, and someone tells them there—that's Sobotka's house, where Slavko is standing on the road with the dog—and off they go, tires screeching. We walk on, walk in murmur, and, walking like that, it doesn't take long. We arrive at the street, and then at the darkness of the house asleep, and once we've arrived I yell and yell from the road, and yelling I laugh at everything—*This is the house that exists!*—and the crowd behind me gasps as if their blood is running cold.

Someone has turned on the lights in the house.

I stand on the road and look at that light in the room where Mother and Father slept, not my father-wreck, but Mother and Father, in the room that was the least mine in the house, where they'd hidden, and there's a light there now, and someone behind me shouts, "Have you no shame?"

"Have you no shame?" shouts someone else. Then the light goes out. A tumult of shouting breaks out, many shouts, human, suddenly becoming angry as if the anger inside them has been released, so they shout all sorts of things. There were a couple of younger people who were probably on their way to a soccer game, so they started chanting—Shitheads! Shitheads! Shitheads! I might have found this funny had it not been going on ever since I'd arrived, all the dizzy coalescing that made me want to sob with rage, because the man was smacked with a metal bat and I came here in a fury-blaze, like a ricocheting billiard ball, with my old rage to boot, with the guttural crowd beside me, so enraged, I cry and fling wide my arms as if I am banishing the evil spirits from the house and the crowd, evil clowns, and my rage is heard, and the other noises go still, only the rage is heard coming from my throat. Like a cat I walk toward the house, hop over the little fence, go to the door, and start banging. We bang on the door and the shutters, and even more people than before seem to be here, and we bang on every aperture, and then from the floor above us a voice is heard, but there's no one in sight, and a voice shouts: I'll shoot!

And a germ of silence forms.

Then I go out onto the clearing. I shout. I hear myself shouting "Shoot!" as if I want the house to kill me.

26

"I AM ANGRY, I'm so angry there are no words to describe it,"
I told Erol in the Blue Lagoon. He was gazing somewhere past me.

The bar was empty. Other people have no money, and I'm
spending Afghani savings.

"I will not let this slide," I said. "Those were Ragan's men,
couldn't be anyone else."

Erol looked at me as if he had only now started paying attention.

"You're sure? What about the seven billion others—"

"So you're defending him?"

"You have to be certain about these things."

"It has to be them. This cannot stand!"

"No offense," he said, "don't think you're going to take care of it,
because you won't. Other things are in store for you."

Erol seemed strange. As soon as they heard about the attack on
Sobotka there were people who wanted to go to where Ragan lived,
armed, but he talked them down. So did Nikola. Admittedly, who
knows what would have happened, but still.

"Sobotka would've told you the same thing. You can take his place."

"It makes me angry, too. Nikola won't explain anything, not where Oleg is, nor why there's no money. He's closed himself off. They say we did things differently, the newspapers rant on about self-management.... It's nothing. As soon as money is involved we're in the dark."

"I asked him the same thing. He told me he can't say anything. Maybe he doesn't know. He looks clueless."

"He always looks that way."

"Yeah. But I think he's sincere."

"Sincere or not, if we continue working without money, that means they owe us for our work. And we don't know if we'll ever get it back. Why grant them credit? It's not ours to grant. This would only make sense if we're all co-owners, and that's what I told him today."

"That's why we need you. What did he say?"

"He shrugged and said, 'Come up with a plan. I'm for it.' So I told him, 'I will. But what will Oleg say?' He looked at me and said, 'Maybe nothing.' He sounded comatose, like Sobotka."

I know, I'm stupid, that is, I don't know how to behave, around men, I mean. Nikola was scared of me, I guess he thought I wasn't all there, because when I start falling for someone, I can't stop. Men tend to gasp for breath around me. I can see them struggling for breath and their eyes wander, because I skip something, a phase. I don't know, I generally don't know how to stop once I start, and then because of that, I'm stuck more or less all the time and hold back, like someone on a chain, and I have to tie myself down or I'll break off and end up all over the place. This is my problem, I know, I have no boundaries, although you can't tell this at first, because everything around me and on me is so shipshape and tidy. My museum is also totally in order, clear, organized, everything spotless, like at my house, and there is order everywhere, but then when someone like him shows up, where you can tell he needs me, he needs order, then hope arises and I lose control and can't stop. I see myself plunging in, everything goes too fast, and I make a muddle. The order all turns into mess and everything goes to hell, because as soon as you destabilize me, I don't know how to take things slowly. I mean, easy and cool, so he doesn't realize how important he is, or feel pressured. And things are like that every time, every time over the last million years since I rush and stop only when I see I've gotten myself nowhere, into my own story, I didn't ask anyone, no one knows where I'm going. I just keep going on my way in my head, and I hate myself for it, really. I'm missing a few marbles, and I keep waiting for someone to fill in the gaps. I wasn't angry at all when I saw he was looking at me like I was missing a few marbles, but I thought—Go ahead, do something, fix it, you're the master, you're the man for me. Well, I really am an idiot, because he's looking at me like I have a few marbles missing, and I say *yes*, to myself, because you can't say that out loud, although it would be, as they say, cool, maybe fun and easy. But I don't say it out loud and he has no idea what I'm thinking. But I need someone, someone to fix me, and it's all wrong, I know it is, and I shouldn't be thinking like this at all. I'm better than that, because I'm smart, even though I may act stupid, which keeps happening, and it takes me by surprise each time, because I freeze in situations—after every hope and after I realize I've been rushing, I freeze for a time, a long time. I guess until I forget. And I'm gone, I don't go out, and again I'm always surprised that I'm like this and I keep rushing like someone who doesn't know how to drive. Then I see everything all at once and feel angry at myself. I need someone, that's what I thought, someone like Nikola, someone who's polite and pretends he doesn't see. I saw he has the emotional room for my confusion. I need to be handled slowly, I don't need short-tempered idiots. When it comes to macho types, I'm in charge, I can put them in their place, there's no doubt that I'm stronger than they are, because I have them in plain view, but I'm not interested, absolutely not interested—if I were even a little interested, I'd have been saved—but I need someone who understands, who will fix me, so parts of me and him fit together like puzzle pieces, and this man seemed like one, but I screwed this up because I couldn't stop, and then he hooked up with the woman named Šeila. I'm explaining this to show how generous I am, and above all that—I know everything's ruined, I'm no maniac—I just want to help somehow, because I see they're in trouble. They don't come to the Blue Lagoon as often anymore, there's no money for rounds, you can tell. But I didn't want to ask Nikola. I get it—we're down to a quick greeting—but I ran into Erol and Branoš that Friday in the empty Blue Lagoon and asked Branoš, because I see he's like the new Sobotka around here, but he didn't say anything specific, so I introduced my friend from the town hall, Jaka, who was with me. I suggested maybe she could help out.

I told them how she stepped forward to handle the paperwork for Slavko's house, and Jaka nodded. She's modest, so she said it wasn't difficult, because the guys at town hall were scared of trouble when his daughter showed up, when Sobotka was attacked, because they thought this might lead to something more, to even more trouble. They can hardly wait to be done with it, they're scared of Slavko's daughter, though she's not doing anything.

Branoš asked Jaka what they could do, what she could do to help them, and she said she'd check some documents; the factory's vacation resort on the coast was lost when the former country was broken up into several smaller ones, so they could possibly ask the country that took it over for compensation, they could initiate a legal process. She also said there are government funds for underdeveloped municipalities, and there is also a chance they could get money from abroad; they could apply for funding to modernize the factory, but that needed to be carefully prepared, because the funding is limited and there are many applicants. "This all sounds pretty long-term," said Branoš, and she nodded. "Long-term" didn't look so promising to him, but, he said, he'd pass this along, good to know these things, but the situation was looking hazy in the short term. Eventually, I guess to lighten the mood, he added more loudly, "And I'm also a bit worried about the Blue Lagoon!"

Rafo, the owner, worked alone and he squinted as he stood behind the bar, which was, I don't know why, funny to us.

"Anyway, thanks, ladies, for thinking of us," Branoš said, and brought us each a drink.

"Karma Chameleon" was playing at the bar, and it was kind of silly, like the old days. We must have looked funny when we started dancing.

Then Rafo treated us to a round of Angebot rakija, which is a strange name for a rakija, but it wasn't bad. He took a shot himself, and said, "While eighties music is still playing at the Blue Lagoon, the factory will not fall!"

He can be funny, I thought, even though I can never tell if it is on purpose.

We toasted, and then once more. This time it was my round, and little by little we got pretty drunk, and hardly being able to describe how, I was making out with Branoš over there by the toilet. No one came across us, but I had the feeling everyone knew when we came back, which was a little embarrassing because I'm older, after all, than he is. He can hardly be right for me—but fine, I kept thinking while we continued drinking—it's better I'm aware of this, better than if I'd rushed things. The museum will always be there, and it would be better, I thought, if I didn't care about anything.

27

YOU NEED TO have nerves of steel and a huge dose of tolerance.

My little secretary left me high and dry. He was a piece of shit, but for some reason—I don't know how—he really didn't smell bad. I even liked the smell of his skin and his soul. Maybe I even kind of loved him, with his scent of half-rotten apples.

He was twisted just like this world, and still he did create some joy. There was something left in him, as if forgotten in the trunk, a respect for the truth, which he had thrown away but it was lodged in the trunk. And he didn't lie to himself, and neither did I. Even if he tried, I didn't let him on our little trip away from the world, this little trip that grew bigger, because he, it seemed, had spiced things up for me. At the last moment, with his last ounce of strength, like a German soccer player, you see, he made a last-minute child for me.

Of course, now there's no word from him.

Luckily, he left me enough money to wait down there until the situation cooled. Luckily I'm not blond, so I didn't stand out on the street, and I was sunning myself every day on the deck, so I tanned like a lamb on a spit. It was convenient for the two times I went down to the port, where I might have yelled too much in my poor English and threatened them with an international court and my American lawyers who were just waiting for my signal. Of course, I also threatened them with the involvement of our great country's embassy, and then later on, when I looked it up online, realized that we didn't even have an embassy there, but consular services were covered by our embassy in the next country over, where Oleg had gone. Well, what can you do? We didn't have any of the other things I threatened them with, either, and I wonder what these frightened men thought of me. A couple of them—who were crammed in this one office, as if they were there to kill time between regimes—kept shrugging, saying the port still wasn't functioning normally, our cargo had been unloaded at a very, very bad moment—very, very bad momentum, one of them kept repeating—after the heroic pro-tester self-immolated. But I didn't get whether this bad moment meant they had also burned the containers in the port, or if they had burned documents, or if they hadn't even received documents, or if these men hadn't even been there so as to avoid being immolated as customs officers of the regime. They just shrugged and, like me, wondered where that turbine might be. Unbelievable! What do you mean it's not here? Well we don't know, either, but we will check momentarily, and they tinkered on the computer. And that moment lasted and lasted. . . . They'll find it sooner or later, they reassured me. So later I kept trying to call them, which gave me a crick in the neck, I don't know why, I held the phone with my head. And shoulder.

For the rest of the time I worked on my tan. I had the time to talk to myself, I talked everything over with myself up in the pent-house, like a forgotten movie star decked out with sunglasses, lying on a sunbed, or like an orphan, depending on the day and my mood. Sometimes I almost died of loneliness, but then I would remember

Ava Gardner reclining on a chaise lounge and say to myself—take this as compensation for all those years without a vacation. But I didn't have a bikini, so I tanned in my underwear, until I realized how good it felt to be naked up there above the revolutionary city.

No one could see me, and it was exciting, both politically and physically, and more than once I wanted to go down and quickly bring up a young man burning with revolution. But who would get rid of him then, I thought, and kept basking until I'd get too hot, and then I'd take a long shower. At first, when I missed my period I didn't even notice because the days were a jumble, they'd become nameless. When I finally realized it was missing, I thought this was from stress and fear, naked sunbathing and giddiness, from a time of carelessness, from forgetting who I was and where I was, and the strange feeling that sometimes emerged there under the sun: as if my body were atop the seething world.

One time I fell asleep like that on the deck with this feeling and had a strange dream—that I was bigger and much fatter than I am, and that I was lying naked atop a plain hill while the sounds of crickets chirped from all around, and everything shimmered in the heat, and in this dream I watched myself from above, wondering why my thighs and belly were so big, while the sounds of crickets turned into the sound of things shattering. Then I opened my eyes and saw a helicopter clattering above me, so I thought that they had been hovering like that and watching me for some time, although maybe they were just circling over the city and woke me up that instant. But I got scared so I ran back inside, imagining the look of the pilot who was surveying the situation in the city, then saw a naked woman and forgot about the situation.

I was afraid he'd remember the building and the apartment and one of these days ring the doorbell in a leather jacket and pants, holding flowers or a gun, saying, in French, that he loved me; or telling me in Arabic that I was a whore who was defying the sky and Allah. I imagined different scenarios, and I planned how to behave around the pilot, how to keep myself alive and well, and how to convince him to give me a lift with the helicopter to the place where the scheduled airlines departed. However, the pilot never did show, that day or the next, even though, in a way, I was still waiting for him, just as I was waiting for Oleg. But the pilot seemed more likely to show than Oleg, since I was watching CNN and saw that things were becoming seriously chaotic where he'd gone, which CNN reported anxiously but also with enthusiasm. It looked as if my little secretary had gone in the wrong direction, I thought, and my period was pretty late, and there was no sign of the pilot. I even started imagining Oleg returning in a flight suit, in a helicopter, and lowering the rope ladder and us leaving at the end of the movie, above this white city, over the sea, all the way to infinity and the final credits.

I was afraid for some time, but in a few days I was soaking up the sun on the deck again, and this time I was careful not to doze off and be surprised by something from the sky, although I was no longer sure if I would run back inside or keep lying like a sleeping beauty under the helicopter's clatter when my pilot came, because I'd already begun feeling familiar about him.

And he did come. I heard him from a distance.

In case I wasn't sure whether to run or stay, I kept a small white towel next to me, to cover my nakedness, and that's what I did as soon as I heard it. He was circling up there, and I watched this flight of the bumblebee through my sunglasses, motionless, and he really did come closer and lower, until I saw him through the open side door of the helicopter waving and grinning, the cheery Arabian pilot, with shiny teeth, probably around thirty-five years old. I didn't move, as if I were asleep behind the sunglasses, and while I was considering whether to wave, he was already on his way back up into the sky with a grin on his face.

If I were allowed to behave like a man, I thought, that is, if I were allowed to behave any way I liked, I'd have waved back. But a woman can't show what she wants because she doesn't know if she'll get beaten like a whore. I'm not free, though I'm freer than others: I don't respond to what I want, but to threats. That's realistic—I've discussed this with the savvy friend in my head.

And so the helicopter and my lover from the sky flew away.

So much for my fling with the pilot.

The next day, they announced the first flights out. I bought a ticket and went once again to the port. I took a cab there, and again, in my poor English, threatened with the international court and my American lawyers sick of waiting for an easy case, and with the involvement of the embassy of our great country, which had actually moved here, because the ambassador had fled the country where Oleg was. And since the ambassador had left to save his skin, I knew there was no chance of doing business with them anyway and Oleg was stuck down there, but I thought: I have to find the turbine and then we'll sell it to someone else.

But the guys killing time in the office at the port between regimes had already grown bolder, it seemed to me, and they started feeling like the authority again, so I annoyed them with my bad English. I think they realized I was making empty threats—a skinny woman on the lookout for a turbine. They started asking where the turbine was supposed to go, why were there no buyers looking for it, and who was I anyway. They looked at me suspiciously, snickered at my yelling, looked me over in a way that left me scared I might disappear like the turbine. Maybe this was all in my mind, but I did start freaking out, so I pulled out my last card, the one that came first to mind, and told them in the most serious tone that I had connections with the Italian prime minister—I don't know where I got the idea, I guess I thought they'd heard of his mistresses—and while leaning on the desk, I got in the lead guy's face and said "Mafia!" I meant to say I was the Mafia, not them, although I saw they didn't get it. But this confused them enough to keep them in their seats while I left the office with my head held high, vigorously slammed the door, stormed down the stairs, and strode out of the port. I didn't run so I wouldn't be stopped.

At the gate, the cabdriver was talking to men in another car. I got into the cab, looking over my shoulder, and they went on talking, which startled me—who the hell are these men?

Then I realized they were asking for directions and my driver was explaining things to them, but they weren't following him. I yelled through the window, "Oh, c'mon! Go ask someone whose meter's not running!"

I didn't even say this in English. I guess they understood "meter." I turned around to see if someone was following me, and then the cabdriver finally got in after a hasty tirade of words, threw the car into first gear, and said, "*Excusez-moi*."

The next day off I flew.

This is the second time I'm meeting with Nikola. He rises to his feet when I walk into the office, where he has, obviously, been smoking a lot and is listening quietly to classical music on the secondhand record player I found for him before I left. The record is creaking, like everything else.

"I haven't had any news from him, either," he says, despondent.

I look at him, so I, too, feel sad, like in a love story, except our story's no good.

For the story to have worked, we'd have had to be meant for each other, but Oleg figured from the start that we weren't meant for each other.

I watched him conclude this right away, because I'm not one to be carried away by stories about love, except when I watch movies, which I really should be banned from doing. If I hadn't watched *Titanic*, and if he hadn't gotten to me by reminding me of it, I wouldn't be pregnant now, thinking about no-good love stories.

This story is no good, and wasn't any good, because I'm dirt poor, and he, you see, is not.

I thought about this over those days out on the deck. It's all about the money: that's why I'm still angry when I think of him and our lousy romance. I know, I'm not a person he'd take to the theater and to places where the acting is first-rate, but if I had money everything would have been different. He'd have taken me, and I'd have learned what to say in that sort of crowd. Then I'd have said something different, but what's important is knowing what's expected, so you can hold your own. Holding my own, I could have taken hold of the tiller. However, he didn't count on me. We both knew this, and that was the best part. It was that kind of love.

Still, watching the news makes me sad, when I see those people on CNN yelling Allahu Akbar, then gunfire, then Allahu Akbar, gunfire, Allahu Akbar, and so on, with no comment, because they're allies, and I find this alliance a strange one between Allah and Washington and Paris.

"When my old man died, I felt it," said Nikola, his face crumpling, "That's why I believe Oleg's still alive."

I wanted to hug him then, but I didn't.

"C'mon, sit down," I say. "I didn't want to say this until I was sure . . ."

"Say what?" he said, sitting down.

"I'm pregnant."

His tongue seemed suddenly shorter, and he looked for it in his mouth. "With Oleg?"

"No, with Hillary Clinton."

He stared at me as if I'd dyed my hair, so I spelled it out. "Yes! With Oleg."

He blotted the sweat from his forehead, and his eyes seemed to be gazing inward instead of out. I said, "I remember so clearly when he walked in that day and said, 'We're bringing in foreign capital.' I knew right away that someone would be screwed over, but not that it would be me. Hats off, he invested in me. I'm thinking whether to keep the baby. There, I've said it."

"Don't get an abortion!" he sat up.

"So, you get to decide?" He pissed me off. "Are you going to be the one who looks after this baby?"

"I will look after it!" he said, without stopping to think.

"So you say."

"Yes!"

"Really? But, look, the child won't have a father. It'll be a bastard."

"But it's Oleg's, right?"

He seemed a little slow. I said, "It is. And you're sure Oleg's coming back? I'm sorry, but it's hard for me to bet on that with this child. Who can confirm it's his, if Oleg doesn't return? Nobody! Or, do you have any ideas? I have to decide now."

"I don't understand. What ideas?"

"Well... If he doesn't come back, you'll declare yourself the father."

"What?"

"Didn't you just say you'd care for it? Did you not say, 'Don't get an abortion'? Don't say what you don't mean."

"I did, but—"

"Well, sign on the dotted line, so you don't forget. Otherwise, this child won't have a father. And that's not a good feeling. Get it? I can tell everyone it's his, but nobody can confirm that. If he comes back, it's his decision whether to accept the kid or not. But if he doesn't, you're it. What do you say?"

"Wait, is this you negotiating a deal?"

"Yes, in the name of my child. That's what his dad did. And I want to have the baby in your country. Can you make that happen?"

He thought about this, then put a pill in his mouth. I guess the pill helped him think. He walked over to the record player, turned up the volume a notch, and then stared out the window. The music was weird. I couldn't tell if it was happy or sad.

"I can make that happen. But this . . . I have to think about it . . ."

"I've thought about it, too. The child will stay with me, but . . . if anything happens to me . . . you'll take it. And in that case it's better to have everything on paper."

He exhaled.

"Why shouldn't it be yours, if you'll be caring for it anyway?"

"But it's not the same . . ."

"It's not the same, it's better. It's better for the child to have a father. Later we can tell the kid we had irreconcilable differences. That much should be obvious, anyway."

"You act as if you know Oleg's not coming back?"

"If he could have, he'd have been back by now. But I don't want to make predictions. I said if."

He halted, as if to catch his breath, and we listened to the record player: a large orchestra on a creaky ship's deck.

"Okay!" Nikola said. "If he doesn't come back, I'll be the father."

Nikola's eyes went red—in the blink of an eye he had a child.

I could cry, too, I thought, but I didn't want to be sad. I got up and gave him a gentle pat. We both looked out the window toward the town where I was born—I didn't want that for my child.

I changed the subject. "I gave you the card. Is there anything in it?"

"You think they'd pay for something they never received?"

"No, but still."

"I'm going to Switzerland in a couple of days to see. The account can't be checked from here."

"Okay."

"Lipša," he said, "please keep quiet about where you've been, about everything, you know, otherwise, they'll block us for good."

"Don't worry. But what about the turbine down there?"

"I sent them the documents I received from the shipping company. Oleg's line: some high-class smugglers. They panicked there. Their story was "Sorry, everybody watches out for their ships." But they did send some papers. We need to call and pester the people at the port. Can you do that?"

"Sure. I already have experience with them."

"The worst part is, now I don't even know what we'd do with it."

"Will you come back from Switzerland if you find money?"

"Come with me, if you don't trust me."

"What for? You could escape on the way."

He almost laughed then, but his face wouldn't cooperate.

"But if you don't find any money . . ."

"What?"

"Don't go killing yourself."

He looked at me.

"Don't kill yourself. You promised me something."

Something came over him again, so he hugged me, like a sister or something similar. I wasn't sure what we were, even though we were having a baby together. His shoulders shook.

"Okay, okay," I said, my throat tightening. "Let's keep this civilized."

28

THE LAST DAY of the conference. She was sitting at the bar of the empty hotel café, gazing out at the street through the window. I'd already noticed her at the conference, when she introduced herself and said where she was from: memories came rushing in, and I felt a thrill, which scared me for a moment because I'd pulled my life together, but this also energized me—perhaps I'd pulled my life together a little too well.

I sat at the bar, leaving a chair between us; the café speakers were singing, *Father, change my name . . .*

"I heard where you're from at the conference. I've been there."

She eyed me before saying, "Really? Whereabouts?"

I told her.

"Yeah," she said as she glanced at her phone. "That's not far. Although it's a little different."

"I was there after the war. It was different from everywhere else."

"That's for sure," she said, granting me another look.

You're pretty and you know it, I thought to myself. I shook hands with her, and we introduced ourselves.

She flashed me a smile, followed by a slightly ironic gaze as if saying: All right then, let's see what you have to say. I almost asked something along the lines of when had she started working for the pharmaceutical industry, but then I thought, That's not why I came over.

Lover, lover, lover, come back to me . . . We shot each other glances during the chorus.

"Can you say something to me in your language?"

She smiled. "What do you want me to say?"

"Have a drink first, please," I said, feeling we were slowly moving into the game, "this will be challenging."

She ordered a martini.

I said, "Talk to me as if I'm another woman."

She gave me a startled yet amused look. She thought I'd said *I was a woman.*

"That's what I want you to say to me in your language," I added.

She instantly looked offended. "You want to talk to me as if I were another woman?"

"No. No. I'm just asking you to *say* the words. There was a moment when a woman who speaks your language asked me for that, to talk to her as if she were another woman, a woman I'd meet years later, here in Washington. She wanted me to talk to the woman about her, just as I'm doing now with you. With you, not with her, see? I didn't do what she asked me to."

She gave me a harsh look, but there was something touching about this for her. "Do you want to talk about it?"

"I don't know. I just wanted to hear it. Where you come from reminded me."

I didn't know exactly what I wanted anymore. I wanted anything, as long as it involved her.

She searched inside herself, and then said, "You ran away?"

Looking at the upside-down liquor dispensers, I remembered my younger self. When I thought about the past I always, not knowing how this was possible, saw myself as a kind of clown in trouble, trying to wriggle out of it, to extricate myself. And I always felt sorry for myself, and for the others. I shook my head between a yes and a no.

"Fine," she said. "First you say something in my language, all right? I'll teach you."

"Okay."

She said, in her own language, *I'm a shithead who shows up and then vanishes.*

"I need to say this in a serious voice?"

"Just don't laugh. Or say it with a smile, or a fake smile, whatever."

That, I don't know why, made me serious.

I said it, and she corrected me a few times, shaking her head, repeating it.

I'm a shithead who shows up and then vanishes.

Then I said it with a smile, and apparently I did it right. While I was saying it, I felt shivers down my spine, a slight cooling, as if a distant wind had swept over me. I didn't know what I was saying, but I saw I was becoming part of her story.

Then she said, "Talk to me as if I were another woman."

She repeated this in her own language.

This rocked me. Unexpected. I'd forgotten I was hitting on the woman. Something was coming back to life, impossible feelings without promise, dead feelings. A tinge of sorrow. Something chaotic about who I am. The misery of my existence, I thought. I ordered a whisky. So did she, flashing two fingers to the waiter. Taking her glass, she said, "I have to go out for a smoke."

I watched her through the wall-sized window—the architect of this hotel really had a thing about glass. My whisky was quickly disappearing in the blur of excitement, and I noticed that she, too, was drinking her whisky restlessly as she smoked. She knew I was watching her, and she turned toward me and shot me a quick glance. I felt the attraction, knowing there was somebody else in her eyes. I wondered what I was supposed to say in her language. It was getting dark, the streetlights were already on. I went out and suggested we go to a better place, not far from there. Her eyes narrowed, as if they were looking at an impostor, and then she said, "All right, let's drink!"

We walked silently to the bar and were already at the entrance when I asked her, "Whose words were those?"

"A phantom's."

"Something happened?"

"Yes. You vanished."

We sat near the wall in a dim corner of the bar, surrounded by waves of chatter and Tom Waits's voice coming from the loudspeakers. She ordered us two double whiskies and water, and then she told me, "Okay, you want to talk to me as if I were some other woman. Or about some other woman. It's hard to understand what you want. But I'll talk to you as if you really were somebody else. And besides I don't know you. And besides all you want is sex."

"No, it's not like that. You are—"

"Don't pretend you're interested in me now!" she hissed, as if I could ruin everything with a lie.

I paused, taking a sip of whisky.

Yes, a lie would take us back to reality, I thought, which seemed a bit unusual.

"All right. I'm interested in . . . all of this. Our conversation. This world. In general."

"This world? In general?" she said with a big laugh.

I felt the warming glow of the alcohol, now we were sailing

away and floating in an interspace, as both of us were here because of somebody else, and it was open, like the entrance to a house of shadows. Waits's voice creaked like rusty hinges.

"It was the biggest love event of my life," I said, simply cutting to the chase.

"The biggest love event . . . Wait, that's not really how you say it, right?"

"If I said that it was the love of my life, that would, I don't know . . . There are too many movies on the subject."

It looked as if she were still thinking about my phrasing. Then she took another sip, held the glass close to her face, and gave me an inquiring look, which was pleasant. The question is always who is looking and do you desire that body, because a long look implies body.

"It wasn't love?"

"It was . . . with slim chances for success."

"Success?" Her smile became twisted. "Yes, I also wanted successful love with you. *Successful love* is what I was after, that's true." She leaned her forehead on her palm like a tipsy version of Rodin's *The Thinker*. "But you knew this. And despised it in a way."

"Success?"

"Success and love, the mix. The only thing I don't know is where the contempt was coming from, but . . . I saw it . . . " She made a brief pause. "The bottom line is that, in a way, you didn't believe I was real. I was a function, a good match. Pretty, successful. I fit all the criteria. See? Merely a sum of highly rated traits. And maybe I really was that, maybe that's how I really look in my world, how I present myself . . . Yes, you made me think."

"I was privileged," I said. "History was kind to me. An American appearing after the Fall of Communism. You arrive as someone who was right, and that's clear now. An incredible situation—you talk, and it goes without saying that you're right. And all around you are losers. Likable losers. Such gullible trust, it gets to you, you know? You kind of feel like a god . . . And then, you came along. So beautiful, and without any pathetic artificiality. You know what I'm trying to say? To find beauty without having the feeling you're looking at a shop window, that's hardly even possible nowadays. And that's what gives life its disgusting taste. You were above that."

She raised her chin and, with her eyes closed, tilted her head first to one side, then to the other, as if relaxing her neck muscles.

"I wasn't above it," she said. "That's just your imagination, you darling prick. I was a part of it and that's why you despised me. You didn't even believe I loved you. But you, on the other hand, were even less reliable. A love event, you say. Yes, well-phrased. But now . . . I have the feeling there's a big story behind this, because you vanished, not only did you run away, but you totally vanished. I can see that by the way your jobs keep failing. Maybe I wouldn't have loved you so much if you hadn't vanished. That redeemed you in a way. Now everything is summed up in you. My supposedly successful life where there is no happiness, except when I lie to people like myself. When I show them pictures from my trips. That is, when you think of it, the closest I get to happiness, lying to people who do the same to me. . . . While we're at it, let's take a picture, let it be known that I had a nice time with a good-looking black guy in America and my life didn't end."

She hugged me, held out her smartphone, and snapped a picture. This part surprised me a little. Good-looking? I hadn't heard that in a while.

"Back home I'd never be saying all of this," she continued, smiling and caressing my cheek. "I sometimes dream of you appearing, neither alive nor dead, naked and suntanned. A hole opened up and everything has been falling through it."

The conversation was growing weirder, but I didn't mind.

"The problems began when everything became real," I said. "While we were lovers, we were on the outside, the world couldn't touch us. Just two people who'd met. There was nothing else. Just us."

"Charming, this love life of yours, darling. I'd rather not talk about everything I'm hearing. . . . But I wanted something from you, a kind of future. I don't know why I chose you, when it was so obvious that you were unreliable. I guess I'm not as normal as I present myself to others, after all. Hey, the future is what I thought about, and that sure as hell was the wrong thing to do, because it kept me from enjoying myself. You had much more fun than I did, I saw that. I overanalyzed everything." She looked at me as if I were someone who understood. "I keep losing. I must be doing something wrong."

I ordered fresh drinks. The bartender asked the customers from time to time, particularly the women at the bar, if they wanted him to play a song off YouTube, and now he asked Lorena that.

She went behind the bar, her movements were much more relaxed than they had been before—the alcohol didn't make her totter; she was growing more graceful.

"This evening," I told her when she came back to her seat, "I must say is so wonderfully hopeless, in a good way."

Ever since . . . I stopped loving you, she was singing the YouTube song in her language.

She translated a few lines: *My sense of taste is slowly coming back, as if after being sick.*

"It was so erasingly beautiful. We erased a whole world and, for a while, we hovered . . ."

"Oh, I love you," she said.

We kissed at the corner of the bar, our tongues full of alcohol, a sour taste of tobacco, exciting, whorish, rotten, European. Everything spun around.

It's good while it spins, I thought.

I woke up in her room, alone.

I think, I feel I recall, that she kissed me silently while I was still sleeping, before she left to catch her flight.

I think she said: "Goodbye Michael, goodbye Oleg."

29

THE TWO OF THEM, one in a yellow trench coat, skinny, one in a black overcoat, sandy-haired and broad-shouldered, stood in front of the bus that was boarding children and women, and everyone was embracing their loved ones, until they saw each other again, after all of this ended.

The one in the yellow trench coat stayed behind with his son, who was taller and stronger than him. The one in the overcoat, the sandy-haired one, was left alone.

They waved, the one in the yellow trench coat, and the one in the black coat with the golden-yellow hair.

One little girl was looking at the man in the overcoat; another little girl was looking at the one in the yellow trench coat, the color of fallen leaves. Both girls waved.

Until the first bend in the road.

An actor, who was famous from TV, was riding with us on the bus, and that caused a sensation. He entertained us over the microphone, singing songs, and we knew the excursion would be fun.

The actor later got off the bus to talk each time we were stopped. Because he was a TV star and they were not allowed to kill him, someone said.

Why not? He also caught the last bus.

Him? No way.

I remember Sobotka's Viktoria. I remember Jasmina, too. She was the older one, I just said I didn't remember her. They kept her for the examination—that's what they called it at first, an "examination," so I thought there was a kind of doctor there. We waited, and she got back onto the bus with bad eyes, they fit her badly, like they were about to drop out. Later, when the bus moved on, her mother was sobbing and cursing, and then she quieted down, and later she stood up and said, "Listen closely, everyone! Whoever says a word about this, I will damn him to hell! Do you understand what the word 'damn' means? Just so you know!"

"What does she mean?" I asked my mother, and she said, "Nothing much."

She was lying, as always.

She often told me a person shouldn't tell the truth. That was because I didn't know how to make things up. I was very bad at the whole making-things-up thing. It's really strange, how it all turned out in the end, that I was the one who wrote a book, and not the others who were better at making things up.

My mother lied whenever she had the chance, not to deceive someone or to sell something—not that—but to hide. That's what she meant. To hide between words so they can't make you out, so they can't see you and know what you think and who you are, because it's dangerous if they know you, that's what she thought. She always told me to lie, and I didn't know how, so since she was always telling me I should lie, I was even worse at making things up, so she kept saying I was that way on purpose, I was telling the truth on purpose and embarrassing her with the truth and putting her in awkward, if not dangerous, situations. "This will end badly, with your stubbornness, when you don't know how to lie and don't want to, I see perfectly well that you don't want to," she said. "Well can't you see, dumbass, that everyone lies? How will you survive in this world that way? How am I supposed to leave you in this world if I don't teach you how to tell lies?" She said these sorts of things all the time, even at the hospital when her end was near.

And she left, and I stayed, like this, defective.

And the actor from the bus acts in America in a sci-fi series. Really. I saw him playing an alien with head thingies and pointy ears. This suddenly dawned on me as I was channel surfing, I didn't recognize him straightaway. I was just watching the series, not sure exactly why; the production wasn't exactly A-list. Then I realized the alien was him and I thought to myself: maybe everyone from that bus has turned into aliens, myself included, it's just that my head thingies aren't visible in this dimension, but sometimes I feel them. The only problem is that I'm not fit for acting of any kind, since I don't know how to lie. Which still doesn't mean I'm telling the truth, as my mother used to think. Because as far as I can tell it's impossible to tell the truth. There's always more. And more. It's a similar situation with lies, only the direction is different, and in the end, I realized, if you really go by the truth, it can also seem made up, which makes me happy for my mom—that in the end people perceive me as someone who is making things up, as if what I'm saying isn't real. What my mother feared turned out to be so useless, because I speak and don't make things up, but this doesn't count as real, which, when I understood this was the case, gave me a certain freedom to tell the truth even more, at least until they sent me to see a psychiatrist. So I told him the truth, too, and so on, right until I realized that the house exists—this distracted me a bit—I don't know why but I felt distracted by the house existing, and I had to make sense of it. That's why I came here and almost, not on purpose, created chaos the first day as if I had come to start some kind of revolution, so even today those fans, who were usually chanting club songs, come to the house where my cousins, the evil clowns, live and yell at them and call them assholes. And I spend my time at Sobotka's place with Slavko—I can't call him my father anymore now that I've seen him—but anyway, I spend my time here cooking for him and wonder—Why did I come, what am I doing, what am I looking for? I can't leave until I figure this out, so I keep my thoughts quietly to myself, because I'm interested in the truth, not in what the old hags are saying, that I came here to look after Slavko because I'm still a stranger, always have been, and don't know how to feel as if I belong here, nor do I feel comfortable, and that is, I think, the problem with the house that bothers me in my very essence as a stranger, that the house really exists here nearby, right around the corner, and I don't know how to be a host, so I no longer, after that first day, go by the house. I haven't gone near it since then, and now I have to work out what this means. Will I now leave for once of my own volition, not driven away like before? It's up to me to stop reproaching myself for having no home, to stop thinking about loss—because I thought about it even when I wasn't thinking, in my own ironies that countered everything in the bitterness of my laugh, and it wasn't freedom, nor was it a new life; it was the continuation of the old denied existence, a life of nonexistence, the vacuum left by the family, the vacuum of everything never experienced on the tail of a decrepit house and a stolen world and place. And it both ended and didn't end, because the bitterness that used to be my pleasure remains, but now it's beginning to bother me, so I stand here and wonder whether to go to a house where there is nothing—it's all in my head—and I think to myself, When I leave again, whichever road I take, I will leave clean of the old story that coiled itself up into unhappiness. So I stay here at Sobotka's place, in someone else's house as usual, and cook cabbage every day and answer the phone when they call from the north, because they are the only ones who call on the landline, and I talk to Viktoria. She thinks I'm ordinary and our talks are ordinary, and she's a lesbian, she was just sorry to tell Sobotka. Well how come you're a lesbian, wasn't Jasmina supposed to be one, I tell her, and then she pauses briefly and says that Jasmina isn't a lesbian, and she is, and she didn't tell him that, though it's stupid, she says, but there you go, somehow I didn't. I don't know him very well, Viktoria says of her father, I would have told him if I'd gotten to know him better, now maybe I won't even get the chance, since they hurt him so badly. So she asks me if there's any point in her coming, and I say not unless you have to. Stay where you are, dear lesbian, this will not be a comfortable place for you, and you can inherit the house that exists and Sobotka's sculptures, they are really good, I'll take pictures of them and send them to you, and I did.

30

I DIDN'T QUITE understand the email Michael sent from his new address. He wrote that he'd done as I asked, he met the woman in Washington. I didn't know who the woman was he referred to. And that's how it all ended, he wrote. He sounded like a Michael who'd started drinking again.

He said they hadn't found anything concrete in the samples Alex brought for now. In short: nothing. But they like collecting samples of isolated groups, especially of white men, because maybe one day they'd see something they hadn't seen before. Therefore, our shares can be sold at a symbolic price.

He thought he'd pass, he said, because maybe these guys would bluff even if they did find something. Sell only if you really have to, he wrote. He said he hoped the money I earned from my fieldwork came in handy.

That's for sure, I thought. The only thing they can still pay for at the factory is the electric bill, and right now it looks like I'll need to lend money to Nikola, who's also drinking, for his trip to Switzerland. Sure, you can imagine the Colonel paying them for a turbine he hadn't seen, but he should check anyway. Especially since they're building a new turbine, because he didn't have the heart to stop the workers. That's my opinion, although today he also gave me his reasons for letting them continue.

"It's like when I couldn't explain to you why it was so important for me to know what you were working on for the Yanks," he said. "I can't admit to the workers that Oleg has gotten trapped with the Colonel, who is under attack from the whole civilized world. Only you and Lipša know. If anyone else found out, someone would spread the word and then we'd stand no chance. Besides that, they have the material for the second turbine, and at the moment, they're working without pay. We may have better luck with the next one, maybe we'll find the first one, find more customers. What good would it do just to send them home? I can't just throw up my hands."

"Maybe you can't deal with the truth," I said.

He fixed his gaze on the floor.

"You came here, you acted like good capitalists, and now you've already gotten used to playing the role," I said, thinking that by now he'd be better off without this. "It may be time to take off the mask."

He looked at me, offended. "I told them: write up what the company owes you as shares in lieu of wages, and we'll see. Okay, maybe I did get used to playing the role. But I am not even an entrepreneur. I just work here, supposedly as the director. They don't need me, unless I manage to pull off some kind of miracle. Something Oleg would do."

He looked at me, then he looked straight ahead again. "What would he do now?"

"From what I know of him, he probably would be drinking and snorting."

"Don't insult him. He had the guts to go down there, who knows if he's even alive."

"I'm not insulting him. I'm sorry. Just be realistic. Who can you sell that turbine to?"

"To the Colonel," Nikola said. "If he wins his war."

"They've got oil there, and his socialism. That doesn't suit either the West or the Islamists. Once they've started in on him, they'll finish him off."

"I've been reading up on him. He's gotten away many times."

"Okay, let's see what else we have. Who else is there to sell it to?"

"I don't know," he said with a reticent smile as he opened another beer. "Maybe the director of the local museum."

I guess he expected I'd laugh, too.

"They exhibit all the historical periods of the town. They could put the turbine under 'The Age of Industry,' you know, the final artifact."

"I doubt they have a big enough budget for that," I said.

"It's too big to fit."

"All right, Nikola. I want you to know that I'm with you in this till the end, okay? I'll help. We just need to be realistic."

"Thank you, sister," he said, and hugged me.

"Don't call me sister."

"I'm joking."

We kissed. We hadn't kissed like that for a while, the way we kissed when we first got together.

Michael's email ended with a P.S. containing information he probably would have disclosed sooner if he had been in his sober phase.

He said that the bosses at his firm didn't like him putting us in the contract, and that his company demanded more loyalty. They might have even read his emails, he said.

So he was in his final days there.

"Oh Michael, dammit, you're in trouble, too?" I said out loud.

Now I'll have the time to fight them, he finished. Michael did sound as if he'd been drinking again. He also added that I could write my own *postscriptum* now, after Washington.

I started writing: Dear Michael, I'm terribly sorry to hear you lost your job ...

You acted incredibly fairly. Thank you.

Anyway, I am doing fine. I'm in a new relationship, after many years. Everything's fine. I'm in my hometown, involved in something of a strange story that my boyfriend got me into (that word sounds so funny as I write it; his name is Nikola). I know this sounds stupid, but we're trying to save a factory in which his cousin invested money to build turbines. But he ... Oof, it's complicated, too complicated even for us, and probably incomprehensible for you. All in all, now I've become a part of it, because of Nikola, and because of the general atmosphere, too, I suppose.

It feels good to write to you again, to talk to you after everything.

I don't know what you meant by what you said about the woman in Washington and the end of the story. Is that something I'm supposed to understand? I forget some things. Maybe I suppress some, too. It took me a long time to forget our love ... love time is strange time. Some of it is so condensed, yet some is very stretched. I lost the habit of being in a relationship, so sometimes I don't feel as if I'm a part of it and am observing it from the outside. I can't say I've had much experience with love, and I'm a little bit afraid, afraid of love time. This is, or so it seems, special time.

You remember when our time was limited? When it seemed to be running out, that we were stealing it, when you ran toward me and I toward you, when it was *now-now-now* ... or never ... Afterward, when you were divorced, we had all the time in the world, and all the future, there were no obstacles between us, everything was ours, for real. And then the "now" disappeared, especially the *now-now-now*. Did you notice?

It's love time number two for me, limitless and too big, like baggy pants. That's what I'm afraid of. I remember how this went in Tbilisi with all the time and it turned out to be too much. Oh yes, it hovered around us, a few sizes too big. The contours of the body got lost and everything seemed so baggy. I was too young to understand, but now I see—love time number two, that's the whole fucking problem. At first it's condensed, like poetry, then it stretches out and loses form. I don't know whether you have this problem now in marriage. I don't want to pretend it's not there, although, as you know, the pretending is mandatory. Now I'm in a loving relationship and the assumption is that it should last a hundred years, and that assumption is the thing that hangs over our heads. Like—security. Although everything else around us is shaky. To say the least.

But somebody has turned things around here. I think society did, promising individual security with eternal love, though love and this baggy eternity thing seem to have problems to work out. Hell, not just problems—deep shit. Security, as you know, Michael, is only stapled onto love as an afterthought. The two have nothing to do with each other. Security is, in fact, an insidious promise, and it suffocates love. And the insidiousness of the promise, Michael, is because society wants to give itself an excuse for all the other security we're missing, they're giving up on me and you and they say to us: There's your love. Happy now? Find your security here, or scram.

Okay, say it like that, just don't drown me in the fake, insidious myths of a love you destroy while piling onto it the burden of fixing all the crap and being a cornerstone, a pillar for mortgages, for rescuing drowning people and for who-gives-a-fuck once you're sick and old. There you have love, it's eternal, believe in it.

I see right through it, Michael, because, as you know, I have a knack for analyzing things. And the thing about not continuing with chemistry, I'm not even so sorry about that: I grew tired long ago of thinking about the formulas we learned at school, so detailed, like we were going to make bombs, but these things I'm talking about: nothing. Not even an intro course. Just some fancy deceptions, so you get to Tbilisi like I did and think to yourself: Here I am, in eternity, love is here and everything will be fine. Yeah, right.

And then for years I chew over this: what did I do wrong? Later, I realize I was wrong because that was all I had, only love, no other supports, so love became the prerequisite for dinner and an evening dress and the future—a source of income, in short, in my specific random case. You have nothing, get yourself some love, that's what my society told me, because it's a bit more direct than yours. The situation was like that, stripped naked. But, as you also know, it's a lie that love can complement and fix everything that's missing. Even if I'd been smart, like some gold diggers I know, and cast a whole net around you, was your shoulder to cry on and a maid and a consultant and an ally and a nurse and I don't know what else, all of this wouldn't be love, but business. It's just business moved into another realm of life, business for unemployed cunts (okay, I know you didn't treat me like that, I'm being ironic), which I knew nothing about, so I just sat there and waited for love to flourish.

I don't know what you told that woman in Washington . . . as I'm writing this, memories are coming back to me, that I mentioned a woman once in Istanbul. . . . Oh yes, that's it . . . When I was dying of grief and couldn't make out what the cause of it was. Yes, yes . . . That's what you're talking about.

You remember it so clearly! I'm impressed, Michael. . . . It must have been troubling you, too, this enigma of our imminent doom, because you knew that you loved me. (I never once doubted your love for me, even in hindsight, for I was certain of your love and that certainty could have been a beautiful thing if it hadn't fallen into the category of things I preferred to forget for being so unbearable. Even now as I write this, it stirs old memories, and once again I feel the endless gulf where once there was something. This no longer has anything to do with you, it's just emotion with no address, emotion I ripped out and discarded; it's like watching Pompeii and reminiscing about death; a death you shared with the person you once were. You know those gulfs—it's dangerous to stare into them for long, so you avert your gaze as if they're suddenly burned.) But what are you going to do when we believe the lie about love being a replacement for other kinds of support, which is being served to us every day, so all the loser boys and girls can hang on to hope.

The problem was mine, but I can see that you, too, were troubled—this proof that love isn't everything, that poetry doesn't last when losers are hooked. Of course, I was a loser with false hopes. Santa Claus didn't come to town, the IMF did; Switzerland didn't come, instead the war over the municipalities did, but—okay—there's still love, and if you keep an open heart, everything will be fine. I'm telling our local version of the story. I don't know the American version. There's probably more Hollywood in yours.

I don't know what you told the woman in Washington, but here, now that it's all over, after all these years of silence, but also of shame, I feel like talking. Everything I'm saying may not seem like the best way to start new love, but the saying is good, I realize this, because I don't want to fall into the same trap twice, the baggy eternity of love time number two. What do you think, Michael, can things be different?

I'm involved in another episode here with Nikola, an episode comparable to a love episode in a way. I said it's complicated, but still—as I already mentioned—the workers here could be said to be waiting for love from investors, and the investors even gave them signs of love. The money's running out here, but the love is in full bloom. Nikola is... No, I shouldn't speak of how he's feeling, telling you about that would be inappropriate.

Anyway everything here is pretty much over, and I have to keep myself from frittering away all the money I earned by helping. I guess I'm a romantic even at this level, but this isn't the sort of thing promoted every day: not a lot of movies about it. Although this, too, is love, it's not a calculation. That is, even if it were a calculation, it hasn't worked. But it has had its honeymoon: the town sprang to life, became better, my town, the one I'd abandoned and stopped caring for. As if I found another one someplace else. But, in fact, I didn't. It was nice seeing this place become less glum and pathetic. I liked that. Maybe that's why I fell in love with Nikola, through that, possibly, although it's better if I don't mention this.

And now everything's going downhill again, and I can tell people are still hoping for a miracle, but realistically I should leave. I can save myself like that rich woman from the *Titanic* while her boyfriend, the poor worker, romantically freezes to death. I'm not only talking about Nikola, he could probably also save himself one way or another, but I'm talking about the people on the lower decks, the people who made the turbines while thinking the *Titanic* was operational again. It isn't. Their last lifeboat was bombed.

They're still coming to work, putting together a second turbine, no money left for paychecks, and Nikola has no clue what to do with this turbine that's antiquated and huge. They're building an artifact. They're more like artists, in my opinion, than the artists today are like artists...

My phone rang.

Nikola.

I saved the email as a draft. Maybe I shouldn't send it, I thought.

3 1

SOBOTKA, THERE'S NOTHING there. Only numbers left. That are called us. And I. I exists and does not exist. As far as I'm concerned, I is the only thing that does exist, but therefore, it also doesn't exist. Only I exists, but therefore, it also does not exist, because my I-self exists to handle the influence of the other numbers. My I, the thing that is spun by the tongue, which lies in grammar, which lies in this body deserted, my I is a cardboard shelter, Sobotka, like your I that lies there and doesn't speak, that lies there with a hole in its head, which I also have, but without the bandages. Then I say our I, because everybody is I, Sobotka, that's the basis for god, because we are all I: you feel it, I feel it, and we are in I united. Have you, Sobotka, thought about the fact that everybody is I? And that everybody says I thinking the same, the thing inside they are protecting, yet which cannot be protected? Does this, Sobotka, mean that we are all the same being, only scattered but the same, the same feeling, the same folly, the same lie of itself? I think reincarnation is not necessary because we are all already I. You are also I. And

I am I. Why should we reincarnate into one another when we would be the same again? No one shall become you, or her, or him. You are always I and are always in the same problem. My plan, Sobotka, was to leave my I. That is my plan, politically. That has been my intent ever since I was fed up, brother, with being I, if you understand . . . it may sound strange to you . . . but for me, think about it, it's strange how others aren't bored by this. How I was the only one bored by it, that's what feels strange to me. Is it simply a matter of the body? I am I, and you are you, because you are another body? Is it that? Seems to me that it is only a matter of the body, otherwise—your I and my I—where's the difference in feeling? I know, you remember something else, you are in your I, but I don't care about remembering, because I have seen through the distinction: it's not a distinction, it's the same thing. You're lying in a coma, I'm speaking in a language, and language makes me exist, but I'm lying dead in language, because I've killed myself, technically, by seeing through the I as an asshole. Everybody's got one, as someone once said. Sobotka, you're in a coma now, I can speak to you frankly. I gave up when I realized there is nothing that binds me to my I, a futile endeavor. Wasting time to experience language. I like you because you tried to live with your I, to wrangle with it, with the belief that you exist. We are complete opposites, Sobotka. But in between are all the others who openly lie. I respect you, but the ones who say I, and there is nobody there, and say I again, and there is nobody there again, and say I again, and there is nobody there again, well, Sobotka, they are unbearable. You have also changed, since I gave up on I—I can see it more easily. You used to be cocky, that is, you were full of life and the courage of life, and then later you became like someone who was grieving for himself. And then again you came back to life for a little while until they killed you. There is even some continuity of I present in you, so you didn't quite lie when you stood up and introduced yourself. But brother, all the rest of them in this country, on TV, cannot utter I, without me laughing, without me going mad from laughter so much that I give up on I, because how could I constantly say hi to false I-selfs all the time—I don't know how you managed it, but for me it was easier to leave the grammar. I, as you have realized, don't care about meaning, because the meaning is I. I don't care that I am not holding on to the logic, because the logic is I. Because I is the thing that makes stories and wants to sustain itself. I only care about the cosmic flow, freedom, seeing as I'm left with nothing else. I would like for you to wake up and for the world to seem to exist again. Because you are, of all the people I know, the only one to try to make the world exist so I can recognize it. You were greatly mistaken, but hats off to you, you really did try to exist. It's a rare ambition, when you think about it. You were ambitious, Sobotka, by wanting to be you, that is, I, wanting to prove there is something behind grammar. My dear friend, you are one of the rare ones I have met on earth. You were a man, something I have surpassed, but nonetheless, that was a touching attempt.

That somebody was shooting strangers on the street, this he could not fathom. He was prepared to walk toward those people with open arms, thinking it impossible for someone to fire on a man walking like that, and he walked like that once.

Zlata went mad, telling him: *No! Don't go!*

But after he saw the people on TV walking like that in the capital city, he got into his car and drove there. At the city limits he was stopped by people with eye slits, faceless, a declaration of a new brand of people. They could have killed him then, he later realized—Zlata was right and he was wrong, because he was still the same old man.

They could have shortened him by a head, but that mustn't have been easy for them, either, a few words could still get to those faceless eyes, when they asked him what he was, and it was already obvious they were referring to his faith and ethnicity. He said, "I'm a workingman, unemployed, a former strike leader. Nothing more."

After observing him silently, the eyes asked him, "Who were you on strike against?"

"I was on strike for the workingman."

The eyes watched him from their slits like the eyes of a lizard. Maybe he, too, was a workingman, so he gestured, let Sobotka through. He must have been a workingman, thought Sobotka, but by the next day he could no longer speak to him that way—by the next day all of that had been erased.

Sobotka came to that city—already under siege and in the snipers' crosshairs—but they were still old people, gullible people from the peculiar system, and stubborn in their naivete, so they walked through the city, sometimes holding hands and singing good-natured, naive songs, trusting a peace that was already gone, but they refused to believe this, so strong was their belief in something else, because it was not only belief. Those people were different from people of today, and they couldn't be convinced of anything, they couldn't be swayed other than by force, iron and bullet, they could not be swayed except by being killed.

Sobotka walked through the city beside them. The squares and streets were full of them, thousands were walking here and there, and not knowing where, they finally convened at and entered the Assembly of the Republic, and not knowing what to do, demanded the government's resignation, and a few hours later the head of the government indeed tendered his resignation. This went so smoothly that Sobotka realized the government didn't matter, this was a faceless thing, and he went out among the people again, just so he could walk with them and be there to the end.

Sobotka walked through this wondrous city, among these people who were walking like Jesus, in this tragedy that seemed beautiful for a moment, in a city most luminous in the moments before its death.

While they were walking across a bridge, a young woman next to him fell. And another. Picked off by a sniper. This could not be explained to them any other way. The start of a new era.

Sobotka saw all this once more, in his nightmare during the coma, and then he felt he, too, had been hit.

32

THIS WAS ALL because Sobotka was lying there neither dead nor alive. Only Slavko came and talked to him. I stood out in front of the room for days, as if I were watching over him, because it was easier for me to stand outside the room than inside, and I heard Slavko talk. If Sobotka can hear anything, he will wake up, crazed by all the talk, I thought. I was thinking about sending Slavko away, but then I remembered how I'd tried to send him away from the factory, and Sobotka blew up, so I told myself to let him be, if he can hear, maybe he's even amused. The rest of us are just standing there silent and waiting anyway.

I waited and picked through my thoughts as I watched over him. I picked through all of them and concluded that I was hooked, that I wasn't free, that I hadn't been free for a long time, but now it was obvious.

I was trying to reassure people like Branoš, because they didn't know what they were talking about.

But the acid started eating away at my throat while I stood guard there and listened to Slavko's words through the door. I was burning up inside, so they gave me pills and told me what I shouldn't eat, and I said to the doctor, "There are things I need to find out and do what has to be done, and then I'll be able to eat what I want."

"What things?" he asked.

"It'll be like an operation for me," I said.

"You'll operate on yourself?" the doctor asked me.

"Doctors can't help with this."

"Really?" He looked at me. "Is this all in your mind?"

"Yes, in my mind, my psyche. But also in my physique."

"So what's wrong?" he asked.

I wanted to tell him I have to get into some other kind of trouble to rid myself of this, though again I wouldn't be free. But it was best just to take the prescriptions and leave.

And then today, Slavko came out into the hallway and said, "Flat."

"Flat?"

"It's flat," said Slavko.

I didn't want to understand, so I said, "What are you jabbering about?"

He was holding his head like he was scared of me, he started scratching his head like he wanted to scrub it, or to avoid my gaze.

I grabbed his arm and he stopped.

He looked at me and said, "He's dead. Sobotka."

I walked in and looked at the monitor—the line was flat.

When I hollered, and my throat stung like I was spewing lava, the nurses came running and then the doctors and they tried something there, I wasn't even looking, I could only see Sobotka's face.

I looked at him for a while, in my unrest. Sobotka's face was peaceful, his eyes closed, without the spasm of surprise I'd seen on the faces of the dead.

I remembered his face looking down at me from above, when he passed me food and books from the upper floor. So I look up and wonder: Is there anything there?

Then I crouched, with my head in my fists, then kneeled as if praying, and the nurses looked at me with pity, thinking I was his son.

Slavko was there again, beside me. He put his hand on my shoulder.

"They killed him," I said.

"Because he existed," said Slavko. He patted me on the shoulder.

Then Slavko seemed saner than me, maybe because we were there, at dead Sobotka's side, and Slavko seemed to understand everything there was to understand, while I knew so few things. I asked him, "Will you tell his family?"

He hesitated a bit then said, "Nedra will."

"I have to go," I said.

Slavko nodded.

I looked at Sobotka again. I never told him how much he meant to me, and for that reason I didn't think he was going to die, that he couldn't leave what with all the words I'd left unsaid.

"Sobotka," I said, "thank you, dear friend. I'll be on my way."

Then I left for home to pack, and prepare.

33

I SAW IT on the Internet.

At first there were the headlines, then came the video.

Did they cut off the man's ear? It was him, bloody on one side of his head. He was under the mob—the phone used to record it was shaking—then he was on his feet again, surrounded by shrieking cries of Allahu Akbar, as if the shouter were overexcited and in a hurry. Did they cut off his ear? I couldn't get a good look. I don't know why I was staring only at that.

I was afraid Oleg would show up somewhere in the video, with one side of his head bloody.

He was dead soon afterward. The Colonel.

The headlines on news sites flickered with excitement.

A not-well-hidden euphoria, an odd kind of happiness, like the one when they started bombing Baghdad. When a meal is long in the making, everybody is happy once it's finally done.

I sat there for a while as if I'd survived a car crash and afterward I was sitting by the side of the road. You were on your way to somewhere, and now you're sitting by the side of the road and you're supposed to be happy to be alive.

But the journey is done.

I tried.

There was no money in Switzerland.

Hanka and I went through all the dusty papers, which included the ones in her attic, and shouted "Yes! They're here!" when we found the contracts from 1980 to 1985. So I began calling old clients—the few who had survived—and in those international, sometimes even intercontinental, telephone calls they spoke to me as if I were calling from some extremely disrupted time zone.

"Turbine 83-N?"

"Yes, you bought one once . . . Could you use another one, new, at a discount?"

"When did we buy that?"

"Hmm . . . 1984."

"Sir, did you find a buried warehouse?"

"No, we manufactured—"

"No, unfortunately, we have no use for it. But, pardon me for asking, why did you manufacture it?"

"It just happened, sir. Might you direct me to someone who could be a potential buyer? Perhaps some of your old clients, partners . . ."

"I don't wish to discourage you, sir, but I believe it belongs in a museum."

"Thank you for the information."

"You're welcome."

I tried everything I could, I said to myself as I went down to the hall.

When I got there, they were all looking at me before I even said a word; a dazed aura was probably exuding from me.

I yelled, "Stop the machines!"

All eyes were on me, and the noise gradually thinned, the machines powered down. And then there was only a little clatter here and there. And then that stopped as well.

Tense stillness.

I began, "Listen, people…" I put my hand to my forehead, feeling giddy, as if pre-stroke. Then I took a deep breath and realized I could press on.

"People… Oleg… Oleg probably won't be coming back… The chances that he's alive are slim. Things took a really ugly turn and now… I don't think we should go on making this turbine."

I stopped, and they must have noticed I was struggling with something that was keeping me from continuing. I waited for it to pass.

"I think everything is over."

I stared at the floor.

"I can't talk about hope anymore…. You're working without pay…. If it means anything to you, I, too, am working without pay…. But… We should wrap this up. There, I've said it!"

"Boss, what do you mean?" asked Branoš after a silence.

"The chances are slim, very slim…. I think they're nonexistent. I don't believe we have a buyer anymore."

"There's no chance?" asked Zulko.

"Look, people, I can't keep you here…. You can kill me, this is horrible for me…. I don't think we have a chance. I can't say it any other way than that."

All the faces looked at me, and all I could do was stand there, maskless. I thought about the day I came here as a stranger and watched Sobotka wandering through the plant, the cobwebs and dust. It will be the same again, I thought, and again I'll be a stranger. I'd been haunted by this moment every night, the moment when we'd have to put a stop to things. This is the relationship in which we were cheating, Oleg and I. How could he say "Trust me" and then dump me here as the scapegoat?

So that's it, I removed my mask, airing everything in the open—I'm just one of the lies they fell for. It was hard for me to stand there, a stranger, and I was ashamed. What right did I have to stand there, what right did I have to speak? I thought they were going to rip me apart, or so imagined the guilty man inside me.

Šeila had been telling me this wasn't my fault. Maybe. Maybe, but somebody will have to take the blame, and there were no other candidates I could see.

Ćamil raised his hand, started turning around frantically, and when he realized that everybody was already looking at him, he said, "I don't buy it! I didn't buy it from the start! But . . . But, since Sobotka is dead . . . those sons of bitches! . . . And since Oleg is, as you say, stuck in the middle of nowhere . . . And since Erol is missing and there's a warrant on his head . . . I'm in favor of . . . of finishing the turbine! You can't walk out on a half-finished job!"

It's just wishful thinking, I thought, rubbing my eyes. Then I heard a murmur, a murmur of approval. This was not how I'd envisioned stripping away the mask. Get it over with and be done with it. But I could feel something else in the murmur. They refused to accept the pointlessness of it, that all of this was pointless. My hand slid down over my eyes.

"No way!" yelled somebody else.

34

SOMETIMES I COME out here and watch from the edge.

I look down, through a gentle, clearing haze to see if there is still movement down there around the factory.

My sheep are bleating; I finally became a shepherd, here, above the first tier of clouds.

My sheep are bleating; sheep which are not mine but belong to two old women who don't speak to each other and to whom, as they say, I am worth my weight in gold, so they will not give me up, should anyone come looking.

And both keep asking how I ended up here, and each day I tell them a different *Hamlet* story, which never bothers them; they tell me different stories about how they ended up here as well. Sometimes I tell them Hamlet was the son of a good king, sometimes that he was the son of a bad king, and sometimes the son of an unknown king. And sometimes Hamlet was the son of all three kings at once—which was not a lie, though it sounds the least true. I say this to them, forcing them to sit together though they don't converse, they just look straight at me.

Hamlet wished to hear the truth from the last living king —I say—and knowing the king would lie, he had to come up with a show.

Hamlet arrived at a lonely manor where the king came to fish by a mountain stream.

Hamlet ambushed the king near the manor, pointed his weapon at him, and proceeded to fire questions at him in rage. But his indecisiveness surfaced so the king let him blow off steam, all the while lying, and then careless Hamlet gave the king the chance to point the weapon at him.

So the king held his antemortem speech for Hamlet, disarmed.

The king's hair was long and black, streaked with gray, his frame big and stout, and his paunch rotund. Crestfallen Hamlet sat in the garden of the manor, as the king said: "It's funny you should come for me to kill you again. And what choice do I have, now that you're threatening me?"

"Come again?" asked Hamlet.

"This, it seems, is your fate. Yours and your real father's, who was once the king of the streets, but whom you never met. You must have come here because of your other father, the king of the paupers, the one who began to punch above his weight and then all of you followed his lead, eh?"

"Yes, I am here because of him. Are you the one who had him killed?"

"What were you thinking? What am I with all of you strutting around? A passerby, a beggar you can send away from your doorstep?"

"Tell me who you are," said Hamlet.

"You really are a fool. You know, ordinary people are all wimps."

"Why?"

"They refuse to admit the truth."

"What truth?"

"That I exist," he raised his arms in the air, thrust out his chin, and shook his head as if declaiming.

Hamlet stared at him as if missing the joke, a chill creeping down his spine.

"I rule this place. I collect my taxes where and when I see fit, and you cannot scare me away, you miserable bastards, because then the other poor bastards will start questioning my authority. Whatever got into you? You've jeopardized my reputation. You are the ones who attacked me. I needed to send a message, as a caution to others."

"I understand now. So what happened to my real father?"

"You won't live much longer so I'll tell you. I am not happy about killing the same man twice. When I first saw you, I thought you'd risen from the dead; do you know what that means? I thought he couldn't be killed, that he'd been resurrected."

Hamlet, disarmed, looked so foolish—he wasn't thought to be overly intelligent anyway—that the king hadn't realized he was deceiving him. But around the corner from the manor, Laertes waved to Hamlet and hid—he was brother to Ophelia who'd perished in the king's castle. Hamlet found her last name and where she'd come from in papers he'd found in the junkyard. He never managed to forget, though he did try. So, thinking about his assistant in the deceit, he visited her town and found Laertes.

Like Hamlet, Laertes hadn't known the truth.

"Your father was the first person I killed. He was my friend and, to be honest, afterward I felt distressed, feverish, as if convalescing. But once that passed I felt no fear. Then you came and reminded me. And I was honestly thinking of sparing you, because I thought this was a sign; I even thought about adopting you. But as you can tell, history will repeat itself."

"What was my father like?"

"He tried to be both bad and good. To be feared, yet not do anything really cruel. You can put on a charade, but once they realize your threats are empty, it's over. It's the same with you coming here. He attacked me, too, for beating up a whore who didn't survive in the end."

"Wait, you said he was the first person you killed."

"I wasn't counting her."

"And do you remember the woman, Ophelia, who perished in your castle? I came, you know, because of her." The king looked at him, puzzled, so Hamlet described what had happened, as a reminder.

"Yes, I remember. . . . But here I am telling you this fine story, and you came here for a piece of ass you picked up along the way? What was she to you?"

"My sister!" said Laertes, coming forward and waiting for the king to see him, throw down his weapon, and look him in the eyes. Hamlet sat there, disarmed, unable to do anything but watch, which was a weak moment in his own play, but he couldn't think of anything better; he watched the king spin around swiftly with his weapon, and then there was a thundering noise.

The king fell. He doubled over sideways, awkwardly. One of his legs miraculously remained in the air. The leg looked as if it were still trying to get away.

Laertes stood.

Hamlet sat.

There was no throne.

Hamlet was the accused, he couldn't betray Laertes, there was no liberty for him. He made his peace with that, his freedom had deserted him years before—as soon as he'd attained it.

Sometimes he comes and stares into the abyss from the edge, through a gentle, clearing mist, fearing each time that he'll find there is no longer any movement down there. That would, he thought, leave him imprisoned in the sky, a dead man.

35

"HELLO TIMA, IT'S Šeila."

"*Heeey*, what's up?"

"You somewhere abroad? Should I Skype you?"

"Yes, in London. Go ahead, I was just responding to emails on my iPad."

Soon Šeila was looking at Tima in one of those cafés where everybody's fumbling around on their computers, doing something, and there's no telling whether what they're doing is work or not.

Tima was looking good, but she seemed a little nervous: too much communication, she said, it never ends.

"It's good as long as your phone keeps ringing," said Šeila.

Tima had made it, so people said.

But only after leaving Šeila.

Collaborating with Tima was one of Šeila's attempts at breaking into the global market, not something many people in her social environment had tried to do, but this idea was probably a carryover from her relationship with Michael. She'd tried her hand at being an art dealer after spending years working part-time in the midst of NGOs, culture, festivals, shows. She was twice on the team that arranged her country's entry for the Venice Biennale, and she felt she understood the vagaries of the art market. She identified seven young visual artists in the hope that she'd represent them, marketing and selling their work, but she didn't yet own a gallery: someday, she figured, she would. Tima was one of the seven—the only one for whom things were looking up: after a few unusual, provocative works, she'd met with a solid international reception.

But then Tima realized Šeila couldn't help her move forward. The worst thing was that Šeila also knew this—she did what she could, but she couldn't help Tima show her work at the best exhibition halls in London and New York nor could she guarantee sensational publicity. She wasn't even close. Šeila accepted what she usually tried to deny: for this kind of job she lacked the know-how to pull strings in the world of culture: the power of the place and the power of the money spinning there. This was what was called "the market," but the word "cash" would have sufficed. She'd tried to create an art market where there was no cash, and her efforts fared well with the critics and the media, but what was supposed to pass for a market was so miserable that you couldn't actually quote the figures in the media; instead, an illusion had to be sustained, and behind it were art managers like herself and artists who could barely eke out a living. Everything was there except the cash, so local fame had to suffice in the realm of this simulation of success. And when ravenous egos were added to the mix, the whole thing tipped over into the grotesque. She saw her artists gossiping and badmouthing Tima, at first quietly, but then louder and louder, envying her success even though she—and Šeila knew this only too well—was earning no more than a low-level clerical worker.

One day, Tima invited her for coffee and then, with delight she could hardly hide despite her best efforts, she admitted she'd received an invitation from a powerful art dealer, a man from London who'd turned a few so-called Neurotic Realists there into international celebrities. I guess he also needs some postwar neurosis in his portfolio, thought Šeila, trying to feel that the news was a shared success. "He doesn't want a third player in the game," stammered Tima. That small piece of information, then silence.

In the silence Šeila saw how, like when you push the wrong key on the keyboard, a mass of files is deleted, whole folders of her illusions went up in smoke.

But she tried to keep this to herself. "All right, my friend, good luck! You've earned this."

Tima looked at her with gratitude, and then added cautiously, "And our contract?"

"We're terminating it orally, okay?"

"Orally?"

"Tima, this is not the best day of my life. But I'm moving on. I'm telling you, you're free."

Šeila's coffee was left unfinished. She remembered Tima's look, with its mingling of hope, guilt, gratitude, and the fear of what all this really meant.

As she was leaving, Šeila thought, I'll contact you again only if you're superrich and I have nothing to eat.

She also thought, Fuck it, there's no point in doing this job, we're done here.

She hadn't called Tima since.

Perhaps that is why Tima was looking a little nervous over Skype, she thought.

"Tima, this isn't related to our contract. That's been voided. But I have a story to tell you. And you must pass the story on."

She did not want to say "You owe me" as she watched Tima, who nodded.

"Art, today, is a story, not a skill. Proportion and perspective were discovered a long time ago," said Šeila, smiling. "Instead of discovering perspective, today we have a story . . ."

" . . . that broadens the perspectives," finished Tima in that café far away, with a smile reminiscent of lost loves. "Our old mantra, I know."

Skype seemed frozen for a moment. There are smiles which are sadly warm, like a memory of parting. Šeila watched Tima's frozen image.

Some more voice crackling, and then nothing.

She waited, and saw Tima again, running her fingers through her light, tangled hair.

"So, I have a story that needs to be passed on. To the person who markets stories."

"Oh? Yeah . . . Hmm."

"Is there a problem?"

Šeila started to question the point of the call. Nothing will come of it, she thought, this woman has forgotten everything.

"Šeila, this is strictly between you and me. . . . Lately Malcolm's attention has not really been focused on me."

Šeila saw in her grimace that Tima still dared be honest with her.

Okay, failure—much better than refusal.

"My lips are sealed, Tima. I assure you. Besides, I don't run in the same old circles. I'm far away. . . . Tell me, how're things going?"

"Well . . . not bad. But . . . I came here and now I'm part of the scene. We've met a few times at exhibits and once he said, 'Wait a minute, you're actually here? What're you doing here?' I realized then that he'd taken me on to represent me as an artist from away. . . . But I wanted to be here. And I've made some things, but . . . Damn it, Šeila, I don't know, I started thinking about what people expected me to be making. I didn't used to think that way. Before, things came to me naturally, pure audacity, and that was that. Now I feel like I'm faking it, selling, overthinking.... There's no playfulness. I'm an artist here, with a career. And there are billions of others like me. What do they think about? They scheme about how to make a name for themselves. They're full of shit. Now I'm here. I guess I'm full of shit. But you can't do that, you can't go around plotting how you'll become famous. Pricks like Malcolm will see right through you. Everything's this big brouhaha over nothing and sometimes I don't know where I am. I need to collect my thoughts. But I can't go home, because the local assholes will gloat, and I still won't have peace. Where are you? I want to go to the middle of fucking nowhere."

"That's right where I am," said Šeila, and laughed.

"You are, eh?"

"You should come here. Then you'll know where you stand. Exactly where you said. I'll tell you a story. You'll tell it to him. You can get involved in it with your work as well. You'll think of something when you get here. There is no competition, no usual suspects ... The idea is so twisted that it requires a shift in perspective. I keep track of what's going on: after Princess Diana with blood dripping from her lips, all those dead animals and the Virgin Mary made of elephant dung, there isn't much room left for provocation. This is something else. I have an audacious story and it needs to be passed on to him fucking audaciously! Because this is exactly what he wants—this will be unheard-of audacity if he does it!"

"All right, the story ... But is there something concrete?"

"Yes."

"You have an artifact?"

"Yes. It's very, very large."

36

WHAT WOULD OLEG say? I imagine this, I imagine his laughter reverberating from the last row of this bright hall that smells of the future and spaceships, supposedly it, too, was a factory before— of course, when you look around, what else could it have been?

I imagine him sneaking toward us, like Van Gogh with no ear, and watching the contorted miracle we're about to perform. I know he'd be delighted with us for trying. I know he'd chuckle at the very idea and say, *Yes! Run with it!*

That's why I agreed.

That, and because we didn't have many aces up our sleeves after the time in Switzerland when I stood on the hotel balcony, holding a bottle of whisky and watching the lake in the night. I repeated several times, aloud, "Wow Lipša sure is a smartass! Can you believe it?" I really meant that, while chugging the whisky straight from the bottle. "You can't even throw yourself off a balcony! What an amazing woman!" And then I laughed at myself.

When a garbage truck rolled past the hotel before dawn, I

thought I saw Oleg standing on the rear steps with the garbage collectors, waving.

I waved at them from the balcony, without a sound.

We'll see if the Malcolm guy can pull off this miracle.

Apparently, he already has.

He's a groundbreaker, he's expected to make shocking moves, Šeila used to say before I even understood who she was talking about. When he says something is art, everybody comes to believe him, she said as I stared at her. He sold some of the work of a few artists for vast sums of money. The artists he has promoted no longer do their art on their own. They have assistants and an entire machinery. What matters is the idea, the story. If we were to tell it on our own, there'd wouldn't be much of a splash, but with him our story is set forth in the context of his other audacious works. And this turbine is art, Šeila said like she feared her thoughts might escape her, so I thought she felt unwell that morning as I watched her groggily, realizing she hadn't slept at all.

"You said we should keep it real."

"Hey, since it was completed after the client had been killed and you found no way to sell it on the industrial market, and since it's, so to speak, an antique, we have to explain all that to him."

"Perhaps there's no chance, but I've dug everywhere to find contracts signed after 1985, to see if there are any other options left," I said. "There are even a few clients who vanished into thin air, there's no trace of them on the Internet, but perhaps the names of the companies changed."

"That is your rational excuse. You know there's no buyer," Šeila said. "You went ahead and built it with other motives. You couldn't stop. You thought you had to go all the way, otherwise everything would have been pointless. Right?"

"True. But don't blame everything on me. I told them—"

"And yet, you finished it."

"We did."

"That's what I'm saying. You don't need to justify yourself to me and undermine my story. This is a would-be commercial product. Actually, it's less of an industrial product than what most of Malcolm's artists sell. They wouldn't even make their art if there were no market. That's the difference in motives. And since things are as they are, we'll generate a great debate by presenting art that's allegedly an industrial product. That's what he's looking for, debate about art."

I watched her, trying to figure out where this torrent of words was coming from.

During our conversations, after Šeila came up with the idea, as she was preparing to call Tima, she paced around the house frenetically, she drank coffee and smoked, and I feared that, after all that had happened we were so desperate that we were succumbing to madness; seriously I didn't think the turbine could become art, and that angered the misunderstood genius in her, so, trying to convince me, she planned her concept out loud and mentioned Duchamp's urinal, which he boldly titled *Fountain*. At the time, she said with fire blazing in her eyes, even his avant-gardists didn't think the piece was art. But eventually it did become art, she continued, smoking one cigarette after another. It's the context, the presentation—there are so many more ways to present this, and believe me, Malcolm knows the ropes. I see you're not bad at it yourself, I said as I began to see a logic behind it, although by then I didn't know whether we were trapped in our thought bubble or what was even real outside the rented guest worker's mansion where I owed rent.

"This is the last card, so we might as well play it," I said. "But honestly . . . I don't think it's art. Can I say that or should I keep my mouth shut?"

"See, this is the debate, what you and I are talking about," her thoughts latched on to each other. "You don't think of it as art, because it hasn't yet become art. It will be art if we place it in the right context, if Malcolm places it in the right context, that is, because I don't have the power or the reputation he has. The fact that many people think what Malcolm is selling is not art, that, too, is part of the game, see?"

"I'm with you . . ."

"Hey, Nikola, you manufactured the 83-N turbine that we're going to make into a global sensation," she said, adding to her smile a spark of jest and a boatload of enthusiasm, the smile of someone with an *idea*. I'd already seen that smile, even on Oleg whose ideas got me into this hopeless mess, so I trembled inside, afraid I was going to believe her, not knowing if the two of us were merely two sleepwalkers from N. sinking deeper into chaos, or actually finding a way out.

"Don't exaggerate," I said. "I didn't do the manufacturing."

"I know, dear. All of you did. So much hope in the midst of ruins. Pure art."

"Now you're messing with me."

"A little. But actually, I'm not."

The first time we talked to Malcolm on Skype, he was sitting next to Tima. As an introduction she told us—while he listened to our language as if he were absorbed in it—that she had not really had the time to pitch the whole story to him, because he was always in such a hurry. She had set out for him a general outline in five minutes just before the call. But he was intrigued. Tima informed us we had an hour. From that moment on, she sat to the side, her arms crossed.

It took Šeila around half an hour to explain the story to him and the way she'd market it, and as her finale she showed him the newspaper article "Self-Management Beyond Seven Mountains." He was silent for maybe half a minute, looking down at them as if peering over eyeglasses, like a professor, even though he didn't wear glasses, and then he burst out laughing and brayed like a donkey—his face even looked a little donkeyish.

After he caught his breath, he said, "You guys . . . You guys *really* are audacious!"

I watched this guy laugh in our faces. And no wonder.

He kept laughing. I couldn't watch him, so I moved out of the Skype frame just as he said to Šeila, "One thing is for certain. You came to the right person."

He grew serious, reverting to the character of an unfeeling man in a suit. He must have had a special talent for these transformations, because on the screen he now looked as expressionless as a computer simulation, and he reminded me of a member of Kraftwerk.

Then he wanted to see the turbine, so we were soon in the plant with our laptop—the people there looked at us askance. We had to interrupt Slavko, who was working on something. When we pointed the camera at the turbine, Malcolm said in an affected manner, "Ooh! This looks, I must say, far better than the usual variety of crap trotted out for me! Yes. Who would have thought? Perhaps we can start. This might just be it. . . ."

We're not in our little bubble, I thought. We are stepping into a much larger bubble.

"What did you say it was called again? *The Last Socialist Realist Artifact*? Who came up with that?"

"Me," said Šeila.

"Oh, you're wonderful," he said, showing his teeth and switching to the role of rascal again.

It won't be long before this man starts hitting on her, and any minute now he'll offer her a job, I thought.

We'd decided beforehand that we weren't going to hold anything back—we'd tell him everything, because the story was the only thing that would entice him, as Šeila said. The whole story, even the Colonel.

We also told him about the turbine that was stuck at a port somewhere in the Maghreb.

This got him thinking.

"So there are two?"

"Yes. Probably," I said. "There will be a hearing in their commercial court, but the date hasn't yet been set. We didn't rush it, because we didn't know where we'd put it anyway. But if someone pressures them ..."

"Hmm. I'll have to think about all of this. Could this be our next big thing? We do need just one, I think. It wouldn't do for another one to turn up later. We should be selling the last one, get it? If another one exists, tell them to drop it into the sea."

"Perhaps they already have."

"No 'perhaps.' We must be certain. And corroborate."

"Okay. But if you folks from London threaten them, perhaps they'll act more quickly."

"Mhm. I just wanted to ask: Is there anybody there who's involved in the project and is, actually, an artist?"

"I was thinking Tima might get involved somehow," said Šeila.

"Of course, but ... You know, I'm trying to picture the whole thing. The story we put together, the context. I have to picture the scene. ... The exhibit, the coverage, the shock, the debates. ... Clearly, it's a product of collective effort, but ... we need a name, a face. Art without an author, well, that would pass muster with young leftists, but we need someone to buy it. ... We must add, attach something to it."

"This whole backstory, there could—"

"Sure ... All the stories need to be told ... And the entrepreneur who initiated it, he is interesting, his fate … and the engineer. We have to commission their portraits, unusual portraits, from a painter on the rise. I'm just brainstorming. Their stories must be there. And the whole history behind it. We must have all of that. The turbine alone won't be enough. We have to do more. An act, a performance, something. …"

Now we'll be selling Oleg and Sobotka as a "story," I thought. This is how far we've come.

This is our last resort, so how was I thinking this wouldn't be prostitution?

Then it hit me: This was going to be disgusting. In my mind, I began apologizing to Oleg and Sobotka. I imagined Oleg's face, and then I realized—he wouldn't mind at all. I could almost hear him saying, Just take their money.

So, this jackass is looking for an artist. I wondered whether it would be stupid …

"Our chief engineer, Sobotka, he was a sculptor, too, for the fun of it," I told Malcolm.

"He was? What did he make?"

"Weird sculptures made of iron."

"Okay, much better than if they were made of wood and if they weren't weird. … Go on. Describe them to me."

"He welded all sorts of things. Car engines and ironware. Each sculpture has car headlights attached to it, asymmetrically. Some have more headlights, some fewer. Many of the headlights were broken in car wrecks. He got them at a garbage dump. It's not clear what they are. Like creatures evolving from vehicles. Beaten-up creatures."

"Really? Where are they?"

"N."

"Are they rusty?"

"Well, kind of …"

"Could you drive there and show them to me?"

"I don't think there is a wireless connection there."

"Send me pictures, then."

He continued talking to Šeila. Slavko soon tapped me on the shoulder and handed me a cell phone—it was Nedra.

"Slavko says you needed pictures?" asked Nedra.

Malcolm received them a few minutes later, a bit surprised at how organized we were.

In the end he said, "You've intrigued me. I'll come with a photographer, a landscapist, Tima . . . Actually, with a whole team. We'll document everything. The whole town. If the story is well-received, we'll split the money from the sale fifty-fifty."

That seemed like a lot to me.

"Fifty-fifty, or no deal," he said. "It's the standard fee, pal. Standard. If it were anyone else, I'd charge even more for this kind of risk. But I see you need the money. I'd like to do something worthwhile."

I said, "That was our story, too."

"Wonderful," said Malcolm. "It's obviously catching."

Then he lifted his finger and became conspicuously serious, saying, "But, to be clear—we'll be splitting fifty-fifty a figure you wouldn't dream of asking, let alone obtaining, on your own! These decorations and additions are okay in moderate amounts, but the turbine. . . . No, we don't want the story to sound humanitarian. We're selling this as art! Just so there's no confusion, I'll price the work so that there can be no doubt! You know, when you add a lot of zeros, it pays off."

"All right," I said. "Fifty-fifty art. What matters is that it's not humanitarian."

"No way! Please, don't feel bad about this. That's important. Take this as a magnificent bank robbery. Only someone who's loaded could afford it anyway. Modesty is no virtue here. Trust me!"

He declared this as if he were Oleg's twin, and it wouldn't have surprised me at all if they were on the same sorts of drugs.

Yes, he will certainly offer Šeila a job and try to bang her as soon as I go around the corner. But this guy, unlike Oleg, is fucking with a condom, I thought.

Now we were there, in London, at an exhibition hall that used to be a factory.

The turbine was on display. It glittered in front of a red curtain. There were very few things in the world as appealing for camera flashes as this was.

Sobotka's sculptures were there, too. Although they had a few rusty parts, they'd been cleaned so well that they were shining: polished ugly ducklings from his cottage yard.

Large-format paintings also hung on the gallery's walls.

One painting was titled *The Arrival of the Investor*. Rio, a young painter for whom Malcolm had high hopes, was asked to paint Oleg and Sobotka meeting for the first time. When he came to see the town, we met over a drink at the Blue Lagoon and I told him how it happened, unaware that he would ask me every day to retell this, perhaps because he noticed that my story was gradually developing and expanding. It could be said that I directed the scene for him, because he needed extras as well. However, in the log cabin bar outside town where we met Sobotka for the first time, on the second day of painting, Rio suddenly dropped his face into his hands, stopped working, approached me, and pleaded, "Please, don't tell Malcolm what I'm going to ask you now."

"Okay."

"Don't tell him it happened here. He wanted the original location... But, but, the place where we were on the first day is much better!"

"The Blue Lagoon?"

"Yes, yes. I immediately saw it there, immediately! Not here."

"But that won't be the truth."

I'd begun to feel sorry for reality.

"I see it there. The disgusting glamour of the eighties, a local version of it, screwed up and shabby, Brooke Shields . . . and when I add all the faces scowling at me . . ."

I looked over at the workers who hadn't been on Rio's wavelength since the beginning, and even though they knew this was our last resort, I could see that the situation was humiliating for them. Yes, it's possible they even hated him a little.

"And all these faces watching . . . And the investor enters and there he is, looking like Steve Jobs and Lenin merged into one; just imagine Jobs portrayed on a socialist realist canvas," concluded Rio.

I actually liked this canvas of his—although he made the Blue Lagoon bar even gloomier than it actually was. Maybe I like it because I'd participated in it.

Next to it was a painting that depicted Sobotka leading the workers. A melancholic piece. Distant perspective, slightly angled: Sobotka and the workers walking toward the factory, the man with the black dog is nearby; fog, a sense of hush. The factory and the town can't be seen. Sobotka and the workers are wearing garish orange vests, which they never actually wore, probably so a train or a crazy Ferrari wouldn't run them down in the wasteland. The painting was at least twenty-three feet long, and the small group is in the middle of it. Sobotka is in the distance; he has a mustache like Lech Wałęsa's, even though he didn't wear one at the time. The painter, Fiona, talked to Slavko, and she told Šeila that Slavko's English was something special: "I can see he knows it, but what he says seems like a different language." She wanted to paint Slavko, but he objected.

The painting depicting Sobotka and the workers was given the title *Self-Management Beyond Seven Mountains*, which almost made me laugh. That journalist wasn't exactly trying to help us, I thought, but the article, a scan of which was included in the exhibition booklet as well, was now a part of *The Last Socialist Realist Artifact*.

What a stretch, I thought and bit my tongue, because we didn't have self-management at the factory, nor did self-management have anything to do with socialist realism. As far as I remembered, our art parted ways with the annoying Soviet doctrine of soc-realism back in the 1950s, just when workers' self-management was first introduced.

Never mind, I thought, nobody here will believe this is an actual "socialist realist artifact," but a play on meanings and a metaphor for "antiqueness." The irony must have been apparent, and with a title like that, as I now saw, the turbine had become something else.

Right, they care about the metaphor, not the details. None of this matters to them: socialist realism, the failed stabs at socialism, the East, Communist regimes, all the newly capitalist countries.... They struggle with remembering their locations and names, let alone which ones were part of the Eastern Bloc and which ones weren't. The moment Malcolm took this on I thought they couldn't possibly care so much about us. There had to be something else to this, in placing industry in a museum, in this story of ruin. Because that's what they're talking about here, too: their industry is now half the size it used to be.

And it's not that the industry is outdated, I thought, it's in flux, the workers are far off in a global fog, and from there they have no power to voice demands for labor conditions. The workers in the West can't voice demands the way they used to, either. It's not the industry that's gone, it's the power of the labor force. Yes, this is also the story of the West, though they'll tell it as if it applies only to us.

Interested in socialist realism, my ass. They care only about themselves. We are merely an alibi for sad, perhaps poetic self-irony. It's easier for them to swallow if the irony is ours.

And our story, I thought, is so fucking twisted in every respect, with these hopeful workers... whereas Oleg was moving capital, and we would probably have vanished from the town as soon as we finished the Colonel's order. I understand it now, but I'm keeping quiet about that, too. So, instead of a showpiece of socialist realism, we could have stood here as a showpiece of globalism and the free market; but they probably weren't prepared to exhibit such an exemplar of self-irony.

This has been a stretch since day one, said Oleg's voice to me in my head, *but just take their money.*

Erol. This image was apparently created digitally, and then enhanced here and there with conspicuously dripping colors. Erol in work overalls, his hand resting on the shoulder of a smiling, black-haired woman whose black shirt read: Walk the Line. With his other arm he's leaning on a heavy yellow drill plunged into asphalt which, upon closer examination, contains elements of a weapon. As if this were based on a photograph; as if the woman wanted to have her picture taken with a worker. Although I somehow doubted that such a photograph existed. A glittery pattern coated everything like snakeskin, but different. Wavy. Like a spinal X-ray, as if you'd taken part of the X-ray with the spine on it, reproduced it, and arranged many of these spinal X-rays, one next to another, in a veil of vertebrae.

Erol. So where is he? At one point I had the impression that Šeila had an inkling. I asked her, only once this time, and she said she knew nothing. Yet here he now was, on display.

Hell, all this is disgusting.

Many large-format photographs were shown in the foyer, I knew, to convey the framework of the story. A panorama of the town.

The iron bridge. The rundown housing. The little square with the Haiduci restaurant. The coppersmith's and the slipper maker's. The Blue Lagoon. Several photographs of the factory. Sobotka's yard, when his sculptures were still there. A special cargo truck with the turbine crossing a bridge.

The photographs all looked like they were taken at rainy dawn.

In the main exhibition hall there was also a painting, at first glance in old-fashioned style, a pseudo-statesmanlike portrait against a dark background, of the Colonel missing an ear, one side of his head bloody. So we've also recorded this victory, I thought. I doubt this will find a buyer.

I hadn't known what would happen after we publicly revealed the story of the Colonel. Malcolm claimed we were safe, and if anyone tried to prosecute us, he would involve a bunch of journalists, and the story would be publicized internationally.

"It's not worth it to them, chasing after artists," he said with a smile, but also with a tinge of sadness in his eyes over the fact that they wouldn't prosecute us, because I noticed he had already started imagining that this would definitely make us famous.

Earlier, I'd discussed the matter with one of Oleg's lawyers. "They'll probably say you didn't go out of your way to battle terrorism," he laughed. "Maybe the secret services will notice you, that I can't know. . . . But legally, as far as I understand, you planned to sell the turbine to the Colonel, but you didn't."

"We failed," I said.

He laughed. "Well, sometimes you'd like to commit an international crime, but you can't pull it off. No problemo. Give me a call when you do."

Tima designed a huge 1983 calendar. It was like a car calendar but with the turbine instead of the cars. Lipša was in the picture with the turbine, leaning with her back against the rotor as if against a wall, staring at the lens as if asking whether they were done yet. Only her pregnant belly was uncovered. It looked glamorous yet troubling. At least to me it was.

On all the posters, the artist of *The Last Socialist Realist Artifact* was officially called Sobotka & Co.

In the front row, on behalf of the artist, sat Šeila, Branoš, and me.

I imagined Oleg watching us, because I knew he'd laugh, to himself, and to the world. This is why I missed him, because laughter wasn't coming easily to me. I was tense. I didn't know if this was because I was afraid it was pointless, or because it was happening. I was haunted by the idea of humiliation. Maybe what we were doing was an audacious act, a great bank robbery, as Malcolm put it, but we were still on display here as people in defeat, the ones they'll place in their museum or private collection as an act of triumph. Will this represent for them the triumph of capitalism, the West, or even triumph over industry and workers? The lucidity of our "art project" must be that we merged all this into one. I am left with the kind of solace Oleg would feel; at least we screwed them good. But his laughter wasn't coming to me, all the thoughts left me uneasily dizzy.

Through the dizziness I perceive the whole charade, this hall, us. I know what's happening next. It would be the picture, brutal.

We agreed to everything, I thought. Everyone agreed to everything. The whole world agreed to everything, and nobody had anything to say against us. But, sometimes you get this feeling... you wish you could step up onto the stage and stop the show.

I looked behind me. There were about two hundred people there. A select crowd, I bet.

Intrigued, intelligent, cynical faces.

Assessors of stories. They knew nothing but stories, they were skeptical of life. I thought they'd spit on this, unless, by chance, it struck them as refreshing. They were thirsty for refreshing. They must have grown tired of the same old same old.

Then, a slender figure in overalls appeared by the turbine, wearing a helmet and safety goggles. It was not possible to tell whether the person was male or female. This person opened a case and pulled out a special metal cutting saw. Once it was turned on, the person approached the turbine, and a murmur of confusion, or maybe disapproval, maybe even a little pain, spread through the room when the sparks started to fly.

I had to get out of there.

It was windy at the exit. Branoš was already there. The smoke from his cigarette was wafting away and disappearing into the neon night.

I didn't say I couldn't watch it, and neither did he; Malcolm needed an *event*, and we knew this. Branoš just stood there smoking into the wind, in a black suit. He gazed in the direction of the Thames. Maybe he was hiding his face.

After a few attempts, I lit my cigarette.

"I was in the emergency room once," Branoš said. "I'd been cut, so I had to get stitches."

He turned his head and looked at me.

"And a man was sitting there in the waiting room, black. I mean, he was a white guy, but he was all purple and black. I didn't ask anything. You don't know what to ask. He explained he'd been electrocuted and was waiting for the test results. Now, check out what the guy asks. He asks me where I go on vacation. I told him, and said I hadn't been on vacation for two years. He said, 'Neither was I last year. The job is good, but you can't take vacations when you like.' Then he said, 'My wife and I decided to go to London this year.' —'That's nice,' I said. —'She's younger than me. She wants to see London, and I've never been there, either.' As if he weren't sure and was asking for confirmation that London was worth a visit. He came to mind a moment ago."

When he paused I wasn't sure if the story was over yet or not.

"So I go in there to get stitched up, and they ask me how I got cut and so on. While they were stitching me, I asked what was up with the guy outside. 'Shocked by high-voltage electricity,' the doctor said, 'we've already called his family. He'll live for an hour, tops. He's falling apart.' So I go out, the guy's still sitting there, asks me if everything went okay. I see the man wants to talk. I said, 'It did'— and I got out of there as if I were on the run. Then for some reason I stopped, outside, to light a cigarette, but I was actually troubled by the thought that I was wrong to run away like that, it would be nicer of me to stay and talk to him casually. When I was already about to turn around... something compelled me again to get away from there. Because what does this man mean to me that I'd have to go through death with him? And so I smoked while thinking, as I am now, and out he comes."

Branoš looked at me, almost as if I were the guy. I wanted to tell him not to look at me like that.

"So the man lights up a cigarette and says to me, 'Maybe I shouldn't, eh?' I think to myself, What should I tell him? I don't want to be the one who makes him realize he's dead, so I go for the logic of a drunk: 'I was told the same... But you only live once.' 'I tried everything,' he said, 'including the nicotine patch, but it didn't work.'—'What I'd give for a beer right now,' I say, and I actually wonder where I might go to pick up a six-pack, because with alcohol, I think, this might all be easier—and he says, 'Sorry, no can do, I drank two or three today, and then got the shock.' So I go back to the London story. I ask him when he plans to go on the trip, if they've already bought the tickets.... Drivel.... He tells me about it, and I realize I'm not listening, I can't, and then he stops and I say to him, 'You should go to London. I've been and it's a must-see.'—'It is, ain't it?' He looks at me, his eyes turning dark.—'Yes, my friend. London's a fine destination. Unfortunately, gotta go now. I have to, there's work to be done,' I say, and shake hands with him. I had to go."

I thought, I probably could have lived without this story tonight. "Yeah," I said. "London."

Branoš lit another cigarette. His legs akimbo, wearing the suit, in the wind, he was like a mobster from a black-and-white movie.

"I'll tell them this is not fucking art," he said.

He was the one Malcolm chose to say something on behalf of the workers. I understood that I didn't look workmanlike enough, and Šeila was simply too beautiful. "Have you talked to Malcolm about it?"

"No. But I'm furious about the turbine being sawed through. It's different when you get to watch."

"I'm not too happy about that, either."

"Good thing our people aren't watching this."

I wondered; did Malcolm know what was coming?

I tried to sound relaxed. "I've known for a long time that I'm not running this show. Whatever you say is fine. Just be calm. Let's keep this civilized."

"Don't worry," he said, drumming his fingers on his thigh. "You think they'll call us when they finish that shit?"

"We're not hard to find."

Šeila came for us. She said the worst of it was over and back in we went. Malcolm was talking, and I noticed some puzzled, perhaps fascinated, faces as the men in overalls carried away the last pieces of the destroyed turbine.

"The initiator disappeared in the revolution. The contractor and the artist behind these sculptures was killed. . . . And the client was killed. This is just a small part of the story. In the exhibition guide you'll find the other details documented," said Malcolm like a stern sovereign.

He paused to look at the audience, as if wondering whether they were worth all this, and then poured it all out.

"This is a blood-filled story about passion, passion for work, passion for investments and risk, passion for survival and hope. This is a story about people from socialism and capitalism, a story about a strange small town between the East and the West, a story about passion for the free market that crosses borders even when that's prohibited, and a story about the passion of workers who rebuilt a factory as their home and couldn't stop even when the project became illusory and pointless by market standards. All this is presented with this antiquated turbine, the 83-N, dubbed *The Last Socialist Realist Artifact*. It combines not only the past and the present, but the future as well, because this event projects itself into the future, the future of art.

"*This* is *The Last Socialist Realist Artifact!*" said Malcolm, and slowly stretched out his hand toward the red curtain being lifted.

There, under the bright light, stood our last turbine.

Louder than before, Malcolm continued. "The first 83-N turbine was manufactured for commercial purposes, an industrial product. They thought they had a buyer. We will exhibit its parts tomorrow. This second turbine remains. It is a pure artifact. It was manufactured even though there was no buyer. The only potential buyer had already been killed. The people who made it never even imagined it would be exhibited here. It was not made for display. Some of them are still against it. The turbine was, nevertheless, manufactured. It was made because it had to be—in the same way art is made. Although this is something we've forgotten."

He said this as if reproaching someone of stature.

"Beyond the incredible history this fascinating artifact has had, today we are building a story. We have dared to recognize this work as art. Our story might seem puzzling today.

"Of course.

"Only to become legendary tomorrow.

"I will not be modest. I will state—this will be a legend! An event which will be remembered as the next among the grand, perplexing acts of the avant-garde."

He waited a moment for his words to sink in, then scanned the audience as if to make sure everyone was following him, and then he said, "With us here is the representative of the team, Mr. Branoš, who will say something on behalf of the authors who built all this."

Malcolm stayed there. The plan was that he would say a few more words after Branoš, and then the event would finally be over.

Branoš slowly approached the microphone, scowling at the audience. "I speak on behalf of the workers who made this turbine which you are calling an artifact. We do not think if it as art."

Silence was heard in the brief pause.

"I was determined to say this, as my colleagues know. If this turbine was manufactured with passion, as said, it was not with the passion of artists, but the passion of workers. I'm not even sure this can be called a passion. I would rather say it was our desire to make everything meaningful. All that has happened. Had we stopped working, we'd have felt incomplete, and even pointlessness looks better when it's finished. If deliberately finished. By making these turbines, one of which we sacrificed here, we became aware of many things. We became aware, again, of ourselves. This is why we wanted to finish the turbine. You know your business, we know ours—this here is your world. Everything the gallery curator said about the history of the turbine is nice, but I have to say that we're not here to sell a story. We're not selling our dead friends. We're selling their work and our work, as always. Ultimately, we don't care if this is art. If someone wants to pay for our work, we'll take their money. My colleague, who is sitting here, thinks the payment itself will be an act of art. Fine, maybe so."

Šeila looked at me and huffed as Branoš stepped away from the microphone. She whispered in my ear, "I did say that. He's really taking this to the edge."

Malcolm listened to all of it almost proudly, as if Branoš's speech confirmed everything he'd just said. It looked as if he wouldn't be speaking anymore. Yes, he, too, stepped back.

"I was so anxious," said Šeila, as the applause erupted. I didn't know how strong the applause should be, but it did not sound indifferent to me.

"Me too," I said. "But it's all good!"

"Let's not get ahead of ourselves," she said.

"Whatever."

Branoš joined us.

"If my daddy could see me nowww," said Branoš, so we started laughing, shaking off the grimaces that had frozen our faces.

The audience murmured while examining the exhibits.

"It's time for a drink," I said, taking three glasses of champagne from a tray a gracious black hostess was carrying, smiling warmly as if to say she was on our side.

Malcolm showed up, took a glass, and toasted, "To the great bank robbery!"

"What do you mean, Malcolm? Have you heard something?" asked Šeila.

"This is an exhibition I know nothing about, believe me," said Malcolm. "I love it. I can't be realistic as to the estimates."

He raised his drink again and we clinked our glasses.

"It would be wonderful if we sold something tonight," he said.

"Anything. That would mean that the whole thing is being, in a way, legitimized. And, strictly between us, I happen to know we'll sell something tonight."

He grinned.

Before he left to mingle further, he said to Branoš, "I had nothing to add!"

"I have to light one up," said Branoš then, and out he went.

"What did he mean by that, that we'll sell something?" I asked Šeila.

"He's probably arranged for an icebreaker."

"Too bad he and Oleg never met."

A few minutes later, Malcolm went to one of Sobotka's sculptures and stuck a red dot on the card next to it.

A murmur rippled through the room.

"Sold," said Šeila.

"Yeah," I sighed. "Sobotka was the icebreaker."

Everybody was watching Malcolm. He was now staring at his smartphone, blinking. He looked around, searching for our gazes, and then looked back at his gadget, blinking like he was counting. Then he raised his hand and lifted his index finger in the air. He went to the painting *The Arrival of the Investor* and put a red dot on the card.

There was an eruption of applause. Only then did I notice Rio, the smile he was doing his best to suppress, so it wouldn't look as if he cared. The Blue Lagoon had become a legend. I lifted my glass to him. He didn't see me.

"You think this, too, was an icebreaker?" I asked Šeila.

"I don't know," she said, without looking at me, following Malcolm as if she were watching Elvis leave the building.

He was heading for the turbine.

37

THE NEXT DAY, at checkout time, they were very hungover. They sat in the hotel lobby, trying to extend their stay, because they'd planned the thriftiest option in case the exhibition was a fiasco; but now they'd decided to stay on a few more days. Cancellation of cheap return tickets would be no great loss.

"No rooms available for us," Branoš said after coming back from the front desk. Then he added, "I spoke to an Englishman who was with me in Iraq. He says I can sleep at his place.... But I have the impression he hasn't slept for some time now."

"A soldier?"

"A plumber. It takes him a lot to get drunk, I think. I'll go check his current condition. I might use my ticket today after all."

"What about us?" asked Nikola.

"I'll look for something online," said Šeila, and went over to the guest computer.

As Nikola watched Branoš slip into a cab, he felt he was watching the closing scene of a movie in a sudden blaze of sunshine; light reflected off the wet street, the parked cars, sparkling. His head throbbed.

He would have preferred a dark room. He thought about asking Šeila out to a matinee showing of a movie as a joke; he hadn't been to one of those since the days of Brooke Shields.

Then he remembered that, after putting it off for weeks, he'd told himself he would tell her after the exhibition. High time. He needed to say, *I made this promise to Lipša.*

She'd say, *What?*

Hell, he couldn't even imagine if the "*What?*" would be the last thing he'd ever hear from her. What does a woman do after finding out her partner is having a child with someone else?

Will she accept all this after he'd explained? He had nothing to compare the situation to. Had anyone else ever done something like this?

Šeila aside, he was scared of the promise. Then he imagined himself in the future, and thought he would probably be glad. Still, he was tempted by the idea of putting off the talk with Šeila.

It would be best if this time in London goes well, he thought. Let this be our little honeymoon.

Yes, we could go see a movie. A naive romance. What are today's romantic movies for teenagers like? he thought. He had no idea.

She came back and said, "Hotels, only some are pretty far away. But there's a site with apartments, I checked."

"Sounds good."

Then she paused, as if about to say something else.

He tipped his chin: Say it.

"I didn't really think about this consciously," she said, "but now when I clicked on the site I began thinking.... Actually, I'd like to stay here for a while. What about you?"

He looked at her and—whether it was her posture, or just his imagination—he felt her slipping away.

"I hadn't thought. How long is a little while?"

"I don't know. . . . It would be kind of strange now to go back. I don't work with you. I . . . I've pulled this off and now what? Sit and wait for you at the Blue Lagoon? You know, I don't know what there is for me to do down there."

"Has Malcolm offered you something?"

"No," she said. "I wouldn't hide that from you. But if he did, I'd consider it. The thing is I have nothing to do back there. See? It's not about Malcolm, it's about me."

He exhaled, and for a moment his temples ached a little more.

He looked at her, as if seeing her in a new light; he thought: yes, of course. And he had the impression that everything was slipping away, the lobby and the front desk, and he was slowly detaching from the world, as he'd dreamed once as a child, after watching a show about deep-space distances and light-years. When he finally understood the years that carried the flickering of stars, they made him feel smaller than a microbe.

He closed his eyes to the glare.

Then, in a swirl of colors, the image of the scorched electrician from Branoš's story appeared, and he opened his eyes.

She put her hand on his shoulder.

"I get it," said Nikola.

"By doing this, I've pulled off something I didn't know I could do. Now I know. I mean, Malcolm pushed the story, but everyone knows the idea was mine. Tima knows, the painters know."

"You think this may open doors for you?"

"This is just a hungover morning. There's been too much since last night. . . . But I cannot leave before I explore this. I'd feel as if I'd missed out on something important. What's more, for the first time in my life I have some money. I can stay here, no panic. Please understand."

"I understand," he said, making the effort not to burden her with his tone.

He thought, This is what success looks like. Yes, things turned out well. She can no longer sit there at the Blue Lagoon.

"Hey, this doesn't mean anything. I'll go search a little more," said Šeila, "and you think about it."

It's true, she did come up with the story, and she rescued me from a nightmare, he thought. We owe her. He had said as much to Branoš the previous night, and Branoš agreed. She took them from rock bottom to the wonder of selling the turbine to a global Internet company. The guy who represented the company told Malcolm they would set it up in the atrium of their headquarters. It clearly had symbolic meaning for them, a reminder of the previous generation's industry, which had been turned into an artifact. "It is a symbol of their victory," said Malcolm. "And the news is already being reported, and they're getting their money's worth of advertising through the news coverage."

Nikola opened his bag and found a pill for his headache.

He went to the restroom.

Šeila noticed.

She was afraid of how he'd react. She understood this had all happened fast, but up until that morning she was caught up with the uncertainty of the exhibition, fully focused on him and the world back there. She hadn't been thinking about anything else. Then all of a sudden this morning she'd realized the whole thing was over; she'd managed to turn everything around, and now felt this other world calling to her; she was already in it.

How strange, she thought. A cut.

But, yes, she'd worked with the factory because of the debts hanging over Nikola, because of her hometown, because of a sort of cosmic justice, and now, she'd done her part. She had no interest in the factory as a factory. They would have to either keep it running or not. She felt like a revolutionary whose revolution had prevailed and now had nothing more to do.

She knew she was smashing Nikola's idea of home. No, he would never even dream of leaving there for good. He'd embraced the story now, strong-armed into it perhaps, but eventually it wormed its way under his skin. He wasn't even thinking about escape, to ditch these people and Oleg's accounts. And he was great at it. Šeila recognized this about him. How strange that he'd become more of a denizen of the town where she was born than she was. The town had become a real town again, she thought, because he'd come, an outsider who chose to live there. But now she had chosen something else, and it was clear to her she'd shaken up his soul.

She thought of Michael, that she was like him. When he told her they were going to Tbilisi, it was like that; he was a man without a home, a global man. She followed him, and later understood she shouldn't have. It wouldn't be okay if Nikola hung around waiting for her in London the way she'd waited for Michael in Tbilisi. Nikola would become the one who'd think love could replace all other stories. But she couldn't tell him all this.

What's the solution? A long-distance relationship? A thousand miles separating them? That sounds so global, she thought. What have I become overnight? But it was all reasonable—choices had appeared, unfortunately. Or fortunately, she thought, though she wasn't feeling the least bit fortunate. If it weren't for Nikola, she'd be feeling fortunate. Had their relationship overnight become a burden? Fortunately? To hell with that kind of fortune. But . . . She now had a choice, which hadn't been the case the day before. And this was disturbing in a way.

413

We're here, she thought, at a turning point. I'm Michael, Nikola is me. And I might be betraying him. Or am I betraying myself? If I—once it's too late—if I realize this was the wrong choice and that I've ditched everything for an illusion, then I'll be the traitor. But if I realize this is the way it should be, then I'll know I'd have betrayed myself if I hadn't tried.

One thing she knew—she couldn't sit idly down there. And there was, in fact, nothing she could do about that. Her fingers were damp with sweat as she pondered all this.

This is the end, thought Nikola. He swallowed the pill over the sink and stared into the mirror. The image shrank and grew.

What were you thinking, he said to himself, that this would all end up *happily-ever-after*? You yourself think those movies are silly; how the hell did you buy this?

What did I think would happen after the exhibition? he thought.

He'd had no idea what was going to happen, nor had he realized that this story that had changed him was drawing to a close. He still had no sense of where he was supposed to be.

He stared into nothing while a man waited for him to finish with the hand dryer, but Nikola never even saw him.

"It's over, I'm free," he said out loud, and looked at the man, wondering where he'd come from. The man shrugged and proceeded to dry his hands.

I can give Šeila the freedom to go her own way. Or do the same for the workers down there?

For the first time he became aware of something: he no longer had to stay there.

The truth is, he wasn't essential.

Should he even be there? he asked himself. Do they need him?

Branoš could take over, he'd be better at it anyway. The manufacturing needed to be modernized or refocused.... What would his role be anyway? Director? Oleg's successor? Oleg never even counted on a future, which he realized when he saw there were no customers out there.

What a morning, he thought. He'd embraced the life there, but maybe he was redundant there as well.

And where wasn't he? he thought.

He went over to Šeila and leaned on the table while she clicked through the sites. He kept his silence and looked at the apartments, opening up like secret caves in adventure films.

The tips of her fingers sweated, while she was thinking: I'm Michael.

"Go ahead and rent an apartment to your taste. I still have to go down there after a few days. To see to everything... Debts need to be paid.... I need to think about what to do and where to go, I really don't know."

"I didn't want to screw up, I'm sorry."

He pressed his lips against hers.

"How long is this clicking going to take?"

"Give me a few more minutes, we need to find something today."

"Okay. How about afterward we go to the movies, and then to the nearest apartment? You know, pretend like you live very close to the movies."

"To the movies with our luggage, huh?"

"These are small bags. I'd like to get away from the light for a little while. Maybe a matinee... About two kids on a Pacific island, something like that..."

She smiled, her eyes sparkling, realizing how much she'd miss him.

"I might even take a nap through a childish romantic lie, if they still make such films. . . . I need some sleep."

"Yeah. Me too," said Šeila.

Although the sun had already hidden behind the clouds, he took the sunglasses from his bag and went out to the curb to light a cigarette.

His headache subsided. He watched the passing of people and cars. He imagined himself taking a long walk down those streets, anonymous and alone.

He could give Šeila the freedom to go her own way, as well as the folks down there.

He could settle up all his debts, walk away, and leave it all to them. He could work everything out with them, throw a big farewell bash at the Blue Lagoon, get staggeringly drunk to Turban-Rap, sing "Those from Here Who've Gone Away," and leave tomorrow with a hangover. They would see him off as a hero and a brother, and he could take the same road back along the river in a Japanese SUV through the fluttering plastic bags. He could stop at Café Strada, order one for Oleg, say—Here, buddy, one for the road—give the waitress a big tip, cross the border, and keep on moving, farther and farther away, and all of this would eventually fade in color and appear to be distant and unbelievable.

Is this how it's all supposed to end? he wondered.

38

AROUND ME THERE'S nothing but a flat line, this is a no-signal area, but I guess today somehow a satellite bumbled into something. and a signal appeared, maybe Allah, maybe Yahweh, maybe Buddha, and or it's that they need to bomb us from above, so they need the signal, so here I am writing you an email, because it seems too late for me to be joining facebook now, although it's a revolutionary tool, and it came in handy for them, or so I hear, in tunisia, and egypt, and here this whole revolution did nicely to get rid of our old client who commissioned the turbine. Fuck 'em all, they picked the perfect moment to oust him after all these years, just when I arrived, because he asked to see me—to see if I was lying or we'd really made the turbine . . . he could read people. I guess the old cocksucker must have known immediately I wasn't lying as soon as I walked in. I wouldn't have come here if I was lying, but it took a while for me to get to him, the rebels had had their first attack by then, no one could get in to see the boss and I had to wait, so I missed the last bus out, goddammit, first went the last plane, then the last ship, and the last bus has already become a legend, who knows whether there even was one, I guess there was, there had to be a last one, at least across the Sahara, I should have been on that last bus, that would have been an adventure, but I missed it, and afterward there was no one left, so I couldn't even hitchhike. I couldn't get in touch because they took my laptop and phone straightaway, in case I was a spy, so I wouldn't call you or anyone else and describe the situation, and my situation was bad, there is no fucking alcohol here, I went through a serious crisis, I think my liver has convalesced quite well, but what good will that do me when I won't have the time to use it. I was in some kind of friendly custody, in this fucking military hotel; I could sit there in the garden in the inner courtyard, so that's what I did, I didn't have anything else to do but think about my life. I was trapped, like I've always been trapped ever since I can remember, only some traps are roomier than others, but still a trap and we lived in it lured by tomorrow it is a fucking trap, always harnessed, like horses . . . you know they killed the colonel, you probably saw that, too, they say the crowd posed around the dead body; that's been broadcast, I hear, around the world, people see it as the death of a gladiator, maybe even spartacus . . . okay, not spartacus, his body was never found and he never held power, too bad, I don't know how crazy he was, but I know how his men were killed, spectacularly, so everyone could see, they lined them up on crosses along the road, and now the internet is serving as the crosses along the road, to show what awaits the enemies of the empire . . . so you see them on the screen, as they die in misery, humiliated and spat upon by your gaze . . . I'm stuck with them but don't think I bought into the legend of the colonel, because I know those faces, though his was a little vague at first, until I realized he'd had botox injections, it took me a minute to figure this out, but I saw he was on cocaine, and I know what that means when you have no corrective, when you're the boss of the universe on coke, boss my ass . . . but the guys on the other side, I don't get why the west would like them so much, unless they were trying to breed worse enemies than the colonel, because he was kind of a jester as he teetered along the edge, so it makes a weird kind of sense that I ended up with him. at the audience I told him we rebuilt the factory and he even promised to pay for it because his accounts were about to be blocked anyway, so it would be better for him to give the money to us. he started laughing uncontrollably, so I thought this was because of something I'd done, but a guy recently told me that his accounts had already been blocked by the time of my audience, only they hadn't told the colonel because he couldn't handle reality all that well. as you know, he was whacked, and I'm still fighting, I mean, I go around with the last of them, with a gun, I've got one, because you have to have a weapon, otherwise some of them might think I'm a prisoner and whack me too . . .

now I'm faced with a dilemma—to fire at them when I see them coming and kill myself with the last bullet; or wait and sell them the story that I can find them a small atomic bomb, they could be interested in that, the ones who catch me, if they speak languages, but I think they are unlikely to forget whose side they found me on, they'll think me a mercenary, and if I introduce myself as an arms dealer, they might torture me for a time, I better not tell you the stories going around. or they'll pick me off with a drone in a few minutes and I'll be freed of my dilemmas by some guy who's several thousand miles away bombing us, a guy who is employed, I mean, he has a job, sits in front of a computer, bombs me from nine to five, goes home to his family, okay, maybe he stops for a beer with friends and, if I'm lucky, maybe he gets drunk and is hungover the next day.

Nikola, brother, I'm just fucking around. such are the times. it's over, for real, I know . . . man, what a stupid story, same as with my ukrainians, those idiots who were anti-communists, pro-nazis, and the last to become Commies, and I, I got here because I'm an entrepreneur, prone to risk-taking, as you know, so it turned out I'm fighting here for the colonel's socialism, though I don't fully get it, but hey, what's here is here, I'm out at the front lines in my last days, here until the end and all through the final credits with the folks who've been smashed in retreat just like the cossack from a hundred years ago, everything's the same, only I'm on the other side. if uncle Martin could see me now he'd have a fine time laughing at me, you know I dream of him sometimes, we've made plans for spending a little time out at the cottage. I might stop by, I say, and now I really could. fuck it, the truth is I was a bare-assed pauper and proletarian, I just wanted to earn some real money, but what can you do, it didn't fly; so remember me as a revolutionary, feel free to lie about me, say I was better than I am.

you know, I only shot a gun for real here once, you won't believe me, when the cat I was feeding was killed, it'd show up, come and go, sometimes it was with me all day long, sometimes it wouldn't be back for ages, and then one morning it could barely walk, I saw blood above one of its legs, I guess from shrapnel, a small piece of shrapnel, why the cat, man, I thought shrapnel couldn't hit a cat, but it did, something tiny, and the cat just lay down beside my legs and died within an hour, goddammit, this dying cat, it looked at me and meowed, as if it wanted to talk, as if it'd been carried away by its story, as if it were summing up its feline life—stupid, but that's the feeling I had—as if I were a cat, a bigger cat, with this little one who's closing its eyes and leaving the world, and I thought about what I'd done in this world, why everything turned out so lame, I started feeling sad, thinking about my life. I was no better than the cat, who'd been struggling to survive until it was hit; I was nothing more than a cat, hiding and jumping back and forth, I never knew god, I don't mean god-god, but light and peace, and now somehow I know it exists because sometimes I see it in the early morning, when I watch the desert and the peeking sun, who's been my friend ever since that cat closed its eyes, and I must be crazy because I talk to the sun at early dawn and I tell it, 'Sup, sun, buddy, how's it going, what's new, how're my friends, how's home, and when I say home, you won't believe it, Nikola, I think of you out there in the middle of fucking nowhere, and of no one else in all the cities I've been to, but of you there in that misery and nothing—if you're still down there, and I somehow feel you are—but it's not misery and nothing, I mean, none of that matters, it's moot, because misery and nothing are over, everything's the same, it's moot where you are and what you are when you're talking to the sun and when you know death is knocking at the door, and darkness is waiting; and I wasn't in the light enough, I was in my fogs with other people in their fogs, it may seem to you that I'm suddenly mysterious, but it's not that, I'm the same old me, and I could joke about all the shit like I used to, and I am joking about it, I don't hide from the shit, but when I say "light" I know what I have in mind, a nice feeling, nice and bright and warm and noble, I have in mind the whore who didn't know she was a whore, the one from Tobolsk, who knows where she ended up, where she was kicked, where a car ran her over; and she was bathed in light, it was with her, she had the light under her skin, some women have it, they're unprepared for life because they don't know how to defend themselves, and you can't, you can't have the light if you're defending oneself, if you clam up like I did; you have to stay open to have the light, and I don't know how I'll stay alive, that's the question, whoever finds a way to stay open and survive the poisons of people is a wise soul because everything gets under your skin when you're open, what can you do, it must be weird for you, me talking like this, you must be thinking, death's nearing so he's rambling about the light, poor old Oleg, but that's how it is, I wouldn't talk like this if I didn't feel death near, I'm rocking it and soothing it like a baby, before it twists into a howl of the universe—what a nice word, universe

and so here I sit at early dawn, and these are the good days, too bad they're my last... it's calm here now, for ten days now, seems like years, since we got away from the crossfire, until they find us again, I can't tell you where we are, just in case, and I could hardly even explain, this is all nowhere for me, and that's good, as a prelude to nothing, because all my life I thought I knew where I was, technically I mean, since we have geography and maps so you locate yourself, but this is a different feeling, and when you think about it, this is how people used to feel, without this business of locating ourselves in the world, on a map, on earth, in states, in the stories that rule countries, broadcast by television, so you think—I'm here—and you always think you're in a place ruled by a story, a stupid story of the moment and place, and you don't see you're under the sky, you're on the ground, you're at a place you know nothing about, and you don't need to know about it, it's fog; because you're on the earth and under the sky and under the sun and this is where you are, this is what people used to know, I see that now; when there were no maps and when they didn't know what the earth was like, where washington or the himalayas were, or where they were except beneath the sky, because that's the main thing, and you forget about it when you see a map and those borders drawn and the cities and you locate yourself using your GPS and you're completely in the human network, in the language of the world which has covered the planet with names you think are real, and you forget you're beneath the sky, same as the cat that was hit by shrapnel, so small and fast, and your piece of shrapnel will find you and all you can do is live beyond the stupid stories, walk on the ground until a piece of shrapnel gets you; and it's a different feeling when you know this, brother, when you know this, the feeling is different, it's not much of a mystery, not any great enlightenment, not a truth you need to ponder on much or solve difficult equations, it is, brother, nothing more than removing the excess from your head, putting two and two together, and the latter two mean you count on death and you immediately know where you stand... it's funny, when you think about it, every day you hear how someone was killed somewhere, died, a bomb blew up one thing or another, and you think how far away it is, beyond your world, it's funny, because even if you think it's right here, close by, you don't know how to handle it, instead, you scratch yourself nervously and talk shit until you forget what upset you and what you can't forgot, so you're scratching yourself nervously and are afraid of your thoughts and you're scared by the stupid small shit that takes you back and you're restless and furious... and if you're furious just because of that, this means it hasn't sunk in yet, if it makes you nasty, that's just rage taking over... for me, brother, the rage is gone, I've put everything down here for you, I'm just sorry how I spent my life—it's true I didn't have much choice, but still, I did have some... then I remember all of you there, and I wonder if there was any use to it all... did Lipša get back, did the guy here actually manage by some miracle to pay you the money... or am I stuck here for no reason...

if anyone asks, tell them it meant more and feel free to say I was better than I am. and I was a little bit better than I am, wasn't I?

let's laugh, Nikola, with an unearthly laughter, wait I hear a sound, I think this might be what brought the signal, it's coming, I'll close now so the message doesn't stay in draft, Johnny B

ROBERT PERIŠIĆ's novel *Our Man in Iraq* garnered rave reviews from the *New Yorker*, the *Times Literary Supplement*, and NPR's *All Things Considered*, among others, and was praised as "a must-read" by the *Guardian*. Perišić has published award-winning nonfiction, fiction, poetry, and criticism in his native Croatia, where both *Our Man in Iraq* and *No-Signal Area* were bestsellers. He began writing short stories in the 1990s with a clear anti-war sentiment, during the days following the devastating war that tore apart the former Yugoslavia, and is now considered to be one of the most important writers and literary critics in the region. Perišić lives in Zagreb.

ELLEN ELIAS-BURSAĆ is a translator of fiction and nonfiction from Bosnian, Croatian, and Serbian. She has taught in the Harvard University Slavic Department and is a contributing editor to the online journal *Asymptote*. She lives in Boston.